FOUL PLAY

OTHER BOOKS AND AUDIO BOOKS
BY BETSY BRANNON GREEN:

Hearts in Hiding

Never Look Back

Until Proven Guilty

Don't Close Your Eyes

Above Suspicion

FOUL PLAY

a novel by

BETSY BRANNON GREEN

Covenant

Covenant Communications, Inc.

Cover photograph by Randy Allbritton, © PhotoDisc Green/Getty Images.
Cover design copyrighted 2004 by Covenant Communications, Inc.

Published by Covenant Communications, Inc.
American Fork, Utah

This is a work of fiction. The characters, names, incidents, places, and dialogue are products of the author's imagination, and are not to be construed as real.

Printed in Canada
First Printing: May 2004

11 10 09 08 07 06 05 04   10 9 8 7 6 5 4 3 2 1

ISBN 1-59156-512-X

*To my daughter Cathy,
who defines pride and joy*

ACKNOWLEDGMENTS

Words cannot adequately thank my husband, Butch, for his love, support, encouragement, patience, and sacrifice. He faces all life's trials with faith and humor and courage. I'm so glad that he's letting me come along for the ride! I owe a special thanks to my editor, Katie Child, for her efforts in my behalf. I feel very fortunate to be associated with Katie and all the other talented folks at Covenant. I'm grateful to my brother, James Brannon, for his technical advice on the game of football. And I express deep appreciation to all my readers across the world who take the time to write and encourage me. You make it all worthwhile!

PROLOGUE

The men sat around the scarred wooden desk in the storage room at the GFL headquarters. They communicated in subdued tones and avoided eye contact. A bare, low-wattage bulb hanging from the ceiling provided the only light. The door opened, and Felix Hummer walked in. He took an empty chair and addressed the others.

"Is everything going according to plan?"

The tax accountant on his right laughed. "Beyond our wildest dreams."

"How so?" Hummer inquired.

"Response to our initial offering has been overwhelming. We are actually having to turn away minor investors and haven't had to touch a penny of our start-up capital," the accountant reported.

Hummer smiled then turned to the city councilman seated at his left. "When will the computer system be up and running?"

The city official swallowed and clasped his hands together nervously. "Days."

"And what about the computer man you've hired? How will you keep him from figuring out . . ." Hummer paused, "the bigger picture?"

The councilman twisted his cuff link. "If he catches on, we'll offer him a piece of the action. I'm sure he'll jump at the chance."

Hummer didn't respond to this, but the orthodontist at the end of the table demanded, "This computer guy isn't one of us! How can we trust him?"

"And why should we share our profits with him?" the retired heavyweight champion wanted to know.

The city councilman raised a hand to forestall further comments. "We aren't sure that he'll figure things out, but if he does and there's any doubt about his trustworthiness, we'll take another, more drastic route." He glanced up at Felix Hummer. "And as for sharing the profits—the amount we would offer the computer man is such a small percentage it's insignificant."

The boxer scowled, but didn't voice any more objections.

"If the start-up capital we all contributed isn't being used, shouldn't it be returned to us?" the orthodontist asked.

Felix Hummer turned cold eyes toward the man. "There will be no disbursements until the plan has run its course. Movements of funds at this stage would attract attention, and that's the last thing we want. Everyone will have to be patient."

"Are there any more questions or concerns?" the accountant asked, obviously anxious to end the meeting. No one spoke.

Felix Hummer pushed away from the desk and stood. "Very well, then. We won't meet again until the exhibition game. If we need to communicate before that, we can contact each other using the secure cell phones I gave you."

Everyone else remained seated as Hummer walked through the door and out into the quiet hallway. Then the others left in turn, each giving the man before him plenty of time to disappear before making his own exit.

CHAPTER 1

Billie Murphy pushed the print button on the copy machine and checked her watch. It was almost seven-thirty. If she hurried, she could finish up by nine and still have time to work on her new novel, *Breathless*, when she got home.

She returned to her cubicle to sort the copies and had just settled behind her desk when there was a knock. She looked up to see her coworker Camille Lockhart standing in the open doorway. Although Billie and Camille both had technically the same job at the Georgia Chamber of Commerce, Camille always received the more glamorous assignments. Billie attributed this to the fact that Camille's uncle was on the city council, and she tried not to be bitter.

"What are you doing here on a Saturday night?" Billie asked, genuinely surprised. Camille rarely put in a full eight hours on regular workdays and never darkened the door of the Chamber offices on weekends.

Camille pushed a clump of honey-blond hair behind her ear. "Marshall Stokes, the CEO of Baptist Health Systems, asked me out to dinner tonight. Since he's such an *influential* local businessman, I didn't think I should refuse."

Billie resisted the urge to roll her eyes. "Is Mr. Stokes meeting you here?"

"Heavens no," Camille answered with a little laugh. "My college sorority is sponsoring a fashion show and dinner at The Summit tonight. Since I have to make an appearance, I told Marshall we could just meet there. He'll pledge a donation so impressive my sorority sisters will be green with envy. Then he wants to watch the fireworks display at Stone Mountain." Camille put a hand up to cover a delicate yawn. "But I'll probably try to talk him out of that since it seems much too cold to be sitting outside."

"Especially dressed like that," Billie observed, pointing at the clingy little dress Camille was wearing. "But if Mr. Stokes is meeting you at The Summit, then why are you *here?*"

Camille walked in to Billie's cubicle and sat down in the chair in front of the desk. "Because while I was driving to The Summit, I checked my cell phone messages. There was one from Frieda telling me that the itinerary for my trip next week was on my desk. She insisted that I come by and pick it up." Camille waved a packet of papers. "Have you seen this?"

Billie shook her head as she stapled the bids she'd gotten from caterers for a literacy event scheduled for April. "Why would I have seen it? It's not my trip."

"Well, it should be," Camille responded. "I don't know if I can do this."

Billie raised her eyebrows. Frieda always booked Camille in the best restaurants and hotels. "What's wrong with it?"

"I'm going to be stuck with a group of Mormons for a whole week!"

This statement caught Billie's attention. "Frieda gave *you* the Blalock Industries tour?" she demanded. She had assumed that this particular assignment would go to her for obvious reasons.

"Can you believe it?" Camille's voice trembled with indignation.

Billie couldn't. Camille was very successful when working with people who enjoyed harmless flirtation and could be swayed by flattery, but the chances of her forging a bond with a couple of straight-laced Salt Lake businessmen were slim to none.

"I guess they had to give it to you since I'm on vacation next week," Billie finally offered as the only reasonable explanation.

"It's so unfair," Camille continued her complaints. "You're going to be in the Bahamas while I stomp through cow pastures with religious fanatics."

"Mormons are not religious fanatics," Billie disagreed. "You've been associated with me long enough to know that."

Camille's lips formed a pretty, well-practiced pout. "But you'll be having fun and I won't!"

"Vacations are supposed to be more fun that business trips," Billie pointed out as she skimmed the itinerary Camille had thrown on her desk. "And the accommodations on this trip are so luxurious, you'll think you *are* on vacation."

"Since you feel that way, why don't *you* give the tour and I'll go on your cruise," Camille suggested with a charming smile.

Billie laughed. "Not a chance. I haven't taken any significant time off in two years, and my mother got me a cancellation, so I'm staying in a honeymoon suite."

"All alone?" Camille demanded.

Billie grimaced. "Since I'm not married, of course I'll have the room to myself."

There was a short pause, then Camille said, "That's one more reason for us to switch trips! Mr. Blalock's son is filthy rich and extremely eligible. If you'd update your hairstyle and buy some new clothes, you might have a chance with him."

"I'm not interested in getting married or changing my appearance," Billie said with flagging patience.

Camille scooted to the edge of the chair. "You know more about Georgia than I do," she said in an obvious attempt to be complimentary. "Switching trips would be a good thing for all concerned."

Especially for you, Billie thought to herself. "It's not happening," she said out loud.

"It's a good idea," Camille insisted in a willful tone.

"It's an awful idea and one I don't intend to discuss further," Billie replied firmly, then changed the subject. "Are you going out of town for Christmas?"

Camille shook her head. "Once I get back from this trip from Hades, I'll spend Christmas with Uncle Conrad. Then I've been invited to the GFL exhibition game as a guest of Jeff Burdick."

Billie was stunned. "The Atlanta Competitors' quarterback?"

"Yes, but you can't tell anyone," Camille pleaded. "His divorce isn't final yet, and if his wife finds out that he's seeing me, she'll demand a bigger settlement."

Billie was at a loss for words.

"But I can't *even* start to look forward to that yet. I still have five days of driving around southern Georgia with a carful of Mormons staring me in the face. I don't know how I'll bear it . . ." Camille's voice trailed off in despair.

"Somehow you will," Billie assured the other woman as she stood. "Now you'll have to excuse me. I have more copies to make."

Billie walked to the copy room and stayed until she heard the elevator start its decent. When she returned to her cubicle, Camille was gone but the itinerary for the Blalock trip was still on her desk. Shaking her head, Billie opened her desk drawer and filed the itinerary under "Junk" before beginning on a detailed summary of her active accounts for her supervisor.

The descriptions took much longer than she had anticipated, and by the time she put the summary on Frieda's desk, it was almost eleven o'clock. Billie walked back to her cubicle, raking her fingers through her long hair. The empty chamber office was starting to feel a little creepy, and the Sabbath was approaching, so Billie cleaned off her desk. There would be no time to work on *Breathless* when she got home, and she accepted the fact that she would leave for vacation on Monday with her unfinished novel hanging over her head.

She was shutting down her computer when the phone rang, setting her nerves on edge. "Georgia Chamber of Commerce," she said into the receiver.

"Billie?" her mother's voice came through the line. "When I kept getting your answering machine at home I decided to check work. It's almost eleven o'clock!"

"Are you going to give me a weather report too?" Billie asked with a smile.

"Cold and dark," Nan replied. "Why are you working so late?"

Billie got her purse out of a desk drawer. "I'm headed out right now."

"It's a good thing you're on vacation next week. You work much too hard."

"Yep, I take after my mother," Billie teased. Nan ran a travel agency from her home, and relaxation was a totally foreign concept to her as well.

Nan continued as if her daughter hadn't spoken. "You put in long hours at the Chamber, then stay up half the night writing books. It's too much pressure for someone your age."

"My job here isn't hard," Billie said. "And my books are formula fiction. They're only a hundred and fifty pages. All I have to do is change the names and the places. The plot stays pretty much the same."

"Other people might believe that, Billie, but I *read* your books. You do a great deal of research on each one and give the characters personalities and—"

"Which is all just a big waste of time since LoveSwift's readers are just looking for lots of kissing and a happy ending."

"Doing a good job is never a waste of time, sweetheart," Nan corrected gently. "That's why you're destined for success."

Billie was grateful for her mother's confidence and hoped that someday soon she would deserve it. She considered telling Nan about the letter she had received from Randall House expressing an "interest" in her political intrigue manuscript, but decided it would be wiser to wait until she had an actual contract.

"I was taught by the best," she told her mother instead. "So, did you have a reason for calling, besides to tell me the time and the weather?"

"As a matter of fact, I did. I made the appointment for our annual family Christmas picture next Saturday at six o'clock, and I want you to put it on your calendar."

Billie rolled her shoulders to release some tension. "Oh, Mama. Can't it just be you and Daddy and the boys this year?" she begged.

"It's not a family picture unless everyone is in it," Nan pointed out logically. "And you'll be fresh from your cruise, so you'll be nicely tanned."

"Six o'clock next Saturday." Billie surrendered without a fight.

"Are you all packed?"

Billie rubbed her tired eyes. "I wouldn't say that I'm *all* packed," she hedged. "But I will be tomorrow night."

"You did buy yourself some suitable clothes with the money I sent, didn't you?"

"Yes, and I felt . . ." Billie paused, looking for the right word, "positively sinful."

"There are dress standards on cruise ships," Nan replied. "I stress that to all my customers, and I certainly couldn't have my own daughter inappropriately attired. It was money well spent—an investment really."

Billie frowned. "Is there any way my new clothes could be considered a business expense so you could take them off your taxes?"

"No, but they *can* be considered one of your Christmas presents. I want you to impress those single-adult men on the cruise."

Billie sighed. Nan rarely interfered in her daughter's life, but when a group of LDS college students from South Carolina booked a cruise through her company, she was determined for Billie to go. Billie dragged her feet until a couple who had reserved a honeymoon suite on the same cruise canceled their wedding. Since the deposit was nonrefundable, Billie was able to get the trip for a fraction of its value. So she agreed to go.

"I'm going for relaxation, not to impress anyone," Billie insisted, trying not to sound defensive.

"I guess it would be too much to expect you to show an interest in a living, breathing human," her mother replied with resignation. "Creating perfect men in your books has spoiled you for the real thing."

Billie laughed. "I may not be looking for men, but I *am* looking forward to the trip. And every time I think about next week, my nose starts to itch." Billie couldn't resist the chance to tease her mother. "It could be a sign."

"I'm thrilled that you agreed to go," Nan answered carefully. "But you know I don't believe in signs." There was a brief pause. "Besides, I thought an itchy nose meant you're going to have unexpected company."

"I thought it meant you had allergies," Billie said. "But Grandma Murphy always claimed that nose itching was a sign from heaven that something good was about to happen," Billie quoted her paternal great-grandmother. "I'm her namesake, and everyone says I look just like her. So maybe I inherited her sign-seeing abilities too."

"Grandma Murphy was a nut," Nan reminded her daughter dryly. "In addition to seeing all kinds of signs, she also heard voices and conversed with spirits. So I don't know how much credence you can give to her nose-itching theory."

"Well, itchy noses aside, I have a good feeling about next week. Hopefully I'll be able to finish my book and get LoveSwift off my back. And if there's any time left over, who knows? I might even fall in love."

"I just hope you have a good time, dear," Nan said.

Billie hooked her purse over her shoulder. "Well, I need to get out of here, Mama. I'll call you tomorrow."

After she ended the conversation with her mother, Billie walked downstairs, and the security guard walked her to the parking deck. "Working late again?" he asked as he watched her unlock her car.

"Somebody's got to do it," she answered with a smile. "Thanks for looking out for me."

The guard waved as she started her car and headed toward her apartment. She stopped at an all-night drive-through for a hamburger and ate it as she drove, saving a few scraps for her overgrown, red fish, even though it wasn't strictly part of Fred's recommended diet. She parked her car in her assigned spot, and after unlocking the front door to her apartment, dropped the sandwich crumbs into Fred's tank, then put up her purse and turned on the computer.

She knew she should go to bed but couldn't resist checking her e-mail one last time. By the time she got connected to her Internet server, there were two messages waiting for her. Her mother had sent one informing her it was now eleven forty-five, still cold and dark, and instructing Billie to turn off the computer and go to sleep. Billie smiled as she opened the other e-mail from her friend Cowboy, a computer programmer for the newly formed Global Football League. The e-mail read:

To the famous authoress Miss Regina St. Claire—

Sorry I didn't write yesterday. I've been installing state-of-the-art computers round the clock with barely enough time to eat and sleep! And I'm having so much fun it hardly seems fair to cash my paychecks (but I still do!). I'm spending the night in Atlanta but didn't bother to call since I'm headed to Cincinnati in the morning. But I'll be back here for the big game in a couple of weeks. I've heard it's a sellout, but I think I could finagle a couple of tickets. Do you want to go with me? Maybe Camille could come too?

Cowboy

P.S. I'll even buy you both a hot dog.

Billie smirked at the words on the computer screen. Even fifty-something computer nerds couldn't resist Camille, although Billie knew Camille wouldn't give someone like Cowboy the time of day. Billie hit the reply button and settled back in her chair.

Dear Cowboy,

A lucky computer genius shouldn't brag about his dream job to poor, hardworking people like me. And I hate football, but the offer of a free hot dog does tempt me. I'll check out the holiday schedule with my mother and let you know about the GFL game.

In other news, my career with LoveSwift Books may be coming to an end. I'm running behind schedule on my new novel. (I know that shocks you.) The manuscript was supposed to be submitted a week ago, and I'm only on chapter 7. My proposal for the next one was due yesterday (and I don't have any idea what it will be about). Oh well. Maybe when LoveSwift cancels my contract, I'll take a course on computer programming and join you with the GFL.

Regina/Billie (something less than famous—but still hopeful)

Billie turned off the computer and bumped the thermostat up a notch. Then she put on pajamas and climbed into bed. After closing her eyes, she thought of playing shuffleboard with young single adults from South Carolina and tanning on white sand beaches until she fell asleep.

* * *

When Billie returned home from church on Sunday, she made herself a peanut butter and jelly sandwich and fed the scraps to Fred, then spent an hour straightening up her apartment. Afterward, she turned on her computer and scanned through a mildly threatening missive from her editor at LoveSwift Books demanding the overdue manuscript. Then she opened an e-mail from Cowboy.

> Dear Ms. St. Claire,
>
> It was snowing in Denver when I left there a couple of days ago, but the sun's shining in Cincinnati. Can't enjoy the weather though. Too busy. Worked so late last night I fell asleep on a computer that cost more than some people earn in a year. Have you thought of a brilliant idea for your next book yet? And have you decided about the GFL exhibltion game? Did you ask Camille?
>
> Cowboy

Billie sighed, then typed a quick reply.

> Dear Cowboy,
>
> I don't have an idea for my next book yet, brilliant or otherwise. But I am going on a five-day cruise to the Bahamas, and surely I can get some work done then (assuming that I don't get seasick). I'm taking my laptop and cell phone, so you can reach me any time of the day or night—voice, text, or e-mail. If you think of a good plot for my next book, I'm open to suggestions!
>
> I haven't had a chance to ask my mother about the GFL game, but pencil me in. Camille is already going with someone else. Sorry.
>
> Next time I write you, I'll be tan.
> Regina/Billie

Billie typed in her cell phone number, then pushed Send.

Once she had finished packing, Billie set her alarm for six o'clock in the morning, settled under the thick covers on her bed, and read until she fell asleep.

Billie awakened from a deep sleep with an uneasy feeling that something was not right. The apartment was very dark and quiet, so she knew it was late. Then a loud pounding startled a scream from her throat. She jumped out of bed and ran to the front door. Through the peephole, she could see Camille's magnified face. Reluctantly she opened the door and stepped aside.

Camille entered quickly, followed by a man with a huge neck. "You sleep like the dead," she told Billie. "This is Jeff Burdick," she added as if Billie wouldn't recognize him. His face had been on magazine covers and cereal boxes ever since he had announced his intention to leave the NFL and play in the new Global Football League.

"Hey." The quarterback flashed her one of his famous smiles.

Billie nodded, struggling to keep both her bathrobe and mouth from gaping open.

Camille moved into the living room and looked around, then shook her head. "I can't believe how small this place is. I've seen closets with more square footage," she exclaimed as she dropped her suede jacket across the back of a chair.

"Everyone doesn't have a rich uncle to finance spacious and expensive apartments," Billie replied with an edge to her voice as the quarterback sat down. His long legs pressed against the coffee table, and his knees were almost touching his nose.

"I think it's cozy," Mr. Burdick tried, and Camille laughed.

"Right, sugar." She gave him a complacent smile then sat beside him. "Just like a coffin."

Mr. Burdick had obviously been taught some manners, since he blushed at Camille's rude remark. He pointed to Fred, who was swimming furiously around the tank. "What's his name?"

"Fred, but it's a her," Billie provided.

"*Her* name is Fred?" Mr. Burdick clarified.

Billie nodded. "I didn't find out she was female until after she was already named, and then it didn't seem right to change."

Camille kicked off her expensive pumps and settled her nylon-encased feet on a needlepoint pillow.

"My mother made that." Billie pointed at the pillow.

"It's cute," Camille said but didn't move her feet. Then she squinted at the brightly colored clothing draped over a kitchen chair. "For your trip to the Bahamas?" she asked, and Billie nodded. "My cruise wardrobe is much nicer." She turned around. "The Competitors are taking a week off from training."

Billie looked back and forth between her guests. "That's good, I guess."

"It's the perfect opportunity for Jeff and me to spend some time together," Camille explained. "But the press hounds Jeff, and now his ex-wife has hired a private investigator."

Jeff Burdick spread his hands. "Everywhere I go, it's like a parade."

Billie shook her head in confusion. "Even if nobody was following him, I don't see how the two of you can spend the week together since you'll be touring southern Georgia with the Blalock Industries representatives."

Camille scooted forward. "There were obstacles, but I overcame them!"

Billie was immediately on guard. "How?"

"We'll take the honeymoon suite on your cruise, and no one will know it's us!"

Billie shook her head in exasperation. "How many times will I have to tell you that you can't have my cruise?"

"Jeff will buy you another one," Camille replied.

"I want *this* cruise!" Billie's tone was adamant.

"Jeff has *this* week off," Camille repeated as if she were talking to a dimwit. "It's our only chance."

Billie was unimpressed. "Wait until after the football season. By then his divorce should be final and his ex-wife won't care what you do."

Jeff Burdick finally felt compelled to make a comment. "Camille, baby, if she doesn't want to sell us the cruise . . ."

Camille stroked the football player's cheek before turning to Billie. "I'm really not here to negotiate, just to inform you of the changes in your situation. Your vacation has been revoked, and you have been assigned to take the Blalock trip. You can either sell us the cruise or let it go to waste. The choice is up to you."

Jeff Burdick blushed again, but Billie was too upset to feel sorry for him. "Frieda wouldn't do that to me," she whispered.

Camille shrugged. "It's nothing against you personally. She's just doing a favor for Uncle Conrad. And don't you think you're being rather shortsighted? Jeff can help me get a job with the GFL, and once I leave the Chamber, all the good assignments will come to you."

Billie very much wanted a chance to prove herself and to be rid of Camille, but sacrificing her cruise was asking too much. She shook her head firmly. "No, I won't do it."

Camille's eyes narrowed. "If you refuse, I'll ask Uncle Conrad to have you fired."

Billie's breath started coming in quick, little gasps. "I don't believe you would really go that far."

Camille moved closer, her expression menacing. "Actually, I'm prepared to go much further. Be glad all I want is your cruise."

Billie flinched as Camille ran her fingers through her hair, then moderated her tone slightly as she continued. "If you'll be reasonable and take care of the Blalock Industries folks next week—life will be better for both of us. And I'm not asking you to give up your vacation, just to postpone it."

Billie wanted to call Camille's bluff, but she couldn't afford to lose her job at the Chamber until she had a contract with Randall House. There was no doubt in her mind that Camille would carry out her threat to have Billie fired if she didn't cooperate. So, feeling like a coward, Billie surrendered.

"I guess I don't have much choice. I'll call my mother . . ."

Camille shook her head. "I've already called her. Everything's arranged. She said the tickets would be waiting for us on the ship."

Billie nodded. "If my mother doesn't receive payment for this cruise by the end of the week, I'll call the press myself and make sure Mr. Burdick's ex-wife is waiting for you when you disembark."

Camille gave her an exasperated look. "For heaven's sake, Billie. I said Jeff will pay for it."

"Full price," Billie added, feeling a measure of satisfaction. "And I want him to start using my mother's agency for all his travel needs."

Camille waved impatiently. "Okay, okay."

"I want Mr. Burdick to give me his word," Billie said. "Yours doesn't mean much."

Jeff Burdick nodded. "I'll tell my personal assistant to use your mother's agency from now on. And I'm sorry about all this . . ."

Camille stood and looked at Billie through narrowed eyes. "Your mother said you had a map and information about the cruise."

"In my purse . . ." Billie's voice trailed off as Camille walked over and studied the contents of Billie's handbag.

Camille removed an envelope from the handbag. She turned and smiled, all sweetness again now that she'd gotten her way. "Do you have one of your mother's business cards you could give Jeff? He'll need her address to mail the check. And now that she's going to be his travel agent, he'll need her phone numbers."

Billie walked stiffly into her bedroom and took a business card from a drawer in her dresser. When she returned to the living room, Camille and Jeff were standing by the front door.

Billie extended the card, and Camille tucked it into her purse. "I couldn't find my itinerary for the Blalock trip, but Edgar will have an extra when you meet him at the airport."

"Edgar?"

"Uncle Conrad's chauffeur," Camille clarified. "He's going to be driving you and the Blalock people around. You'll need to be at the airport by four o'clock. Call if you need me." Camille stepped forward and whispered into Billie's ear. "But only if you *really* need me." Then she turned to Jeff Burdick. "Come on, sugar." She took the quarterback by the hand and led him outside.

Billie locked the door behind them, then took several deep breaths, refusing to cry. It wasn't that big a deal, she told herself. She needed time to work on her book, but she figured she could do it in her hotel room at night during the Blalock trip. The only reason she had to believe that a week spent on the cruise ship might be significant was the nose-itching theory of her crazy great-grandma.

Since it was only five-thirty in the morning and the Blalock reps didn't need to be picked up until later that afternoon, Billie retreated to her room to get some more sleep. She fell back into bed and burrowed under the covers. Then, once her head was buried deep into the pillow, she allowed a few tears to slip from her eyes.

Billie was awakened fifteen minutes later by a phone call from her mother. "I can't believe the Chamber canceled your vacation!" was

Nan Murphy's first comment. "But it did work out nicely that Camille and her cousin could use your ticket."

Billie realized immediately that Camille had given Nan a fictionalized version of the situation, but in order to set the record straight she knew she would have to upset her mother, so she sighed and answered, "Yeah, that was a real stroke of luck."

"And I'm sure the LDS businessmen will appreciate the fact that a member of the Church will be showing them around."

Billie murmured a noncommittal, "Hmm."

"I've already booked another cruise for you that can be taken anytime during the next twelve months. Since Camille said money was no object, I put you in a stateroom with a balcony."

"Thanks, Mama," Billie said softly.

"Are you all right, sweetheart?" Nan asked. "You sound kind of stuffy."

"I told you my nose was itching. Maybe I'm catching a cold," Billie replied. "And let me know if you don't get a check from Camille's *cousin*."

"Camille said he was a very responsible sort of person. I'm sure he'll pay me promptly. She also said that he'll be giving me a lot of business in the future."

As Billie ended the call, she marveled that her mother could be so shrewd in business and yet such a bad judge of character. Billie took the last Pop-Tart from the box, then sat in front of the computer and worked on chapter 8 of *Breathless* until two-thirty. At that point, she turned off her computer and stared at her luggage.

She didn't have the heart to repack, even though she would be going on a tour of southern Georgia in December instead of a cruise to the Bahamas. Hoping she could adapt her wardrobe, she stepped into the shower. As the water sluiced down her, she realized that Camille and Jeff Burdick were probably just getting settled in to what should have been her luxurious honeymoon suite.

Billie let the water run until it started to get cold. After drying her hair, she put on a business suit and sensible shoes. As she covered the sprinkling of freckles across her nose with makeup, she wondered if she *should* cut her hair. It hung almost to her waist, and though she'd always thought it was her best feature, Camille's remark about updating her appearance still stung.

Once she was ready, she slipped on her red, down-filled coat, gave Fred a generous helping of fish food, and picked up her purse. She reached inside and felt for her keys but couldn't find them. After several fruitless seconds of searching, she walked over to the kitchen counter and dumped the contents out for closer examination. There were still no keys.

Grinding her teeth in frustration, Billie stalked to her room and opened the jewelry box she had inherited from Grandma Murphy. As she grabbed the extra set of keys she kept there, she saw her emergency hundred-dollar bill. Since the Chamber would pay expenses on the trip and taking her own money might tempt her to spend it unnecessarily, she started to close the jewelry box. Then, she had the overwhelming feeling that she should take the money with her. Whether it was Grandma Murphy or the Holy Ghost or her own imagination, she didn't dare ignore the prompting. So she tucked the bill into her purse and rushed outside into the cold winter afternoon.

Billie made it halfway down the sidewalk before she realized that her car was not in its regular parking space. Dumbfounded, she stared around the crowded lot. Her Taurus, while dependable, was certainly not enviable, and she doubted that a thief would choose to steal it over the other cars in the apartment complex. Then her eyes settled on a silver Volvo, which looked very much like Camille's, parked where her Taurus should have been. Closer inspection proved that it *was* Camille's car. Furious, Billie pulled out her cell phone and dialed quickly.

She had to call three times before Camille finally answered. "Billie!" She sounded delighted to hear from her coworker. "This suite is incredible! It has a huge hot tub and a skylight and a big screen television—"

"You stole my car!" Billie interrupted.

"I didn't steal it," Camille said with a laugh. "I just traded so that the private investigator wouldn't follow us. When you leave my car in the long-term parking lot at Hartsfield International, he'll assume I've gone on my business trip as planned."

Billie took a deep breath. "You could have at least asked me."

"You would have said no," Camille replied blithely. There was a noise in the background, then Camille giggled. "Just a second, sugar!

Billie, I've got to go. The keys to my car are under the front passenger seat." The line went dead.

Billie stared at the cell phone for a few seconds, then turned it off and got into the Volvo. Once she got the car started, she noticed that the gas gauge was below empty, so she had to stop at the nearest gas station. Then, with evil thoughts of Camille thrashing around in her mind, Billie finally headed to the airport.

CHAPTER 2

Cowboy finished packing his carry-on suitcase and checked out of his hotel. As he drove his rental car to the Cincinnati airport, he sighed. After months on the road, he would finally be back in Atlanta for good. The complicated computer system was in place, and his job with the GFL was ending. His supervisor had told him today that they were bringing in someone else to take it from there. Cowboy felt no regret at being replaced —only relief.

Once he was settled into his seat on the airplane, he quickly typed a text message.

> The exhibition game is a sellout, and I heard a rumor that 10,000 bogus tickets will be printed and distributed to scalpers. You think that's what we're looking for?

He pushed Send, then waited for a response. It came a few seconds later. Cowboy's contact in Atlanta replied:

> Hummer wouldn't waste his time on a small scheme like that. You can bet if he's involved, it will be something much bigger.

Cowboy sighed as their exchange continued.

No sign of Hummer yet. Are we sure he's involved?

Pretty sure.

You still watching Camille Lockhart?

Yeah. She may not be a part of whatever's going on at the GFL, but she's definitely working for Hummer.

She's been lying low. Haven't seen her in a while.

Maybe she knows we're on to her?

Maybe so. Since my time's running out, I'm going to have to get more aggressive.

How aggressive?

I'm going to activate the listening devices I installed in all the computers at the GFL headquarters.

Very dangerous. If anyone catches on, they'll know it was you.

It would take a computer genius to find my eavesdropping system, and I haven't met anyone at the GFL with the computer literacy of a third grader.

After a short delay, a final message appeared on the tiny screen.

Just be careful. These guys don't play nice.

Roger that.

Cowboy put away his PDA and leaned his head back against the seat. Maybe he could catch a couple of hours of sleep before he hit Atlanta.

* * *

An hour of fighting the heavy Atlanta traffic did not improve Billie's mood. She turned into the long-term parking lot at Hartsfield International Airport and pulled into the closest space available. As she unloaded her suitcases from the trunk of the Volvo, her cell phone vibrated. She checked and saw that she had a text message.

Billie,

I should be back in Atlanta late tonight. Know you're headed to places tropical, but thought I might try to meet up with you when you get back. Could we go to dinner or something? And if you don't mind my asking, who is taking Camille to the exhibition game?

Cowboy

Billie leaned against the Volvo as she typed a quick reply with numb fingers.

Cowboy,

Camille Lockhart has skipped town with a new boyfriend (sorry, I'm sworn to secrecy or I'd tell you his name) and left me to do her job. So I'm headed to

southern Georgia, and I won't have a tan anytime soon.
I'll call you when I get back and we can split a pizza.

Billie

She locked the car and resisted the urge to kick the expensive vehicle. Holding the collar of her coat with one hand, Billie stacked the suitcases onto a collapsible dolly with the other, then dragged them behind her into the terminal.

A man with graying hair, reading a paper and wearing a chauffeur uniform, was sitting in one of the plastic chairs of the waiting area. He glanced up as Billie approached and smiled. "Edgar, I presume?" she said, and he nodded. "Billie Murphy."

"A pleasure to meet you," he replied in a British accent. Whether it was real or affected, she couldn't tell. "I was beginning to wonder if I dreamed Miss Camille's phone call about impersonations and intrigue."

"Unfortunately, it's a real-life nightmare," Billie mumbled.

Edgar smiled indulgently. "Miss Camille has put us on the spot, I'll admit that. But we'll do just fine on our little assignment," he said as he reached over and took the handle to her luggage carrier.

Before Billie could reply, the arrival of the plane from Salt Lake was announced. Taking several deep breaths, she stood beside Edgar and watched passengers walk into the public area. There were businessmen, a couple of families, several young students, and a youth group from Silver Springs who were all wearing T-shirts emblazoned with a picture of the Grand Canyon.

Billie was just beginning to think that maybe the Blalock folks had missed the plane when she spotted the two men from Salt Lake. Wearing conservative suits and carrying standard leather briefcases, they looked like full-time missionaries just a little past their prime.

Edgar held up a discreet sign that stated simply *Blalock Industries*, and the Mormon businessmen veered toward them. As she waited with resignation, Billie's eyes drifted to the two men walking directly behind the Blalock reps. Their resemblance to each other was so remarkable that Billie assumed they must be brothers. Each wore faded blue jeans and a denim shirt, and both had a backpack slung casually over one shoulder. Their hair was longish and light blond, their eyes were sparking blue, and both had natural tans. Smiling to herself, Billie wondered if they had come to Atlanta to film a commercial for DoubleMint gum.

The Blalock reps had come to a stop in front of her, so Billie dragged her eyes away from the mirror-image men and tried to concentrate on the business at hand.

"You must be Miss Lockhart," one of them said to Billie. "I'm Cliff Reynolds, and this is Neal Talbot." He waved toward his suited companion. Billie absently acknowledged the introduction while covertly watching the matching men who had come to a stop beside Mr. Reynolds. "May I call you Camille?"

"Oh, please don't," Billie said, and Mr. Reynolds gave her a startled look. "Miss Lockhart had a . . ." she searched for the appropriate term, "a conflict. My name is Billie Murphy, and I'm taking her place as your tour guide."

Mr. Reynolds recovered quickly. "Nice to meet you, Billie."

Billie couldn't resist another glance at the blond men, and the one on the left gave her a brilliant smile. He was a little taller than his counterpart, and she was sure that his baby-faced good looks had broken many hearts over the years. The man on the right was watching her as well, but his gaze wasn't flirty. Although his coloring was identical and his features similar, upon closer examination Billie realized that he wasn't really that handsome. His eyes were too far apart, and his nose looked crooked, as if it had been broken. His jaw was a little too square, and his lips too full. Billie reached up to scratch her nose as he nodded politely in her direction.

Mr. Reynolds went on, "I'm the managing attorney for Blalock Industries, and Neal is in charge of the accounting department."

Billie raised her eyebrows. "I'm surprised that a paper company would have more than one lawyer and accountant."

Mr. Reynolds laughed at this comment. "The paper company is just one of the business enterprises owned by Blalock Industries. It's one of the largest conglomerates in Utah."

At this point, the handsome twin leaned forward, recapturing Billie's attention. "I'm Kip Blalock, heir to the conglomerate. I hope you don't mind if I crash your tour."

"Of course not," Billie said with a quick look at Edgar.

"No problem whatsoever," the chauffeur assured them. "We'll adjust our hotel and restaurant reservations accordingly."

Kip Blalock smiled. "Great." Then he looked at his companion. "Oh, and this is Nathan Turner."

"The heir's bodyguard," Mr. Turner provided.

Billie clasped Kip Blalock's palm. "You need a bodyguard?" she asked.

Kip laughed. "Naw, Nathan's exaggerating to make himself sound important. He's just head of security for Blalock Industries."

"I thought you were brothers," Billie admitted. "Or even twins."

"In my father's dreams," Kip exclaimed with a grin in Nathan Turner's direction.

Mr. Turner cleared his throat. "Kip's father hired me specifically because of my resemblance to his son, and while I do have other duties at Blalock Industries, my major responsibility is Kip."

"Why would your father want his head of security to resemble you, Mr. Blalock?" Billie asked.

"Please call me Kip. We all prefer to be on a first-name basis," the heir to Blalock Industries requested. "And my father is a worrier. He insists that Nathan and I dress alike so that if there was an assassination attempt, I would have a fifty percent chance of survival."

Billie's eyes widened. "Someone wants to *kill* you?"

Kip transferred his backpack to the other shoulder. "It's a long, boring story."

Billie turned back to Nathan Turner. "And one that sounds very dangerous for you."

"The danger is minimal." Nathan looked around the busy airport, then returned his bright blue eyes to Billie.

"We appreciate you filling in for Miss Lockhart," Kip said.

"Miss Murphy canceled her vacation to escort you," Edgar informed them, then gave Billie a covert smile.

"How kind!" Cliff interjected. "Although I regret that I won't be able to meet Miss Lockhart. I served a mission in Hong Kong and was anxious to talk to her about the Buddhist religion."

Billie raised an eyebrow. "Camille knows about Buddhists?"

Cliff nodded. "Miss Lockhart told me she that she had recently converted to the Buddhist faith."

Billie controlled a laugh. "I'm sure you would have found discussing Buddhism with Camille fascinating."

"I read my itinerary on the plane and was very impressed," Cliff continued. "The Georgia Chamber of Commerce is really giving us the royal treatment."

"Georgia is a very hospitable state," Billie replied with confidence as she scanned the itinerary that Edgar had slipped into her hand.

"What I can't figure out is what's in it for the Chamber of Commerce," Nathan Turner said bluntly. "Why are they willing to invest so much money in us?"

Cliff Reynolds opened his mouth, then closed it again, apparently unable to think of a suitable reply. So Billie faced Nathan Turner.

"When you build your new plant in Georgia, the Chamber will take all the credit."

Nathan blinked, then said, "What makes you so sure that we will choose a site in Georgia?"

Billie returned his stare. "Because given a choice, only a fool would choose to build elsewhere."

A smile played at the corner of Mr. Turner's mouth. "Well, I like someone who is forthright."

"Especially if they're also beautiful," Kip added, stepping forward. "And you, Miss Murphy, are definitely both. I love it here already."

Billie couldn't help but laugh as Edgar reached for her luggage and started toward the escalator. "If you'll all follow me, please, I need to get you checked in to the Peachtree Center Marriott before dinnertime."

"I'm glad to see you have a tour of the Georgia Dome built into our schedule," Kip said as he fell into step beside Billie. "I'm a big football fan and am particularly interested in the new GFL."

"Mr. Conrad Lockhart is Edgar's employer and he was instrumental in bringing a franchise of the GFL to Atlanta," Billie explained to the Blalock men. "So we had inside connections."

"Even though their practices are closed, we've arranged for you to meet several of the players," Edgar added with pride.

"I thought the Competitors weren't practicing this week," Billie said with a frown, remembering her discussion with Camille that morning.

Edgar nodded. "They aren't, but some of the players are going to attend the tour on Thursday as a special favor to Mr. Lockhart."

Kip smiled. "I love having friends in high places."

Edgar cleared his throat. "Yes, well, once we collect your luggage, we will take it out front where I have a rental car waiting." He then asked the men to point out their suitcases and instructed airport valets to collect the appropriate bags and take them to a black Yukon parked in the deck.

"Traffic will be bad this time of day," Edgar predicted as Kip chose the front passenger seat. The accountant and lawyer climbed into the far back while Edgar helped Billie into the middle row by the window. Nathan Turner took the seat beside her and pulled a sheaf of papers from his backpack, then started making notations.

The huge vehicle eased into the rush-hour traffic, and Billie took advantage of the time to study the itinerary. They had rooms at the Peachtree Center Marriott and dinner reservations at the Atrium, a critically acclaimed restaurant on the top floor of a downtown skyscraper. In spite of her brave words to Nathan Turner, Billie was surprised by the luxury level of the accommodations. Maybe the Blalock Industries paper plant was more important to the state of Georgia than she had initially realized.

Edgar was pointing out Atlanta landmarks to Kip, and Billie could hear Cliff and Neal conversing quietly in the back. She glanced at Nathan, who was scowling at the papers in his lap.

"What are you working on?" she asked.

"A new security system for Blalock Industries," he replied.

She squinted at the notations and remarked, "It looks complicated."

"It is," he acknowledged.

Then Kip addressed her from the front seat. "Billie is an unusual name," he said. "Is it short for something?"

She nodded. "I was named after my great-grandmother, but thankfully my older brother couldn't say her name, so I've always been called Billie."

"And what is your real name?" Kip asked.

Nathan looked up from his figures, the conversation in the backseat ceased, and even Edgar glanced at her in the rearview mirror. She shook her head. "Sorry, but I never tell anyone my real name."

Kip's eyebrows arched. "I think you just issued a challenge."

Billie shrugged. "It wouldn't be that hard to find out what my legal name is," she admitted. "But it will be impossible to get me to *tell* you."

"Hmm," Kip murmured. "We'll have to see about that."

"How many brothers do you have?" Cliff asked.

"Four. One older, three younger," Billie told him.

Neal Talbot spoke for the first time. "I have three sons, and my wife is expecting our fourth child any day now," he divulged, then blushed.

Billie smiled. "I love big families. Are you hoping for a girl this time?"

The color in Neal's cheeks deepened. "Honestly I don't care, but I think my wife would like a daughter."

Anxious to keep the shy Neal talking, Billie asked, "What are your responsibilities at Blalock Industries?"

"Just boring stuff like tax reporting and budgets," Neal replied.

"Boring but very important," Billie guessed. "What about you, Cliff?"

"Acquisitions mostly, but I handle other things as they come up."

Billie considered the information she had collected thus far, then said, "When I meet a group like yours I always try to determine who the decision maker is. That helps me to direct my sales pitch." She turned to Kip. "Based on your relationship to the owner of the company, I presume I should try to impress you."

There was a moment of awkward silence before Kip laughed. "Actually, I'm just along for the ride."

Nathan abandoned his figures to say, "Cliff and Neal are the ones who have been looking for property to build the new plant, and they'll be the ones to choose the site."

Kip nodded. "When I found out our guys were coming to Atlanta, where the GFL headquarters is located, I decided to tag along. Nathan is here to keep me out of trouble."

"And alive," Billie teased, trying to recover from her blunder.

Kip smiled. "That too."

"Yes, Kip wanted to see the Georgia Dome, so I had to drop everything and fly to Atlanta." There was an edge of resentment in Nathan's voice. "Even though I have bugs to work out of a multimillion-dollar security system being installed on January 1."

In an attempt to lighten the mood, Billie said, "Well, it should be easy to impress you two with Georgia's magnificence since you haven't seen the competition." She looked into the backseat. "And while this trip may not be your first, it will definitely be your last. Once you've seen how beautiful Georgia is, you'll forget that you even have other options."

"There's that brutal honesty again," Kip said with a smile. "And total loyalty to the state of Georgia."

Cliff leaned up and told Billie, "It's not beauty that will make the decision for us, though."

"No," Nathan agreed. "They're looking for bargain land prices, cheap labor, and reduced transportation costs in a state that doesn't mind sacrificing their forests."

Billie stared at Nathan's profile. "Mr. Turner, I believe that in one sentence you have managed to insult the entire state of Georgia."

Nathan seemed surprised by her remark.

"What Nathan meant to say is that . . ." Cliff began, but Kip interrupted.

"Who cares what Nathan meant to say? Let's talk about you, Billie. Where did you go to school? What's your goal in life? What's your favorite flower? And what is that perfume you're wearing?"

"My favorite flower? Perfume?" she repeated in confusion.

Kip laughed. "That information might help in my campaign to make you tell me your real first name."

Billie shook her head in mock despair. "I graduated from the University of Georgia. My goal is to one day have a houseful of beautiful children. My favorite flower is the lily, and I don't know what kind of perfume I'm wearing." She paused to sniff her wrist. "It's something my mother gave me for my birthday."

"A houseful of kids?" Cliff said. "You'd make a good Mormon."

"Actually, I *am* a good Mormon." Billie smiled at their surprised reactions. "And I'd much rather hear about Blalock Industries than discuss myself."

Cliff didn't need any more encouragement. "We're one of the top ten paper producers in the country," the lawyer told her. "As Nathan mentioned, Mr. Blalock is interested in profit, but he's also environmentally aware. We have a very ambitious replanting program, and our emission standards are above those set by the state or federal government."

"But there are some very extreme conservation groups in Utah," Neal contributed. "And they won't listen to reason when it comes to cutting down trees, even though making paper is a business that provides jobs and tax revenue."

"So we're hoping for a more friendly working environment in the South," Cliff concluded.

"In a state that doesn't mind sacrificing its trees," Billie added with a glance at Nathan Turner.

"I would have said it a little differently, but that's it basically," Cliff agreed with a smile as Edgar pulled the huge SUV to a stop in front of the Peachtree Marriott. Two hotel valets collected the luggage, then led the way inside. Stepping into the luxurious lobby, Billie stayed with the visitors while Edgar walked to the registration desk.

"I met Jeff Burdick today," she told Kip in an effort to make conversation.

He looked back blankly. "Who?"

Billie frowned. "The Competitors' quarterback," she clarified. "I thought that since you loved the GFL and all . . ." Her voice trailed off in confusion.

Now it was Nathan's turn to smile. "Kip's real interest in the GFL is gambling, not football. That's why he doesn't know the name of the Competitors' most famous player."

Kip admitted the truthfulness of this with a shrug. "It's not that I don't like football. It's just that I *really* like to make easy money."

Just then, Edgar returned and began issuing keys. "They were able to give us two more rooms without any problem," he announced. "Mr. Reynolds, you and Mr. Talbot will have adjoining rooms." He turned to Kip and Nathan. "And Mr. Blalock and Mr. Turner will be neighbors."

"Oh!" Kip groaned as he accepted his plastic card key. "I got stuck beside Nathan, Mr. All-Work-and-No-Play." He appealed to Billie. "Don't you feel sorry for me?"

Billie's eyes skimmed from Nathan Turner's blond head across his broad shoulders and past the little scar just below his left eye, settling on his too-full lips. *This is the stuff formula fiction heroes are made of,* she thought. Then she turned to Kip. "You have my deepest sympathy."

"Onto the elevator now," Edgar encouraged. The men stepped back and let Billie precede them. Once they were moving upward, Edgar continued, "Your dinner reservations are for seven o'clock. The Atrium, where you will be eating, is a very exclusive establishment, and in order to feel appropriately dressed, I suggest that you gentlemen wear a coat and tie."

Kip leaned toward Billie. "Is he trying to tell me that I have to change clothes?"

Billie smiled. "I think that's it exactly." Her eyes moved to Nathan, who nodded.

"If Kip changes, I change."

The elevator stopped on the eighteenth floor, and they walked together to a group of rooms at one end of the hallway. Edgar supervised the distribution of luggage to the appropriate rooms, then tipped the valets and left with a promise to meet in the lobby in an hour.

Billie stepped inside her room and paused to appreciate the opulence. The carpet was thick, the walls were covered with linen fabric, and a fruit basket wrapped in delicate white netting rested on the coffee table. She walked into the bedroom and sat on the edge of a large, four-poster, king-size bed with a polished cotton comforter. From her perch high on the massive bed, she could see the Jacuzzi in the bathroom, lined with scented soaps and bath salts. Billie smiled to herself. Maybe doing Camille's job wasn't going to be so bad after all.

* * *

Cowboy threw his carry-on bag into the corner of his small office at the GFL headquarters in Atlanta. Then he collapsed into the chair and ran his hand lovingly across the sleek LCD monitor on the desk. In all his years of working with computers, he had never seen a system quite so exquisite—or quite so expensive. He turned the system on and ran a few tests, made some adjustments, then pulled up his e-mail. He barely had time to enter the familiar address when he heard voices in the hall.

"So, you folks been having nice weather in Nevada?" a vaguely familiar voice asked.

"Hot and dry. Same as always," another man answered, and Cowboy smiled. He was reasonably certain that the voice belonged to an underworld kingpin named Felix Hummer. "Is everything still on schedule?" the man from Las Vegas continued.

"Perfectly," the voice Cowboy couldn't place replied.

Cowboy held his breath, hoping they'd say more, but instead their footsteps echoed down the hall. When he was sure they were gone, Cowboy returned his attention to his e-mail.

* * *

After a soothing bubble bath, Billie left her hotel room at exactly six-thirty, wearing a simple black dress she had purchased for the formal dinners on her cruise. When she reached the lobby, she found the men from Blalock Industries assembled in a sitting area near the door. Cliff and Neal looked pretty much the same as they had earlier. Billie had to smile, wondering if they had an endless supply of dark suits. Her eyes moved to Kip and Nathan, who both looked predictably identical in khaki pants and navy blue sports jackets.

"Am I late?" she asked with a quick glance at her watch.

"No," Kip assured her. He stepped forward and clasped her elbow. "But you *are* gorgeous."

This was certainly an overstatement, but Billie just said, "Thank you."

"You're a little underdressed for the cold weather," Nathan commented with a frown. "Don't you have a coat?"

"Just that huge red parka I was wearing earlier," she replied. "And it doesn't match my dress."

"If Billie gets cold, I'll let her wear my jacket," Kip offered gallantly.

"Thanks," she told him with a smile. "But they won't let you into the Atrium unless you're wearing your sports coat and tie." She looked at Nathan. "And if you take your coat off, Nathan will have to remove his as well, and then you'll both be cold."

Kip laughed. "I love a woman with a sense of humor!" He tucked her hand around his arm.

Edgar led them out to the SUV and helped Billie into her seat by the window while the men took their previous positions. It was cold in the Yukon and she wanted to rub her hands up and down her bare arms, but Nathan was watching so she resisted.

As they drove, Edgar gave a detailed description of the Atrium's cuisine.

"It sounds like you eat there often," Kip finally said.

Edgar nodded. "I've been Mr. Lockhart's guest on several occasions."

"Then you'd better go over that menu again and let me take notes," Kip said with a smile, and Edgar complied.

During the recap of the Atrium's best dishes, Billie leaned toward Nathan, who was still staring into space. "Is something the matter?" she asked.

He looked up as though he were coming out of a fog. "No, I just have so much work to do. And this whole hospitality thing is pointless. It doesn't matter how nice our dinner is or how luxurious the hotel is or how beautiful you are—" Nathan paused abruptly, and Billie could tell he regretted this last remark. With a sigh he continued, "Cliff and Neal will recommend the property that best meets the needs of Blalock Industries, whether it's in Georgia or Mississippi or Timbuktu."

Billie leaned closer and lowered her voice to match his. "So you're saying the Georgia Chamber of Commerce is wasting time and money?"

He gave her a little smile. "Well, it's not a complete waste of time. I guess we do have to eat."

"And the Atrium is supposed to be very good," Billie agreed.

"You've never eaten there?" He seemed surprised.

She shook her head. "Oh, no. I'm more of a Wendy's kind of girl." She took a deep breath, then pressed on. "You're here now, and this trip has already been paid for, so why don't you relax and be a good sport?"

Nathan nodded. "Okay, I'll try to forget about the work that's piling up on my desk in Salt Lake."

Billie smiled her approval. Then they heard Kip invite Edgar to join them for dinner. "Oh, thank you very much," Edgar said with obvious discomfort. "But the Atrium is very strict about reservations, and I've already had to ask them to add two people for tonight."

"Cliff or Neal will go back to the hotel and eat room service," Kip offered generously.

Billie had to control laughter again when she glimpsed the surprised looks on the faces of the occupants of the backseat. Nathan glanced at her, and she thought she saw amusement in his eyes as well.

"That won't be necessary," Edgar declined more firmly. "Part of my job is to stay with this rented vehicle."

Kip abandoned the subject as quickly as he had picked it up and asked where the Georgia Dome was in relation to their current position. "It's to the east," Edgar responded.

There was a little lull in the conversation, and then Kip asked, "So, Billie, have you met any of the other Competitors besides the quarterback?"

Billie shook her head. "No, but I've had contact with a lot of the GFL's lower-level employees. As I said earlier, Edgar's boss, Mr. Lockhart, was instrumental in getting the franchise here in Atlanta, and since his niece works with me, we've been involved from the first."

"Do you think the GFL can really compete with the NFL?" Cliff wanted to know.

Billie considered this. "I had my doubts at first, but I have to admit I've been impressed with the setup. There's lots of money behind the new league, and they're well organized. They have franchises all across the country and a lot of community support. Their ads are appealing, and the exhibition game here in Atlanta is reportedly a sellout." She shrugged. "So I think they might have a shot."

"I'm going to try to come up with a ticket to that game," Kip said. "It would be worth a trip back to Atlanta if I can make a few well-placed bets and win big."

Billie was surprised that a member of the Church would openly admit to gambling, but she tried to keep the disapproval from her voice. "Tickets to the exhibition game are hard to come by," she told him. "But maybe Conrad Lockhart could get you one."

"I'll ask Mr. Lockhart to check," Edgar volunteered as he stopped in front of the Carlisle Building, where a new set of valets began opening doors. "I hope you enjoy the evening," he added. "I'll be waiting right here when you're finished."

Assuming the role of hostess, Billie led the way to the elevator with as much confidence as she could muster. She told the attendant that they had reservations at the Atrium. He pressed a button, and the impressive distance was traversed quickly. When the door opened, they approached the elegant maître d' guarding the entrance to the exclusive restaurant. As soon as Billie mentioned Conrad Lockhart, his expression brightened.

"Oh yes, we've reserved a very special table for you." With a flick of his wrist, he summoned a younger man. "Ramón will provide you with excellent service for the duration of your visit tonight," he promised. "Ramón, please escort Mr. Lockhart's guests to table nine."

They were seated along the wall of windows and had a breath-taking view of the city. "And there's the Georgia Dome," Billie pointed out for Kip's benefit. "The lights are all on."

"Probably getting the field ready for the big game," Kip guessed.

Billie agreed that this was very likely the case, then Ramón recommended the poached salmon and white wine. Everyone chose the salmon with soft drinks. Looking a little disappointed, Ramón went off to fill the orders.

After the waiter left, Nathan Turner's arm brushed against Billie's. She rubbed her nose, then apologized for the necessary action. "I must be catching a cold, but I'm not congested."

"It could be allergies," Cliff suggested.

"I hope you're not allergic to me," Kip said, pushing his chair a little closer to hers.

"I'm allergic to shellfish," Neal told her shyly. "When I eat them, I break out in hives."

"Allergies can be very serious," Cliff continued. "A bad reaction can cause respiratory failure or even death. You really should see a doctor."

Billie cleared her throat. "So far my symptoms are very mild. Just an itchy nose." She pointed out the window. "Isn't the view spectacular?"

"Very nice," Cliff responded politely.

"Gorgeous," Kip agreed, but he was looking at her, not out the window.

"Pretty," Nathan allowed, "but I prefer mountains to skyscrapers."

"We have Stone Mountain," Billie said as Ramón returned and distributed tiny bowls of cold asparagus soup. "But I'm sure that's nothing compared to the Rockies."

"The Rockies are magnificent," Nathan told her, enthusiastic for the first time since she'd met him. "There are no words to adequately describe them."

Kip looked up from his soup with a smile. "Why don't you come visit us in Salt Lake sometime, Billie?" he suggested. "Nathan and I will take you skiing."

Nathan looked startled by his inclusion in Kip's invitation, and Billie had to laugh. "Sounds like fun. But I'd better wait until Nathan gets his security system in place so he'll have time for recreation."

Nathan seemed relieved, but Kip frowned. "No point in that. Once he's through with the security system, he'll just get busy with something else."

"This soup is delicious," Cliff said in an obvious attempt to avoid an argument. Billie didn't care for it particularly, but nodded as good manners dictated. A few minutes of awkward silence followed, then Ramón picked up the soup bowls and gave everyone some carrot salad surrounded by sprigs of asparagus. Cliff asked about a skiing trip Kip was planning to Switzerland, and while they talked Billie stared at her plate.

"Not exactly food that would appeal to a Wendy's kind of girl," Nathan whispered.

She smiled. "It's colorful but not very appetizing." She poked at it with her fork, then turned to Nathan. "You seem young to be responsible for the security of a large corporation. Mr. Blalock must have a lot of confidence in you to trust you with the safety of his company and his son."

"Oh, yeah, my dad's crazy about Nathan," Kip answered.

"It's just my good fortune that I look like Kip," Nathan replied, a slight undercurrent of irritation in his voice. "Otherwise I would never have landed the job." He looked up at Billie. "Although my credentials are decent, and I hope to eventually prove myself to Mr. Blalock," he added as the main course arrived.

"So, Billie," Cliff said with a sigh. "When did you join the Church?"

Billie swallowed a bite of flaky fish. "I was born a into the Church, Cliff. In fact, I have ancestors who crossed the plains in a handcart company."

Cliff blushed. "I'm sorry. I just assumed that you were a convert since you live in the mission field."

"It was a natural assumption," Billie told him.

While they ate, Cliff and Neal took turns asking questions about Mormonism in the South. Billie was relieved when Ramón arrived with pieces of the Atrium's world-renowned chocolate almond pie for everyone, although she felt obligated to remind Ramón that they hadn't ordered pie.

"Compliments of the house," he replied as he served her with a flourish. He then encouraged everyone to have a cup of gourmet coffee with their dessert, but they all declined. "Without the coffee, our famous pie won't be the same," Ramón pleaded.

"It's against our religion to drink coffee," Cliff explained.

"So the pie will have to stand on its own," Kip added with one of his most charming smiles.

"This pie is delicious," Cliff said after a few bites.

"I don't know how it could be any better, even with gourmet coffee," Billie agreed as Kip's cell phone started ringing.

"If you'll excuse me," he said, then stood and hurried toward the entrance.

While they finished dessert, Billie addressed Neal. "It must be difficult for you to be away from home right now with the holidays coming up and your wife about to have a baby."

A shadow crossed Neal's face, and Billie knew the trip was a personal sacrifice for him. "Yes, but Mr. Blalock wants the paper plant location settled before the beginning of the year. So . . ."

At this point Kip returned, and Neal let his voice trail off. Everyone finished their pie, and then the maître d' came to their table.

"I hope you have found our cuisine to be satisfactory," the man said with confidence.

"Everything was superb," Cliff assured him.

"Well, on behalf of your host, Mr. Lockhart, I wish you all a pleasant trip and a good evening."

As they moved toward the elevator, Billie looked up and saw Nathan staring at her. "Is something the matter?" she asked.

Nathan shook his head. "You're just so different from the other public relations reps I've dealt with."

She nodded, thinking of Camille. "I know I'm not glamorous or particularly witty."

He shook his head. "No, I meant that as a compliment. You're honest and genuine, and I find it quite refreshing."

She gave him a tentative smile. "Thanks. And I'll admit that you aren't exactly what I expected either." She pointed at Cliff and Neal, who were a few steps ahead. "Now *they* fit the Mormon stereotype."

Nathan grinned as they stepped onto the elevator. Then Kip spoke from behind them. "Nathan would look just like them if he could. I grew my hair out to aggravate my dad."

Billie glanced at Nathan with sudden understanding and sympathy. "Then you had to grow your hair out to match Kip's?"

Nathan nodded as he rubbed the golden curls at the back of his neck self-consciously.

Kip laughed. "The funny thing is that my long hair doesn't seem to bother my dad, but it drives Nathan crazy!"

When they walked outside, Edgar was waiting in the Yukon. Once they were seated, Billie regarded Nathan seriously. "So you weren't kidding about enhancing the similarities in your appearance to confuse a would-be assassin?"

The men exchanged a glance, then Cliff spoke up. "About a year ago, Blalock Industries announced their intention to cut trees in what a militant conservationist group considers an 'environmentally fragile area,' and the group took them to court. When the judge ruled in favor of Blalock Industries, Kip started receiving death threats."

Billie was shocked. "They've really tried to kill you?" she asked Kip.

"Nothing we could prove," he said casually. "But my dad was still nervous when he met Nathan at a big security convention in New York a few weeks later. He thought the resemblance could be used to our advantage and offered Nathan a job."

Billie looked over at Nathan. "I'm not sure that was such good luck for you."

"Sure it was," Nathan assured her. "Even if Mr. Blalock never sees me as anything but a glorified bodyguard, head of security at Blalock Industries looks good on my résumé."

"You won't need a résumé if you get killed," Billie said earnestly. "And being so far from home doesn't seem wise."

"Nathan can protect me in Atlanta as well as he can in Salt Lake," Kip said with an amused expression.

Cliff cleared his throat. "Nathan's presence is merely a precaution. We have no reason to believe that Kip is at risk."

Nathan agreed with a nod. "The police investigated the death threats thoroughly, and other than some minor incidents . . ."

"How minor?" Billie asked.

Nathan shrugged. "A few slashed tires, nuisance phone calls, a small fire in an equipment shed—nothing life threatening. And the last letter was received over six months ago."

"But like I said, my dad worries," Kip said with a sigh. "So wherever I go, Nathan goes too."

"My security job, however, stays in Utah," Nathan told her. "Besides the new security system, I'm remodeling a house, and I have a Church calling that I'm neglecting."

"Nathan thinks that the whole world depends on him," Kip said in mild derision.

Billie looked at Nathan's broad shoulders. *He's well qualified to carry the weight of the world,* she thought.

During the drive back to the hotel, Kip quizzed Edgar about the GFL. Billie heard Cliff and Neal making discreet cell phone calls to their families. She stifled a yawn and noticed Nathan staring aimlessly out the window. She leaned across and whispered, "You didn't bring your diagrams with you tonight."

"I knew I wouldn't be able to see them in the dark."

"Are you trying to figure out where to put alarms?" she asked, much more interested in this subject than the various components of the Global Football League.

"It's a little more complex than that," he said, but he didn't seem offended.

"Why would a thief want to break into a paper plant?"

"Blalock Industries is a big operation composed of sixteen separate locations that contain millions of dollars of equipment."

"Sixteen locations?" Billie was surprised.

"There are administrative office buildings, warehouses, manufacturing plants, and lumberyards. We have to defend against different types of theft at different locations. At the offices, we're mostly concerned about corporate theft."

"You mean you have to keep employees from stealing paper clips?" she asked.

He gave her a small smile. "Paper clips haven't been a big problem so far. But we can't have our people selling Blalock strategies or technologies to other companies."

Billie frowned. "It's hard to believe that employees actually do that."

"When there's enough money involved, people will do most anything," Nathan told her grimly. "But a larger concern is the people who steal from the outside. We have the nuisance vandals who want to break in and set a fire or just make a mess. Then there are the common thieves who want a coil of copper wiring or a box of expensive paper."

Billie arched her brow. "How expensive can a box of paper be?"

Nathan regarded her seriously. "A case of our finest, 100 percent cotton paper is worth almost a thousand dollars."

"Paper?" Billie confirmed in astonishment.

"Paper," he assured her. "On top of that, we have those militant conservationists to deal with."

"The ones who want to kill Kip?"

"The ones who want to save Utah's trees and will go to astounding lengths to do so."

"What kind of security system could protect Blalock Industries against all of that?" Billie asked, daunted by the scope of his task.

Nathan shifted in his seat to face her more directly. "I'm trying to combine three separate systems and coordinate them with computers. Phase one uses brilliant lighting, motion detectors, and cameras, which should be enough to discourage small-time thieves. Our second layer of defense is audible and silent alarms, electrical fencing, and miles of barbed wire."

"And the third?" Billie prompted.

"The human factor. Well-trained security guards with attack dogs will be on each site, and we'll have a central computer room where it can all be monitored twenty-four hours a day."

"You've thought of everything," she said, impressed.

He smiled. "I've tried to anyway. But no matter how good my plan is, things aren't secure at Blalock Industries until I have it all installed and coordinated."

"And you need to be in Utah to accomplish that," she sympathized.

He nodded. "Yes. I want to be involved in each step."

"You're very dedicated, and I think Mr. Blalock is lucky to have you, whether or not you look like his son."

Nathan seemed pleased by this remark. "Thank you."

Billie's cell phone started to vibrate, and she pulled it out automatically. After glancing to see that she had one text message, she started to put it back in her purse.

"Go ahead and answer it," Nathan spoke from the shadows beside her. "We don't mind."

"Oh, thanks, but I'll check it later."

Nathan turned back to stare out the window, apparently brooding about his security system. The men in the back were still talking in whispered tones to their families, so Billie listened as Kip questioned Edgar about the GFL.

When they stepped back into the lobby of the Marriott, Billie glanced up at Nathan, who was right beside her. "I hope your room is all right," she said, "even though your view is of the Atlanta skyline and not the Rocky Mountains."

Nathan looked surprised by her comment. "The room is fine. In fact, it's much nicer than what I'm used to. The house I'm renovating is old and in bad shape, so I've been without running water for almost two weeks."

"Why did you decide to renovate an older house?" she asked as they moved toward the elevators.

"The price was right," he told her.

"It's a financial nightmare," Kip chimed in. "And Nathan says I can't manage money! That place has already cost him as much in renovations as he paid for it, and he's still nowhere close to being finished."

Nathan looked a little embarrassed, and since Neal and Cliff didn't rush to defend him, Billie had to assume that they agreed with Kip's analysis.

"It *would* have been cheaper to buy a new house, but this old place had a sense of dignity that you can't put a price tag on," Nathan explained. "And if I hadn't bought it, the city was going to bulldoze it."

"You helped to preserve a little piece of history," Billie said with approval as she reached up to scratch her nose.

"Still itching?" Nathan asked, and she nodded.

"My great-grandmother claimed that an itching nose was a sign from heaven that something good was about to happen."

Nathan's eyebrow rose in skepticism, but Kip seemed intrigued. "Like what?"

Billie shrugged. "We'll just have to wait and see."

Edgar ushered them onto the elevator, and Kip situated himself between Billie and Nathan. Edgar reminded everyone about the plans for the next day. "You'll have breakfast in the hotel restaurant, then we'll depart at ten o'clock. I'll be here at nine-thirty to get bags loaded into the Yukon."

After this arrangement was agreed to, Kip invited Billie to his suite to watch a movie. "It's much too early to go to bed," he coaxed, and Billie recognized the antics of a practiced flirt.

"I appreciate the offer," she said politely. "But I can't."

"Oh please," Kip begged. "Cliff and Neal will be on the phone to their wives for the rest of the evening, and I'm sure you've realized by now that Nathan is as dull as dirt. The minute he gets to his room, he'll hook up his laptop, so I can't count on him to keep me company. Besides," Kip added with a smile, "I'd much rather look at you than Nathan."

Billie shook her head. "Unfortunately, I also have work to do, but thanks."

Kip frowned. "The Georgia Chamber of Commerce makes you work from your hotel room at night?"

Billie laughed. "No, the work I have to do tonight is, well, personal."

"You just don't want to watch a movie with me," he said. "Probably afraid that I'll convince you to tell me your real name."

Billie wasn't concerned that she'd hurt his feelings, but all the men were watching her and she knew she would have to give an explanation. "Actually, I write books to supplement my income, and my new one is seriously overdue to my publisher. In fact, if I disappear during this tour, you'll know that they've kidnapped me, locked me in a room, and chained me to a computer."

"You're an author?" Cliff asked.

Nathan was staring at her. "You write books?"

She waved a hand. "We're not talking *War and Peace* here," she was quick to assure them. "I write short paperback romances. All the heroes are tall, dark, and handsome; all the heroines are thin and beautiful. The novels themselves have about as much literary value as a comic book."

"But you *are* a published author?" Neal clarified, and she nodded.

Nathan tilted his head and regarded her with interest. "How many books have you written?"

"Twelve," she told him, and when his eyes widened, she wished she had lied. "My contract is for a book every quarter."

"Twelve books. That's quite impressive," Neal praised her.

"I don't think I could write twelve *paragraphs*," Kip contributed as they stopped by the door to her suite. "But maybe I could come to your room and watch you type. I'd be willing to help you with the love scenes," he added with a wink.

She laughed but shook her head firmly. "I think I can manage alone. Good night, everyone. I'll see you in the morning." With a wave, she unlocked her room and walked inside.

Billie barely had time to pull off her shoes before there was a quiet knock on her door. Thinking that Kip Blalock had come to pressure her into spending the evening with him, she squared her shoulders and opened the door. In the hallway stood Nathan Turner. He put a finger to his lips and slipped into her room.

"Is something wrong?" Billie asked in surprise.

Nathan shook his head. "No, I just wanted to give you a little warning about Kip." Billie frowned as he continued. "Collecting women is a hobby of his, and he's very good at it, but the conquest is all that matters to him. He's got 'girlfriends' across the world, and I didn't want your name to be added to the impressive list."

Billie stared back, dumbfounded. "You think I'm taking him seriously?"

Nathan shrugged. "Kip has an amazing success record with attractive, otherwise intelligent women." He paused for a second. "I just don't want you to get hurt."

"Then I guess I should thank you," Billie responded as she rubbed her nose with the back of her hand. "But you don't have to worry about me. There's no room in my life for romance, and honestly, even if there were, Kip Blalock doesn't appeal to me."

This caused Nathan to smile, and Billie's toes curled against the thick carpet. "You'll do fine, then. It's the girls with tender hearts and subscriptions to *Modern Bride* that I have to watch out for."

It was Billie's turn to smile. "And what about you, Nathan? Have you left disappointed girls all around the world too?"

Nathan shook his head. "I make it a point to avoid romantic entanglements."

"Too early in your life to consider marriage?" Billie studied the tiny wrinkles at the corner of his eyes and guessed his age to be close to thirty—not exactly young.

His eyes became serious. "No, I had a bad experience . . ."

"You mean a woman broke your heart?" Billie asked, half-teasing.

"She destroyed me," he told her without smiling. "I don't trust women or get involved in relationships. I stay busy instead."

Billie studied him carefully, trying to imagine a woman who could destroy someone so strong and capable. "She must have been something else."

Nathan broke eye contact. "She was."

"I'm sorry," Billie said finally.

He gave her a little smile. "Me too."

Nathan pushed away from the wall and reached for the doorknob. "Well, I've taken enough of your writing time, and I've got work of my own to do. But I'll admit that it's kind of nice to know that someone else besides me will be bleary-eyed with fatigue in the morning," he said as he stepped into the hall. "And if you do get desperate for help with your love scenes, Kip really would be an excellent resource."

Billie smiled as she watched him disappear into his room. Then she locked her door and changed into pajamas before setting up her laptop and checking her e-mail. She responded to one from her mother and deleted her bulk mail, then put in a disk to begin working on chapter 9 of *Breathless*.

Progress was slow and tedious until she got an idea. Using the search and replace feature of her word-processing program, she changed the description of her hero. Instead of dark hair and eyes, she gave him longish blond hair and bright blue eyes, a jaw too square, and a nose that had been broken. Finally, she added an intriguing little scar just below his left eye. As she began again, the words seemed to flow effortlessly from her fingers.

Billie had written ten pages before she looked up and saw the time. It was almost two o'clock in the morning, and she knew she had to get some sleep in order to function the next day. So she checked her e-mail once more and was pleased to find a short message from Cowboy.

Billie,

Sorry about your cruise. I'm back in Atlanta with time on my hands. If you'll e-mail me your itinerary, I might take a drive down south and meet you for lunch.

Have fun,

Cowboy

Billie smiled grimly, then started typing her reply.

Dear Cowboy,

It's been so long since I've had "time on my hands" that I can't imagine what it would be like. And as much as I'd like to have lunch with you this week, I need to concentrate on my clients. So we'll save our lunch date until I get back to Atlanta.

I still haven't finished my book or come up with an idea for the next one. Maybe when I finish this trip, I'll just change my name and disappear off the face of the earth.

Billie

Just to show Cowboy how much fun she was having, Billie summarized their itinerary at the bottom of the e-mail, then sent the message before climbing into the big bed. She barely had time to appreciate the softness of the feather pillows before she fell asleep.

CHAPTER 3

It was late, and Cowboy was alone at the GFL headquarters. From the computer in his office, he started running a systemwide test program, which gave him an excuse to be in other offices. For the next two hours, he went from room to room, activating the listening devices in each computer monitor. He was headed back to his office when he remembered the control computer he had been instructed to install in a storage room. He followed the dark hallway to the service area, then tried the door. It was locked, so he picked the door with a practiced hand, and it opened easily.

Inside the storage room, a makeshift office had been set up. An old desk was pushed against the wall in a corner, and a comfortable-looking chair was beside it. On the desk there was a phone console with four lines and the computer that he had installed. His instincts told him that he had found Felix Hummer's temporary office. Knowing that if someone caught him there he would probably be killed on the spot, Cowboy moved quickly to activate the listening device.

By the time he returned to his office, he was sweating profusely. He put on his headphones and pulled up the program that would allow him to monitor all the offices at once. Then, to keep from falling asleep, he opened his e-mail and read the most recent message from Billie.

* * *

On Tuesday morning, Billie and the group from Salt Lake met in the hotel's main restaurant for breakfast. While they ate, Billie asked Neal how his wife was doing.

"She's having some contractions but thinks she can hold off until we get back."

"Maybe you should go home early," Billie said with a frown. "I'm sure Cliff and the others can handle things here."

Neal smiled. "The minute she says she needs me, I'll be on the next plane to Salt Lake."

Billie sighed at the sweetness of this remark, touched that a nerdy accountant could be so romantic.

In an effort to be a good hostess and keep the conversation going, Billie continued, "So, I know that Cliff served his mission in Hong Kong. Where did you other guys go?"

"Paraguay," Neal answered promptly.

"Germany," Nathan contributed.

Billie looked at Kip, and he shrugged. "I couldn't spare the time from the ski slopes." There was an awkward silence, then Kip continued, "Religion never has really interested me. Now if you want to talk skiing . . ."

"Let's do that," Billie said, giving him her full attention. "Start with your first ski trip and don't leave out a single detail," she added as she took a big bite of her cheese omelet. Nathan glanced up again, but Kip complied without further encouragement and Billie was able to enjoy the rest of her meal while he talked.

Edgar met them in the lobby as they left the restaurant and said that their luggage had already been transferred into the Yukon. He led the way outside, and once everyone was settled, they headed south with Edgar at the wheel. For the first little while, Kip questioned Edgar about Atlanta while the men in the back discussed the upcoming end of Blalock Industries' fiscal year. Nathan got out his laptop, and when he saw Billie looking at it longingly, he smiled.

"You could work on your book while we drive."

"I'd love to," she admitted, "but it seems rude."

Nathan discounted this comment with a wave. "Cliff and Neal could discuss taxes and year-end reports for hours, and Kip will be happy as long as the driver lets him talk. No one will even notice."

"I'll give it some thought," Billie said, and Nathan returned his attention to the small computer's screen.

Billie watched the Georgia countryside fly past her window and tried to think of a way to retrieve her laptop from her luggage without making a big deal. At twelve-thirty they stopped for lunch at a restaurant called Dream Time.

"According to a survey in the *Atlanta Constitution*, this place has the best barbecue in Georgia," Edgar informed them all as he picked a space in the crowded parking lot. "And after you eat, we'll tour the first prospective plant site."

All the men were staring at the restaurant and made no comment about the afternoon's activities. The establishment resembled a ramshackle barn. The weathered exterior was gray, and the roof was covered with an assortment of different-colored shingles. A fifty-gallon drum propped open the door—a piece of plywood—and hickory smoke billowed from behind the building.

"Looks like we're in for a unique experience," Cliff said optimistically as they approached.

"Looks like this place should be condemned," Nathan muttered, and Kip laughed.

"I like to live dangerously," he said with a wink at Billie.

The interior of the restaurant was dim, and they paused in the doorway to let their eyes adjust. Some of the hickory smoke from outside had found its way in and hovered above them like a thundercloud. Edgar asked a man in a grease-splattered apron if they could have a table for six. The man pointed to a vacant booth at their left.

"Help yourself," he said inhospitably. Dirty dishes were still piled in the middle of the table, but everyone slid gingerly into the seats nonetheless.

"You're sure this is the best barbecue restaurant in Georgia?" Neal clarified after everyone except Edgar was settled.

"The article said they have the best barbecue, not the best atmosphere," the driver replied serenely. "I'll be waiting in the Yukon when you're finished."

"You're not eating in here with us?" Nathan demanded.

"No, sir. I told you I have to stay with the vehicle, so I packed a lunch."

"That's ridiculous, Edgar," Billie said firmly. "No one is going to bother that SUV while you eat."

"I don't know." Nathan glanced around the room. "Some of these folks look pretty shady to me."

Edgar spoke again before Billie could respond. "It's part of my job." He moved toward the door. "You folks enjoy your meal."

"It's not a good sign that the driver doesn't want to eat here," Cliff pointed out as they watched Edgar disappear through the broken door.

"I wonder what their health rating is," Neal whispered.

"Do you suppose they have a bathroom?" Cliff wanted to know.

"I'm sure they have one, but it might be in a little house out back," Kip replied with a pleasant smile.

A waitress rushed up at that moment and handed out a few cardboard menus. "Hey, I'm Willa Sue and I'll be serving you today." Her eyes zeroed in on the dishes in the middle of the table. "Harold!" she screeched. "Get over here and clean this place up!" Willa Sue shook her head, turning back to her new customers. "That lazy boy won't keep my tables clean, and it's cutting into my tips."

They reviewed their limited menu options, then Nathan asked, "All you serve is pork ribs and white bread?"

"And your choice of draft beer or fountain drinks." Willa Sue pointed to the bottom of the menu where beverages were listed.

"No potato salad or coleslaw or fries?" Kip gave the waitress a charming smile, and she blushed with pleasure.

Willa Sue took a step in Kip's direction. "No, honey, just ribs and bread—and really the only reason you need bread is to sop up our famous sauce. Once you taste our barbecue, you'll understand. Putting anything else on the menu is, well, a waste of time."

Harold arrived and exchanged a few cross words with Willa Sue, then threw the dirty dishes into a plastic tub. Nathan ducked as a pork bone flew off a plate and narrowly missed his left arm. Billie tried unsuccessfully to control a laugh, and the whole table joined in, even Willa Sue. Nathan resisted for a few seconds, then smiled too.

"This had better be good," he said as they began placing their orders.

When Willa Sue delivered the plates, she recommended that everyone roll up their sleeves. "And tuck your napkins around your necks. Making a mess is half the fun," she promised Kip as she settled his plate in front of him.

The food was good but left Billie feeling as though she needed to have her teeth cleaned. Edgar distributed toothpicks to everyone as they stepped into the parking lot.

"I know it's hard to believe," he said. "But in a few hours you'll be hungry again. And tonight you will be eating at Hugbustles in Columbus. They have a standing offer that anyone who can eat an entire twenty-four-ounce steak with all the trimmings in one hour or less doesn't have to pay for their meal." Edgar opened doors and watched while everyone climbed inside the Yukon.

"I'll gladly pay for my own meal if we can eat somewhere that doesn't leave me feeling like I need to take a bath afterward." Nathan studied the barbecue sauce under his fingernails.

Edgar closed the door, then climbed behind the wheel. "We'll be at the first site in about thirty minutes, then to our hotel in about two hours."

* * *

In the early afternoon, Cowboy took a break and walked across the street to a deli. While they prepared his Reuben sandwich, Cowboy went into the rest room and sent a text message to his contact.

Hummer's here and the ears are working.

After a few seconds his contact replied, and their exchange began.

Learn anything yet?

All about the GFL's concession contracts and mainte-nance fees and labor-relation problems—hopefully I'll learn something useful soon.

Use extreme caution. Pull out if there's trouble.

Roger.

Cowboy turned off his cell phone and left the rest room. He paid for his sandwich, then carried it back to his office and ate after the headphones were back in place.

* * *

Once they were headed down the interstate, Billie wished that she had retrieved her laptop. Instead of working on her novel, she had to make conversation with Kip Blalock. Nathan glanced up occasionally and gave her sympathetic smiles, then slipped back into deep concentration.

When Edgar stopped the Yukon, Billie looked around in wonder. They were parked in front of a nice, Victorian-style house surrounded by acres of overgrown lawns. Several pieces of play equipment and a glassed-in gazebo adorned the backyard.

"Why would anyone want to sell this place?" Neal spoke her thoughts.

"Especially to a company that is going to bulldoze it all and build a smelly paper plant," Nathan added.

"Here comes the owner, Mr. Mabeus," Edgar told them. "I guess you can ask him."

Carter Mabeus was in his early thirties, wearing khaki pants, an expensive-looking polo shirt, and leather loafers with no socks. He greeted them warmly.

"We were just admiring your place here, Mr. Mabeus," Nathan told him as they shook hands.

"Call me Carter," Mr. Mabeus insisted as he followed Nathan's gaze to the house. "It belonged to my parents. They were killed in a car accident at the first of the year, and the assets have just been released," he said as if selling the place were the obvious next step.

"How many acres do you own?" Neal asked.

Carter looked around. "Eighty-five, give or take a few."

"Good farmland?"

"Used to be," Carter acknowledged. "Nobody's tried to grow anything in a couple of decades."

"I'll bet it breaks your heart to let it go," Nathan said with a suspicious look at Carter.

The man shrugged. "My wife and I are both attorneys in Columbus, and this house is too far out for us to consider living here. If we leave it empty, it'll be a target for vandals, so we've decided to sell."

Nathan looked like he wanted to say more, so Billie put a hand on his arm and said to Mr. Marbus, "Why don't you give us a tour?"

He took them through the house after Billie expressed interest in seeing it, even though she knew it wouldn't influence the decision made by the Blalock folks. "Isn't it incredible?" she asked Nathan and Kip as they walked along.

"It's almost a hundred and fifty years old and in good shape, but he's going to let someone tear it down," Nathan muttered resentfully. "And they don't even *need* the money."

"Nathan has a thing for old houses," Kip teased. "If it was up to him, nothing would ever be torn down."

Billie smiled at Nathan, absently rubbing her nose. "It's good that someone is looking out for the old places."

When they walked back outside, Carter showed them a Civil War historical marker hidden in a copse of trees behind the house. "This house was used as the Union Army's headquarters for a few weeks," he told them as if it were nothing more than a useless piece of trivia.

"The man has no sense of history or decency or respect for his ancestors," Nathan whispered as they left the trees.

Carter offered to drive the businessmen around the perimeter of the farm, so Neal and Cliff climbed into the Yukon, asking Carter questions regarding the land.

"I think I'll just wait here," Nathan told Edgar.

"Me too," Kip added quickly.

Billie shrugged at Mr. Lockhart's driver. "I guess I'll stay with them."

Once the Yukon disappeared down the dirt road, Kip took Billie by the arm and led her to the glassed-in gazebo. "Isn't this romantic?"

he asked. "Can't you just picture all those Southern belles, swooning as they said good-bye to their beaus for what might be the last time?" His dimple came clearly into focus as his lips grew closer. Billie tried to hide a grimace, torn between amusement at his audacity and irritation at his arrogance.

She stepped aside just in time, and Kip accepted the rejection with a good-natured smile. Before either of them could speak, his cell phone started to ring. Kip retrieved the phone from his pocket, then walked out of the gazebo to stand near a large tree. He gave Billie a smile as he put a finger over one ear. Billie smiled back, then left the gazebo to join Nathan, who was standing on the front porch of the old house, scowling.

"I'm ready to get out of here," he told her when she reached him.

"I'm sure the others will be back soon. Why didn't you want to go on the rest of the tour?"

"Because even if this turns out to be the best location, I will strongly advise Mr. Blalock not to buy it for the paper plant."

"To protect the house?" Billie asked.

Nathan nodded. "Carter Mabeus can destroy history if he wants to, but I won't be a part of it." He looked over her shoulder. "Where's Kip?"

Billie pointed to the tree where Kip remained in deep discussion. "Kip certainly stays busy, even away from the office," she commented.

Nathan laughed. "His phone calls might be from his bookmaker or one of his many girlfriends, but not from a business associate," he assured her.

Billie didn't know how to respond to that remark and was saved from the necessity by the return of the Yukon. Carter Mabeus climbed out, and Cliff promised that they would be in touch as soon as a decision was made.

"We're kind of anxious to go ahead and get this settled," Carter said, causing Nathan to make a little growling noise in his throat.

With effort, Billie controlled the urge to laugh as they climbed into the SUV. Kip was still under the tree, talking on the phone, but Nathan closed the door in Carter Mabeus's face. "Jerk," he muttered as the young man waved and walked toward the new Jeep Cherokee parked in the gravel driveway.

"I find your Georgia weather fascinating," Cliff said to Billie. "It's almost Christmas, but we're out walking around in shirtsleeves. At home there's snow on the ground."

Billie nodded. "Georgia weather is usually mild, but we do have occasional spurts of bad weather and the temperature can drop suddenly and without much warning. I recommend that you carry a coat and umbrella with you, just in case."

While they were waiting for Kip, Billie got Edgar to open the back of the Yukon and let her dig her laptop out of her suitcase. By the time Kip reached the SUV, they were all settled and Billie was happily typing. Kip apologized for causing the delay as he climbed into the front seat with Edgar, and he was quiet as they began their trip to Columbus.

"What chapter are you on?" Nathan asked quietly.

"Ten—the last one," Billie answered.

"So you're almost done," he said.

Billie nodded. "I'll have to go back through and iron out some rough spots, but I should be finished by the end of the week."

Nathan gave her one of his rare smiles. "Congratulations."

"Unfortunately, finishing is not a reason for much celebration," she told him honestly. "This book was due to my editor a couple of weeks ago, and I've already missed my deadline for my next proposal."

"Why do they need a proposal?"

"There are so many people writing these books they have to check out the story lines in advance so they don't end up with absolute duplicates," she explained. "Submitting my proposal late will delay approval and put me in a bind with my next book too."

Nathan gave her a sympathetic smile, then went back to work, allowing Billie to do the same. For the next hour, she worked on chapter 10 while Edgar entertained Kip.

When Billie typed *The End* she was tempted to start immediately on her self-edit, but she noticed that Kip was staring out the window and started feeling guilty. She put away her laptop and leaned forward.

"I've been remiss in my hostess duties," she told him. "You don't look like you're having fun."

He flashed her a warm smile. "I'm having lots of fun. I'm sorry if I gave the opposite impression."

"Did you get some bad news?" she asked, and he gave her a sharp look.

"What do you mean?"

"The phone call at Mr. Mabeus's house." She gestured to the little phone poking out of his shirt pocket. "It seems like it upset you."

Kip shook his head. "No, that was nothing. I guess I'm just a little tired."

"Lean your seat back and try to catch a quick nap," Edgar advised. "We'll be in Columbus soon."

Kip nodded, but he didn't adjust the car seat or fall asleep. Instead, he remained quiet until they reached their hotel.

The Redmont Inn in downtown Columbus was not as grand as the Peachtree Center Marriott, but Billie realized it was a good choice. It had all the modern conveniences, along with plenty of old-fashioned charm, and its central location in the city made it very convenient.

Billie had time for a quick shower, then pulled her long hair back into a loose French braid. She put on a pair of white cotton slacks and a hot pink shirt before hurrying to the lobby to meet her traveling companions. As she stepped onto the elevator, she realized that she was actually enjoying this trip. Refusing to consider what this said about her real life, she pushed the appropriate button and watched the elevator doors close slowly.

Once again, the men had arrived before her. Neal and Cliff had dressed down for the evening by removing their ties. Nathan was wearing khaki pants and a blue, button-down oxford left open at the neck. Scratching her nose, Billie turned to Kip, who had on an outfit that matched Nathan's exactly.

"Lovely as usual," Kip said, seemingly restored to good humor.

"Thanks. You don't look bad yourself," she told him with a smile.

"And as usual, you don't have on a coat," Nathan pointed out with a frown. "It may not be freezing outside, but it's chilly enough for a sweater."

Billie recognized the wisdom of his words but refused to let her less-than-appropriate wardrobe become an issue. "I have thick blood," she assured him. "I'll be fine."

"Well, if everyone is ready," Edgar prompted, then gestured toward the door. Kip made a point to walk beside Billie as they followed Edgar out of the hotel and down the sidewalk.

"Are you feeling better?" she asked.

"Great," he promised.

Hugbustles was two blocks down from the hotel. It was an upscale steak house with plenty of side dishes and a variety of desserts, so there weren't any complaints about the food or the atmosphere as they took their seats at the table. No one wanted to try to win a free meal, so they settled for the house special. Their waitress was a buxom girl named Ivy who was almost sitting in Kip's lap by the time the dinner ended.

Afterward, Edgar suggested that they walk up the street and see a collection of animated Christmas displays. The temperature had dropped even further, so Nathan insisted that they stop by the hotel for Billie's coat. When she returned to the registration desk, the group, minus Kip, was waiting for her.

"The waitress arranged to get off work early, and Mr. Blalock is going to take her to a movie," Cliff explained.

Billie raised an eyebrow at Nathan. "You let him out of your sight?"

Nathan shrugged but didn't look happy. "He didn't exactly ask permission first. He just left a note at the front desk."

Edgar held the door open for everyone, then led the way toward downtown and the Christmas displays. Cliff and Neal mentioned they wanted to do some souvenir shopping, so Edgar escorted them, which left Billie and Nathan alone. She expected him to mention Kip, but when he didn't, Billie finally brought up the topic herself. "Are you worried about Kip?"

He shook his head. "This is typical behavior for him. He disappears occasionally, but he always stays in contact by cell phone." Nathan patted the small bulge in his shirt pocket. "If I don't hear from him every hour, he knows I'll call his father."

"I'm curious," Billie said carefully. "Kip doesn't seem to fit the Mormon mold."

Nathan considered this for a few seconds. "Kip is the classic example of someone 'kicking against the pricks,'" he began. "He has wonderful parents, plenty of money, and he was raised in the Church.

But he doesn't value or appreciate those things at all. It doesn't make any sense to me, but . . ." He shrugged. "And there's nothing immoral about going to a movie, nor is it my place to judge him."

"I'm not judging him," Billie clarified. "I just find him a puzzle."

"His parents can't figure him out either, and I don't even try. I just keep an eye on him like I was hired to do." Nathan looked down at her. "You're not jealous of the waitress, are you?"

Billie laughed out loud. "Certainly not." They remained quiet for a few minutes, looking at animated elves making toys, then she said, "It's quite a coincidence that Mr. Blalock found in New York a staunch member of the Mormon Church who looks like his son," Billie commented. "And that you would want to relocate in Utah."

Nathan shrugged. "It was kind of a lucky break for both of us, but my reasons for wanting to live in Utah are natural enough. I went to college in New York, but I'm originally from the Salt Lake area." He saw the surprise on her face. "Nowhere near the neighborhood the Blalocks live in. I was raised in a poor community close to downtown. In fact, when I first started working with Kip, he theorized that we really are brothers."

Billie raised an eyebrow.

"Knowing my parents, I had to concede the possibility," Nathan told her. "But once I met the Blalocks, I knew that was out of the question. Neither one of them would have been involved in an extramarital affair."

"What school did you attend in New York?" Billie asked.

"Cornell."

Billie was impressed. "Wow."

"Scholarship," he admitted.

"Your grades and SAT scores must have been . . ." Billie searched for the right word, "perfect."

He grinned. "They were pretty good."

"So you met Mr. Blalock at a security convention?" she prompted, wanting to keep him talking.

"During my senior year, I did an internship at a firm on the cutting edge of security technology. After graduation, they offered me a job, and I took it. A couple of years later, we hosted a big convention and Mr. Blalock attended. When we met, my resemblance to Kip gave him all kinds of ideas. Then he found out that I was a temple-recommend-carrying member of the Church and hired me on the spot."

"Because he knew he could trust you?"

"And I think he had hopes that close association with me might help Kip develop some interest in religion."

"But it hasn't?"

"Not that I can tell, but religion is a funny thing. Even though he was raised by devout parents, Kip rejected the gospel. My parents never took me to church, and yet I can't imagine life without it."

Billie was surprised and pleased by this additional comment about his personal life. Before she could think of a reply, Edgar caught up to them. He said that Cliff and Neal wanted to call their wives before it got too late, so he was walking them back to the hotel. He asked if Billie wanted to cut her tour short as well.

"We'll just see that last display on the next block," Nathan answered for her. "Then I'll make sure Billie gets to the hotel safely."

Edgar looked to Billie for confirmation, and when she nodded, he hurried back to the other men. The last Christmas scene was an intricate display of elves loading Santa's sleigh. The detail and animation were amazing, and the two of them stared at it until Billie began to shiver. At that point Nathan suggested that they head back to the hotel.

On the way there, he stopped at the Hot Chocolate Hut, and Billie enjoyed the warmth while he placed his order. When he rejoined her, she eagerly extended her half-frozen fingers to accept the styrofoam cup he gave her.

She took a sip, drawing comfort from the warm liquid and Nathan's pleasant company. "Is that good?" he asked.

"Delicious," she answered with stiff lips. He laughed, and the sparkle in his eyes made her lose her breath for just a second. "Absolutely delicious," she repeated. Only this time she wasn't referring to the cocoa.

* * *

By late Tuesday, Cowboy was numb with fatigue and had yet to hear anything useful. He was just about to call it a night when a light started flashing on his screen, indicating activity in the storage room. He typed in a few commands, then settled down to listen.

Apparently they were having a meeting of some kind. When Cowboy recognized Felix Hummer's voice, he picked up a pencil to take notes. The men in the meeting were careful to avoid using names, and Cowboy wished he had installed a device that could take voiceprints.

As the meeting progressed, Cowboy took so many notes he wore down the lead on his pencil and had to get another out of the desk drawer. Just as he began writing again, one man slipped and addressed another as "Conrad." Cowboy's heart pounded. *That* was the voice he couldn't place a few nights before. An Atlanta city councilman was involved in the scheme to steal billions of dollars through the GFL.

Once the meeting ended, Cowboy hid his notes, then tried to figure out the next step. He needed to get the information to his contact but couldn't risk running into any of the men from the meeting as they left the GFL headquarters. Finally he decided the safest course was to wait until he was sure everyone was gone.

He opened his e-mail account and read the last message from Billie. He laughed at her continued problems with LoveSwift Books, but the smile left his face as an idea started to form. Maybe he could help Billie and give himself a little insurance at the same time. He rolled up his sleeve and hit the reply button. An hour later, he was rereading the e-mail when a voice spoke from behind him.

"What are you doing here?"

Startled, Cowboy pushed *Send,* then turned around to face a tall man with dark, curly hair and a deep tan. He had seen enough surveillance pictures to know that he was meeting Felix Hummer for the first time. Conrad Lockhart stood beside Hummer, and both wore grim expressions. The security guard at the door looked terrified.

"I don't think we've met." Cowboy used every ounce of training he'd ever had to remain calm. "My name is Milton Bagley, but folks call me Cowboy." He extended his hand toward the tanned man.

Hummer didn't respond. "This building is supposed to be empty."

"I always work crazy hours. Mitch can verify that." Cowboy pointed at the security guard, who was nodding vigorously.

"It's true, sir," the guard confirmed, his eyes wide. "Half the time Cowboy sleeps at his desk."

"I know that a new computer guy is on his way," Cowboy explained with what he hoped sounded like easy confidence. "I've been running a few tests to be sure everything is ready for him to take over."

Felix Hummer pointed at the computer screen. "Who's Regina St. Claire?"

Cowboy felt his heart pound but kept his voice light. "Girlfriend, sir. I hope you don't mind me e-mailing her on a company computer."

Hummer shook his head. "Not in the least. So, the computers are all hooked together and coordinated and everything?"

Cowboy nodded. "Yes, sir."

"Are you prepared to prove it?"

Cowboy raised an eyebrow. "How could I do that?"

"Do another test—only this time practice moving money," Felix Hummer replied as he reached into his pocket and pulled out a card. "I'll make sure these financial institutions cooperate."

Cowboy studied the card Hummer had given him. It listed the names of several banks with accompanying account numbers and contact people. Surprised that Hummer would allow him to see such sensitive information, Cowboy glanced back up.

"I want to make sure our computer system can handle it," Hummer explained. "When real money is involved, we can't afford any glitches."

"You want me to do this now?" Cowboy asked, mentally calculating the hours of work it was going to require.

Hummer nodded. "Since you're here, you might as well be busy."

"Okay. I'll get started right away. I'm pleased you have this much trust in me."

Hummer gave him a cold smile. "I don't trust anyone, but I need these tests. So hurry."

Cowboy felt his mouth go dry. "Yes, sir." He waited until his uninvited guests had left, then turned to his computer. Before beginning the test, he deleted all his personal files.

* * *

On Wednesday morning, the tour group ate a leisurely breakfast in the hotel restaurant, then toured the second possible paper mill site. It looked like miles and miles of scrubby backwoods to Billie, but Nathan, Cliff, and Neal seemed interested and asked the owner endless questions. Kip spent most of his time on his cell phone. He seemed distracted and edgy, but every time Billie inquired, he assured her that everything was fine.

An hour into the tour, Nathan offered to walk her back to the car to wait with Edgar, but Billie doggedly refused. When the tour was over, Edgar suggested that the landowner join them for lunch at a place called the Home Cooking Buffet. Kip said that he had plans for the afternoon and asked Edgar to drop him off at the hotel. As Billie watched him climb out of the Yukon, she was certain that the lovely waitress, Ivy, would somehow be involved in his afternoon's activities.

The fried cuisine at the Home Cooking Buffet was too heavy for Billie's taste, so she just pushed her food around on her plate. She noticed that Nathan didn't eat much either, but she couldn't tell if it was the fat content of the food or the businesslike nature of the conversation that suppressed his appetite. After lunch, Nathan explained that they had another site to look at but would be in touch when they had made a final decision. There was a round of hand-shakes, then Billie led them out to the Yukon.

"If you'll refer to your itinerary, you'll see that this afternoon we're visiting a local botanical garden, and tonight we have tickets to the Columbus Symphony Orchestra's performance of Handel's *Messiah*," Edgar told them as they drove.

"I confess, I'm surprised that a rural area like this *has* a symphony orchestra," Nathan whispered to Billie.

She tried to ignore the sensation of his breath on her neck and answered, "It will probably be a couple of guys playing the spoons and a lady with a harmonica."

Nathan's eyebrows shot up. "I can hardly wait to hear them perform the 'Hallelujah Chorus'!"

The botanical gardens were spectacular, and the Blalock Industries people were very complimentary. "I had no idea Georgia was so beautiful," Cliff said enthusiastically.

"I'd like to bring my family out sometime," Neal seconded the endorsement.

"When Blalock Industries builds the new paper plant here, you'll probably get plenty of opportunities to visit," Billie told Cliff with a confident smile. "And once the new baby is old enough to travel, you can bring your family and make a vacation out of it," she added for Neal's benefit.

When they got back to the hotel, Billie looked through her limited wardrobe. She didn't want to wear the black dress again, so she was forced to wear one with a blue tropical print. The material was thin and the colors a little loud for dinner and the symphony, but it would have been perfect for a cruise. It also clashed with her red jacket, so she didn't wear her coat, even though she knew Nathan would comment on it.

When she met the others in the lobby, Kip wasn't with them.

"So, where's the heir to Blalock Industries?" she teased.

Nathan frowned. "Apparently he drove back to Atlanta with the waitress from last night. He's staying with her in a friend's condo for a few days."

"And Mr. Blalock doesn't mind that?" she asked as they walked.

"He's not happy, but as long as I'm in cell phone contact with Kip, Mr. Blalock won't fire me."

Billie stepped into the small entry area of the restaurant. "Why would Kip leave if he knew it could cost you your job?"

Nathan took her by the arm and pulled her out of the doorway so the people behind them could pass through. "Kip doesn't consider other people," Nathan said. He paused while the hostess showed them to their table, then he took a seat beside Billie. When the hostess had left after handing out the menus, he leaned forward and said quietly, "But as a precaution, we've agreed that Kip will use my name and I'll use his until we board the plane in Atlanta."

"So, does that mean I have to call you Kip?" she whispered.

Nathan shook his head. "Only if you're introducing me to a stranger."

Billie frowned as the full implication of Nathan's impersonation dawned on her. "But if anyone *is* trying to kill Kip, this means they'll kill you instead."

Nathan shrugged. "No one is trying to kill Kip."

The waitress stepped up just then and asked for their orders. Billie chose a large green salad with boiled shrimp, and after everyone else had made their selections, she turned back to Nathan. "If you're worried about Kip or your job, we could all just go back to Atlanta."

"Before we've seen the other available plant site?" Cliff asked.

"We'd have to come back later," Neal added in alarm.

"We're going to see all the sites and make a decision before we go back to Utah," Nathan said. "I've got to get this settled so that I can get back to work on the new security system."

"And your old house," Billie added with a smile.

"That too, although I'm getting used to the convenience of running water."

Cliff turned to Billie. "The last two appointments are tomorrow. It's my understanding that we'll spend the night in a resort town called Eureka, then head back to Atlanta on Thursday."

"The tour of the Georgia Dome and a photo shoot with a couple of the Atlanta Competitors is scheduled for Thursday afternoon," Billie reminded them.

"And since Kip won't miss that, we know we'll be reunited by then," Cliff said with a smile.

Nathan nodded. "And the only real danger that Atlanta holds for Kip is the GFL."

"The GFL?" Billie repeated.

Nathan sighed. "Kip mentioned that he loves to gamble—"

"I don't know why," Neal interrupted. "He always loses."

"I guess that proves that practice doesn't always make perfect," Nathan agreed, then gave everyone a smile. "But there's nothing I can do about it, so let's try to forget about Kip and enjoy our dinner."

Billie reached up to scratch her nose as the food arrived. Then she leaned toward Nathan. "You're still worried about him."

He nodded as he cut his steak. "But that doesn't mean everyone else has to be."

After the meal, they walked several blocks in the mild evening air into the theater and were seated in a private box once they arrived. The building was lovely and the music beautiful. During the intermission, Billie asked Nathan if he was having a good time. "It sounds okay," he allowed. "I'm not overly fond of the symphony, so for all I know they could be playing the wrong notes."

"Of course they're playing the right notes," Billie said indignantly.

He smiled as he glanced down at her dress. "Since you seem determined to underdress, I'm sure you're cold. Would you like me to get you some hot chocolate from the concessions area?"

Billie rubbed the thin material that covered her arms and shook her head. "No, but thanks anyway."

The temperature had dropped into the thirties by the time they stepped out of the theater, and Billie couldn't keep her teeth from chattering. Nathan removed his suit coat and draped it over her shoulders while they waited for Edgar and the Yukon to reach them. She knew she should decline the coat, but the warmth was irresistible, so she clutched the lapels together instead. It made her feel close to Nathan, so even after they were inside the cozy confines of the Yukon she kept it.

"How was the concert?" Edgar asked once everyone was settled.

"It was nice," Cliff said from the backseat.

"The Christmas music made me miss my kids," Neal admitted.

Nathan smiled and shook his head at Billie. "Family men." He turned to the men in the back. "Don't worry. You'll be home in a couple of days."

Billie looked out into the night, wondering what it would be like to have someone waiting for her at home besides Fred. When they reached the door to her room, she told everyone good night. Cliff and Neal went immediately into their room, but Nathan paused. "Thanks for letting me use your jacket," she told him as she returned it.

"You're welcome," he responded with a smile. "For a girl used to unpredictable Georgia weather, you didn't pack very well."

Billie laughed. "Remember at the airport when Edgar told you I had to cancel my vacation to take this tour?" she asked, and Nathan nodded. "Well, I was supposed to be on a cruise this week, and these clothes would have been *perfectly* appropriate."

Nathan looked concerned. "I can't believe the Chamber of Commerce asked you to give up a cruise to show us around."

Billie decided not to go into all the complexities. "I was sorry at first, but this has been very . . . pleasant."

He massaged the back of his neck. "I feel the same way. I didn't want to come, but I can't say I'm sorry I did."

She laughed again before assuring him, "And the best is yet to come!"

He gave her half a smile. "See you in the morning."

"At breakfast," she agreed, then slipped inside her room.

CHAPTER 4

Billie changed into pajamas, then set up her laptop and opened her e-mail. There was a message from her mother and one from Cowboy. She scanned through her mother's message, which asked if her brother and father could spend the night when they came to Atlanta for the GFL game. Billie quickly replied that they were welcome, then opened the next e-mail.

Billie,

Thanks for the mini-itinerary you sent me, and you're right—it did make me feel sorry for you. My free time has kind of evaporated anyway. The GFL is replacing me with a new computer expert, but he hasn't gotten here yet and they've got me running all kinds of tests on the system—so I'm stuck at the GFL headquarters.

But the good news is that I've thought of an idea for your new book. I've attached it to this e-mail so you can send it on to your editor even if you think it's awful. It will get her off your back for a few days anyway. Enjoy the rest of your cow pasture tour.

Your friend, Cowboy

Billie opened the attachment and scanned it quickly. The plotline was about a group of sinister men who started a new professional football league. They solicited money from private investors and munici-palities across the country, hired coaches and players who quit their real jobs in good faith, but in the end the whole thing was really a scam. There was no intent to actually follow through with the new league. Instead, the planners intended to skip town during the first exhibition game, taking all the start-up capital and ticket proceeds with them.

Billie laughed out loud thinking how many comparisons could be drawn between Cowboy's idea and his employers. If she were to actu-ally write something like he suggested, they would probably both be sued, along with LoveSwift Books. And besides the possible legal problems, one of the cardinal rules of romance writing—even in her realm of formula fiction—was to never, ever use a sports story line.

However, she was desperate, and as Cowboy had pointed out, any proposal would buy her some time with her editor at LoveSwift Books. So Billie forwarded the attachment to her editor, then deleted the message and composed a response.

> Cowboy,
>
> You're not missing much. We're just making a quick tour of farmland in southern Georgia, but I think the Blalock folks have been impressed so far. I'm sorry you're so busy—but thanks for the book idea! I'll call you when I get back into town.
>
> Billie

She pushed Send and waited for the confirmation to appear, but instead she got a notification saying that the address she had used was invalid. Surprised, she double-checked her address book, then care-fully retyped the message and sent it again. A second time, the e-mail came back undeliverable.

Chastising herself for her hasty decision to delete the original e-mail so she couldn't check the address, she tried her response a third time with the same results. Finally, she stared at the stark words as they glowed ominously in the warm, comfortable hotel room. Was something wrong, or was it just a computer glitch of some kind?

Billie decided to go to bed and try again in the morning, but after tossing and turning for thirty minutes, she got up and put her jeans and sweater back on. She peeked out into the hallway, then walked a few steps to the door of Nathan's suite. He answered to her third series of quiet knocks wearing cutoff sweatpants and a Cornell T-shirt.

She opened her mouth to speak, but words failed her as she stared at his well-developed biceps.

"Billie?" he prompted, obviously surprised by her presence.

She dragged her eyes up, where they settled on his longish blond hair.

"Did you need something?" Nathan tried again.

"Sorry to bother you," she forced herself to say. His feet were bare and his calves tan and muscular. Her heart started pounding, and she had to swallow hard before she could continue. "I need your help. Is your laptop on?"

He nodded suspiciously as she stepped into his hotel room. "Why?"

Billie sighed. "I have this friend named Cowboy," she began, and Nathan's eyebrows rose. "Well, that's not his real name, of course, but it's the one he uses on the Internet."

"What is his real name?" Nathan asked.

"Milton," Billie responded, regaining her composure and confidence.

Nathan looked even more confused. "You struck up a friendship with a guy you met on the Internet?" he asked. "Surely you know better than that."

Billie was mildly offended. "I *do* know better than that. I met Cowboy at the GFL headquarters," she told him primly. "He works for them, and when they were first setting up their offices, I was over there a lot. Then he had to start traveling and . . ." She paused. "Well, it's a long story, but over the past few months we've become friends, and we e-mail each other almost daily."

Nathan raked his hair back from his face. "Okay, so you've got this *friend* named Cowboy Milton, and you need my laptop because . . ."

Billie laughed. "His name is Milton, and I call him Cowboy. He's about sixty years old—so *friends* is all we'll ever be. And I need your laptop because I got an e-mail from him, but when I replied it was returned as undeliverable." She glanced up at Nathan to see if he was following. His blue eyes glowed in the lamplight, and she had the oddest desire to reach up and see if his hair was as soft as it looked.

"How can my laptop help you?"

"I want to be sure mine's not malfunctioning," she explained. "Would you mind sending him an e-mail from yours?"

"That sounds like a long shot," he told her with obvious skepticism. "But if it will make you feel better—"

"It will," she assured him. Nathan gave her another hard look, then waved for her to follow him to the back of the suite. As they walked she said, "At least things are quiet for you now that Kip's gone."

"I'd sacrifice quiet for peace of mind any day." Nathan turned in to the bedroom. She couldn't help but notice that his bed was neatly made and the suit he'd worn to the symphony was draped across a wing chair. His laptop was set up at the desk, and he took a seat in front of it. "What's his e-mail address?"

Billie provided the information, then stood back and watched Nathan's hands move gracefully along the keyboard. "You type pretty fast," she said, and he looked up briefly. "That's just not a skill that many men I know have gone to the trouble to develop."

"I didn't have anyone to type papers for me when I was in school, so I learned to type them myself," he told her. "What's your message?"

"Just say for him to contact me as soon as possible," Billie said. "And that I'm worried," she added.

Nathan typed in her message, and they waited for a few seconds. Finally a message popped up. "The address you entered is invalid. Please check your information and try again," he read the words out loud. "Sorry, it looks like either your friend has closed his e-mail account or is blocking your address for some reason."

"I can't imagine why he would do either one," she whispered, the feeling of anxiety returning. While biting her lower lip, she looked around to see his diagrams spread out on the hotel desk, suddenly realizing he was trying to work and she was disturbing him. "Well, I've taken up enough of your time," she said with false cheerfulness.

Nathan followed her back to the small sitting area. "Sorry I couldn't help you."

"Me too, but I appreciate you trying."

He opened the door for her and watched until she was safely back in her own room.

Still uneasy, Billie put her pajamas on and got into the bed. But her dreams were disturbed by visions of Cowboy being chased by unseen villains and Kip smiling at her, his dimple amplified as his face grew nearer. As the night progressed, her dreams became weirder and more unsettling. Finally she dreamed that Kip was Cowboy, and he was running for his life from militant conservationists. When she woke up from that nightmare, Billie abandoned all hope of getting any sleep. She climbed out of bed and watched the Home Shopping Network until dawn.

* * *

At five o'clock on Thursday morning, Cowboy finished the test of the computer system. Because of the early hour, the building was deserted, so his plan was to put the test results on the desk in the storage room. Then he would leave the GFL headquarters and go straight to the Treasury Department office, where he would figure out a way to stop Felix Hummer and his conspirators.

He had just put his hand on the doorknob to the storage room when he heard voices from the other side. He raised his hand to knock, then he heard a remark that temporarily paralyzed him.

"That computer guy, Cowboy, will have to be eliminated," Felix Hummer was saying.

"Now?" Conrad Lockhart asked.

"There's no point in putting it off."

"Do we have to *kill* him?"

Hummer laughed harshly. "Of course we do, and I want his computer checked. We might be able to recover his e-mail files even if he's been wise enough to delete them. That will give us an idea of how much he knew and whether or not he shared it with his girlfriend, Miss St. Claire."

"Surely we wouldn't consider taking any drastic action against the girlfriend," Conrad Lockhart began.

"No loose ends," Hummer cut him off. "That's the way I operate."

Cowboy didn't wait to hear the other man's response. Instead, he backed silently away from the door. Once he reached the main hallway, he headed straight for the service elevator, leaving his duffel bag and other personal effects behind in his cubicle. As he stepped onto the loading dock, he glanced around to be sure that no one was waiting for him. All was still and just beginning to get light.

Even though the air was cool, he was sweating. He threw the results of the computer tests into a garbage can, then wiped his forehead with his right shirtsleeve. Finally he stepped away from the building and hurried toward the silver Mazda Protegé parked several rows down.

While he walked, he used his cell phone to send Billie a brief text message. It would take some time for Hummer to determine that Regina St. Claire was a pseudonym for Billie Murphy—so he didn't invest precious seconds in a detailed message. He'd arrange for Billie's protection once he got to the Treasury Department, but for now he did want to scare her into caution, just in case Hummer moved quickly.

As he pushed Send on his cell phone, he pulled the car keys from his pocket and pressed the unlock button. He considered it a good sign when the car didn't explode. He covered the last few feet at a fast trot, and when his hand closed around the handle of the car door, he heaved a sigh of relief, then pulled the door open. He never saw the gunman hiding in the shadows, and he never heard the soft click of the trigger. He also never felt the bullet that entered his skull just below his left ear, causing death instantly.

* * *

After breakfast on Thursday morning, Edgar herded the tour into the Yukon. Cliff assumed Kip's place in the front passenger seat while Neal climbed into the back. Nathan helped Billie inside, then sat beside her and took out his laptop.

Billie tried to edit her book, but her thoughts drifted regularly to the man sitting next to her. They drove to a parcel of land owned by an iron pipe company about thirty miles outside of Columbus. A real estate agent and a lawyer representing the owner met them as arranged.

While they walked, Nathan observed that it was a good location, near the pipe plant in what was obviously an industrial area. There would be no complaints from neighbors about construction or traffic. Billie thanked the real estate agent for conducting the tour, and Cliff said that they would be in touch.

During lunch, Billie turned to Nathan. "So, do we need to continue our search, or are you ready to make an offer on the pipe plant property?"

He smiled. "The asking price is within our range, and it's definitely a good prospect."

"Better than the others you've seen?" Billie included Neal and Cliff in her question.

"Definitely," Cliff answered for them both.

Billie was pleased. "Then my success is assured?"

"Do you get a new car or something if we choose Georgia?" Nathan asked with a quizzical look.

Billie frowned, thinking that Camille would probably find a way to take credit for the Blalock Industries sale even if Billie was able to swing it. "No, all I get is the satisfaction of a job well-done."

"Then let's say that satisfaction is probably in your future," Nathan told her. "But we want to see all the prospective sites here in Georgia before we make a final decision."

She gave him a smile as their sandwiches arrived. "Suits me." She turned to Cliff. "Since you've assumed charge of the itinerary, tell us about our next stop."

Cliff took this request very seriously. "It's a defunct dairy farm about thirty miles from here. The acreage is adequate, and the price is a real bargain. It's in a rural area, though, and we have concerns about access roads and neighbor relations."

These drawbacks didn't phase Billie. "If you get a good enough deal on the land itself, you could build your own access roads, and if the area is rural, there won't be enough neighbors to cause a fuss."

Nathan laughed at this. "Is there no obstacle you can't work around?"

She gave him a tolerant smile. "I haven't found one yet."

When Edgar turned off the county highway onto a poorly maintained dirt road, they all exchanged glances.

"I did say the dairy farm was *defunct*," Cliff reminded them.

They pulled up at the old farmhouse, and Neal looked around in wonder. "It reminds me of a Western ghost town." Besides the house, there was a dilapidated barn, two ancient milking facilities, and countless little sheds and outbuildings—but no people.

"I'll bet a stiff wind would level everything on the place," Cliff agreed.

Billie was in a good mood since they liked the pipe plant, so she said, "In which case, think of the money you'll save tearing things down!"

"This is a waste of time," Nathan muttered. "The other site was more convenient, and we wouldn't have to fool with clearing off all this junk."

Before anyone could respond, an elderly gentleman walked out onto the sagging front porch. He was wearing baggy blue shorts and a bright orange T-shirt that proclaimed *War Eagle* on the front. Knee-high dress socks and a pair of running shoes completed his ensemble.

"He looks like a troll," Nathan whispered as the old man approached the car.

Billie covered her mouth to control a giggle, and Edgar lowered his window.

"Hugh Warren," the little man said, sticking his hand through the driver's side window. After shaking hands with Edgar, Mr. Warren withdrew his arm, then cupped his hand around his mouth and hollered toward the house, "Come on out, Thelma. There's folks here to meet us."

All eyes turned to the porch as a tall, sturdy-looking woman in her seventies emerged. She had bright red hair that, considering her age, could not be natural. "Bring them in, Hugh. I've got fresh cookies made," Thelma said, wiping her hands on the bottom of her apron.

Mr. Warren turned back to the occupants of the Yukon. "Now that's an offer you don't want to turn down. Come on in."

"We don't have much time," Billie told him.

"Oh, please come in for just a minute," Mr. Warren pleaded. "Thelma's a great cook, and we never get any company out here. It will break her heart if all those cookies go to waste."

Billie conferred with the men, and they finally decided to go in for a few minutes. Edgar said he would wait in the Yukon as they climbed out and followed Mr. Warren. Nathan stepped onto the porch, checking each board for soundness before committing his full weight.

The interior of the house was even drearier than the outside. "This place is in *serious* need of renovation," Billie whispered as she looked at the crumbling plaster walls.

"Or demolition," Nathan replied.

"And if Nathan thinks it's hopeless, it's really bad," Cliff said with a smile.

Billie was relieved to see that the kitchen was in better shape than the rest of the house. Thelma insisted that they sit around the large table, then bustled around distributing warm oatmeal cookies.

"These are great," Cliff praised her efforts as he finished off a cookie.

"And this room is nice and cozy," Billie added.

Hugh nodded. "We spend most of our time in here, so we kind of fixed it up."

Cliff took another bite of cookie, then asked, "Have you been raising dairy cows all your lives?"

Thelma laughed. "Oh, no. We're from Eureka originally. Hugh worked in the coal mines there."

"A couple of years ago, the city of Eureka bought our house and built an athletic complex," Hugh explained.

"Real nice," Thelma interjected. "A football stadium, soccer fields, baseball diamonds, and a running track."

Hugh picked up the dialogue. "Since we didn't have a house or yard to care for anymore, we bought us one of those Winnebagos and took off to see the country."

"But we found out right soon that the only part of the country we really wanted to see was here in southern Georgia," Thelma explained as she poured everyone a glass of milk.

"So we sold our motor home and bought this place." Hugh waved toward the farm outside. "The previous owner was making money hand over fist, or at least that's what he told us."

Thelma refilled the plate with more cookies fresh from the oven. "We figured we could work the farm for a few years, then sell off the cows and spend the rest of our days here in prosperous comfort."

Hugh sighed. "But once the sale was complete and we got here, things was different than we expected."

"For one thing, dairy farming is hard work," Thelma told them. "Much too hard for Hugh."

"I'm *retired*," Hugh defended himself. "I spent forty years breaking my back in the coal mines, and I'm through with all that. That fellow who sold us this place said the farm would run itself. But all the workers were Mexicans, and I don't speak Spanish, so we couldn't communicate. It was frustrating, I can tell you."

"Then after a couple of weeks, they all disappeared," Thelma announced. "Didn't come and give us notice or anything, just up and left."

"Not that giving us notice would have done much good since we couldn't understand a word they said," Hugh pointed out, and Billie had to struggle to keep from laughing.

"I tried to hire some more help, but all the experienced folks were already working on other farms."

"So we sold off our cows before they died of neglect," Thelma told them. "More cookies?"

Cliff held out his plate. "I'll take a few."

The others shook their heads. "We'll be eating dinner in a few hours and need to save some room," Billie told their hostess.

"We were going to fix up this house and just stay here even without the cows," Hugh continued. "But the house is in pretty bad shape."

"And it's so far out in the country!" Thelma exclaimed. "I'm used to having neighbors and grocery stores. Here, if you forget something when you're shopping, you just have to do without until the next week."

"And we got off on a bad foot with the local Baptist church, so we haven't been to services in a month of Sundays," Hugh added.

Thelma pulled a chair in from the living room and sat beside Billie. "We attended for the first time on Easter Sunday, but instead of having a nice cantata or reading from the scriptures, they were holding their annual business meeting."

Billie frowned. "Why?"

"Figured on Easter they'd have a nice big crowd and get lots of pledges," Hugh explained.

"But it just didn't feel right, sitting there talking about new choir robes and building a canopy over the front entrance when we should have been celebrating the Resurrection of the Savior," Thelma told them as she added a few more cookies to Cliff's plate.

"Thelma might have been able to overlook taking care of business on Easter, but the next week when she went to her new Sunday School class, a woman asked Thelma to get out of her grandma's rocking chair."

Billie was struggling to follow this part of the story. "Did the grandma want to sit in the rocking chair?"

"Mercy no!" Thelma exclaimed. "The grandma is dead and the rocking chair was donated to the church by the family."

"But the woman said it was a delicate antique and she was afraid that Thelma was too heavy for it!" Hugh told them.

"Can you imagine the gall of that woman?" Thelma demanded. "Calling me fat right there in front of the whole Sunday School class!"

Billie saw a corner of Nathan's mouth turn up in a slight smile. Then she looked back at Hugh, who was obviously enjoying himself. "Even that might have been allowed to pass, but after Sunday School, the same woman showed Thelma a poster advertising the Weight Watchers group that meets every week."

"That was the last straw!" Thelma declared. "I don't have to go to church to be insulted!"

The guests exchanged a glance.

"I do miss it though," Thelma continued. "Church I mean. The sermons and socials and spiritual enlightenment."

"You mostly miss the gossip," Hugh said with a smile. "And I miss seeing all those pretty ladies dressed up in their Sunday best."

Thelma reached over and slapped her husband on the shoulder. "Hush and behave yourself."

Hugh rubbed his shoulder. "I always behave myself," he assured the group. "But I'm not blind, and I figure the Lord would want me to appreciate *all* His creations."

"Anyway," Thelma went on with a stern look at her husband. "We decided just to sell the whole place and find us another house."

"One that doesn't need so much work," Hugh added.

Thelma nodded. "And one that's a little closer to a town."

Hugh winked at Billie. "Near a nicer church."

Thelma ignored this. "Where Hugh can have a little garden."

Nathan looked at his watch. "Well, I hope things work out for you, but we're on a pretty tight schedule."

Hugh laughed. "Sorry that we've been running on and on. What do you want to know about the place?"

Nathan glanced at Cliff, who asked, "What time will your real estate agent be arriving, Mr. Warren?"

The older man shrugged. "Don't have one. I'll show you around the place, and if you want it, you can draw up the papers. I'll read them, and if they sound okay, I'll sign."

"That's a very unconventional way to do business," Cliff said with a frown. "As an attorney, I strongly advise you to have a lawyer review the papers before you sign *anything*."

Hugh Warren studied Cliff through narrowed eyes. "Never been crazy about lawyers."

Cliff Reynolds blinked, then looked at Nathan.

Billie expected the security director for Blalock Industries to respond with annoyance, but instead Nathan smiled and said, "Why don't you show us around?"

Mr. Warren beamed. "Come on, Thelma. We're going for a ride."

They walked out to the Yukon, where Edgar was reading the newspaper. When he saw the Warrens, he got out and devised a new seating arrangement, putting Mr. Warren in the front passenger seat, Mrs. Warren in the middle row beside Billie and Cliff, and Neal and Nathan in the far back. Then they spent the next thirty minutes driving around the desolate dairy farm.

"Have you tried selling this to another dairy farmer?" Nathan asked as they rode.

"Yeah," Hugh admitted with a sigh. "They said the equipment is worthless. That's why I figured if we offered a bargain price, we could sell to someone who just wanted the land—"

"A family would have the same problems we're dealing with," Thelma interjected. "Too far from town, too many repairs . . ."

"And awful television reception," Hugh added. "We don't get cable, and the satellite dish only works half the time. Something about the farm being built on the wrong side of a slope."

"And it's nearly time for the bowl games!" Thelma said with emphasis.

"You fellows like football?" Hugh asked the men in the back, and they all nodded. Then he pointed at Nathan. "Based on those breaks in your nose, I'll bet you played in high school and maybe college."

Nathan shook his head. "No, sir, I never played football. I just got into a lot of fights."

Mr. Warren seemed to think this was very funny. While he laughed, Thelma continued, "Hugh is a huge Auburn University football fan. He won't wear anything but orange and blue unless he's going to a funeral."

Edgar pulled to a stop in front of the old farmhouse, and the cheerful mood inside the Yukon evaporated.

"You folks don't have to rush off," Thelma tried to delay their departure. "Why don't you come in for more cookies?"

"Thelma'd be glad to whip up some dinner," Hugh expanded the invitation.

"Thank you, but we've got to get checked into our hotel," Nathan declined for the group.

With a disappointed nod, Hugh climbed out of the SUV, then opened the side door for Thelma. "So, you folks are spending the night in Eureka, did you say?"

Edgar nodded. "We have reservations at a hotel on the lake."

Hugh's eyes lit up with interest. "I've spent many pleasant hours fishing there."

"We can't thank you enough for the cookies," Billie said in an effort to disengage them from the Warrens.

"We'll be in touch once a decision is made on the paper plant site," Cliff called from the backseat.

Hugh nodded, then started to close the door, but Nathan reached out and stopped it. "Do you folks have plans for tonight?" he asked, and Billie wasn't sure who was more astonished—the old couple or the occupants of the Yukon. Nathan continued calmly, "Because I was thinking if you're not too busy, it would be nice to have you go along with us, as sort of tour guides."

Billie couldn't imagine why Nathan wanted the Warrens to go to Eureka with them. They already had Edgar to drive and a well-prepared itinerary.

"Would we have to dress up?" Hugh asked as he peered in at the constantly suited Cliff and Neal.

"The dress code for tonight is casual," Edgar replied.

"Which means that Cliff and Neal will take off their ties," Nathan teased his business associates. "I personally plan to wear a comfortable pair of blue jeans, and you can wear orange and blue."

"The dinner reservations are at a restaurant called The Lure," Cliff provided after referring to the itinerary.

"According to the *Columbus Journal*, the food is good, and live entertainment is provided nightly." Even Edgar seemed to be encouraging the Warrens.

Thelma's very red head was bobbing. "We've been to The Lure! A friend of ours used to be a waitress there." She looked at Hugh. "We haven't been out to eat in ages."

"And after dinner, you two can have my hotel room," Nathan offered. "I'll double up with Cliff or Neal."

"I'm sure we can arrange an extra room," Edgar said quickly.

"Then we can drop you off back here on our way to Atlanta tomorrow," Nathan concluded with a look at Edgar, and the chauffeur nodded in agreement.

"Well, now, that's a deal just too good to turn down," Hugh said with a smile. "What do you say, Thelma?"

"That I can pack so fast y'all won't even have time to miss me," Thelma replied, already heading toward the house.

"You folks want to come inside while you wait?" Hugh offered.

All eyes turned to the ramshackle dwelling. "Thanks anyway," Nathan answered for everyone. "But we'll just stay here."

"Suit yourselves," Mr. Warren told them. "Let me go give Thelma a hand."

Once Mr. Warren had disappeared inside his house, a surprised but pleased Billie addressed Nathan. "That was nice of you to invite them."

Nathan looked a little uncomfortable. "It helps to get an insider's view of an area before making a purchase."

"And the Warrens will provide some interesting dinner conversation, I'm sure," Edgar contributed.

"I hope it won't be an imposition for you to bring them back here on our way to Atlanta," Nathan said.

"None at all," Edgar assured him.

Cliff and Neal decided to walk around while they waited for the Warrens. Edgar got out as well and spread a map on the hood of the Yukon, leaving Billie and Nathan inside alone.

Billie turned to the backseat and said, "You know what I think?"

He regarded her suspiciously. "What?"

"I think you don't care about getting an insider's view of this area. I think that you're just a nice guy and *that's* why you invited the Warrens to come with us. They seem lonely, and they were swindled into buying this awful dairy farm, and they're from Eureka and . . ."

"Okay, I'll admit it." He smiled and held up his hands in surrender. "I'm a nice guy."

The little scar under his left eye caught her attention, and she asked, "Did you really get into a lot of fights when you were in high school?"

The amusement left his face as he murmured, "A few."

The side door opened then, effectively ending the conversation. While Cliff and Neal climbed into the backseat with Nathan, Billie turned to look out the window. Nathan seemed so calm and in control of himself. The idea of him being a troublemaker in school was nearly unfathomable.

The Warrens came out of their house a few minutes later, and Edgar helped them stow their overnight bags in the back. Mr. Warren then reclaimed his seat in the front, and Thelma settled beside Billie. As the Yukon drove to the town of Eureka, the two of them provided educational and entertaining commentary.

When they reached the lakeside resort, Edgar handled check-in, and the concierge led them personally to their suites on the third floor. After agreeing to meet in the lobby at six o'clock for dinner, they separated.

* * *

The phone on the scarred, wooden desk rang, and Felix Hummer picked it up. "Your computer guy is here," a voice said.

"Send him in," Hummer commanded, then put down the receiver. A few seconds later, the door opened, and Hummer looked up with a smile. "Mr. Blalock, glad you could join us."

Kip stepped into the room followed closely by Conrad Lockhart. "I'd say it was a pleasure, but I don't like to lie."

Hummer laughed. The young man was afraid and trying to hide his fear with bravado. "I have a project for you. I want you to examine a computer and try to recover any deleted files. I'm especially interested in any e-mails sent to someone named Regina St. Claire during the last forty-eight hours."

Kip nodded. "Piece of cake."

"Conrad, please show Mr. Blalock to the computer in question," Hummer requested. "I'll be waiting anxiously to hear what you find."

* * *

As Billie walked around the sumptuous room, eating a complimentary apple, she wondered how she was going to adjust to living in her little apartment after a week of luxury. She took a shower, then put on a pair of jeans. Wishing she had packed a Christmas sweater, she settled for a turquoise blouse covered with pink orchids. As she applied her makeup, she studied her reflection in the bathroom mirror.

Her eyes were shining, and there was color in her cheeks. As she reached up and scratched her nose she remembered that tomorrow they would return to Atlanta. Nathan would find Kip, and on Saturday the men from Blalock Industries would fly back to Salt Lake.

The others were waiting for her when she stepped off the elevator. Edgar was wearing his uniform, as always. Thelma was wearing a denim pantsuit with a huge poinsettia painted on the shirt, the stem extending down one leg. Mr. Warren, predictably, had on a navy Auburn sweatshirt. Both Cliff and Neal had taken off their ties, and Cliff had actually donned a cable-knit sweater over his white dress shirt. Nathan's hair was still damp from his shower and curling up in the back. He looked comfortable in a plaid flannel shirt and well-worn jeans.

"Well, is everyone ready to go?" Cliff asked, rubbing his hands together anxiously.

Billie nodded and then followed the men as they walked down the street to The Lure. A tall, blond waitress wearing a Santa hat and a name tag identifying her as Carmella met them at the door, and Thelma immediately threw her arms around the woman's neck.

"It's been so long since we've seen you!" Thelma cried.

"I thought Sydney told me the two of you had bought a dairy farm out in the country!" Carmella responded with equal amazement.

"We did," Thelma confirmed. "We're just in town for a visit."

"Well, you're in luck," the waitress told them as she led the way through the crowded room. "To commemorate the holidays, tonight our manager is having a hoedown."

"That's a dance," Mr. Warren provided helpfully for the out-of-towners.

"That's why all the tables are pushed against the wall," Carmella explained further as they reached an empty table by the stage. "Y'all have a seat and get comfortable. I'll be back in a few minutes for your order." She distributed menus. "And maybe we'll get a chance to visit," she added to Thelma, then disappeared into the crowd. Edgar made an attempt to leave, but everyone absolutely insisted that he stay.

"This is the kind of place that attracts criminals," Edgar argued. "So I should watch the vehicle."

"That's silly," Billie replied. "You need to eat, and the Yukon will be perfectly safe."

"It's a rental," Nathan added with a wave of dismissal. "If it gets stolen, they'll give you another one."

Edgar frowned and sat stiffly in an empty chair.

"I'm kind of in the mood for a steak," Hugh commented as he scanned the menu.

"The catfish is always good here," Thelma told everyone. "It's fresh-caught daily."

"It looks a little pricey," Hugh noted with a frown.

"Don't worry about the cost," Billie said. "The Georgia Chamber of Commerce is picking up the tab."

Hugh chuckled. "In that case, I *know* I'm in the mood for a steak!"

A huge black man stepped onto the stage and introduced himself as Pinkie Howton, The Lure's manager. He expressed his hope that everyone would enjoy the music and encouraged the crowd to make use of the temporary dance floor. Then he turned the stage over to the band, and as the twang of electric guitars filled the air, the waitress took their orders and disappeared.

A few minutes later she reappeared and pulled a chair over from a neighboring table. "I turned in your orders," she announced. "Now tell me how you like dairy farming," she said to the Warrens.

"We don't like it much," Thelma admitted.

"In fact, we're trying to sell the old place," Hugh added.

"So tell me about Sydney," Thelma requested. "I haven't talked to Nelda in ages."

"She's as big as the side of a barn, ready to have that new baby any day now," Carmella replied.

"Is she complaining?" Thelma asked.

"Is she Sydney? Of course she's complaining! But it'll be over soon, and they say it's another boy."

"Good," Thelma said with a nod of her head. "Sarah's had the position of princess in that family too long to give it up now."

The band struck up a rousing tune, drowning out Carmella and the Warrens. Billie leaned close to Nathan and hollered, "Cliff and Neal look almost as miserable as Edgar."

He glanced at the men across the table, then yelled into her ear, "I guess being at a dance without your wife would stink. And Edgar just misses that Yukon."

Billie had to laugh. "How about you? Do you wish you were back in your quiet hotel room, working on security systems?"

He shook his head, and they were so close that his curls brushed her cheek. "No. This is fun."

Carmella ended her conversation with the Warrens and went to get their food. The meal was delicious and the music was invigorating. By the time Billie finished eating, she was as happy as she could remember being in ages.

"We used to square dance every Saturday night," Thelma informed them during a brief lull in the musical din. She glanced over at Hugh. "I wonder if we remember how."

"Only one way to find out," he said, then stood and extended a hand to his wife.

"Anyone care for dessert?" Carmella asked as she returned to their table and stacked their plates on her arm. "Our fresh peach pie is out of this world."

Hugh nodded. "Bring a piece for everybody. In fact, bring two for me. Dancing always gives me an appetite!" He turned and winked at Billie. "Might as well get our money's worth out of the Chamber of Commerce." Then he led his wife onto the dance floor.

The others turned their chairs around so they could watch. In spite of their age, Hugh and Thelma proved to be graceful and proficient dancers. They organized the throng of people into a Virginia reel, the bunny hop, and finally the hokey pokey before they returned to the table, flushed and out of breath.

"Pass me some of that pie, quick," Hugh requested. "Thelma has sapped every ounce of my strength. I kept trying to sit down, but she wouldn't let me."

"You crazy old man," Thelma said as she bit into her own piece. "I finally had to drag you off the dance floor."

"The pie was delicious," Billie told them. "Didn't you think so?" she asked her other companions. "In fact, the whole meal was great."

"Well," Nathan began thoughtfully, a smile playing in the corners of his mouth. "I didn't have to wear it in order to eat it, and it didn't quadruple my cholesterol level, so I guess I'd have to say yes."

Before Billie could respond, the manager announced a country line dance and Hugh stood up. "I've gotten a second wind. Would you like to dance, Miss Billie?" he asked.

She smiled at the little man. "Sure."

He turned to Nathan. "Good. Nathan here will dance with you while I dance with Thelma."

Billie turned to Nathan, embarrassed. "You don't have to dance with me," she assured him softly. "I'm perfectly happy watching."

"Nonsense," Thelma said as she took Hugh by the hand. "Dancing is much more fun!"

Nathan stood and pulled out her chair. "I'd be honored."

"What about you boys?" Hugh asked the other men sitting around the table. "Why don't you grab a girl and join us?" Cliff and

Neal both turned crimson, and Edgar looked like he was on the verge of cardiac arrest.

"I, well, I mean we," Cliff began nervously.

"What Mr. Reynolds means to say is that they are ready to return to the hotel," Edgar interjected, then turned to Billie. "I'll return with the Yukon whenever the rest of you are ready to leave."

"Don't hurry back," Hugh called after Edgar as he led Cliff and Neal out of the crowded room. "The night is young!"

Billie allowed Nathan to guide her to a relatively private corner. "You really don't have to do this," she tried again to let him off the hook. "We can go sit in the lobby, and Mr. Warren will never know."

Nathan smiled as he drew her close. "Actually, Hugh did me a big favor. I've been wanting to ask you to dance."

"So why didn't you?"

He shrugged. "I didn't want to give you the wrong impression."

Billie frowned. "You thought I would read too much into a *dance* invitation?"

"I guess it was a silly concern," he said as he drew her into his arms.

Billie was so distracted by the feel of his embrace that they were halfway through the next song before she realized it. "We're still dancing!" she hollered into Nathan's ear.

"Are you in a hurry to get back to the table and discuss dairy cows with Hugh?" he countered.

"No," Billie replied.

He smiled, then pulled her a little closer. They kept dancing through a third song and then a fourth. Finally the manager announced a new band, and Billie and Nathan headed back to their table. The only person sitting there was the waitress wearing the Santa hat.

"You two look great together," Carmella proclaimed cheerfully as they approached her.

"We're not together," Billie clarified with a blush. "I mean, we're just here on business."

Carmella smiled. "Yeah, sure."

"Where are the Warrens?" Billie asked, hoping that the dim lighting hid the heat that rose in her cheeks.

The waitress shrugged as she got to her feet. "They said they were going to the hotel and for you to call when you were ready for the driver to come back and get you." Carmella stretched, then pulled her order pad from her apron. "Well, my break is over, so I'd better get to work. Can I bring you something? Cheese fries? Mozzarella sticks? Oysters on the half shell?"

Billie started to decline, but Nathan told the waitress to bring them fresh Sprites. "I'm not anxious to get to the hotel unless you are," he said after Carmella left.

"No, I guess I'm not," Billie admitted. "Since even my Internet friends are ignoring me," she tried to joke about Cowboy's defection.

Nathan leaned toward her. "Surely a girl like you can find dates a more conventional way."

Billie decided to take this as a compliment. "Thanks." Then, after a brief pause, she asked, "What about you? Do you date?"

Nathan turned his gaze toward the band. "Rarely."

Billie cleared her throat and changed the subject. "So, are you going to recommend that Blalock Industries build their plant on the Warrens' property so they can move?"

"No." Nathan shook his head. "Our best bet so far is the land owned by the pipe company."

Billie knew she shouldn't feel disappointed. Nathan and the other men from Blalock Industries had a business decision to make, and there was no room for sentimentality. At least the plant would be built in Georgia, but she felt sorry for the Warrens.

Nathan looked over at her and smiled. "Don't worry about the Warrens. They'll sell their land. In fact, I'm going to recommend to Mr. Blalock that he buy it personally. The asking price is below market value, and Mr. Blalock could make his money back immediately from the trees on the property. Then he could turn around and sell the cleared land to a developer for a mint. But if Mr. Blalock doesn't want it, someone else will. And I thought on the way back to their place tomorrow, we might drive by that nice house with the gazebo owned by the ungrateful yuppies."

Billie smiled at the thought. "Wouldn't that be perfect?"

Nathan nodded. "Pretty close."

When a soloist took the microphone and started singing with a guitar, Nathan led her to the dance floor again. The room was dark and crowded, which oddly made her feel as if they were completely alone. "I understand that you don't do serious relationships," she whispered. "But just for tonight, I'm going to pretend that you don't have a broken heart."

Instead of responding, he gathered her close and they moved together in time with the slow music. When the soloist finished, Billie suggested that they head back to the hotel. "Should we call Edgar or do you want to walk?" she asked.

"Let's just walk. It's not that far, and since the temperature outside is mild, I don't think you'll freeze to death, even though you refuse to wear a coat."

She smiled as they moved toward the entrance. Nathan reached for her hand and led the way to the sidewalk along the lakefront. *This is just for tonight*, she reminded herself as she savored the feeling of Nathan's fingers wrapped around her own. They reached a pier, and Nathan pulled her down it until they were at the end, surrounded by water.

"It's such a beautiful night," he said.

"Almost magical," she agreed. "Although I'm surprised to hear you admit it. I didn't think you liked much of anything about Georgia."

Nathan looked up at the star-filled sky as a slight breeze blew strands of light blond hair around his face. "If I've seemed rude, I apologize. Kip's sudden determination to take this trip upset my timetable, but I shouldn't have taken my frustrations out on Georgia." He reached over and took her other hand in his as well. "Or you. I'm sorry."

"I understand completely," she told him, wishing that time would stand still. Music from The Lure drifted toward them, and Nathan drew her back into his arms.

"One more dance," he said softly. They moved together on the small pier, and as the last sweet strains of the song hung in the air, Nathan's head lowered toward hers. She watched his lips get closer and could actually feel his breath when a carload of teenagers yelled from the street, startling them apart.

"What are you thinking?" he asked as they started back down toward the sidewalk.

"That I wish tonight could last forever," she told him wistfully.

Nathan squeezed her hand. "But it can't and it won't."

Billie pulled him to a stop at the end of the pier. "If you met someone who understood that you have issues from the past, someone who would be patient while you work through them," she began, careful to avoid looking into his eyes. "Maybe . . ."

Nathan shook his head. "It's too big a risk to ask anyone to take." He stared at the stars for a few seconds.

Billie's heart began to ache as she looked at Nathan. He seemed like such a good man. It pained her to think of him living his life alone. A breeze blew off the water, and Billie shivered. Nathan pulled her forward.

"I shouldn't have kept you out in this night air," he apologized. "You might catch pneumonia."

"If I get sick, it will be worth it," she answered, holding his hand tightly.

He gave her a small smile, but as they walked up the sidewalk toward their hotel, she noticed that his eyes looked sad. When they reached her door, he leaned down and whispered, "Sweet dreams."

As she went inside her room she fought back tears. Camille had tricked her, Cowboy had abandoned her, and now Nathan had put himself out of her reach. As she rubbed her itching nose, she wondered how much worse her luck could get.

* * *

There was a knock on the storage room door, and Felix Hummer looked up from his computer screen. "Come in."

Conrad Lockart stepped into the room and approached the old desk. "Kip Blalock recovered portions of the final e-mail Cowboy sent to Miss St. Claire. I've made you a copy." Conrad put it on the desk and watched while Hummer scanned the pages.

"She will need to be eliminated. Immediately."

Conrad cleared his throat. "It turns out that Regina St. Claire is the pen name for a Chamber of Commerce employee named Billie Murphy." He paused. "I *know* her."

"This is business, Conrad. You can't let your emotions get involved," Hummer replied without a trace of sympathy. "She's a threat to everything. Have you located her?"

"She's on a cruise in the Bahamas right now."

Hummer frowned. "The Bahamas?"

"Yes," Conrad confirmed. "She'll be driving back from Savannah on Friday evening."

Hummer steepled his fingers, thinking. "I don't want to draw attention by bringing in anyone else from Las Vegas. Talk to our friend, the former heavyweight champion. Tell him we need her car fixed to explode during the trip home. I'm sure he has the right connections for a job like that."

"I'm sure he does," Conrad acknowledged.

"I want her apartment searched and her computer equipment seized. If a hint of this e-mail gets into the wrong hands, our whole plan is ruined."

"Mr. Blalock is asking to see you," Conrad told him.

"Stall him."

Conrad nodded miserably and left the room. Once the door closed behind the city councilman, Felix Hummer picked up the phone and dialed a number. "Can you talk?" he asked when the other party answered.

"Yes."

"The opportunity we've been looking for has just fallen into our laps. Listen very carefully." He then proceeded to outline a series of instructions. After having them repeated back to him, he smiled. "I'll see you soon." Then he hung up the phone. After several seconds of careful consideration, he made another call.

"Atlanta Police Department," the voice on the other end answered.

"It's time you started earning your retainer," Hummer said.

There was a brief pause. "What do you want me to do?"

With a smile, Felix Hummer explained his plan.

* * *

On Friday morning Billie woke up feeling tired. She had finished *Breathless* about two o'clock in the morning and had e-mailed it to her editor. Thanks to Cowboy, she had also submitted a proposal, albeit a bogus one, for her next book. It had been a very productive week, and she knew she should be happy. But soon Nathan would be on a plane headed back to Salt Lake, and that was a depressing thought.

After the romantic hours they had spent together the night before, Billie's initial meeting with Nathan at breakfast was a little awkward. They were both quiet, but Neal and Cliff filled the silence by discussing politics with Mr. Warren. Billie let her mind wander during the good-natured debate, but when Edgar came to collect them, the conversation shifted to the GFL, and she started listening.

Edgar mentioned that the new league was offering very favorable odds for the exhibition game the next weekend, and Nathan frowned.

"What do you mean they're offering very favorable odds?" he asked Edgar.

"Ordinarily the odds are set based on who the Las Vegas experts think will win," the driver explained. "But in this game, the backers of the GFL are subsidizing the odds so that no matter who wins, everyone can make money."

"Why would they do that?" Nathan asked in confusion. "I mean, isn't the whole point for them to make money on the losers?"

"And eventually they'll make plenty, believe me. But for this first game, they just want people to bet and to buy tickets and concessions and to watch the game on television. So they're covering part of the spread, basically eliminating most of the risk."

"No wonder Kip has been so interested in all this," Nathan muttered.

"You think he's going to bet on the exhibition game while he's in Atlanta?" Billie asked and their eyes met.

"He'll risk every cent he can beg, borrow, or steal," Nathan predicted grimly.

"So when will your company make a decision about where to build their paper plant?" Mr. Warren asked the men from Blalock Industries.

Nathan leaned forward and answered the question. "Soon. By the end of next week you should get a notification of some kind."

After breakfast, the group checked out of their hotel, then took the Warrens home. On the way they made a detour to show them the Victorian-style house for sale. "This is lovely," Thelma breathed.

"And this garden has the potential to be unparalleled," Hugh agreed.

"I wish you could see the inside of the house," Billie told them. "It's in good shape and so charming."

"When you sell your dairy farm, you can get this place at a bargain price," Nathan told them. "The owners are anxious to sell, and I think they'll negotiate."

"It's something to think about," Hugh replied.

When they got to the Warrens' house, it looked drearier than Billie remembered. The Warrens begged them to come in for a while, and Billie was considering it when Edgar reminded her that they needed to keep on schedule. So they waved good-bye to the Warrens and headed toward Atlanta.

CHAPTER 5

The trip to Atlanta passed too quickly, and soon they were checking back into the Peachtree Center Marriott. There was a line waiting for valets to take luggage upstairs, so Edgar picked up Billie's suitcases and the men carried their own into the elevator.

Before he carried Billie's luggage into her room, Edgar reminded the others that they had tickets for the Hawks game that night and reservations at a restaurant in Centennial Park. "So, did you enjoy trip, Billie?" he asked politely as he deposited the suitcases on the thick carpet of her suite.

"Actually, I did," she admitted with a smile. "But I couldn't have done it without you."

"All a part of my job," the driver answered.

Before Billie could respond, there was a knock on the open door and Nathan joined them, a look of concern on his face. "Kip's not answering his cell phone or the number he gave me here in Atlanta," he told them. "He was planning to go on a tour of the Georgia Dome this afternoon," he addressed Edgar directly. "Can you find out what time it starts?"

"Of course," Edgar agreed, already pulling out his cell phone. He stepped a few feet away and carried on a quick and quiet conversation. "The tour began at one o'clock."

Nathan checked his watch. "That was about thirty minutes ago. Is there any way to determine whether Kip showed up for the tour?"

Edgar nodded. "I will certainly try."

Billie and Nathan waited in anxious silence as Edgar made phone calls. Finally he closed his phone and addressed Nathan. "I'm sorry, but Mr. Blalock is not on the tour."

Nathan shook his head. "I can't imagine what would have distracted him from something related to the GFL."

"Unless he's sick or hurt," Billie whispered.

"He probably just lost track of the time," Edgar offered with optimism. "Keep trying his cell phone. You'll get through eventually."

Nathan nodded. "Right now I'm going to have to call Mr. Blalock, which I dread."

"Surely he won't be mad at *you!*" Billie was offended in his behalf. "None of this was your fault."

Nathan gave her a small smile. "He won't be happy with me, but he's going to be furious with Kip, and I hate to see their relationship deteriorate any further."

Billie was touched once again by his compassion.

Edgar stepped toward the door. "I've got a few details to check on for tonight," he told them. "But since we don't have to leave until around five o'clock, I suggest that both of you try to catch a quick nap."

Nathan followed Edgar out into the hallway. "I guess I might as well get it over with."

"Call if you feel like talking after your conversation with Mr. Blalock," Billie told him.

Nathan nodded, then moved on to his own room.

Billie removed a complimentary ginger ale from the little refrigerator, then stretched out on the couch. She had only been watching *Gilligan's Island* for a few minutes when there was a knock on her door. She opened it to find Nathan standing in the hallway.

"What did he say?"

"I've been relieved of my duties where Kip is concerned."

"He fired you?" Billie was outraged.

Nathan sighed heavily as she led him to the couch in her small sitting area and turned off the television. "Not yet. I'm still in charge of security at Blalock Industries, but he's hired an entire private investigation firm to find Kip—and he's notified the police as well."

"But he doesn't want you to help?"

"Mr. Blalock doesn't think that Kip has been kidnapped or injured in any way. He thinks his son is hiding in Atlanta so that he can stay and attend the GFL exhibition game next Saturday instead of returning to Salt Lake."

"What do you think?" Billie asked.

Nathan shrugged. "Makes sense to me."

"So what will you do?"

"I'll continue to impersonate Kip, and if anyone is looking for *him*, it will be easy to find *me*."

"So you'll still be protecting Kip, in a way."

"Yes, just not actively involved in trying to find him." Nathan stood and stretched. "Well, I guess I'll let you rest for a while."

She followed him to the door. "I'm here if you need me."

He waved, then walked out into the hall.

Billie closed the door and looked around the beautiful room. It was identical to the one she had been so impressed with on Monday, but now all she could think about was Nathan. He was only a few feet away, but they might as well be a million miles apart. On Saturday he'd leave and she'd never see him again.

She kicked off her shoes and started toward the bedroom when the phone rang. She picked it up absently.

"I didn't wake you up, did I?" Nathan's voice came through the line.

"The most exhausted person in the world couldn't have fallen asleep that quickly," she replied.

"So, are you planning to follow Edgar's advice and take a nap?"

"Sleeping during the day gives me a headache."

"Are you going to work on your book?" Nathan pressed, and Billie laughed into the receiver.

"My book is finished and submitted to my publisher," she told him proudly. "Why all these questions?"

"Edgar says the hotel has a nice indoor pool, and I was thinking of trying it out. Do you want to come along?"

Billie smiled. "I may not have warm clothes or a coat that matches, but I do have a *new* bathing suit."

Nathan laughed. "Is that a yes?"

"I'll be ready in ten minutes."

Nathan knocked in eight. Billie glanced one last time in the mirror, pleased by what she saw. The bathing suit was the most expensive one she'd ever owned. It was a tropical print in hot pink and neon orange and designed to be attractive yet modest. Tying the matching sarong around her waist, she joined Nathan in the hallway.

"You like it?" she asked, making a little turn for him to get the full effect.

"It's very nice," he told her with a smile. "And for the first time since we met, I don't need to suggest that you wear a coat."

She rolled her eyes and led the way to the elevator. The pool took up most of the seventeenth floor, enclosed in a room with glass walls on all sides and a skylight. The room was also full of indoor trees and greenery.

"If I didn't know I was inside, I'd think I had walked into a rain forest," Billie whispered in awe.

"This is very nice," Nathan agreed as he picked out a table and hung his towel over the back of a chair. "Let's race," he challenged as he took three long strides and dove into the deep end of the pool.

"You win," she said with a smirk as he resurfaced.

He shook his long hair out of his eyes. "Aren't you coming in?"

"Not like that," she assured him. "I'm cautious and prefer the one-step-at-a-time approach."

She took off the sarong and put it on the chair beside the one Nathan had claimed, then walked sedately to the steps and eased herself into the warm water. "Oh, this is wonderful," she exclaimed.

"Are you also one of those finicky women who don't want to mess up their hair, so they won't go under water?" Nathan asked with a teasing smile.

Billie ducked beneath the surface and came up beside him. "No."

He had little drops of water clinging to his eyelashes that fell off as he laughed. "Good."

"How's the water?" Edgar asked from the edge of the pool, and they both looked up in surprise.

"It's great," Nathan answered. "Thanks for suggesting it."

Edgar nodded with a smile. "I've asked the hospitality department to provide you with some light refreshment." Edgar indicated toward a pair of waiters who were busy putting food on the table they had chosen. "If you need anything else, just call the desk, and they'll be happy to arrange it." With a wave, he stepped toward the door.

"You're the best, Edgar," Nathan called after him.

After the waiters left, Nathan pulled himself up on the side of the pool and climbed out. "Wow, we're really getting the royal treatment."

He held out a hand. "We don't want all that good food to go to waste."

The image of him dragging her, dripping wet, from the pool was too much, so Billie shook her head. "Thanks, but I'll use the steps."

When she joined him by the table, she wrapped the sarong around her waist and draped a towel around her shoulders, then they filled their plates from the impressive array provided by the hotel. "Kip sure is going to be sorry he missed this," Nathan said as they settled in their seats.

"The swim or the food?" Billie asked with a smile.

He grinned back. "Both."

They ate in companionable silence for a few minutes, then Billie asked, "Do you think Kip will contact his father?"

Nathan nodded. "Eventually. He doesn't have the financial ability to survive on his own. He likes to test his father's limits sometimes, but he won't risk serious trouble." Nathan took a big bite of an éclair.

"And Kip's little trick won't cost you your job?"

"I'm trying not to worry about that until I have to."

"Because you have an expensive house to maintain," she teased, and he agreed with a tip of his head. "Tell me about it."

"It's just an old house," he said, wiping his mouth on a linen napkin with *Marriott Hotels* monogrammed in the corner.

"It can't be *just* an old house if you're investing so much time and money in it," she disagreed. "Not to mention living without running water."

"I just couldn't stand the thought of the city tearing it down. Does that sound crazy?"

She shook her head. "Not at all."

"The house will never be worth what I've already put into it. The neighborhood is shabby at best, but it gives me great satisfaction to see the improvements."

"Almost like you're turning back the hands of time."

Nathan nodded, then took a bite of crab cake. "This stuff is great."

"It is very good," she agreed.

After eating, they lounged for thirty minutes, then swam around for a while longer. Finally Nathan took her hand and pulled her toward the steps. "If you want to have some relaxation time before dinner, we'd better head back to our rooms."

Billie nodded. "Not that we'll be able to eat any dinner after this little *snack*." She waved at the table.

"So what's on tap for tonight?" Nathan asked as they stepped into the elevator. "I'll bet it's a restaurant built around a basketball theme. They throw you your food, and you get to eat whatever you can catch."

Billie laughed. "Actually, I have heard of a place sort of like that, but it's not on the itinerary. We're eating at the Fountainside Café."

"Sounds safe enough," Nathan remarked as they reached her room. "See you at six o'clock."

* * *

"I assume that you have arranged for Miss Murphy to have a nasty little accident on her way home from the cruise?" Hummer asked Conrad Lockhart when the older man arrived with lunch.

"Yes. The car has been rigged to explode when it reaches a certain speed. But there might be a problem, and that's why I wanted to talk to you."

"What kind of problem?"

"According to the man who was watching when the cruise ship disembarked, Jeff Burdick was with Miss Murphy."

Felix Hummer feigned surprise. "The Atlanta Competitors' quarterback?"

Conrad nodded. "When the car blows up, he'll be killed along with Miss Murphy."

"The Competitors have a backup quarterback, don't they?" Hummer asked.

"Yes," Conrad gasped. "Of course."

Hummer took a bite of his seafood salad. "Then I don't see a problem. Close the door on your way out."

* * *

Billie took a shower to wash the chlorine out of her hair, then curled up on the big bed, intending to rest for a few minutes. She closed her eyes and woke up later to the sound of someone banging on the door. When she jerked it open, she saw Nathan standing in the hallway.

"I was just about to call security," he told her sharply. "You said you didn't sleep during the day, and when I couldn't get you to answer I was afraid you'd drowned in the bathtub."

Billie pushed a clump of her still-damp hair over her shoulder and clutched her bathrobe close around her neck. "I guess I dozed off."

Nathan glanced over her. "Cliff and Neal are already waiting in the SUV with Edgar. How long will it take you to get ready?"

"I'll hurry," Billie promised, then closed the door. There was no time to pick and choose, so she pulled on a pair of jeans, a long-sleeved T-shirt, and tennis shoes without socks. Then she ran a brush through her hair and rinsed her mouth with some of the complimentary Scope. After a quick application of mascara and blush, she rushed into the hall.

Nathan was leaning against the wall beside her door. She reached up to scratch her nose as he did a slow perusal of her from head to toes. "Do I look *that* bad?" she asked with concern.

"You have freckles," he said as if she'd been hiding something important from him.

"Guilty," she admitted, keeping her tone light. She'd been teased her whole life about the sprinkling across her nose and was particularly sensitive about them. "I usually cover them with makeup, but because of my unplanned nap, I didn't have time tonight."

He seemed at a loss for words, and Billie was beginning to wonder if he had a strange prejudice against freckles when he smiled. "You shouldn't cover them up. They give your face character."

"My brothers used to beg me to let them connect the dots," she told him as they moved down the hall. "The kids at school would tease me that my face was dirty."

"That's just the price you pay for having a nose with character." He reached for her hand and drew her onto the elevator. They stood close together during the descent, but once the doors started to open, he gave her fingers a short squeeze, then released them.

Her heart was pounding as they joined Edgar in the lobby. He gave them a speculative look, then herded them out to the Yukon waiting by the entrance. As they reached the Georgia Dome area, Edgar gave the guests from Salt Lake educational commentary.

"This is actually a huge, interrelated complex," Edgar told them. "To your left is the Centennial Olympic Park, one of the largest city parks in the United States. You'll get a chance to walk around there some tonight before the game. Then ahead on your right is the Georgia World Congress Center. It has a huge exhibition hall, and, well, just about everything else imaginable. That's where the GFL has their headquarters."

Billie saw that Nathan was studying the massive edifice with interest and gave it a cursory glance to be polite. The whole place looked like a parking attendant's nightmare to her. "That is Philips Arena, where we'll come for the basketball game tonight." Edgar pointed out his window. "And the Georgia Dome is there. It's all an interrelated sports complex."

"I'll bet this can't compare with the stadiums in Utah," Billie teased Nathan, but he didn't rise to the bait.

"To be honest, I've never seen anything like this before in my life," Nathan responded. "You Southerners certainly take your sports seriously."

Billie laughed as Edgar continued. "This is the recently completed Phase IV of the World Congress Center, and it has a parking deck underneath. But parking is expensive and not always convenient, so many people either come in by taxi or ride the Marta." Edgar indicated toward the tram station on their left.

It was starting to get dark when they reached Centennial Park. Edgar dropped them off at the Fountainside Café and promised to come back once he had the vehicle situated. Billie led the group inside and presented Conrad Lockhart's name as naturally as if he had been her uncle.

Once they were settled around the table, Billie asked, "So, have you chosen a site for your paper plant yet?"

"It's going to be in Georgia," Neal told her cheerfully.

Billie gave him a confident smile. "I fully expected that much. Georgia was a given. I just wondered which site you chose."

Cliff cleared his throat, then said, "I think we'll build our paper plant on the site owned by the pipe company."

Billie tried not to sound disappointed. "Nathan told me that it was the best location all the way around."

Nathan leaned forward. "But Mr. Blalock authorized us to buy the Warrens' farm too. He'll recoup most of the purchase price by selling the lumber and depreciate the rest as a tax write-off. So your time with us has been well-spent."

She reached up and scratched her nose. "It certainly has," she agreed.

Cliff and Neal began discussing the intricacies of purchasing the two parcels of land while Billie and Nathan concentrated on the menu. The waitress returned, and everyone placed their orders. Nathan seemed distracted, and finally Billie asked, "Are you worried about Kip?"

He sighed. "I guess I am, which is ridiculous because it's none of my business. But if you sat down and made a list of the qualities that would make up the perfect mother and father, you would have described Mr. and Mrs. Blalock. They've dedicated their lives to Kip and making him happy. He repays them by gambling and disappearing and refusing to take an interest in their business or religion."

"They deserve better than that."

"Yes, they do," Nathan agreed. "Sister Blalock has spent months planning a family Christmas up in the mountains, but now Kip's ruined the whole thing over a chance to gamble on a football game." Nathan looked at her. "It makes no sense."

Billie shook her head. "Maybe Kip will eventually learn to appreciate what he's got."

Nathan shrugged. "Maybe so."

Once the food arrived, everyone started eating, but Nathan remained pensive. Billie determined that if this was going to be their last night together, she was going to make it one Nathan would always remember. She began entertaining everyone with anecdotes about her family, and when she told them that she was required to participate in the annual family portrait on Saturday night, Cliff and Neal pulled out their wallets and passed around photographs or their respective families. Nathan was conspicuously quiet during the family discussion although he did give her warm smiles from time to time.

Wanting to include him more, she changed the subject. She told them about her years at college and got him to admit to being on the debate team at Cornell. "Arguing was always one of my strong points," he confessed.

"Is that how you broke your nose?" she whispered as the conversation moved on.

"No," he replied in low tones. "I got into a fight with a nosy, freckle-faced girl."

She smiled. "Who won?"

He grinned back. "Guess."

After their meal, Cliff and Neal wanted to visit the Chamber of Commerce offices on the edge of the park—the last place Billie wanted to go. She sent Edgar with them and asked Nathan to take her on the quilt walk.

The park was busy, and as they were leaving the Quilt of Remembrance, a pair of cyclists almost ran them over. Nathan grabbed Billie's hand and pulled her to safety. It took Billie a few minutes to regulate her breathing before she realized that his arms were wrapped tightly around her. For the second time in as many nights, she thought he was going to kiss her, but instead he dropped his arms and stepped back. "Sorry."

"Don't apologize for saving my life," she said.

"Saving your life might be an exaggeration," Nathan replied. "But I kept you from a painful series of skin graphs for sure."

Billie led the way to the front of the park where the others were waiting. They walked together to the arena, and Edgar distributed tickets, then led them to the appropriate entrance. "I'll be parked out front when the game is over," he told them.

They bought peanuts and Sprites and settled in their seats. While watching the game, Billie cracked peanuts and carelessly threw the shells on the floor. This seemed to amuse Nathan, so she did it often. The Hawks were losing badly at halftime and Neal was anxious to check on his wife, so they decided to call Edgar to come get them. Billie pulled out her cell phone and found that the battery was dead.

"I guess I left it on by mistake," she said, frowning.

"Use mine," Nathan offered, and she accepted the phone from his hand.

She made a quick call to Edgar, then returned the phone to Nathan.

"Do you have a charger in your room?" Cliff asked, apparently concerned about her lack of cell phone access.

She thought for a second. "I'm not sure I even packed it. The Chamber just bought them recently, and I'm not used to having one, so I won't miss it until I get back to my apartment."

When they reached the lobby of the hotel, Nathan walked up to the registration desk and she followed.

"Can you tell me whether or not Mr. Nathan Turner has checked in?" Nathan asked.

Billie was momentarily confused by this question before she remembered that Nathan and Kip had "switched" identities for safety reasons.

The desk clerk checked her computer, then shook her head. "No, I'm sorry, sir."

Edgar said good night in the lobby, and Cliff turned to Nathan. "Are you two coming up now?"

"I thought we might sit around the indoor pool for a while," Nathan responded with a glance at Billie. "Unless you're tired."

She smiled. "The pool sounds nice."

Billie let Nathan lead her outside, content to just be in his company. Instead of taking her to the indoor pool, though, he guided her down the elevator and out the back entrance into a garden. "I thought you said we were going to the pool," she reminded him.

"I told Cliff and Neal that's where we *might* go," he clarified. "But I don't want either one of them to join us, so I brought you here."

"It's a little chilly," Billie said, rubbing her hands up and down her arms.

He pointed toward an ornate wrought-iron bench and they sat close, his arm draped around her shoulders. "Cool temperatures present certain opportunities." He pulled her closer, and she didn't resist. "I'm crazy about freckles," he told her. "And with your nose all red and the wind making your eyes water, you're almost irresistible."

Billie gave him a weak smile. "If you think I'm cute now, you should see me in the springtime when the pollen is everywhere."

"I'd like that." He stroked her cheek. "Seeing you in the spring, I mean." He looked at an arrangement of poinsettias at the foot of the bench. "I guess you'll go home for Christmas."

"My mother would kill me if I didn't," she answered, then could have kicked herself when she remembered that Nathan had no family to spend the holidays with. "I could tell that you were uncomfortable when we were talking about our families tonight," she said. Even though she was anxious not to upset him, no true intimacy could develop between them unless he was honest with her. "Have your parents been dead for a long time?"

He didn't respond immediately, and she was beginning to wonder if he would. Finally he said, "My mother has been dead for two years. My father died a few months ago, but he's never been a part of my life."

"They died young," Billie remarked.

"Yes, that kind of runs in our family." He glanced down at her. "Another reason I don't plan to marry."

Billie closed her eyes and snuggled a little closer to him. "Aren't you ever tempted to give it a shot?" She felt his gaze on her but didn't raise her eyes to meet his.

"Until now, I can honestly say that I haven't been tempted," he whispered against her ear.

Billie sat beside him until her fingers and toes lost their feeling. Afraid she was on the verge of frostbite, she suggested that it was time to go inside.

"I had fun tonight," he told her as they stood in the hall outside her hotel suite.

"I did too," she admitted.

"And after I get the security system at Blalock Industries up and running, maybe you *could* fly out to Utah for a friendly skiing trip."

"I'm not very athletic," she warned him.

"Then we'll just sit by the fire and sip hot chocolate for a few days."

"Now that should be within my ability!" She leaned closer, giving him an opportunity to kiss her. He took a step forward, but as his head descended toward hers, a door down the hall opened and an elderly couple stepped out into the hallway.

"I guess it's just not meant to be," Nathan murmured with a rueful smile.

Billie smiled back. "Not tonight anyway," she told him, then opened her door and slipped inside.

Feeling slightly encouraged, Billie pulled off her coat and was about to call her mother when the phone rang.

"You're never going to believe this," Nathan said, and she could hear the laughter in his voice.

"What?" she demanded.

"I just got a call from Mr. Blalock. He said he wants to get the site purchased before the end of the year, and since we're already here . . ."

"He wants you to do it?" Billie asked in astonishment. "Now?"

"The meeting is set for eleven tomorrow morning at an attorney's office in Columbus. Mr. Blalock wanted Neal to go, but since his wife's about to have her baby . . ."

"You volunteered?" Billie chest swelled with pride. He was so sweet.

"Actually, since I have a complicated security system to install, I suggested Cliff, but he has all kinds of year-end reports that have to be filed on time or Mr. Blalock goes to jail. So that left me."

Billie swallowed hard to hide her disappointment. "Oh."

Nathan laughed. "I'm just kidding. I more than volunteered—I begged."

Billie's good humor was restored. "So you're not flying home tomorrow?"

"No, I'll fly home on Monday. But Edgar is driving me to Columbus tonight, and I was sort of hoping you would come too."

Billie pressed a hand to her pounding heart. "Me?"

"To represent the Chamber of Commerce and make sure that everyone knows where credit is due."

Billie laughed. "When do we leave?"

"Edgar says within the hour."

"You and Edgar sure have been talking a lot."

"Only about unimportant stuff. As soon as we got to a crucial decision, we called you," he teased. "Edgar's arranging for the hotel shuttle to take Cliff and Neal to the airport in the morning. I told him we'd be waiting in the lobby at ten o'clock."

"I'll throw my inappropriate wardrobe into my suitcases and meet you down there in a few minutes," she told him, then hung up with the sound of his laughter lingering in her ears.

The phone rang again and Billie grabbed for it, thinking it might be Nathan. Instead it was Camille. "We're just a few miles out of Atlanta, and before I see Uncle Conrad I wanted to check and see how things went with the Mormons."

Billie sighed. "Blalock Industries is going to build their paper plant in Georgia."

"I knew you could do it!" Camille sounded genuinely pleased. "Will the deal go through before the end of the year?"

"I imagine so, since the closing is tomorrow. Edgar is driving me and a representative from Blalock Industries back to Columbus in a few minutes."

"Perfect. That will look so good on my annual production report."

"Don't you mean on *my* APR?" Billie clarified.

"Let's not nitpick," Camille suggested. "It's a big success for the Chamber as a whole. So tell me about Kip Blalock."

"What's to tell?" Billie answered as she packed.

"Is he handsome?"

"Who?" Billie was thinking of Nathan and finding it hard to concentrate on Camille.

"Kip Blalock," Camille clarified impatiently.

"He's absolutely gorgeous." *And missing in action*, Billie thought to herself.

"Really?" Camille sounded almost jealous. "So, are you in love with him?"

"Not in the least," Billie replied. "But I am in a hurry. Leave my car parked in front of my apartment, and I'll see you after the holidays. Merry Christmas," she added as an afterthought as she hung up.

When Billie was finished packing, she checked the time and placed a quick call to her mother. "I'm sorry to call so late," she apologized. "But I've got good news and bad news. Which do you want first?"

"You've thought of a way to get out of the family picture," Nan guessed correctly.

"Yes, and you owe it all to Camille. I did such a good job on her tour that the paper plant people are buying not one site but two."

"Your boss at the Chamber will be so impressed!" Nan cried in excitement.

"But they want to close tomorrow, which means that Edgar and I have to accompany their representative back to Columbus."

"I'm pleased that your trip was a success, but I hate for you to work right up to Christmas Day." There was a brief silence, then Nan continued, "I guess I can reschedule the family portrait for early January if you'll promise to wear red and green."

Billie laughed. "I promise."

"So, are the Blalock people nice?" Nan probed.

"They are very nice. In fact, one of them is so perfect, if I wasn't an extremely sensible girl, I would have fallen in love with him at first sight."

"Oh, dear." Nan sounded apprehensive.

"You know how sensible I am, Mama. Anyway his plane leaves on Monday afternoon, so once I get him to the airport, I'll check on Fred and grab my presents, then head for Coopersville."

"So the perfect, almost irresistible man is going to Columbus with you?" Nan asked.

"Yes, but Edgar will chaperone."

"That's very wise on the Chamber's part," Nan praised.

Billie doubted that the Chamber cared one way or another. Edgar's participation was more than likely his own idea. "Yes, well, I'll see you on Monday night."

"I'm cooking all your favorite foods."

Billie thought of Kip and his lack of appreciation toward his parents. Feeling a little insensitive herself, Billie said, "I can hardly wait to get there, Mama."

"You've always loved Christmas," Nan said. "So I go all out."

"See you soon."

Billie disconnected and thought about her large, boisterous family and all their love and support that she had taken for granted. She thought about Nathan and the way he had infiltrated her thoughts. Not an hour of the day went by that she didn't think of something she would like to tell him or a comment she knew would make him smile. Maybe she should push him a little, make him reevaluate his decision not to get involved in relationships.

There was a knock on her hotel room door as Billie hung up the phone. She opened it to find Edgar standing in the hallway.

"I'm sorry!" Billie apologized. "Nathan told me we were supposed to be waiting in the lobby at ten."

"No problem," Edgar said as he picked up her luggage. "And congratulations. This is quite a feather in your cap." He glanced down at a piece of paper in his hand. "I got a memo from Mr. Lockhart a few minutes ago confirming that you will represent the Chamber at the closing."

Billie took the paper from his hand. The memo was addressed to Camille, and in it her uncle praised *her* for a job well-done.

"So, Camille didn't tell her uncle that I was taking this trip for her," Billie stated the obvious.

"No," Edgar admitted. "And she made me promise not to mention it either."

"In fact, I'll bet my vacation wasn't revoked," Billie thought aloud, furious with herself for not calling Camille's bluff. The uncomfortable look on Edgar's face confirmed her suspicions. "She *tricked* me into doing her job and giving her my cruise!"

"I'm sorry." Edgar seemed ashamed of Camille's behavior.

"Does everyone at the Chamber think I'm really on vacation?" she demanded, and Edgar nodded. "Well, I'm not going to let her get away with this." Billie's voice trembled with anger. "I'm going to tell Conrad Lockhart myself."

"I don't blame you one bit," Edgar said in a rare alignment against Camille. "But for now, let's take care of business. There will be time for retribution later."

With a frown, Billie agreed. She watched Edgar load her luggage onto a dolly, then followed him down to the lobby. After he loaded the suitcases into the Yukon, Edgar asked if they wanted something to eat. "If so, we'd better stop now. It will be quite late by the time we reach Columbus," he explained.

Nathan laughed. "I'm not hungry, but if you and Billie want to stop . . ."

"Are you kidding?" Billie asked. "All we've done is eat all day. If anyone gets hungry, I've still got half a bag of peanuts in my pocket."

"But watch out if she resorts to eating them," Nathan warned Edgar. "She throws the shells on the floor."

While they drove, Billie remembered about Fred. "Oh, I need to call my landlady and ask her to keep feeding Fred."

"Fred?" Nathan asked, arching one eyebrow.

"My fish." She pulled her cell phone from her purse, then realized that it didn't work. "My battery is still dead," she said as she let it fall back into the bottom of her purse. "Can I use yours again?" she asked Nathan.

"And when we get to the hotel in Columbus, I'll loan you my charger," Edgar added.

Billie made her phone call and was thankful to get the landlady's answering machine, since leaving a message took less time than a conversation would have. Then she returned the phone to Nathan. "Thanks."

"The traffic is even worse than I expected," Edgar said as they were inching along I-85.

"It's a good thing we're not trying to go that way," Nathan pointed to the oncoming traffic that was at a standstill for as far as they could see. "The problem seems to be over there, and our side is just slowing to satisfy morbid curiosity."

"Do you mind if I turn on the radio and find out what's going on?" Edgar glanced around. Neither Billie nor Nathan expressed an objection, so Edgar turned on the radio and adjusted the channel until he found the local news. For the next thirty minutes, they listened to various descriptions of an eleven-car pileup on I-85 north-bound. "Sounds like we got out just in time," he said.

Billie looked out her window, worry lines forming between her eyes. "I hope no one was hurt."

"If they close down the entire interstate, it usually means a fatality," Edgar told her.

Once they were outside of town and progressing effortlessly down the interstate, Billie leaned back in her seat. "Tired?" Nathan asked from across the vehicle.

"A little," she admitted, then looked around the interior of the SUV. "There sure is a lot of *space* in here without Cliff and Neal."

"And Kip," Nathan added.

"I sort of miss them," Billie mused.

"Yeah, they did help move the conversation along. Like Kip said, I'm just plain boring."

"I didn't mean that."

Nathan smiled. "I know. Why don't you tell me all about your new book?"

Billie started shaking her head. "Now *that* would be boring."

"Let me be the judge," Nathan suggested.

With a sigh, Billie began. At first she was self-conscious, but eventually she warmed to her subject and began describing characters and plot and setting with enthusiasm. She finished her narrative just as they reached Columbus.

"I am very impressed," Nathan told her.

For once, Billie didn't hide behind false modesty. "Thanks."

"If I wanted to buy one of your books, would I just walk into a Borders or Barnes and Noble and ask for all the books they have by Billie Murphy?" Nathan asked.

She laughed. "They'd have to special order my books for you, and I don't write under my real name. I use a pseudonym."

Nathan raised an eyebrow. "And what would that be?"

"Regina St. Claire."

Before Billie could provide any additional information, the Yukon swerved onto the shoulder. Billie and Nathan sat in tense silence as Edgar fought to return the big vehicle back onto the road. Once the SUV was under control, Edgar reduced his speed and apologized to his passengers.

"A deer ran across the road," he told them, his face very pale. "I know that you aren't supposed to swerve to avoid an animal, but it was an automatic reflex."

"We understand," Nathan answered for both of them, and Billie was glad. Her heart was still in her throat, and she couldn't have responded if her life had depended on it.

When they reached the Tutwiler, Edgar handled the arrangements with the desk clerk, then took Billie's bag up to her room while Nathan followed behind. When they reached their rooms, Edgar apologized again. He was obviously upset, and Billie wondered if he was afraid they would report his driving error to Mr. Lockhart.

"We all make mistakes," she tried to reassure Edgar. "And you never lost control of the car."

"And now we don't have the death of an innocent deer on our conscience," Nathan pointed out.

Edgar seemed relieved as he deposited Billie's suitcases into her suite. He offered to do the same for Nathan, but he shook his head. "I can handle it myself," Nathan told the driver.

"I'll say good night then," Edgar said as he moved down the hall. Then, as an afterthought, he added, "Rather than drive back to Atlanta tomorrow, I thought we'd stay here until Sunday morning, if that suits you both."

"Fine with me," Billie agreed.

"Whatever." Nathan was cooperative. After Edgar left, Nathan whispered, "Where does he sleep?"

"I'm not exactly sure," Billie replied. "He seems to make a point of keeping himself separate."

"Why?"

"Edgar's somewhat of an enigma," Billie said thoughtfully. "I think it's his way of making sure that we realize that this is just a job. He's our driver, not our servant, and when he's on his own time, he doesn't have to spend it with us."

"You mean he prefers his own company."

She smiled. "Something like that. Or maybe he's trying to give us some time alone."

Nathan raised an eyebrow.

"Matchmaking," Billie clarified. "Because he doesn't know what a hopeless case you are." She was just teasing, but Nathan's expression tensed and she wished she could take the words back.

He glanced at her door, then his own a few feet away. "Well," he began awkwardly, "I know you're tired."

"Yes, we should try to get some sleep."

He leaned toward her but hesitated.

Unable to stand the thought of another near miss, Billie stood on her tiptoes and pressed her lips against his. Then she stepped back and looked up at him with anxious eyes.

"I guess now I owe you an apology," she told him breathlessly.

"That kiss was nothing to apologize for," he replied with a smile.

"I just didn't want you to be looking *too* forward to going back to Salt Lake," she said with a shaky laugh. "A little something to remember me by."

Nathan reached out and touched her cheek. "I have a feeling that you're going to be very difficult to forget."

Billie was unaccountably pleased by this remark as she slipped into her hotel room.

CHAPTER 6

The door to the storage room and makeshift office at the GFL headquarters opened without warning, and Felix Hummer looked up. He smiled when he saw his local conspirator collapse into one of the chairs in front of the desk.

"So, it's done?" he asked. "Billie Murphy is dead?"

Conrad nodded grimly.

Hummer shook his head. "Tragic."

The city councilman's voice trembled as he replied, "May the Lord have mercy on our souls."

Felix Hummer sighed. "Don't be so dramatic. When you decided to try a life of crime, you knew that this sort of thing was part of the deal."

Conrad put a hand to his forehead. "I didn't. I swear I didn't. I thought we could just make huge amounts of money without anyone getting hurt."

"Then you were a fool."

"Aren't you afraid that too many bodies will cause suspicion?" Conrad asked.

Hummer waved his hand in an impatient gesture. "This is Atlanta. People turn up dead every day, and I'm sure you told our boxing friend to make sure Miss Murphy's demise looked accidental."

"If I could go back—" Conrad began.

"Well you can't," Hummer cut off this pointless reverie. "In a few days, all your financial problems will be over, and that should dull your pain."

"Kip Blalock is getting insistent about talking to you," Conrad reported listlessly.

"Have him brought in."

With a defeated nod, Conrad stood and left the storage room.

* * *

Billie's phone rang at seven o'clock the next morning. The desk clerk told her that Mr. Blalock had arranged the wake-up call for her so that she would have plenty of time to get ready for their breakfast date at nine o'clock. Smiling with determination, she thanked the clerk and climbed out of bed.

She was dressed and ready when Nathan knocked on her door a few minutes before nine. "Thanks for the wake-up call," she told him as she joined him in the hall. "I don't know what I can ever do to repay you."

He laughed. "I'm afraid you'll think of something."

Billie ordered blueberry pancakes, and Nathan had waffles. After the waitress delivered their food, Billie asked if he'd heard anything about Kip.

"No," Nathan replied with a frown. "I talked to Mr. Blalock this morning, and he said both the police and the private investigators have drawn a blank."

"Well, at least that proves how hard Kip is to keep up with."

"I'd rather they found him safe and sound even if it costs me my job."

She smiled. "I know, and I think that's very commendable of you."

"Have you seen Edgar this morning?" Nathan asked a few minutes later, and Billie shook her head.

"No, but we won't have to leave for the lawyers' offices for more than an hour. Edgar is never late, so I'm sure he'll be here soon."

Nathan pushed away from the table. "Mr. Blalock faxed me the contracts this morning, and I need to go over them before the closing," he told her as he got the attention of their waitress. Nathan tried to pay the bill, but the waitress told them that it had already been taken care of. "I guess we don't have to worry that Edgar has disappeared too," he told Billie with a smile as they walked to the elevator.

He left her at her door, then moved on to his own room. After repacking, Billie stretched out on the big bed. A few minutes later, there was a knock on her door. Billie pulled it open to find Edgar standing in the hall. "There you are," she said, drawing him inside. "We missed you at breakfast." Then she noticed that he was pale.

"What's the matter, Edgar?" she demanded, knowing that something must be very wrong to have shaken the unflappable chauffeur.

"You remember that traffic accident that we passed on the way out of Atlanta last night?" he asked in a faraway voice.

Billie nodded and motioned for him to sit on the couch. "Of course."

"One of the cars involved was yours. Miss Camille and her companion were both mortally wounded."

"They're dead?" Billie cried in horror. "Camille and Jeff Burdick?"

Edgar put a trembling hand to his temple. "I'm afraid so."

"I can't believe it." Billie sat beside him on the couch. "What happened?"

Edgar held out a part of the *Atlanta Constitution*, and her eyes focused on the bold type that described the eleven-car crash that had brought Atlanta traffic to a standstill the night before. She scanned the article and found her own name listed among the casualties, then looked back up at Edgar. "They don't know that Camille was driving my car?" she asked.

"They do now," Edgar replied dully. "This was printed shortly after the accident happened, and I guess they used the license plate for identification. I tried to reach Mr. Conrad, but he's not answering his phone, so I called a friend of mine who works for the Atlanta Police Department. He confirmed that Camille died in the crash."

"This says my fuel pump malfunctioned." Billie pointed at a part of the article. "But that's not possible. I just had my car serviced a couple of weeks ago, and the mechanic recommended that I have the fuel pump replaced, so I did!"

Edgar looked up. "Maybe the new fuel pump was defective."

"If there was something wrong with the fuel pump, how did Camille and Jeff Burdick drive my car all the way to Savannah and most of the way back to Atlanta without a problem?"

Edgar shook his head, looking even more confused. "I don't know. I just don't know."

"Something's not right here, Edgar. Camille said that Jeff Burdick's ex-wife was very vindictive. I wonder if she found out that they were spending the week together and had my car tampered with."

"That sounds somewhat far-fetched."

Billie gasped. "I was probably the last person to talk to her before the accident! She called me on her cell phone just before we left Atlanta last night. Maybe I should call the police and tell them in case they need help establishing the time of death."

"I'm sure they know the exact minute the crash took place, and Camille must have died instantly," Edgar told her. "But I'll mention it to my friend at the Atlanta PD, and he'll call if he needs to talk to you."

Billie took a deep breath. "Well, the only thing we can do is leave immediately for Atlanta."

"But what about Mr. Turner and the Blalock closings?" Edgar reminded her.

Billie frowned. She hated the thought of leaving Nathan under such hurried and disturbing circumstances. Without time to make plans for the future, there was a good chance that she would never see him again. But she said, "I'm sure Nathan can handle the closings alone."

After a few seconds of consideration, Edgar shook his head. "It would be unconscionable to abandon Mr. Turner in a strange city. I will go and see about Mr. Lockhart. You stay with Mr. Turner, and once the business has been taken care of, the two of you can come to Atlanta."

"But Camille . . ."

"There's nothing you can do for her now. There will be plenty of time for you to pay your respects later."

Billie sighed. "I guess you're right. But please tell Mr. Lockhart how sorry I am."

Edgar agreed with a nod. "I'll arrange for the delivery of another rental car and then be on my way."

After Edgar left, Billie reread the article from the *Atlanta Constitution*, shaking her head in wonder. Camille wasn't the nicest person she'd ever known, but it was difficult to imagine her still and cold. With a shiver, Billie picked up the phone and called her mother.

"Billie!" Nan cried when she heard her daughter's voice. "I've called your cell phone at least a hundred times!"

"I'm sorry, Mama," Billie said. "The battery in my cell phone is dead, and I left my charger in Atlanta. I guess you heard about Camille?"

"That's why I've been trying to call. The highway patrol came here in the middle of the night and told us *you* were dead. We had a horrible few minutes until your father got the details and realized that it couldn't be you since you were on your way to Columbus. Such a terrible tragedy right here at Christmastime! Have you talked to Camille's uncle?"

"No, we've been trying, but he's not answering his phone," Billie said.

"Well, when you get through, give him our deepest sympathy," Nan requested. "Are you headed back to Atlanta now?"

"Not until later today."

"I can't tell you how much peace of mind it gives me to know that you'll have a professional driver at the wheel."

Billie decided not to mention the fact that Edgar would not be with her when she returned.

"Oh, there's someone at the door, so I'd better run." Nan said a hasty good-bye and disconnected.

With the phone still in her hand, Billie decided to call her landlady and make sure she had gotten the message about feeding Fred. Mrs. Lloyd picked up on the second ring, sounding more agitated than usual. "Yes!" she demanded.

"Mrs. Lloyd, this is Billie Murphy."

"Of all the unmitigated gall!" the landlady screeched. "You may think it's funny to frighten and torment an old lady, but I consider it the lowest type of behavior. Since I am a Christian woman, instead of telling you just what I think of you, I will pray for you instead." With this decree, Mrs. Lloyd slammed the phone down.

Billie was too surprised to react for a few seconds. Then she realized that Mrs. Lloyd still thought that she had died in the traffic accident. She considered trying to explain the truth to the landlady, but since her time was limited, she decided to use a little evasion. She dialed the number again, and when Mrs. Lloyd answered, she said she was a friend of Billie's, that she had read the article in the paper, and she was calling to check on Miss Murphy's beloved red fish.

"Oh my," Mrs. Lloyd wailed. "This has been the most terrible time of my life. First I got the news that Billie had been killed in a car crash, then I came up to feed Fred and found that her apartment had been plundered."

"Plundered. You mean *robbed?*" Billie clarified.

"I mean torn to pieces. There was paper strewn everywhere, the couch cushions had been ripped open, the walls have huge holes in them. It was the work of particularly destructive thieves."

"What did they steal?"

"As far as I could tell, only her computer."

Billie felt a little chill run down her spine. "Did you call the police?"

"Of course! They said they would handle it."

"And what about the fish?"

She heard Mrs. Lloyd sniffle. "They turned the tank over and left the poor thing to die of suffocation."

Billie's hands were trembling as she hung up the phone. She knew it was foolish to be more affected by Fred's death than by Camille's, but she was. She was trying to make some sense of it all when the phone rang again. It was her mother.

"The strangest thing just happened, Billie," Nan told her.

"Mama, can you speak up? I can barely hear you."

"That's because I'm whispering," Nan explained. "A policeman from Atlanta is here and he wants the boxes you have stored in our garage."

"Why would the Atlanta Police Department want my stuff in the garage?" Billie asked.

"I can't imagine how they even knew you had things stored here."

Billie frowned as she replied, "I don't understand that either, unless they've recovered my computer. I had an inventory of the things in your garage on my hard drive."

"Recovered your computer?" Nan repeated. "Where was it?"

Billie took a deep breath and explained, "My apartment was robbed last night, Mama. The thieves killed Fred and stole my computer."

"Oh, Billie." Nan seemed at a loss. "I'm so sorry about Fred."

Billie blinked back a fresh wave of tears. "Me too."

"And I can't believe you were robbed!" After a brief pause, Nan asked, "Are you in trouble, dear?"

"I'm not sure, Mama. Did you let the policeman take the boxes from the garage?"

"Since he's from the police, we didn't have a choice!" Nan replied. "He's loading them up right now."

"That's okay, really," Billie assured her mother. "There's nothing important in those boxes. But if he asks you where I am . . ."

"I'll say I don't know," Nan finished the sentence. "Which I don't—exactly. Can you tell me what's going on?"

Billie sighed. "I'm not sure myself, but once I get back to Atlanta, I'll figure it out. Just tell the policeman that I'm out of town and you haven't been able to reach me on my cell phone. I'll be back in touch soon."

"I think we should discuss this with your father," Nan hedged, obviously having second thoughts.

"I don't have time for that, Mama. Good-bye, and try not to worry."

* * *

Kip Blalock was escorted into the storage room by two armed thugs. "I feel like I'm in prison," he exclaimed when he saw Felix Hummer.

"I'm sorry if I gave you the impression that you'd be an honored guest here," Hummer told him with sarcasm, and Kip blushed.

"I didn't expect to be 'honored,'" Kip assured the career criminal. "But you've locked me in a room without so much as a transistor radio for days."

Hummer frowned. "I gave instructions for you to have a television, a VCR, and a wide variety of movies. If there's something you want to watch that we haven't provided, just tell your guards."

"Why can't I watch regular television channels and choose for myself?" Kip asked. "And why do I have to stay in that little room all the time?"

"I make the rules here, Mr. Blalock. Watching videos for a few days won't kill you, and I can't risk someone recognizing you before Saturday. Security must be maintained, but we'll keep you as comfortable as possible until our business with each other is finished."

"Can I at least have a newspaper?" Kip begged.

"I'd rather you keep your mind clear so that you can concentrate on the money transfers."

An angry flush stained Kip's cheeks. "I guess I don't have any choice in the matter."

Hummer smiled. "You're right—you don't. But look on the bright side. It will all be over soon." Then he waved to the guards, who took Kip by each arm and led him from the room.

* * *

After Billie hung up from the conversation with her mother, there was a knock on her hotel room door. She opened it to admit Edgar, and if anything, he looked worse than he had the last time she'd seen him.

"Did you get through to Mr. Lockhart?" Billie asked.

Edgar shook his head. "I did talk to his secretary, though, and she says he's taking it very hard—blaming himself."

"I guess that's a natural if unreasonable reaction," Billie replied. "And on a different unhappy note, I just called my landlady and she said my apartment was robbed last night."

Edgar reached out to pat her hand. "A lot of that kind of thing happens around the holidays. I'm sorry that you were victimized."

"I don't think it was a regular robbery," Billie told him with rising anxiety. "My landlady said they tore the place up—even made holes in the walls—but all they took was my computer. They left a nice television set, a stereo system, and a DVD player."

Edgar frowned. "That is strange."

"Then my mother said an Atlanta policeman drove all the way out to my parents' house in Coopersville to confiscate several boxes I had stored in their garage."

"What was in the boxes?"

Billie shrugged. "Old manuscripts, textbooks from college —just a bunch of junk. The important question is how did the Atlanta PD know I had things stored there? The only place I kept an inventory was on my computer."

Edgar looked alarmed. "The *police* stole your computer?"

Billie shook her head. "No, I think one of the thieves—posing as a policeman—got the boxes from my parents' garage."

Edgar sighed. "This is a very disturbing situation and I hate to add to your worries, but I'm afraid I have more bad news."

Billie braced herself. "What?"

"I talked to my friend at the Atlanta Police Department, and he said that Camille's death has been categorized as a homicide."

"So my fuel pump didn't malfunction?"

Edgar shook his head. "No, it was definitely tampered with."

She collapsed beside him on the couch. "Why would someone try to kill me, Edgar? Who does things like that?"

Edgar shrugged. "Apparently someone thinks you pose a threat to them. And it must be someone very powerful with an important secret."

"I don't know anyone powerful *or* important!" Billie insisted. "Much less their secrets!"

Edgar sat quietly for a few seconds, thinking. Then he said, "Since they stole your computer we can assume their secret is somehow related to information stored there."

"I only use my computer to write books and e-mail friends," Billie whispered.

"I don't see why they'd be interested in your manuscripts. Maybe we should look through your old e-mails for a clue," Edgar suggested, but Billie shook her head.

"I have limited storage space, so I delete my messages as I receive them," she explained. "Although I did get an unusual e-mail the other day." She told him briefly about Cowboy and his failure to answer her recent e-mails. "But Cowboy never gave me details about his work or his employers. The only thing remotely negative that he ever said about them was an idea he sent me for my next book. He suggested that I write about a group of men who start a new football league but never intend to actually administer it. They just plan to take the money from ticket sales and investors and gambling bets and leave the country."

"Could that possibly be what the organizers of the GFL are planning to do?"

"It seems unlikely."

"Outrageous even. But a scheme like that, if successful, would net billions of dollars for the crooks." He glanced at Billie. "Unless someone got wind of the plan before next Saturday," Edgar thought out loud. Then he shook his head as if to clear it. "Well, I've got to head toward Atlanta. The other rental car will be parked in front, and the keys will be left at the desk. I'll also leave directions to the attorneys' offices where the closing is being held."

Billie nodded. "We'll come back as soon as the closing is over."

They stood and walked to the door, then Edgar put his hands on her shoulders. "Listen to me, Miss Billie. Whoever sabotaged your car was not just trying to scare you. They meant to kill you, and they will succeed if you're not careful."

Billie rubbed her hands up and down her arms as a cold chill shook her. "I wish you could stay with me."

"You'll be safe with Mr. Turner." Edgar reached into his pocket and pulled out his cell phone charger. "I keep meaning to give you this. Charge your phone so I can call and check on you. And you have my number?"

Billie nodded as she accepted the charger and his Chamber Gold Card. "The car is already taken care of. Charge the hotel and any other expenses to this."

Billie nodded again.

"I'll call you," he promised. "Be a brave girl." Then he was gone.

* * *

The phone rang, and Felix Hummer answered it. He listened in silence for several minutes, then said, "It sounds like you have things under control. Remember, I'm counting on you." Seconds after he hung up, Conrad Lockhart burst into the storage room. Hummer resisted the urge to smile when he saw the city councilman's unhealthy pallor.

"Is something wrong, Conrad?"

Conrad's lips were trembling too much for him to speak, and there were tears in his eyes.

"Our boxing friend killed the wrong girl," Hummer guessed for him.

"He killed my niece!" Conrad cried, his hands twisting in frustrated fury. "How could he make such a mistake?"

"He was going on information *you* provided," Hummer pointed out. "And he confirmed with the Chamber of Commerce and the cruise ship."

Conrad was sweating profusely even though the storage room was quite cool. "He should have looked at the picture I sent!"

Felix was losing patience, so he turned back to his computer screen. "What's done is done. We have to turn our attention to the future."

"The future?" Conrad repeated dazedly.

"Miss Murphy is still alive and poses a potential danger to us."

Conrad spread his hands in supplication. "No, please. She can't be that much of a threat, and the game is only days away."

"Which is precisely why we can't take any risks," Hummer told him. "I want her eliminated immediately. And this time, make sure you give the hit man a better picture."

Conrad raised a handkerchief to his perspiring head with a trembling hand. "How in the world can we commit another murder without drawing attention?"

Hummer gave him hard look. "That's your problem."

* * *

Billie handled the checkout procedures and picked up the keys to their new rental car. She was just about to go in search of Nathan when he arrived in the lobby.

"I can't believe your friend was killed in that car crash last night," Nathan said, concern in his eyes. "Edgar seemed very upset."

"I think he's worked for the Lockharts for a long time, and he was pretty close to Camille."

Nathan frowned. "You should have gone with Edgar. I could have handled the closings myself."

"Camille and I weren't really friends, so there was no reason for me to rush back," Billie responded.

Nathan rubbed the curls at the back of his neck. "Well, if you're really not in hurry to get to Atlanta, I have a suggestion."

"Which is?" Billie prompted.

"We've been driving around a lot, and my plane doesn't leave until Monday afternoon."

"And?"

"Maybe we could spend the rest of the weekend here in Columbus."

Billie considered this. Another day or two in Columbus would give her some time to figure out what was going on.

"I guess I'm just reluctant for our time together to end," Nathan added.

Billie smiled. "Me too."

Nathan checked his watch. "Since neither one of us is familiar with Columbus, we should probably leave soon."

Billie pulled the keys to the rental car from her pocket. "It won't upset you if I drive?"

Nathan looked startled. "Why should it? Are you a bad driver?"

She shrugged. "No, I was just afraid it would wound your macho ego."

He laughed. "My ego is impenetrable, and I don't have a prejudice against women drivers."

"Good." She pointed to her bags by the door. "Let's go."

He picked up his suitcase and one of hers, and together they walked through the front door. They hurried outside, where a new Infinity was parked by the curb. Nathan opened the trunk, and they put their luggage inside. Once they were settled in the front seat, Billie followed the directions the hotel manager had given her to an office building near the county courthouse.

* * *

The phone rang in the makeshift office, and Felix Hummer answered it quickly. "Yes?" It was both a question and a demand.

"My driver is on his way back to Atlanta. He left Miss Murphy and a representative from Blalock Industries in Columbus to complete a signing," Conrad Lockhart replied.

"Why would he do that?"

"Because he thought I would need him to help make arrangements for Camille's funeral."

"So how will you take care of Miss Murphy?"

"The people who have been hired for the job are already on their way to the lawyers' offices. They'll follow Miss Murphy when she leaves and handle things when they are a discreet distance away."

"Let me know when it's done," Hummer said before hanging up the phone.

* * *

Billie parked the rental car on the street, then a security guard directed them to the eighth floor, where a paralegal met them, explaining that the people from the pipe company had already arrived and were waiting in the conference room. The Warrens were due at noon.

The meeting went smoothly, but Camille's death put a damper on the whole occasion for Billie. Once it was over, everyone shook hands and Billie and Nathan went back to the lobby to wait for the Warrens. The paralegal they had met earlier was at the reception desk, and Billie asked if it would be all right for her to charge her cell phone.

The woman shrugged. "It's okay with me. I don't pay the electric bills here."

Billie and Nathan exchanged a glance as Billie plugged her phone into a wall socket.

"I get the impression that she isn't thrilled to be here on a Saturday," Nathan whispered.

Billie nodded as the Warrens walked in. After hugs, they told Billie and Nathan that they had made an offer on the Victorian house. "The young couple wants to think about it over the weekend, but I feel hopeful," Thelma said.

"They'll take your offer," Nathan predicted. "They can't wait to get away from their heritage."

"You folks had lunch?" Hugh asked.

"No, but we ate a late breakfast," Billie replied.

"Thelma packed boiled ham sandwiches and potato salad. Thought we could have a picnic."

Thelma looked back and forth between them. "Oh, Hugh, I don't think they want to spend their time with a couple of old folks like us." She pressed the bag into Billie's hands. "After we're through signing all these papers, you two go have your own picnic."

Billie gave Nathan a wide-eyed look as the door to the conference room opened and one of the lawyers stepped out. "We're ready for you now," he said in his undertaker's voice.

The meeting began just like the one before it—solemnly. After a few minutes, the paralegal stuck her head in the door. "Sorry to disturb you," she said, although she didn't look sorry, "but your phone is making all kinds of noises," she told Billie.

"Excuse me," Billie said with embarrassment as she hurried into the lobby. She unplugged the charger and answered her phone.

"Billie!" It was her mother. "Are you okay?"

"Fine, Mama. What's the matter?"

"I just had another visit from that policeman. He insisted that I give him your cell phone number and kept questioning me about where you are."

"Did you tell him?"

"I don't *know* where you are," Nan reminded her. "So I *couldn't* tell him."

"I'm not sure if cell phone calls can be traced or not, but it would probably be better for you not to call me," Billie suggested. "I'm going to stay here until Monday, then I'll drop Nathan off at the airport and head home. By then Edgar should have everything straightened out with the police or . . . whoever."

"I'm not really comfortable with all this," Nan began.

"I've got to go, Mama," Billie interrupted. "Don't worry. Everything will be fine."

She disconnected, then glanced at the paralegal, who was playing solitaire on the receptionist's computer. Billie hated to interrupt the closing, and since her presence was unnecessary anyway, she decided to check the rest of her messages on her phone. Settling into a chair in the lobby, she played them all. There were a few from the Atlanta Police Department, and one was from her editor at LoveSwift wanting to discuss her most recent book proposal. Billie smiled. *I'll just bet you want to talk about that,* she thought to herself. Then she frowned, since her proposal reminded her of Cowboy.

She cleared all her voice messages and saw that she had one text message sent on Thursday. She stared at the words on the small screen. *You are in grave danger. Disappear. Trust no one. Cowboy.* Even though it was oppressively warm in the law office, Billie shivered. She knew Cowboy wouldn't take any pleasure from playing such a cruel joke.

Turning away from the paralegal at the desk, Billie called directory assistance and got the number for the GFL headquarters in Atlanta. She dialed the number, and when a pleasant female voice answered, she asked to speak to Milton Bagley.

"Hold please," the voice requested. Billie waited impatiently, her thoughts in turmoil. A few days ago her life was boring and completely safe. Now her car had been rigged to blow up, her apartment had been robbed, her parents had been visited by a fake policemen, and Camille was dead. That was more than enough evidence to prove she was in danger. Cowboy's message just emphasized the fact.

The voice came back, "May I ask who's calling?"

Billie chewed her lower lip for a second, then responded, "Regina St. Claire."

"One moment, please."

Billie considered her options. She could stay in Columbus and hope that the people who were trying to kill her didn't find her. She could go to her parents' house, but whoever meant her harm was sure to be watching for her there. With a sigh she realized that her best course of action was to follow Cowboy's advice. She would disappear until Edgar could assure her that she was safe.

"I'm sorry to keep you waiting, Miss St. Claire," the woman apologized. "But I'm afraid we don't have an employee by the name of Milton Bagley."

Billie was stunned by this reply. If she had said that Cowboy wasn't in, that would have been plausible. If she'd said he was on another line, that could be believed. But Billie had seen Cowboy at the GFL headquarters herself and knew he was an employee.

"If you'll leave a number where you can be reached, I'd be glad to have someone else return your call," the voice offered.

Billie disconnected abruptly, then started to call Edgar, but Cowboy had warned her to trust no one, and unfortunately that included the chauffeur. So she put her phone and Edgar's charger into her purse and pulled out a pen and piece of paper.

She felt terrible about leaving Nathan without an explanation, but she didn't fully understand what was happening herself. She wrote a quick note of apology and walked toward the desk, intending to leave it with the paralegal. Before the exchange could be made, however, the door of the conference room opened and Nathan stepped out.

"I was starting to get worried about you," he told her.

She slipped the note into her pocket and gave him a nervous smile. "I didn't want to disturb the meeting twice, so I just sat out here and returned phone messages. Are they almost through?"

Nathan nodded. "They're finished with me. Since Hugh doesn't trust lawyers, he reads every piece of paper in its entirety before he'll sign. Which means they could be there for hours."

Billie felt an urgency to leave immediately. Getting away from Nathan could prove difficult, so she decided she had no choice but to take him with her. "I have an idea," she told him, thinking furiously.

"What kind of idea?"

"First, let's leave a note for the Warrens telling them that we couldn't wait and will call them later."

Nathan glanced at the conference room door. "That's okay with me."

Billie took another piece of paper from the tablet in her purse and wrote a note to the Warrens. She handed it to the paralegal, then led Nathan into the hallway. He came to a stop in front of the elevators, but she waved him on to the stairs.

"I need the exercise," she told him as they began their descent.

He gave her a suspicious look, then asked, "So what's the rest of your idea?"

"Well, I was thinking that since you arrived in Georgia, all you've seen is the glitzy, superficial side."

He frowned. "I know you're not going to try and convince me that the barbecue place was glitzy."

She gave him a nervous laugh. "Well, *glitzy* was a poor choice of words, but you have to admit it wasn't your regular, everyday kind of experience."

"Where will we find the 'everyday experience'?"

"Off the beaten path," she responded with confidence she didn't feel. "Instead of staying here in another luxury hotel, we'll take some back roads and head in the general direction of Atlanta. We'll find some genuine southern towns and let you meet a few real people." She glanced up with challenge in her eyes. "That is, if you're man enough."

He laughed. "You're talking to a *man* who's been living without running water for weeks. There's nothing Georgia has to offer that could be worse than the current condition of my house in Salt Lake."

"So, are you game?" she asked as they stepped outside.

"I'm game."

Billie looked around nervously, then grabbed his hand and hurried to the parking deck.

* * *

Felix Hummer drummed his fingers impatiently on the old desk as he listened to the other man explain the latest episode of incompetence. "So, what you're telling me is that they lost the girl," he said finally.

"The men our friend sent missed her by just a few minutes," Conrad replied as if this made a difference. "She left the meeting early."

"Any idea why?"

Conrad shook his head.

Hummer bit back a reprimand. "How long will it take them to find her?"

"Not long."

Hummer studied the other man. "Your niece's death was a terrible shock. Maybe I should arrange for someone else to take over your duties . . ."

"I can finish what we've started," Conrad insisted. "Miss Murphy and Mr. Turner from Blalock Industries left together. My driver says that they are romantically involved, but I don't think Miss Murphy has any suspicions about the GFL."

"She called the headquarters asking about Cowboy," Felix Hummer reminded his cohort.

"Just checking on a friend," Conrad suggested.

"I won't take the risk."

Conrad nodded in acquiescence. "If they're headed back to Atlanta, it shouldn't take long to locate them."

* * *

Billie wanted to get far away from the law offices quickly, so she pulled out of the parking deck and drove north for several miles. Finally Nathan asked, "Do you know where you're going?"

She laughed. "Not really."

"Just how much of an adventure do you have planned?"

She pulled over and parked along the curb. "Let's see if there's a map in the glove compartment." There was a map, a flashlight, a mini first-aid kit, and a box of complimentary tissues. Billie and Nathan studied the map together, finally determining that they should back-track to Interstate 85 and from there they could pick any exit and look for their genuine southern town.

Billie felt conspicuous on the interstate, so she took the second exit after they were out of Columbus. They drove for a couple of hours, turning onto county highways randomly and eating the sandwiches provided by Thelma Warren.

"She put cookies in here too," Nathan announced with pleasure as he searched the sack. "We could probably survive on this for a week."

Billie nodded, hoping they didn't have to.

"You've been quiet and tense ever since we left the attorneys' offices," Nathan observed finally.

She gave him what she hoped was a reassuring smile. "I'm sorry. I guess I'm just a little upset about Camille."

"That's understandable. Maybe it would help to talk about it," he suggested. "And I'm a good listener."

She wanted very much to tell him everything, partly to ease her guilt over misleading him but mostly to share her fears. She felt tears fill her eyes. "I want to talk about it, but I don't think I'm ready yet."

He nodded. "Just know I'm available."

Feeling guiltier than before, she concentrated on the road. As it was starting to get dark, they pulled into a little town called Green Pond. There was a banner across the main street advertising a live Nativity production. "This is it," Billie whispered, feeling certain. "This is where we'll spend the night."

Nathan looked out the window. "You're sure?"

"Not only will you get to see small-town Georgia, we can go to the live Nativity tonight." She pointed at the sign. "But first we've got to find a hotel."

"Which could be quite a challenge," Nathan murmured.

Billie smiled. "I love a challenge."

They drove through town twice and soon discovered that the only motel was a squat cinder-block building with peeling turquoise paint. The flashing sign was missing several bulbs and advertised rooms for $19.95 a night.

"Maybe if we keep driving up the highway we'll find another hotel," Nathan suggested.

Billie frowned. She felt a peace in this town that she hadn't experienced since Edgar told her that Camille was dead. She believed that the Lord had led them here, and she wasn't willing to give up. So she shook her head. "No, this looks fine to me."

Nathan stared at the motel. "You're sure?"

She nodded and pulled to a stop in the deserted parking lot.

"I wonder why it's called the Pink Flamingo since it's green?" he commented as they climbed out.

Billie joined him on the sidewalk. "I don't know, but I'll be sure to ask."

A teenager was watching *Wheel of Fortune* on a small black-and-white television behind the desk when they walked into the minuscule lobby. The boy introduced himself as Bernie and asked how many rooms they needed and how long they would be staying.

Billie decided to take each day one at a time and said they would need two rooms for one night. She reached into her purse to get the Chamber Gold Card, then stopped suddenly.

"What's the matter?" Nathan asked.

She shook her head. "Nothing."

"You look pale."

"I'm fine," she said, her mind racing. Charges put on the Chamber Gold Card would be easy to trace, which made it useless to her. She took the emergency hundred-dollar bill from her wallet and paid for the rooms, grateful for the cheap rates. Nathan, who out of necessity was standing close to her in the cramped space, saw her pay with cash and offered to put the rooms on his company card.

"Since this part of our trip is personal, I don't feel right letting either of our companies pay," she whispered.

"Then I should at least pay for my own room." Nathan took an American Express card from his wallet.

Billie shook her head regretfully. Nathan's card would be as easy to trace as the Chamber's. "No, this was my idea, and I'll pay."

As a safety precaution, she wrote her name as Priscilla Glover and his as Homer Sandler. She angled the registration forms away from Nathan and hoped that he wouldn't notice the false information, but when she saw the strange expression on his face, she realized he had. With a grimace, she stuffed her change into her purse, mentally calculating how much they could spend on meals and still be able to get a room the next night. She said a silent prayer of thanks for Thelma and her sack lunch as Bernie led them down the cracked sidewalk to rooms 3 and 4.

"These rooms are *adjoining*," the boy informed them with something approaching a leer.

"Thanks for the information," Nathan replied crossly. "But we wouldn't be paying for two rooms if we only planned to use one."

Bernie looked abashed as he gave the keys to Nathan and returned to the lobby.

"Smart-aleck kid." Nathan pushed open the door to room 3. "Do you have a preference?" he asked as they stepped inside. The air was musty and cold. The carpet was orange, and the red curtains looked like geometric figures at war. "Are you sure you want to stay here?" He gave her another chance to change her mind.

"This is fine," she told him. Somehow the unattractiveness of the room made her feel even safer. Who would think to look for them here? She walked in and put her bag on the Mediterranean-style chest of drawers, noting that the television actually had an On/Off button and dials for UHF and VHF channels. "*I* don't need luxurious," she teased.

"I'll bet the word *luxurious* has never been uttered in this room before," he said, but when she looked up he was smiling. "I can stand it if you can." He moved closer, and the air seemed to leave Billie's lungs. "But why did you use phony names when we registered?"

"You fly back to Salt Lake in less than forty-eight hours," she said. "Until then, I want to have your undivided attention. I don't want us to be bothered by the Georgia Chamber of Commerce or Blalock Industries or anyone."

Nathan considered this for a second. "Do you think the Chamber of Commerce would really track you down?"

"I doubt it, but no point in taking chances," Billie answered.

"Are you going to have to call me Homer?"

She smiled. "No."

"Good," Nathan said as she walked over and turned on the wall heater. The fan noise was impressive, but the output less so. "Is that steam or smoke coming out of there?" Nathan asked, and Billie sniffed.

"Hard to tell. I'll keep an eye on it. You go ahead and get settled in your own room." She pushed him gently outside and watched while he entered room 4, then she closed her door. If she let herself think she'd cry, so she turned on the television instead. After adjusting the rabbit ears, she was able to get a fairly clear picture and listen to the local news.

The weatherman said rain was predicted for that night and then the weather would remain mild for the next several days. He was just beginning his five-day forecast when there was a knock on the adjoining door. Billie opened her side to find Nathan leaning against the door frame. "So, is your room as nice as mine?" she asked.

"My carpet is mud-brown shag and our bedspreads are twins," he returned with a smile that took her breath away.

Before she could respond, there was a knock on her outside door. They exchanged a quick look, then Nathan came in and opened the door to admit Bernie. The boy muttered something unintelligible as he walked into Billie's temporary bathroom. He came out a few seconds later carrying a plaid bathrobe, a toothbrush, and an electric razor. After Nathan had the door closed and locked behind their host, he turned to Billie.

"Looks like this is Bennie's favorite room."

Billie gave the bed a dubious glance, and Nathan frowned again.

"I think we'd better switch rooms in case our new friend walks in his sleep and decides to come home to roost during the night."

Without an argument, Billie picked up her suitcase and met him by the adjoining doors. "You just like my orange carpet better," she accused him.

"How did you guess?" After putting down his suitcase, Nathan returned to room 4. "So, what sounds good for dinner?"

"I was thinking we could sit in here and eat the rest of Thelma's ham sandwiches," Billie suggested.

"I'm being a good sport about this test of manhood you're putting me through." He waved at the room. "I may be willing to sleep in this squalor, but I won't eat here."

Billie had to laugh. "Okay, we'll drive around until we find a picnic table and eat outside."

"Don't you think those sandwiches have passed their prime?" he asked as he held the door open for her.

"The weather's been cool. I'm sure they're fine."

CHAPTER 7

They found a nice little park in the center of town and spread out the remaining contents of Thelma's sack on a picnic table. Nathan bought soft drinks from a vending machine, and when Billie tried to reimburse him, he declined firmly. "I'm an old-fashioned kind of guy. I like to pay for things when I'm on a date."

"A date?" Billie repeated, her voice faint.

He leaned a little closer. "Since this isn't Chamber of Commerce business, I'd say it's a date."

She smiled at him. "In that case, I'll take the root beer." He passed the can across the table, and they ate quickly. "We only have about thirty minutes before the Nativity program starts," Billie reminded him.

"And it's getting kind of chilly."

"Maybe we could go by the hotel and get the bedspreads to wrap up in."

Nathan shuddered. "Those things are irreverent in the hotel room. I can't imagine taking them to a solemn occasion."

After they finished eating, Billie scraped all the leftovers into the brown grocery sack. "I thought we might get hungry later," she explained when she saw Nathan watching her.

He stood and led the way back to the car. "I'll bet the rats and cockroaches at the Pink Flamingo will invite all their friends over when they see that you've brought home a feast."

Billie looked down at the sack and dropped it into a nearby garbage container.

They followed the signs to the live Nativity being held in an amphitheater on the outskirts of town. They arrived as the production was about to begin. A big crowd had gathered, so they had to take seats near the back. The lighting was bad and the sound system even worse, but the costumes were imaginative and the actors enthusiastic, so Billie thoroughly enjoyed the production. And sitting next to Nathan under the starlight with his arm protectively around her made her wish the play would never end.

When the last notes of the finale faded into the night, the lights were turned onto the crowd to help them exit. Nathan stood and pulled Billie to her feet, then kept her hand in his as they walked to their car. They could see Bernie in the office when they drove by, but there were no other cars in the parking lot. They both went in through room 4, then Nathan crossed over into room 3.

"I want you to close and lock your adjoining door," he told her. "But I'll leave mine open just in case you need me."

"Thanks." Billie nodded, feeling a little nervous at the thought of being alone.

Nathan paused in the doorway and turned back. "So, did you have fun tonight?"

"I had a wonderful time."

"You know, there's an age-old custom used by women to show their appreciation to men who take them on nice dates."

"And what is that?" she asked breathlessly.

"They give them a good-night kiss."

Billie walked over to stand beside him. "I kissed you last time."

He smiled. "You're right. It's my turn." Their lips met in a soft, sweet kiss, then he pulled back. "Good night, Billie."

"Good night," she echoed. Then she closed the door gently.

* * *

Felix Hummer was pacing when Conrad entered the storage room. "Have you found her?"

The older man shook his head. "No. We have a detailed description of the rental car and the tag number, but it hasn't been seen on any of the major roadways leading toward Atlanta."

"Maybe they aren't using the major roadways," Felix Hummer said with flagging patience.

The other man looked stunned. "But why wouldn't they?"

"That's the question you should be asking yourself."

* * *

On Sunday morning, Nathan woke Billie at seven o'clock by knocking on the adjoining door. "I'm starving," he called through the wood. "We've got to go get some breakfast."

Billie moaned and rolled to the edge of her bed. Pushing her hair out of her eyes, she stood and opened the door. Nathan was already dressed, his damp hair combed neatly away from his face. "Why are you wearing a tie?" she asked, pointing to his attire.

"It's Sunday, and I'm planning to go to church."

"I doubt we'll be able to find a Mormon congregation in a small town like this."

He shrugged. "It doesn't have to be an LDS church. But it's the Sunday before Christmas, and it just doesn't feel right not to go."

She nodded. "I'll get dressed and we'll drive around until we find something."

"That sure has worked out well with hotel rooms," he murmured before leaving.

When Billie reopened the door thirty minutes later, Nathan was packed and ready to go. They checked out of the Pink Flamingo, then got into the car, where several foil packets of Pop-Tarts and orange juice in small glass bottles were arranged in the storage compartment between the front seats.

"Want some breakfast?" he offered, then opened a pack of frosted blueberry.

"Where did you get these?" she asked, looking through the assortment of pastries.

"From the vending machine in the lobby, so they're probably expired. I didn't dare look," he said, then took a big bite.

Billie checked the date on the apple cinnamon package before she opened it. "They still have almost two months of freshness," she informed him. "And these are my favorite."

"Glad to hear it." He offered her a swig of bottled orange juice, but she declined.

"What's your favorite?"

"Pop-Tart?" he clarified, and she nodded. "I don't have a favorite. I hate them all equally."

"It's un-American to hate Pop-Tarts," she told him with complete seriousness.

"I was raised on Pop-Tarts, and I swore when I got old enough to buy my own food, I'd never eat another one." He glanced down at the wrapper in his hand. "Except when I'm staying under a false name with a beautiful woman in a hotel that should be condemned."

"The beautiful woman part is all that saved you," she told him as they pulled out of the parking lot.

"I thought it might," he responded with a grin.

"Have they found Kip?" she asked, and his expression hardened.

"Not yet."

They stopped at the first church they came to, a small building with a sign claiming to welcome everyone. They waited in the car until they heard the choir singing, then walked in and looked for seats near the back. The chapel was crowded, and it became immediately obvious that slipping in unnoticed was going to be impossible. Billie was about to give up when she saw an empty row near the front. She led the way to the middle aisle and stopped by the unoccupied seats. Affixed to the end of the pew was gold nameplate that said *Reserved for the Whitlow Family.*

Billie stared at little metal square in bewilderment. In the congregations she had attended, most people sat in the same seats every week, but never had she seen them actually assigned. She was about to suggest that they go back to the car when an elderly lady came to stand beside them. She was dressed in black and had a little hat with netting perched on her gray hair.

"Are you visiting?" she asked, and they nodded. "Then I'd be honored if you sit with me." She waved toward the bench labeled *Whitlow* as the preacher stood and gave them a pointed look.

Nathan accepted the invitation by moving into the row. Billie scooted in next to him, and the little woman sat closest to the aisle. The service began and consisted of choir numbers interspersed with sermonettes. Throughout the proceedings, their hostess conversed with them as if they were the only people in the room. At first Billie was uneasy, but none of the other members of the congregation seemed disturbed, so finally she relaxed.

The lady introduced herself as Essie Faye Whitlow, widow of the late Reverend Whitlow, who had built the church in the 1930s. She asked where they were from and nodded sagely when Nathan said Utah. "I thought I recognized the accent. I had an aunt who lived in Greene County, Alabama, and we used to drive through Eutaw when we visited her."

Nathan gave Mrs. Whitlow a blank look, but she rushed on, oblivious.

"After the services today we're having a covered-dish dinner, and I'd be so pleased if you'd join us as my guests."

Billie caught Nathan's eye and gave him a subtle "no" signal. He smiled politely at Mrs. Whitlow but told her that they had to be on their way immediately after the meeting ended. Mrs. Whitlow looked disappointed but nodded. "Well, it's been mighty nice having someone to sit with at least. Eldon and I weren't blessed with children, and since he passed on it's been downright lonely on Sundays."

Billie reached over and patted the old lady's hand. "You've made us feel very welcome. Thank you."

The preacher stood and announced that the congregation would join the choir in singing some Christmas carols. Billie and Nathan shared a hymnal, singing the familiar songs and sharing in the spirit of the occasion. After a few minutes, they noticed that Mrs. Whitlow was gone.

"Do you think we offended her by declining her dinner invitation?" Nathan asked with a look of concern on his face.

Billie shrugged. She hoped Mrs. Whitlow wasn't upset, but she had a restless feeling, like they should stay on the move. "Being part of a congregation is one thing. Attending a covered-dish dinner with a bunch of strangers is something altogether different."

Nathan was smiling as he bowed his head for the benediction. Afterward they walked quickly out to the parking lot. On the passenger seat of their rental car, they found several sturdy paper plates covered with foil. Nathan looked under the protective wrappings and reported, "Turkey, mashed potatoes, green beans, rolls, and red velvet cake."

Billie picked up two sets of plastic dinnerware wrapped in Christmas napkins, tears blurring her eyes. "I guess this explains why Mrs. Whitlow had to leave the meeting early."

Nathan smiled. "I guess so."

"How did she know this was our car?" Billie wondered out loud.

"It's got that little rental sticker on the windshield," Nathan pointed out.

Billie frowned as they climbed into the car. If sweet little Mrs. Whitlow could identify their car, assassins would be able to as well. They drove away intending to find a park or rest area, but Billie spotted a little pond just outside of town, so Nathan pulled the car over. They spread their coats on the grass and ate their lunch.

"Mrs. Whitlow not only showed us a great deal of Christian kindness, she saved us from having to buy on Sunday," Billie said as they ate. She didn't mention that it also preserved some of her dwindling amount of cash.

After the food was gone, Nathan demonstrated his prowess in skimming rocks across the pond while Billie cheered or ridiculed as the toss deserved. Finally he stretched out on the grass beside her while she checked the map and suggested various routes.

"I don't care which way we go," he said drowsily, "as long as I get to pick the hotel."

She agreed to this arrangement, then studied the map carefully, praying for direction in finding a safe place to spend the night. Finally she decided on the town of Heflin. It had a population of 8,000, was three hours to the northeast, and would not give them a difficult drive to Atlanta on Monday. She turned to show the map to Nathan and saw that he was asleep. Her breath caught in her throat as she watched him. His hair was falling away from his face, his lips were slightly parted, and he looked completely relaxed for the first time since she'd met him.

She let him sleep for a while, but as each minute passed her anxiety increased. Either inspiration or self-preservation told her they needed to be moving on, so she reached out and shook Nathan gently. His eyes flew open, startled.

"Time to wake up," she told him with a smile. "We have more of rural Georgia to see."

"Did you find a place for us to stay tonight?"

She nodded. "I've chosen the quaint country town of Heflin, and I'll stay in any hotel you want to there as long as you pay."

"It's my turn," he agreed as he sat up.

"Cash," she added without looking him in the eyes.

She felt his penetrating gaze. "Why?"

"Just because I asked you to?" she tried.

"There's something you're not telling me."

Billie knew he was suspicious but not on to anything, so she decided to cling to the idea of adventure. "Why do you say that?"

"You're paying with cash and staying in hotels only someone truly desperate would even consider. I know something's going on; I just don't know what."

Tears gathered in Billie's eyes. "I'm sorry you're not having fun. We can go on to Atlanta now."

He sighed. "I didn't mean to hurt your feelings, and I don't mind staying in dumpy hotels." Two tears slipped onto her cheeks. "And driving on back roads has been great!" he continued with more enthusiasm. "The Georgia countryside is beautiful. I think there's more to this little detour than meets the eye, but since my plane doesn't leave until tomorrow afternoon, I'll play along."

"Are you sure?" she asked, and he nodded.

"Positive. I'm having the time of my life!"

He didn't look as optimistic three hours later when he pulled in front of the Traveler's Delight Motel in Heflin.

"I didn't think that it was possible for a place to be worse than the one we stayed at last night, but I was wrong." Nathan's tone was one of disgusted awe as he stared at the pitted-stucco edifice. "We'd probably be more comfortable sleeping in the car."

Billie laughed. "Be a man," she encouraged as they climbed out of the rental car.

The office door of the Traveler's Delight was locked, and the clerk, an older woman with overprocessed hair, was on the phone. It took them a few minutes of knocking to get her attention before she finally ended her phone call and let them in.

"I'll tell you from the start that I don't put up with monkey business in this motel," the woman said in the gravelly voice of a longtime smoker. "I don't rent to couples who ain't married."

"Billie and Nathan Turner," Billie said, extending her hand. *It wasn't exactly a lie*, Billie comforted herself. She had merely omitted her own last name. Pointing at Nathan, she continued, "Nathan will pay."

She stepped back, and Nathan moved up to the counter. The woman quoted him a price, and he took a hundred-dollar bill from his wallet. She then started grumbling about having to get change from the convenience store next door. "Don't you have anything smaller?" she demanded.

Nathan returned the hundred to his wallet and pulled out two twenties.

The clerk smiled, exposing nicotine-stained teeth. "That's better." She made change with money in a shoebox, then stood. "I'll give you my best room, 216." She extended a key with a plastic rectangle declaring the room number attached.

Since Billie estimated there were only about twenty rooms in the entire complex, the numbering system seemed grandiose. Instead of remarking on this, she simply said, "We'll need two rooms."

The woman pulled the key from Nathan's palm and studied them through narrowed eyes. "If you're married, why do you need two rooms?"

"We've been arguing," Billie said, skirting the truth once again.

The woman looked at Nathan, who smiled. "Give us adjoining rooms in case we make up during the night."

Nathan pulled loose bills and coins from his pockets and piled them on the counter. Stifling a giggle, Billie added some of the money she had left to his collection, and together they came up with enough money for another room. The clerk reluctantly gave him the keys for 216 and 218 before they walked outside. They retrieved their luggage from the car and when they pushed open the door to 216, it was pretty much the same as the rooms at the Pink Flamingo—only colder—and the bed tilted obviously to one side.

"Remind me again why we can't stay in nice hotels," Nathan requested as they looked around.

"Because nice hotels are for sissies?" Billie tried.

"You'll have to do better than that. No male ego is that fragile."

"I wanted a spoiled rich boy like you to have a real, down-to-earth experience?"

"I'm not spoiled or rich," Nathan muttered as she walked over and looked into 218. "What are you doing?"

"If 216 is her *best* room, I've got to see what the other one looks like." Billie couldn't tell much difference in the rooms except that she had a black rotary phone and Nathan had no phone at all. They ate the leftovers of their church dinner in the car, then went back into the motel room and tried to watch television, but the reception was terrible. Finally Nathan hooked his laptop up to his cell phone and checked his e-mail.

When he was finished, Billie asked if she could check hers. She had a message from her mother and one message from her insurance agent. There was nothing from Cowboy, and this seemed ominous based on his text message. Still frowning, she opened the e-mail from her insurance agent. The woman expressed polite condolences over the loss of Camille and Billie's car, respectively. Then she explained that until the police eliminated any question of foul play, no settlement could be made.

Billie hadn't had time to think of the practical effects of Camille's wreck but realized now that once she got back to Atlanta and turned in the rental car, she would be without transportation. She was deep in thought, and when Nathan spoke, he startled her.

"Camille Lockhart was driving *your* car when she died?" Nathan asked. Billie quickly signed out and nodded reluctantly.

"There was a problem with my fuel pump," she said, hoping that he hadn't read the entire e-mail.

"What did that mean about foul play?" he demanded, destroying this hope.

Billie pasted a smile on her face. "You know how insurance companies will use any excuse to try to keep from paying a claim."

He frowned. "No, I don't know that. And I can't imagine them mentioning foul play and the police unless they had reason to."

"I'll deal with that when I get back to Atlanta. For right now, I'm still having fun." She stepped away from the laptop and stretched. "So, what are we going to do with the rest of our evening?"

She could tell that Nathan wanted to pursue the topic, but he didn't press. Instead he pulled a well-worn deck of Old Maid out of his briefcase. As he shuffled and dealt the cards, Billie tried to ignore her conscience. It was wrong to mislead Nathan, but she'd been warned to trust no one. Of course, she did trust Nathan, but . . .

They played cards until midnight, then said good-bye at the adjoining doors before turning in for the night. As Billie climbed under the thin blanket on the crooked bed, she shivered. She sensed danger all around, and once Nathan was on his plane the next day, she would be alone. With this dismal thought, she drifted off into a troubled sleep.

* * *

"Still no sign of Miss Murphy?" Felix Hummer asked in a sharp tone when Conrad walked into the little office.

The other man shook his head. "None."

"She's got to be eating and buying gas and staying in hotels. Why can't you trace her through credit card transactions?" Hummer demanded.

"Because there aren't any. Not on the Chamber's card, her personal cards, or the cards of Mr. Turner."

Hummer pounded the old desk in a rare show of temper. "She knows we're looking for her."

"I doubt that," Conrad replied. "But finding her is not that essential."

Hummer raised an eyebrow. "And why not?"

"Because tomorrow afternoon, she'll bring Mr. Turner to Hartsfield International to catch his flight back to Salt Lake. We can take care of her then."

Hummer seemed to relax a little. "Take out the Blalock rep as well. She may have said something to him."

Conrad put out his hands in supplication. "All this unnecessary death has to end somewhere."

"I will determine what is necessary and what is not," Felix Hummer said coldly. "And based on the way you've handled this so far, I have little confidence in your opinions."

* * *

At nine o'clock on Monday morning, Nathan banged on their adjoining door. "Don't people in Utah ever sleep in?" Billie grumbled when she opened it and saw him all dressed and ready for the day.

Nathan smiled. "Never. I guess it's because we breathe all that invigorating mountain air."

Billie grimaced. "That explains the annoying cheerfulness too." He raised an eyebrow. "High altitude—lack of oxygen," she elaborated, then closed the door and turned toward the bathroom.

After checking out of the motel, they ate breakfast at a local café. Billie picked at her French toast, too worried to have an appetite, but Nathan ate his egg sampler plate ravenously.

"You're quiet this morning," he said finally.

"I'm worried about my friend Cowboy," she admitted.

"I think you should forget about him," Nathan advised. "He sounds unstable to me."

"And I'm also afraid that once you get on that plane you'll never want to see me again," she confessed.

She wasn't sure how he'd react and was relieved when he smiled. "Utah is not another planet, Billie. We can call each other and e-mail."

Billie nodded in resignation. "And pretty soon you won't be able to remember my name." She looked out the café window at the shoppers rushing along the sidewalks. "I almost envy the woman who broke your heart," she muttered. "At least she made a lasting impression on you."

Nathan covered her hand with his. "Billie . . ."

She removed her hand gently but firmly. "It's okay," she assured him with as much bravado as she could muster. "You warned me in advance, and you can't be held responsible for my recklessness."

They were quiet for a few minutes, then he said, "Her name was Diana, and believe me, you have no reason to envy my memories of her."

Billie blinked back her tears. She knew that even this small admission had cost him, and she appreciated it. Nathan paid for breakfast, then led the way out to the rental car, which Billie had parked between a Ryder truck and a dumpster.

"My flight leaves at three-thirty, so I need to be at the airport by two," Nathan said. "Since you're more familiar with Atlanta, do you want to drive?"

She shook her head. "No, you drive. I'll navigate."

They got into the car, and Billie consulted the map before instructing him to follow Highway 69 until they reached Interstate 85. A little before noon, they stopped on the outskirts of Atlanta for gas. When Nathan went inside to pay for the gas, he asked if she wanted something to eat.

"Thanks, but I'm not hungry," she told him. He stared at her for a second, then shrugged and went inside to pay for the gas. When he returned he had a cup of homemade peach ice cream, which he offered to share. "It's too cold for ice cream," she declined. She knew he thought she was pouting, but the closer they got to Atlanta, the more nervous she got and the more difficult it became to pretend to be carefree.

Nathan pulled off the highway onto a dirt road and finally parked under a tree. Once they were out of sight of the main road, Billie sighed with relief. Nathan took advantage of this momentary relaxation to slip a spoonful of ice cream into her mouth. He surprised her and managed to smear the sticky, frozen mixture all over her mouth.

"What a mess!" she cried, licking her lips.

"But it sure is good," he countered. "And it's giving me the urge to kiss you again."

"I don't kiss in broad daylight," she responded primly. "Especially not men I'll never see again."

"Billie . . ."

She smiled. "Just kidding." He seemed relieved. "I fully intend to see you again," she added, and he raised both eyebrows. "If you don't come back here to see me, I'll accept Kip's invitation to come skiing in Utah."

He smiled. "In which case I'll have to go with you to the slopes to protect you from Kip."

She nodded. "Exactly."

They arrived at the Hartsfield International Airport a few minutes before one o'clock, and Billie drove through the long-term parking deck. She was pleased to see Camille's Volvo just where she had parked it almost a week before.

"There's Camille's car that I drove to the airport," she told Nathan. "Either in all the confusion no one's thought to look for it or Edgar has thoughtfully left it here for my use."

"My money's on Edgar," Nathan replied.

Billie smiled, then turned toward the terminal. After returning the rental car to the check-in station, they stood in the parking deck.

"There's no point in me going inside," Billie said brightly. "We can just say good-bye here."

Nathan checked his watch, then waved over an airport valet. "I'll walk you to the car."

While the man stacked Billie's luggage on a dolly, she tried to protest. "I don't want to make you miss your plane. I can make it across the parking lot by myself."

"It won't take long, and I'll worry if I don't see you safely situated before I leave."

With a sigh, Billie handed Camille's keys to a valet and gave him her parking slip, where the Volvo's location was written. He led them to a shuttle, which deposited them about a hundred yards from Camille's Volvo. Nathan took Billie's hand and waited until the valet was far enough ahead of them before he spoke.

"All kidding aside, I've had a lot of fun this past week, and I don't think I'm going to be able to file you away as a pleasant memory."

She had to smile in spite of her anxiety over their pending separation. "I don't give up easily when I see something I want," she warned him, only half teasing. "I plan to take Diana and your memories of her head-on. You may learn to hate me, but I won't let you forget me."

He shook his head. "You shouldn't waste your time on me." But he was smiling, and she took courage from that. He stopped and took both of her hands in his. "I've never told anyone about Diana, but I'd like to try and explain it to you," he said slowly. "I'll need some time to organize my thoughts—and gather my courage. Once I feel like I'm ready, I'll call you."

He leaned forward, and she knew he was going to kiss her. Her attention was focused on his lips, but in her peripheral vision she noted that the valet had come to a stop behind Camille's car. He fumbled with the keys, then bent to insert one into the lock on the trunk just as Nathan's lips touched hers, blocking the valet from her vision.

Billie had written many times of earthshaking kisses, but as the ground trembled beneath her feet, she wondered if such a thing actually could occur. She was still a little dazed when Nathan pushed her to the ground as Camille's Volvo and the unfortunate valet disappeared into a ball of fire. Billie screamed, but Nathan put a hand over her mouth. They heard several people shouting and footsteps running toward them.

"Whoever is coming might be wanting to help us," Nathan whispered. "Or it might be someone sent to make sure we're dead. I don't think we can take a chance."

Billie whimpered through his fingers.

"Follow me," he instructed, then scooted to the edge of the car they were hiding behind. He shifted to a crouching position and she did the same, then they ran between the parked vehicles, putting some distance between themselves and the flaming Volvo. The air was full of black smoke, and approaching sirens wailed. After several minutes, Nathan held out his hand. "Something's coming. Sounds like a parking tram."

They stood as casually as possible and stepped from behind a parked Pathfinder as if they had just gotten out. It wasn't an airport tram, but a shuttle bus with *Holiday Inn Express* painted on the side in big green letters. Nathan waved, and the driver stopped beside them.

"Do you have room for two more?" he asked as the man pushed open the door.

"You got reservations at the Holiday Inn Express?" The driver looked suspicious.

Nathan gave him a charming smile. "Not yet."

The driver checked the available seating in his bus, then nodded. "Come on, but hurry. We're already behind schedule."

As they boarded the minibus, Billie heard heavy footsteps approaching. "Don't look," Nathan whispered and pulled her quickly to an empty pair of seats in the back. Once they were seated, the driver closed the doors and moved forward. Someone pounded on the side of the bus, but the driver shook his head.

"Sorry buddy. All full," he said through the window, then accelerated.

Nathan pushed Billie low in the seat and leaned down beside her. They maintained this position until the minibus passed through the tollgate and moved out onto the streets of Atlanta. When they sat up, Billie was horrified to see most of the other passengers staring at them.

Nathan looked around, then turned back to Billie and pressed a firm kiss on her unsuspecting lips. "Newlyweds," he said, smiling sheepishly. Some people nodded and others smiled tolerantly, but everyone turned their attention elsewhere.

"They'll follow us, won't they?" she whispered to Nathan.

"Yes," he replied. His lips were against her cheek but his eyes were looking out the window.

"I've never been so scared in all my life."

"*Now* is there something you'd like to tell me?" he asked.

She looked away. "I still don't want to."

He put his fingers on her chin and made her face him. "Well, I'm afraid I'm going to have to insist."

She sighed. "I'm not sure why people are trying to kill me, but I think it has to do with my friend Cowboy and the GFL."

Nathan studied her for a few seconds, then nodded. "We'll talk about it more later. Right now we'll just concentrate on staying alive."

"If you're smart, when we get to the Holiday Inn you'll check into a room and forget you ever met me," she said miserably. "I'm a hazard to your health."

He considered this for a few seconds, then muttered, "I've never been all that smart."

When the Holiday Inn came into view, Nathan stood and pulled Billie toward the front of the van before the driver came to a complete halt. Other passengers followed close behind, and a valet met the group at the door.

"Would you like me to get your other luggage?" He pointed at the overnight case in Nathan's hand.

Nathan peered down at the suitcase as if he were surprised to see it. "This is all we've got," he responded vaguely, and the valet gave him a startled look.

They followed their fellow minibus passengers as far as the lobby, but once the group dispersed Nathan led Billie back over to the front door and motioned to the valet. "We've just realized that we're at the wrong hotel," he said. "Could you help us get a taxi?"

"Sure." The man gave them another skeptical glance, then pulled a walkie-talkie from his pocket. "Someone will pick you up in a few minutes."

They thanked the valet and stood in the lobby, waiting anxiously until the cab pulled up to the curb. Nathan took Billie's hand and they walked out to the taxi. He opened the back door. Billie got into the backseat.

"Name a big mall," he whispered as he slid in beside her.

"Lennox Square," she answered.

"Could you take us to Lennox Square, please?" Nathan addressed the driver.

"Have you there in fifteen minutes," the man promised.

"Are we taking time out for a little Christmas shopping?" Billie asked as Nathan settled back against the seat.

"No, but the people who were chasing us at the airport know we went to the Holiday Inn Express, so they're probably already there questioning the valet."

Billie nodded. "Who is sure to remember us since we didn't have any luggage."

"Right. It won't take long to track down this cab and figure out where we were dropped off."

"Won't they come looking for us at Lennox Square?" Billie asked in alarm.

"Of course, but we'll have a big crowd of shoppers to hide in. And I don't plan to be at the mall for long." He looked down and smiled. "Trust me."

"I do," she told him.

After the cab driver dropped them off at the mall, they went inside and Nathan called a different taxi service, then ripped several yellow pages from the phone book. "I've never done that before in my life," he said as they walked back toward the entrance. "You've got me lying *and* defacing property."

She hung her head. "I'm a bad influence."

Nathan squeezed her hand. "I wish we had time to buy some clothes that whoever's trying to kill us hasn't seen." He found an inconspicuous spot near a side entrance and studied his stolen yellow pages while they waited for the cab. "But we can't stay here long."

"I could just take off my coat and put it in a garbage can," Billie suggested.

Nathan frowned. "You'd catch pneumonia and we'd really have problems. We'll have to postpone shopping until later."

Billie nodded and pointed out the glass doors. "I think this must be our cab."

"You wait here," Nathan said as he picked up his bag. "I'll wave for you to come if it looks okay."

Billie held her breath as she watched him walk out and exchange a few words with the driver. He turned and motioned for her to join him. Once they were settled, Nathan gave the man an address, then they slid down in the backseat so they couldn't be seen from outside.

Twenty minutes later, the man dropped them off in front of an adult bookstore. As they stood on the sidewalk, Nathan watched the taxi disappear while Billie stared at the store. "I'm afraid to even ask what we're doing here," she said when she was satisfied that the taxi was gone.

"You can ask questions later. Right now just follow me," he responded briefly. They walked three blocks and into a pawnshop. "We need cash. Put anything you can bear to part with on the counter," he instructed as he removed his watch and Cornell class ring. He pulled his cell phone from his pocket, so Billie dug hers out.

"I need to send my mother a quick text message first," she said, glancing at him. Nathan nodded, so she typed, *I'm safe but probably won't make it home for Christmas. Don't let the boys open my gifts. See you soon. Billie.* She then added the phone and the watch her parents had given her for graduation to the pile on the counter.

They walked out of the shop with a hundred and twenty dollars more than when they had walked in. "That stuff was worth much more than a hundred and twenty dollars," Billie fumed as they stopped at a phone booth.

"Pawnshops don't stay in business by giving people fair market value for their possessions," he said while inserting coins. He pulled her into the booth with him and shut the door. He made several phone calls as she leaned against him, drawing comfort from his closeness. Finally he hung up the phone and opened the door. "Another taxi will be here in a few minutes."

"I feel a little better," Billie told him. "Since I don't even know where we are it seems unlikely that anyone else could find us."

Nathan looked less optimistic. "I hope I've given us some room to work, but they'll know exactly where we are when I buy a used car with my credit card."

"Why are you going to do that?"

"Taxis are too expensive, and we won't want to be dependent on anyone else for transportation." His eyes searched up and down the street. "That taxi better get here before dark or we'll have local residents joining the effort to kill us," he said, and Billie suppressed a shudder. "You said all this has something to do with the GFL?"

"I think so, but it's complicated and I don't understand most of it myself."

Just then, a vagrant came up and asked for money. "We're broke," Nathan said with a shrug. "But we can at least give you our coats." He removed his and motioned for Billie to do the same. He handed them to the man, then took Billie's hand.

"Now we're going to freeze to death before *anyone* has a chance to kill us," she whispered as they watched the man walk away with a smile on his face.

"We'll buy more, but that red one of yours was too distinctive. It made you easy to identify, even from a distance," he explained. "Taxi's here."

This time Nathan had the cab driver leave them in front of a Salvation Army thrift store. They quickly purchased coats and stepped back outside. The temperature was still dropping, and as Billie pulled on the coat, she was too grateful for the warmth to consider whom the previous owner might have been. Nathan led her down the street and over a block before finally stopping in front of Eddie Frank Roper's Car Barn.

"Start saying your prayers, Billie," Nathan recommended as they started for the office housed in a small trailer.

"Are you kidding? I've been praying for days."

Eddie Frank was a huge man with a booming voice and a horrible toupee. After introducing himself, he sat them in folding chairs in front of his desk and asked what he could do for them.

"We need a car," Nathan explained. "Something inexpensive yet dependable."

Eddie Frank's eyes narrowed shrewdly. "So, you kids in trouble?" he guessed.

Billie searched her tired mind for a response, but Nathan spoke first. "Yes, we're in a bad situation, and we need transportation quickly with no questions asked."

"How do you plan to pay for this dependable vehicle I'm supposed to sell you without any of the regular formalities?"

Nathan took out his American Express card and handed it to the used-car dealer.

Eddie Frank studied it carefully. "What's your credit limit?"

"Theoretically, there isn't one," Nathan responded.

"You pay off the balance every month?" Eddie Frank asked, and Nathan nodded. "You looked like that kind of guy to me." He waved the card. "I'll have to check this out."

"Could you wait until the last minute?" Nathan requested.

Eddie Frank thought for a second, then hefted himself out of the swivel chair. "Let's go find you kids a car." He led the way outside and stopped by a bright orange Dodge. "This one's in good shape, and I could give you a reasonable price on it," he said. "But the color would be a drawback if you're trying to keep a low profile."

Nathan nodded. "What else do you have?"

"This here's a fine automobile." Eddie Frank pointed at a dark blue sedan. "It has two fuel tanks and several hidden compartments that the police never did find."

Billie shuddered to imagine the kind of person who would want a car with such features.

"It's a little pricey, though," Eddie Frank added, still looking at the dark car with admiration.

"We don't need anything fancy," Nathan told him, his eyes searching the lot. "Just a car that is mechanically sound and won't draw attention to itself."

"I think I've got it." Eddie Frank showed them a fifteen-year-old Honda Accord with 200,000 miles and sang its praises until Nathan nodded.

"We'll take it."

Back in the office, Eddie Frank filled out a simple bill of sale and passed it across the desk to Nathan.

"That car costs five thousand dollars?" Billie was shocked into asking when she saw the sales figures.

Nathan ignored her and addressed Eddie Frank. "I'm going to change the amount to six thousand, but I'm trusting that you've given me the best car on your lot since our lives may depend on it."

The used-car dealer stared back for a few seconds, then took the bill of sale from Nathan's hand and ripped it in two. He pulled a fresh form out of his desk and started over. "Let's make it the 1995 Impala that was delivered yesterday," the man suggested.

Nathan watched as the new bill of sale was completed, then signed it and the charge slip. While Eddie Frank waited for confirmation of Nathan's credit card, Billie leaned toward Nathan and whispered. "When this is over, I'll pay you back." *Somehow*, she added silently.

He nodded as Eddie Frank handed him a set of keys and led them to the back of the lot and waved at an unimpressive vehicle. The hood was wired shut, and the back door on the passenger side had a dent. "My mechanic checked it out and said it's in good shape, but the thing I like best about it is the color."

Billie squinted at the car. The color was something between gray and green. Or maybe it was blue—she couldn't tell. "What color *is* it?" she asked, and Eddie Frank smiled.

"Exactly. The accelerator is a little touchy, but she's fast. Used to belong to an escaped convict."

"Did he get caught?" Billie couldn't help but ask.

Eddie Frank smiled. "Heck no." He watched as Nathan put the suitcase into the backseat, then opened the front passenger door for Billie. "You think someone will be dropping by soon, asking questions about you?"

Nathan nodded. "I think there is a very good chance of that."

"Police?"

Nathan shrugged.

Eddie Frank frowned. "I think I'll go ahead and close up a little early tonight, maybe take my wife out to dinner and forget to bring along my cell phone. So it'll be hours before anyone can reach me. And then with my record keeping the way it is, it could take me a while to find the paperwork on this sale."

Nathan appeared to relax slightly. "Thank you."

"I run a legitimate business here," Eddie Frank explained. "I can delay them, but eventually I'll have to tell what I know about you and this," he paused to squint at the car, "tan Impala."

Nathan nodded. "We appreciate any help you can give us."

"One last little piece of advice," Eddie Frank said as Nathan started the car. "There's a junkyard out on Highway 20 at the Ensley exit. The owner keeps a wheelbarrow full of nearly new plates. He'll sell you several pretty cheap, and since even he won't know the ones you choose . . ."

"He can't tell anyone else the numbers," Nathan guessed, putting the car in gear.

Eddie Frank stepped back. "You kids take care now."

Nathan waved, then pulled out of the lot and headed east. After four blocks, he turned right and circled back to the west. A few minutes later, they risked driving by Eddie Frank's Car Barn. The place was locked up for the night. Billie sighed with relief as Nathan found the entrance ramp for I-20.

* * *

Felix Hummer answered the phone. "Well?"

"We located their cell phones at a pawnshop in downtown Atlanta. Then they used Nathan Turner's American Express card to buy a car."

"Where are they *now*?"

"We're working on that."

Hummer thought for a minute, then said, "Bring your driver in here. They might try to contact him, and if they do, we can turn that to our advantage."

"He may not cooperate willingly," Conrad replied.

"He will cooperate nonetheless," Hummer returned.

"Very well."

"Keep me informed," Hummer concluded. After disconnecting the call he dialed a number in Las Vegas. When someone answered, he said, "Round up some guys and put them on a plane headed out here. I'm not sure these local amateurs can handle the situation." Once his instructions were confirmed, Hummer disconnected and placed another call.

"Atlanta Police Department."

"So you've done as I asked?" Hummer inquired.

"I've been assigned to investigate the murders," the voice replied. "So far no one is asking any questions."

Hummer smiled. "Let's keep it that way."

CHAPTER 8

"Where are we going?" Billie asked once they were safely on their way.

"To get an assortment of license plates," Nathan replied, adjusting the mirrors. "Then to Tennessee. From there I hope we can come up with a plan to stay alive."

"Why Tennessee?"

"Because I don't think anyone would expect us to go there." He glanced over at her. "Now, would you please tell me *why* people are trying to kill us?"

"Maybe we should wait until after we get our new license plates," Billie tried.

"I want answers, Billie. Now."

She took a deep breath and stared at the brake lights on the car in front of them. "My life was as calm and normal as anyone's until Monday when Camille came over with Jeff Burdick. She told me that my vacation had been revoked and I'd been assigned to the Blalock tour. Looking back, I should have called my supervisor to make sure."

"She lied to you?" he asked.

Billie nodded. "Then she offered to buy my cruise from me since I wouldn't be able to use it."

"Why would she want your cruise?"

"Because Mr. Burdick's ex-wife was having him followed by a private investigator, and if they found out that he was spending the week with Camille, the wife would get more in the divorce settlement. They wanted my car and my cruise so they could slip out of town unnoticed."

"And she talked you into this?"

"I know it sounds stupid now, but Camille is," she paused, cleared her throat, and continued, "*was* the consummate Southern belle. She was beautiful and spoiled and could be ruthless when she saw something she wanted. And she wanted my cruise, so she took it."

"It doesn't sound like you liked her very much," Nathan remarked.

Billie considered this. "We weren't friends."

"So she tricked you into giving her your cruise."

"And taking the Blalock trip by threatening to have me fired."

Nathan's eyes cut to her quickly, then looked back at the road. "How could she have gotten you fired?"

"Her uncle is on the city council and is quite powerful in Atlanta. One word from him to the Chamber director, and I would have been gone."

"It sounds like you need to find another job anyway," Nathan advised.

Billie took a deep breath. "I've submitted a real novel—not one of my formula romances—to Randall House, and I should know soon whether they are interested in publishing it."

"If they are, were you planning to quit your job at the Chamber?"

She nodded. "But I couldn't afford to lose it before then. Besides, Camille told me she was trying to get a job with the GFL, and if she left the Chamber, staying there wouldn't have been so bad."

"But instead she got killed." Nathan glanced over at her again. "In your car. And the police suspect foul play."

"I took my car in for a safety check just over a week ago. The fuel pump needed to be replaced, so I had them put in a brand-new one."

"So someone rigged the car to blow up?"

She nodded. "At first I thought maybe Jeff Burdick's ex was even more vindictive than Camille had said. But then Edgar pointed out that Camille and Mr. Burdick were driving in my car and using my reservations on the cruise while I was handling Camille's business trip."

"So someone was trying to kill you, not her."

Billie spread her hands. "It doesn't make sense but apparently it's true."

"And why did we sneak toward Atlanta like fugitives instead of going to the police?"

"Because of Cowboy."

Nathan sighed. "Your Internet boyfriend."

"I told you that he's just a friend, but one whom I corresponded with almost every day." Billie paused. "Emphasis on *friend*. We weren't involved romantically. We just talked about his work and my books and just . . . things."

"Until the other night when you tried to e-mail him and the message came back as undeliverable." Nathan turned on his signal and took the Ensley exit off I-20.

"He was just about to finish his job with the GFL, and he even talked about meeting up with me on our business trip. Then, all of a sudden, nothing."

"Maybe he just wanted to end the relationship?" Nathan suggested gently.

"We didn't *have* a relationship," Billie said in exasperation. "We were just friends. You don't have to end something like that! You just start making your e-mails shorter and go a few days before answering and finally it just goes away!"

Nathan pulled to a stop in front of the junkyard. A five-foot chain-link fence extended as far as they could see, and two cranky-looking Rottweilers paced inside. "I guess this is it."

"How are we supposed to get inside?" Billie whispered.

"I think this gentleman is going to help us."

Billie looked out the windshield to see a tall, thin man wearing greasy overalls. His face was almost completely obliterated by a bushy beard and unkempt hair. "Don't get out," she told him urgently, but Nathan was already opening the door.

"You stay here," he said as he hit the automatic lock button and closed his door behind him.

Nathan spoke to the tall man, then followed him inside the gate. Billie cringed as she waited for the dogs to attack, but the owner yelled something at them and they cowered against the fence. Nathan and the man talked, then she saw money change hands. Finally the man led Nathan into a shed. A few minutes later, Nathan emerged carrying several license plates. The junkyard owner provided a screwdriver for Nathan to make the change. Then the men shook hands.

Billie reached over and unlocked his door. Nathan slid in behind the wheel and started the car. He turned around and headed back toward the interstate. "Okay," he said once they were underway. "Now back to your story of death and deceit."

"Well, I thought it was odd when Cowboy apparently changed his e-mail address without telling me and didn't write for several days. But I wasn't worried or afraid at that point," Billie explained. "But then Camille and Jeff Burdick were killed in my car. And when I called my landlady to ask her to keep feeding my fish, she told me that my apartment had been robbed."

Nathan looked over, startled. "Robbed?"

"*Destroyed* would be a better description. She said they tore open the couch cushions and made holes in the walls and killed my pet fish." Billie forced herself to continue past the lump in her throat. "But all they actually took was my computer. Then my mother said a man dressed like an Atlanta police officer came to their house in Coopersville and took some boxes I was storing in their garage."

"How do you know it wasn't really a policeman?"

"I don't know for sure, but the only way anyone could know that I had boxes stored in my parents' garage was to look at the inventory I kept on my computer."

Nathan frowned. "Your parents didn't ask the policeman for identification or a warrant or anything?"

Billie shrugged. "They are law-abiding citizens who respect the police. I'm sure it never occurred to them that he was an imposter. So they just let him take my stuff."

"Was anything important in those boxes?"

"No." She took a deep breath, then pressed on. "Then when I came out of the closing in Columbus, I checked the messages on my cell phone. The battery had been dead for several days, so I had a lot. Most of them were from my mother. Then I saw that I had a text message from Cowboy."

"What did he say?" Nathan asked.

"He said that I was in danger and should disappear and trust no one."

"And you're sure this was really from your friend Cowboy."

"Pretty sure, so I called the GFL headquarters to confirm it. They said they didn't have an employee by that name." She paused, then gave him a perplexed look. "Now why would they tell me that? I know he worked there."

"That's why you were in such a hurry to leave the attorneys' offices," Nathan said as he turned to study her for a second. "And you weren't planning on taking me with you, but I surprised you before you could escape."

"I didn't want to involve you in my problems. Although now I'm very glad I did," she added. "But . . ."

"The message said to trust no one—even me."

She winced. "I do trust you, Nathan."

"I know and I understand why you didn't tell me all this earlier. What I don't understand is why people are trying to kill you."

Billie twisted a long strand of hair as she replied, "I think I told you that I was late with a proposal to my editor for my next book?"

Nathan nodded, and she continued. "Well, last week Cowboy sent me a suggestion. He said I could write a book about a group of men who form a football league. They hire coaches and players and attract investors from all over the country. But they don't actually plan to run the league. They plan to steal the money put up by investors, ticket sales, and gambling proceeds from the big exhibition game—which is a ridiculous idea for a romance book. Women as a general rule aren't interested in sports themes."

"But if it was just a bad book idea, why is someone trying to kill you over it?"

"Because I think it wasn't just a poorly thought-out romance plot. I think it's what is really going to happen to the GFL."

"The organizers are criminals?"

"Maybe not all of them, but some."

Nathan considered this for a few seconds. "You said your friend's job was ending at the GFL. Maybe he's just a disgruntled employee trying to mess things up for the new football league?"

"He didn't sound upset," Billie said thoughtfully. "He sounded glad. He's had to do a lot of traveling, and I think he was looking forward to a more settled life."

"I'd like to see his e-mail about the GFL."

"I don't have a copy. I delete my e-mails as I get them."

"So you have no proof that we could take to the police or the FBI or whoever handles things like this."

"None."

"In fact, the e-mail may have been a product of Cowboy's imagination and the GFL could be perfectly legitimate."

"That's possible. We won't know for sure until after the exhibition game in Atlanta on Saturday." Billie paused and looked out the window. "But someone is trying to kill me."

They were quiet for a few minutes before Nathan took an exit off the interstate and pulled into a gas station. "If you need to use the bathroom, do it now. It may be a while before we stop again," he told her as he got out of the car. While he filled up the gas tank, Billie made use of the rest room, then waited for him in the car. When he got back into the front seat, he handed her a brown paper sack. It contained a road atlas of the United States, bottled water, snack foods, and a pair of scissors.

He pulled the car around to the back of the gas station and parked in the shadows. Then he turned to face her. "First let's determine exactly how much money we have left to work with." He twisted onto one hip and removed his wallet from a back pocket, fishing out a handful of crumpled bills and change from his front pocket as well and piling it all on her lap.

Billie added her money to the pile. "One hundred fifty-eight dollars and sixty-three cents," she reported.

"Well, that's not going to last," Nathan said with a frown. "We'll have to figure a way to get some money wired to us." He started the car and eased onto the highway.

"We'll keep to side roads, which whoever's after you will expect, but they won't know the direction we're headed and there are a lot of side roads. We'll try to be unpredictable by eating and sleeping at unusual times. With a little luck, we should be able to hide out until Saturday."

"And the crooks will get away with their scheme."

He shrugged. "If there really is one." He looked at the clock on the dashboard. "It's seven-thirty now . . ."

"Is that all?" Billie asked in surprise. "It seems so much later."

"We'll drive for a few more hours, then find a hotel."

"I wonder if they've found Kip," Billie mused as they drove along.

Nathan shook his head. "Mr. Blalock would have notified me."

Billie frowned. "You don't have your cell phone anymore."

"I checked my voice mail from a pay phone in the gas station," he told her.

After a while she said, "I don't think I can live with myself if we don't at least try to warn someone about the accusations Cowboy made about the GFL."

"Who would we notify and what would we tell them?"

"I don't know. The Atlanta PD is looking into the deaths of Camille and Jeff Burdick. Edgar has a friend who's a policeman, and he was going to see if he could find out anything about that."

Nathan glanced over. "So did he?"

"I don't know. After I got the message not to trust anyone, I didn't return his calls." She looked out the window. "The FBI maybe?" she suggested. "Even if we just leave an anonymous tip. I can't just sit back and let it happen."

Nathan considered this for a few minutes, then nodded. "How about this: First we'll look out for our own safety. Once we've lost whoever is trying to kill you, we'll call both the FBI and the Atlanta police and tell them what we think we know."

"Fair enough," she agreed.

"Okay, now why don't you try to get some sleep."

She snuggled down into her used coat, feeling almost safe for the first time in days. "I don't know how I can begin to thank you."

"Don't thank me yet," he replied.

* * *

Billie awakened with a start when the car came to a halt. She sat up straight and saw that they were parked outside a Motel 6.

"I want the hotel people to think that I'm traveling alone, so keep down," he said softly. "Lock the doors, and I'll be right back."

Billie slid low in the seat and watched him enter the lobby of the hotel. He smiled as he talked to the clerk at the desk, then reached for his wallet and took out some of their dwindling cash. When he returned to the car, he was carrying a key for room 110. They drove around the building and parked. Nathan backed into the space ten feet away from their room. She gave him a questioning look, and he explained, "I backed in so nobody can drive by and check our license plate, in case they've traced us to the junkyard."

"How would they be able to do that?"

Nathan shrugged. "Eddie Frank took a bribe from us. He might from someone else too."

This was such a sad thought that Billie was afraid she might cry.

"And I parked down from our room so that if they find us during the night, they might try the room in front of the car first. That would buy us a few minutes anyway."

Billie looked up at him in amazement. "How did a paper company executive learn so much about avoiding detection?"

"I learned everything I know about hiding from criminals by reading Robert Ludlum books."

"Great."

"But if it's any comfort, I did read a *lot* of Robert Ludlum books," he said with a smile as he climbed out of the car and approached room 110 with caution. He unlocked it, walked inside, and looked around. Then he came to the door and waved for her to follow. She hurried inside and he closed the door, then locked and bolted it.

"I only got one room to save money," he explained as she looked around the warm, pleasantly decorated suite. "But it has a little loft." He pointed to a twin bed in an open space above them.

"This is nice," she said, running her hand along the glossy surface of a wooden desk.

Nathan climbed the stairs and put his bag on the twin bed. He unzipped it and removed his shaving kit, then walked into the bathroom. "There's soap and shampoo and a toothbrush in here. Be sure and take them with you since the next place we stay might not provide extras."

Billie looked at the shower longingly. "I need a bath."

"You go first," he offered. "I have some sweatpants and a T-shirt you can sleep in. Rinse out your clothes and hang them up to dry. We can go shopping tomorrow, but we'll want to keep purchases to a minimum."

Billie took a long, warm shower, then dressed in the clothes Nathan had loaned her. She brushed her teeth and left the bathroom to give him a turn. She switched on the television and watched part of *It's a Wonderful Life* before falling asleep. She wasn't sure that Nathan slept at all. Every time she opened her eyes, he was peering out the window or pacing in the loft. Finally he woke her up just before dawn.

"It's time to go," he whispered, his face very close to hers.

"Well, we lived through the night anyway," she said as she pushed herself up into a sitting position.

"Looks that way," he responded with a weary smile.

She went into the bathroom and washed her face. After brushing her teeth, she carefully put all the complimentary hotel products into the plastic laundry bag. She added the plastic cups and box of Kleenex, then changed back into her own clothes. "Thanks for the loan," she told him as she returned his sweatpants and T-shirt.

"You're welcome. One item of business today will be to find a thrift store and get you some more clothes and a hat to hide your hair. I'm going to get mine cut so we'll hopefully look like two men traveling together."

"We could just wear our hair down and look like two women traveling together," Billie suggested with a smile.

Nathan ran his fingers through the curls at the back of his head. "I've been trying to find an excuse to cut my hair for over a year. I won't waste this chance." He pointed toward a pair of scissors on the dresser. "Will you trim it?"

Billie looked at the scissors with trepidation. "I cut my younger brother's hair once with terrible results. Maybe we could just find a barber?"

"Until we alter our appearance, anyone who sees us up close might identify us."

"But the people who are searching for us don't know where we are."

"We can't be sure."

Billie nodded. "I am. I've been nervous ever since I read that text message in the lawyers' office. But last night I felt at peace."

He smiled. "That's reassuring, and I do think we've put some distance between us and our pursuers. But we want to keep them looking in a lot of different towns. If they know we were here last night, then that narrows their search considerably."

"And increases our danger."

"Exactly."

Billie walked over and picked up the scissors. "I guess I'm willing to try it if you are."

He smiled. "Let's wait until we get in the car. If they trace us to this hotel room I don't want them to know I've cut my hair."

She stuck the scissors in her pocket, then helped him collect their meager possessions. "I guess I'm ready," she said, although she hated to leave the safety of the comfortable room. "But I think there's something else we need to do before we leave."

Nathan paused, his hand on the doorknob. "What?"

"I think we need to pray."

Nathan looked perplexed. "I've *been* praying, and so have you."

"You know that old saying about two heads being better than one?"

Nathan nodded.

"And there's that scripture in Matthew that says, 'Where two or three are gathered together in my name, there am I in the midst of them.'"

He nodded again.

"I think we need to pray together."

Nathan smiled. "In the hopes that a combined prayer might get the Lord's attention faster?"

She shook her head. "I know the Lord heard us the first time, and I know He'll answer our prayers. I just think praying together will help us to feel better about the decisions we make."

"Decisions that will keep us safe?"

"We're in the Lord's hands, Nathan. We'll do all we can and then accept His will."

"Okay," Nathan agreed. "Who'll say our joint prayers?"

"We'll take turns," she replied.

"Ladies first."

She bowed her head and offered a short but sincere prayer asking the Lord to direct and protect them. After the "amen," she looked up to see Nathan watching her.

"Ready now?" he asked.

She took a deep breath, then nodded. "Do we need to check out?"

Nathan unlocked the door and glanced outside. "No, the sign on the door says you can just leave your key in the room if you don't have any additional charges." He looked back at her. "I'll motion for you once I'm sure the coast is clear."

"I'm familiar with the routine by now," she assured him as she moved to stand beside the door.

He circled the car once, then opened the trunk and put his suitcase inside before he waved her over. He started the car as she climbed in but didn't turn on the headlights until they were on the road in front of the hotel.

"Are you hungry?" he asked.

"A little," she admitted.

Nathan pulled behind a strip mall and parked. "After my haircut, we'll find a truck stop." He turned his back to her and slumped down so she could reach his head. "Breakfast is usually a good value and truckers tend to mind their own business."

Billie forced herself to concentrate on his words as her fingers moved through his hair. It *was* just as soft as it looked.

"Trim it around my ears and along my neckline," he instructed. "When we get to Chattanooga, we'll find a barber."

"So that's where we're going? Chattanooga?"

He nodded. "I believe that's our best bet. Strangers stick out too much in small towns."

At first Billie was nervous with her role as barber, but she soon warmed to her task and finally Nathan glanced over his shoulder with mild alarm. "That's probably enough."

"Well, what do you think?" she asked as he took the scissors from her and examined himself in the rearview mirror.

"It's a good thing for you that I'm not vain," he said with a smile.

"It's a good thing for you that you already took those scissors back," she countered.

They found a Flying J a few miles out of town. Nathan parked between two eighteen-wheelers. As his eyes searched the area, he said, "I'll go and buy you a knit hat to cover your hair. Once you're semi-disguised, we can both go in and eat."

"I could just cut my hair too," she suggested. "Instead of fooling with a hat."

He lifted a heavy lock of her long hair with his hand. "I'd like to save that as a last resort."

"Be careful," she admonished as he left the car.

She watched him walk across the parking lot until he disappeared behind a group of huge trucks. It seemed like forever, but according to the clock on the dashboard only ten minutes had passed by the time he returned. He slipped into the front seat and handed her a fuzzy white hat. She pulled her hair up into a bun and put the hat on. Nathan readjusted it a couple of times, then nodded.

"That should do, and this place is perfect. It's busy and all the employees are too tired to be curious."

They both ordered a big breakfast and while waiting for it to be prepared, Nathan bought a newspaper. After reading the article together about the investigation into the death of Jeff Burdick, they split the paper and read separately. While flipping through her portion, an article about the GFL caught Billie's eye. It was titled "GFL Critic Fails to Appear." She scanned the column while the waitress delivered their food.

"Find something interesting?" Nathan asked as the waitress moved away.

Billie sprinkled salt on her eggs, then nodded. "Apparently a man had expressed concern about the way money was being accounted for by the GFL. When the backers refused to produce documentation, he filed a complaint in federal court accusing the league creators of racketeering. On the date he was to present his case, he failed to show up in court. His lawyer was astounded, the judge was irritated, and the newspaper used the incident to fill a few inches of empty space in the business section."

Nathan put a forkful of pancakes into his mouth, his expression dark. "I'd be willing to bet the GFL is somehow involved with organized crime."

Billie suppressed a shudder as she tried to eat her meal.

After he paid for their breakfast, Nathan bought some snack foods and bottled water. Once they were back in the car, he said, "Now we'll get some gas and contact the FBI."

"How?"

"I'll bet they have a toll-free number listed in the phone book for crackpots like us who want to warn them of doom and destruction."

Billie gave him a worried look. "You don't think they'll take it seriously?"

Nathan sighed. "All we can do is try. Then, after we call the Atlanta police, our civic duty will be done."

"While we're calling people, do you think we could call my parents?" she asked. "Just to let them know I'm okay."

Nathan shook his head. "Whoever is looking for us is sure to have your parents' phone tapped."

"But we're leaving here," she pointed out.

"We can only get so far away in this car. If they pinpoint our location, we'll be sitting ducks."

"I could mail them a postcard," she suggested.

"That would give us more time to get away but would still tell them where we *were*."

Billie thought out loud. "I could mail a postcard to a friend and ask them to call my parents."

"That might put whoever you send the postcard to in danger. Besides, it could take days." Nathan chewed his lip in concentration. "Maybe when we talk to the FBI, we can ask them to contact the Atlanta police and get word to your parents that you're okay. That will reduce the number of calls we have to make and our chances of getting caught."

Billie smiled. "That sounds like a very good idea."

They found a pay phone off the main road, and Nathan dialed directory assistance.

"Well?" Billie asked when he disconnected.

"She gave me a 1-800 number for the Atlanta office of the FBI." He passed the receiver to her. "Since you're the one who got the e-mail from Cowboy, I guess you should be the one to place the call." He dialed the numbers, and she waited for the first ring.

"Should I use my real name?" she wanted to know.

"I don't see why not."

She listened as a recording started playing in her ear. "It says to press One if my call is emergency related and I will be connected to an operator. Otherwise I can stay on the line and leave a message," she whispered to Nathan.

"Leave a message," he suggested. "That way they can't ask questions."

Billie nodded, then after the beep said, "My name is Billie Murphy, and I have reason to believe that the organizers of the GFL are planning to steal the money they take in at the exhibition game on Saturday. Everyone who invested in the league or bet on the exhibition game will lose their money. There won't ever *be* a GFL. They don't intend to play the games scheduled across the country. It's all a hoax that will make billions of dollars for the criminals who set it up. The deaths of Camille Lockhart and Jeff Burdick are connected to the hoax, and a computer programmer for the GFL named Milton Bagley can corroborate my story. Please pass this information on to the Atlanta Police Department and let my parents know that I'm okay." Billie recited her parents' phone number, then looked toward Nathan. He nodded and ended the call.

"Now, let's get out of here," he said, pulling her toward the car.

Once they were driving down a winding county highway, Nathan said, "Our other critical problem is the fact that we have no money."

"Could we use your credit card and get a cash advance?"

"By now our criminal pursuers have probably put a stop on my account. If we try to use it, we'll be tipping them off for nothing. I could ask Mr. Blalock to wire me money, but I hate to bother him while he's searching for Kip. Besides, the people following us would probably expect that." Nathan frowned. "I think we should look for someone who is on the periphery of our lives. That way we can be fairly certain that our pursuers won't be watching for us to contact them."

"And that they aren't involved in . . . whatever this is."

"Right. It will have to be someone who has access to several hundred dollars in cash and the ability to wire it."

"That eliminates my college roommates. They're all as poor as I am." Billie thought hard. "How about my bishop?"

"I'd rather not involve the Church in this if we can help it. There's a girl I dated about a year ago . . ."

Billie shook her head. "Forget it. I don't want you to be in her debt."

Nathan gave her a little smile.

"I could call Edgar," Billie suggested. "I'm sure he'll help me."

"I thought you didn't trust him."

"I didn't say that," Billie hedged. "I said that Cowboy warned me to trust no one and so I didn't call Edgar. But I have no reason to distrust him."

Nathan nodded. "Edgar it is, then."

"When will we call him?"

"We'll wait until we're set up in Chattanooga."

* * *

A clerk at the FBI office in Atlanta listened to the day's hotline messages. Most of them were from people reporting to have seen fugitives. A few messages requested information about available job positions. One threatened to blow up the state capitol, and another claimed that the GFL was a hoax. The clerk typed them all up and distributed them to the appropriate department.

* * *

As they drove, Billie watched the heavy traffic. "It's Christmas Eve," she remarked finally. "I guess everybody's trying to get home." Billie looked out the window and thought about her mother, cooking and making last-minute preparations. There would be stockings hanging over the fireplace, and presents surrounding a huge tree . . .

"Tell me about your family, Billie," Nathan requested.

"There's not much to tell. We're just regular, boring, all-American folks."

"It will help pass the time," Nathan insisted. "Start with your dad. What does he do for a living?"

"He manages a T-shirt factory."

"And your mom?"

"She runs her own travel agency from home. She's a perfect housekeeper, an excellent cook, she quilts and sews and . . ."

"Bakes cookies?"

"Every variety known to man."

"How did they meet?" Nathan asked. "Your mom and dad, I mean."

"At church. My dad says he fell in love with Mama in Sunbeam class." Billie rolled her eyes as she related this.

"And after all these years they're still in love?"

"Oh yeah. They're crazy about each other. When I was a teenager, it used to make me sick the way they would hug and kiss." Billie paused, frowning. "In fact, if I think about it too much, it *still* makes me sick. But I'm glad they're happy."

"How was it growing up with all those brothers?"

"Something got broken every day," Billie told him. "Either a plate or a family heirloom or a bone. It was beyond anything you can ever imagine."

"You might be surprised," Nathan remarked without smiling. "I have a good imagination," he added when he saw that she was watching him. "I guess your mom's pretty busy now getting ready for Christmas."

"Oh yeah. My mother is a fanatic about Christmas. She starts buying gifts in January and hides them all over the house."

"And you don't peek?"

She gave him an incredulous look. "Are you kidding? I've known every present that I was going to get since I was six. But we don't want to spoil it for Mama, so we pretend to be surprised on Christmas morning."

"I guess she fills stockings and makes a turkey dinner too."

Billie nodded. "I tried to tell her that Santa doesn't have to keep coming since my youngest brother is thirteen, but she won't listen. When we wake up on Christmas morning, our stockings are bulging with candy and fruit and little gifts. She feeds us cinnamon rolls and hot chocolate while we open the presents Santa brought. Then she lets us sleep for a few hours until our grandparents come over with more presents."

"Sounds like quite a day."

"It goes on forever—people coming and going, presents, food, wrapping paper everywhere." She looked over and decided to risk a personal question. "What are the Christmas traditions in your family?"

"We never had any that I can remember," he said softly as he came to a stop in front of an old-fashioned barber's pole. "This place looks obscure enough."

Billie pulled her hat back on and followed him inside the tiny shop. "Do you have time to give me a haircut?" Nathan asked the elderly gentleman who was sitting in his barber's chair eating lunch.

The man waved a half-eaten banana at Nathan's head. "Don't know how to do any of those fancy layered haircuts."

Nathan ran his fingers through the uneven ridges Billie had inflicted on his hair with the scissors. "All I want is a regular cut."

The old man smiled. "Now that I can do."

Nathan took a seat in the chair, and the barber went to work on him. When he was done, Nathan paid the man, then asked if he could borrow the phone book. After checking the business section and writing some information down on the back of his hand, Nathan closed the phone book and led the way outside.

"You look like a completely different person," Billie whispered as they climbed into the car. His hair was now military short without a hint of curl.

"That was the general idea," he responded.

"What did you look up in the phone book?" she asked as he pulled out into the traffic.

"I found a Winn Dixie store in eastern Chattanooga that has a Western Union office. We're going to pull over in a few minutes and call to find out the information they need in order to have money wired there. Then we'll call Edgar."

They stopped to use a pay phone at a busy strip mall. Once Nathan had the wiring information, he stood beside Billie as she dialed Edgar's cell number. "Remember, keep it short," he cautioned.

She nodded as Edgar answered. "Edgar, it's Billie."

"I've been so worried about you!" the chauffeur replied.

"We're okay, but we need money. Will you send five hundred dollars to the Western Union office in a Winn Dixie grocery store in Chattanooga?"

"Of course," Edgar agreed eagerly. "And if there's anything else—"

Billie interrupted him. "That's all we need." She gave him the wiring information, then said, "Please do it as soon as possible and put the money in Nathan's name."

"I'll take care of it right now," Edgar promised. "But we need to talk. A Detective Davenport from the Atlanta Police Department has been calling me trying to reach you. He says it's urgent."

Nathan shook his head, and Billie broke in again. "I'm sorry, but I've got to go."

"How can I get in touch with you?" Edgar asked, his tone pleading.

Billie thought for a second. "Leave a message on my Chamber voice mail. I'll find a way to check my messages." Then she hung up the phone. After taking a couple of deep breaths, she looked at Nathan. "What should we do about the detective from the Atlanta police?"

He frowned. "I guess we'll have to call them."

He dialed directory assistance again and soon had her connected to the Atlanta Police Department. Holding the phone away from her ear so Nathan could hear the conversation too, Billie identified herself and asked for Detective Davenport. After a brief pause, she was connected to the detective. He verified her name and asked for her social security number.

"I'm sorry, but I don't give out that information over the phone," she replied automatically, then felt obligated to explain. "You know, identity theft and all that."

"I assure you I'm not trying to steal your identity," the detective responded rather testily. "I'm trying to save your life." Then he asked several other personal questions, including her exact location. When she told him that she wouldn't give him that information because of safety concerns, he demanded that she go immediately to the nearest police station. Finally Nathan reached over and disconnected the call.

"He didn't ask a single question about the GFL hoax," she said.

Nathan frowned. "He didn't care about the GFL. He was trying to keep you on the phone long enough to trace the call."

"Why?"

He shook his head. "I don't know. Maybe he really was trying to save your life. Or maybe he's working with the criminals."

Billie's heart started to pound. "Did I talk too long?"

"I don't think so, but let's get out of here just in case." He grabbed her hand and led the way back to the car.

"Now what?"

"Now we go to the Winn Dixie and see what happens."

* * *

"We've found them," Conrad told Hummer, but he didn't sound particularly pleased.

"Where?" Hummer demanded.

"Outside of Chattanooga. They've arranged for money to be wired to a grocery store there."

"I assume we'll have a warm welcome waiting for them."

The older man sighed. "It will all be over in a matter of hours."

* * *

Billie and Nathan drove past the Winn Dixie for the first time just before dark. Nathan stayed in the flow of traffic and circled the block twice.

"What are we doing?" Billie asked.

"Trying to get a feel for things," Nathan replied.

"Is that what Robert Ludlum would do?"

Nathan smiled. "My plan isn't as ingenious as one of Mr. Ludlum's, but I hope it will work. I think we'll leave the car there." He pointed to the Peaceful Rest Cemetery to their right. "Then we can walk over to the Winn Dixie."

Billie nodded as the knot of anxiety returned to her midsection. He parked, and they put on their jackets. Nathan offered a prayer and took her hand in his. "We're not going to rush into anything. We'll watch from the outside for a while. If everything looks okay, I'll go in and try to get the money. If there's a problem, meet me back here." Billie nodded again but with less enthusiasm. She didn't like the idea of separating, even for a few minutes.

Nathan pulled the keys from the ignition and took one off the ring, then extended it to Billie. "Here's an extra key in case you make it back and I don't." He put the other set of keys in his pants pocket. Then they got out of the car and started walking toward the street. The cemetery caretaker met them by the wrought-iron gate. He approached them shaking his head in agitation.

"You folks can't park in here!"

"We're not parking," Nathan responded. "We just need to leave the car for a few minutes."

"That's *parking*." The caretaker was adamant. "Move your car or I'll call the police."

Billie smiled at the man. "We don't mean to be any trouble, but we've come to visit a grave." She waved vaguely at the markers behind them. "I forgot to bring flowers, so we were going to walk up to that grocery store and come right back."

The caretaker looked as though he might be softening.

"I wanted to get some poinsettias since it's Christmas Eve," she added.

Finally the man nodded. "Okay, but hurry. I'm supposed to lock the gates in thirty minutes."

Nathan took Billie's hand, and they walked briskly down the sidewalk toward the store.

The air was chilly, but not really cold. "Everything seems pretty normal to me," Billie whispered finally.

"And busy. The crowd should help hide us."

"Do you think we should risk it?"

Nathan sighed. "We have no choice. We don't have enough money for even a cheap motel tonight." He looked around, then pointed to a little stand where a troop of Boy Scouts was selling Christmas trees. "Why don't you wait over there? Act like you're searching for the perfect tree. You can see into the store from there so I can signal you if there's trouble."

"How will you do that?"

He thought for a second, then said, "If I put both my hands in my back pockets, run. Find a policeman or a security guard or a meter maid and tell them to get you someplace safe. And don't worry about me. I can take care of myself."

"And what if someone tries to grab me while I'm standing out here alone?"

"Scream. All these people won't allow you to just be dragged off."
He exhaled, and she could see his breath. "Well, we might as well go
on in. You first. I'll be right behind you."

Billie made it to the grouping of trees, then walked along,
pretending to consider the limited selection while watching for
Nathan. A few minutes later, he passed behind her and walked into
the store. Out of the corner of her eye, Billie saw a man step out of
the shadows and follow Nathan inside. She was sure that the man
had been waiting for Nathan to arrive, so without pausing to
consider the risks, she rushed to the entrance and pushed inside the
store.

Nathan was a few feet ahead of her, moving toward the customer
service counter. The man was right behind him, closing the distance
between them quickly.

"Homer!" she called loudly, and everyone in the front part of the
store turned to stare. The man behind Nathan moved to the left and
picked up a magazine off the stand. "I can't decide on our Christmas
tree all by myself! Come help me right now!" She didn't have to fake
the strident tone in her voice and knew he recognized the fear in her
eyes when he turned around.

"Okay, honey," he responded, then joined her quickly. He took
her hand as they hurried outside.

"A man followed you into the store," she whispered frantically,
and Nathan picked up his pace.

"If there's one, there are more," he said with certainty, and they
started across the parking lot. They heard shouting behind them.
"Run!" He pulled her straight into the busy traffic. Horns honked
and tires screeched, but they made it to the other side without
injury.

"Are we being followed?" Billie asked breathlessly as they ran up
the sidewalk.

"Afraid to look," he answered. They made it into the cemetery
and ran past the startled caretaker. "Call the police," Nathan told him
as a bullet flew over their heads. The caretaker ducked into his little
office and picked up the phone. "This way." Nathan dragged Billie
onto the grass. "We'll try to lead them away from the car and hope
that when the police arrive they'll run."

Another bullet whizzed past them as Billie ran in a zigzag pattern to keep from stepping on the graves. "What are you doing?" Nathan finally demanded in exasperation. "You have to stay low!"

"I can't step on dead people!" she cried.

"You're going to *be* one of the dead people if you don't stop dancing around up there." He yanked her down on a grassy mound as sirens started wailing in the distance. The gunfire ceased suddenly, and they rose to a crouch and ran for the car. "Now the trick is going to be getting out before the police can stop *us*."

"That looks like a back entrance." Billie pointed to a small chain-link gate beside a utility shed, and Nathan shot her a smile.

"You get the car, and I'll open the gate."

Billie ran to the Impala and unlocked it with trembling hands. More sirens were approaching, and she could hear the caretaker calling to her as she jumped into the car. She started the motor and spun gravel when she pulled the car onto the road and drove toward Nathan. She slowed as she passed through the gate. Nathan took the time to close the gate before he ran to the car. As soon as he was inside, she drove down the street and out of sight.

"Don't turn on the headlights," Nathan instructed, looking behind them. Then he gave her a series of instructions. "Turn right at this corner, then take the next left. When you reach the light, turn to the left and stay on this road until it intersects with the main street."

After a few minutes, Billie realized that she had been clutching the steering wheel so tightly that her hands were aching with the strain. She took a deep breath and forced herself to relax. "Is anyone following us?" she asked, almost afraid to know the answer.

"Not that I can see," Nathan responded. "The Christmas Eve traffic probably saved us."

"But we still need money," Billie pointed out.

"Yeah, we seriously may have to spend tonight in the car." He frowned at the windshield.

Billie considered this depressing thought as she drove. "Nathan, what about your laptop?"

"What about it?"

"We could sell it or pawn it or something."

He paused briefly and nodded. "We're almost into downtown. We should be able to find a pawnshop." He reached into the backseat. "I'll save everything important on disks."

Billie continued to drive as he worked. The traffic thinned when they reached the downtown area. "Everything's closing down early for Christmas," she said.

"Some places never close," he promised her. His words proved to be prophetic, and a few minutes later they were parked in front of a pawnshop with a neon sign that flashed "Open 24 Hours."

"You stay here," Nathan said as he studied the sidewalk. "If I run into trouble, promise me you'll leave."

Billie nodded to avoid an argument, although she knew she would never desert him. He gave her a smile of encouragement before tucking his laptop under his arm and getting out of the car. She watched him disappear into the pawnshop and waited anxiously until he returned.

He came to the driver's side door and she slid over, glad to let him take over. He handed her two hundred dollars as he pulled out of the parking lot.

"This is all you got for a thousand-dollar computer?" She was appalled.

"Yeah, the guy said he was being generous since it was Christmas Eve," Nathan responded.

"I shouldn't have suggested that you sell it."

"I just pawned it," Nathan reminded her. "Which means that after all this is over, I can reclaim it for twice what they loaned me on it."

"That was supposed to make me feel better?"

He smiled. "No, the fact that we now have a little money should make you feel better. And it *was* a good idea," he added. "I don't know why I didn't think of it!"

He stopped for gas just as they reached the Alabama state line. They studied the map and charted a course, then started driving again. It was almost midnight when Nathan stopped in front of a motel called the Good Sleep Motor Lodge.

"It looks very similar to the Pink Flamingo," Billie whispered.

"Yeah, it feels like coming home," Nathan agreed as he went in to pay for their rooms.

He returned a few minutes later with two keys and drove around to park a few spaces down from rooms 12 and 14.

Once they were inside her room, Billie tested the mattress.

"Hard as a rock or lumpy?" Nathan asked.

"Better than the car," she responded with a tired smile.

"Are you hungry? There's a Wendy's up the street."

"All I want is to take a shower, change into your sweatpants and T-shirt, then get into this uncomfortable bed."

He tucked a lock of hair behind her ear and pressed a kiss to her forehead. "Keep your door locked and call if you need me."

* * *

"If you've got bad news, I don't even want to hear it," Felix Hummer said as the other man walked into the storage room.

"They got away again."

"These are regular, everyday people we're dealing with, not super-heroes," Hummer replied. "I don't understand why we can't kill them."

"Their luck will run out soon," Conrad predicted wearily.

"For your sake, I hope so," Hummer said.

CHAPTER 9

Billie woke up on Wednesday morning to a strange combination of smells. With her eyes closed, she tried to identify them. One was the aroma of rich chocolate, one was peppermint, and the other was evergreen. She smiled, hoping it had all been a bad dream. She was safe at her parents' house. Her mother had been up since before dawn making cinnamon rolls and hot chocolate. There were stockings full of candy over the fireplace and a huge Christmas tree surrounded by hundreds of presents.

Slowly she opened her eyes. There was no Christmas breakfast awaiting her, no candy, no presents—just a shabby hotel room and another day of danger. She moaned and turned over, then realized that Nathan was knocking on the adjoining door. With a sigh she pushed back her covers.

"So, you don't sleep in even on Christmas," she said as she opened the door.

"Merry Christmas to you too," he replied with a smile, then pulled her into his room.

On the bedside table was a tiny fir tree decorated with twine bows. Little pieces of hard peppermint candy were balanced on the sparse boughs, and several presents wrapped in newspaper were nestled below it. Beside the tree was a small red and white felt stocking with a Hershey bar and a candy cane sticking out of the top.

Billie's hand flew to her mouth as she tried to suppress a sob. "Nathan!"

"It's not much."

She threw her arms around his neck and let the tears fall freely. "It's beautiful. I don't know how I can ever thank you!" Then she turned her eyes to meet his. "I didn't get you anything!"

He pulled her down on the edge of the bed. "Don't worry about that. I never get anything for Christmas." Her expression grew even more alarmed, and he laughed. "Except a big bonus from Blalock Industries." She knew he intended this to make her feel better, but it didn't. "Really, I don't care about Christmas. I never put up a tree or anything. But you're used to the big family deal, and I didn't want you to wake up this morning to nothing."

He pointed at a box of honey buns and two steaming styrofoam cups. "Hot chocolate was easy, but that was the closest I could come to homemade cinnamon rolls."

She accepted the cup with both hands and sipped the warm liquid. "Delicious."

He tore the cellophane wrappers off two honey buns, and they ate them hungrily. "Want another one?" he asked when she started licking the sugar coating off her fingers.

"Actually, I'd rather have the Hershey bar," she requested. "And I want to open my presents."

"The selection at the gas station wasn't very wide," he explained as she tore the newspaper off her gifts—a pair of socks, a comb, and two packs of gum. "And my budget was extremely limited. I hope you're not disappointed."

She pulled the socks onto her feet and smiled. "Are you kidding? This is the first time in over twenty years that I haven't known what my presents were before I opened them!"

He laughed.

"So, when do we have to leave?"

"Not for a while," he said. "There won't be much traffic this morning, and it would be dangerous for us to be on deserted highways. I thought we'd wait until this evening and drive through the night."

Billie scooted up and settled against the headboard of his bed. "Well, that gives us plenty of time to talk."

His expression became slightly wary. "About what?"

"Nobody doesn't have Christmas, Nathan, even children in hospitals and homeless shelters. I think it's time you told me about yourself."

"I'd rather watch television," he tried, but she shook her head.

"I want the whole story—every last detail. Consider it part of my Christmas."

He stood and paced around the room, obviously agitated. "You don't know what you're asking for." He stopped in front of the window and looked out. "I *never* talk about my childhood."

"That's because you don't trust anyone, especially women. But you don't have to worry about me divulging your secrets. I probably won't live out the week."

He gave her a rueful smile, then sat in the chair and took a deep breath. "My parents married when they were teenagers, and I was born a few months later. We lived with my dad's mother. My grandmother took care of me while my mother sat on the couch all day watching television and drinking cheap wine. My father worked as an auto mechanic when he wasn't drunk or hung over."

"My grandmother died when I was five. My parents were always fighting, and my dad got fired a lot, so there was never enough money. Finally he started selling drugs to make ends meet. He got caught and was thrown in jail a few months after my grandmother died. From that point on, my mother depended on a steady stream of boyfriends for her support. By the time I was seven, family services wanted to put me in foster care, but my mother sobered up for her court appearance and charmed the judge into letting me stay with her."

"It was good that she wanted to keep you." Billie was glad for a chance to make a positive comment.

Nathan waved this remark aside. "She just needed me to keep the house clean, answer the phone, and make excuses for her if the bills weren't paid—that kind of thing. So for the next several years, she went from one bad relationship to another. She wasn't choosy about her boyfriends as long as they could give her booze and drugs, so she got beat up a lot. When I was small there was nothing I could do about it, but as I got older, I tried." His fingers moved absently to the small scar under his left eye.

"That's how your nose got broken." It wasn't a question.

He nodded. "Every time a guy would go too far and she'd throw him out, she'd cry and promise me that there would be no more men. She'd swear she was going to stop taking drugs and get a real job so we could be a regular family. That would always last about a day. Then she'd need a fix and find herself another bum.

"I learned about Christmas at school and developed some expectations, but nothing ever happened at our house. Sometimes my mom would be sober enough on Christmas Day to apologize for not getting me anything, and if her current boyfriend had given her candy, she usually shared it."

Billie wanted to cry but instinctively knew that if she expressed sympathy, he'd stop talking. "What about your dad?"

"In the really bad times I'd dream about him being released from prison and coming to get me. He'd take me to a new house with something besides Pop-Tarts in the kitchen. I'd do the laundry and dishes for him, and he'd be glad to have me around." Nathan gave her a wry smile. "Then I found out that he'd been out of prison for years and had never even bothered to call. I didn't see him again until my mother's funeral."

"What did he say?" Billie asked.

"He told me when he got out of prison he wanted to take me with him, but he was afraid my mom would kill herself if he did. Besides, he had no job, no place to live . . ."

"He didn't have anything to offer you," Billie completed the sentence.

Nathan shrugged. "Maybe."

"He could have at least come to visit you."

"He said he had a bad time with alcohol and drugs after jail too. He'd been in several detox programs and was finally clean. He brought his new wife to the funeral and a little boy about two. He said he was trying to be a good father." Nathan's tone was derisive.

"So you have a little brother," Billie said gently.

"I guess you could call him that. Poor kid."

"What's his name?"

"Cody."

"That's cute," Billie said, trying the name out a few times. "How often do you visit him?"

Nathan looked up in surprise. "Never. Why would I?"

Billie frowned. "I can understand you being resentful. Your father didn't live up to his responsibilities to you, but Cody is your *brother*."

"The kid will have to make the best of life, just like I did." Nathan wouldn't meet her eyes when he added this last part, and she wondered if he was really as indifferent as he sounded. "I'm afraid I might have inherited a tendency toward chemical dependence, emotional instability, inability to sustain a relationship, and refusal to live up to responsibility. All of those traits can be passed from a parent to a child, and all of them can really mess up a kid's life. I'm living proof of that."

"You're living proof that people can overcome their circumstances and make a success of their lives," she told him firmly. "Tell me the rest of the story."

He shrugged. "My mother's parents were members of the Church, and she was baptized as a child, although I don't think she was ever active. Every few years a new elders quorum president would be called in the ward she was a 'member' of and he would send home teachers out. It usually didn't take long for my mom to scare them off, but about the time I started high school we got a home teacher named Vince Hudson. He also happened to be the Young Men president, and he didn't scare off easily. He started coming by when my mom wasn't home and eventually got me involved in youth activities. After a few months, he arranged for me to take the missionary discussions, and when I was ready, Vince convinced my mother to let me be baptized. He helped me get a scholarship to Cornell, and when it was time for me to go on a mission, he paid for the whole thing."

Billie blinked back unexpected tears. "He saved you."

Nathan nodded. "I owe everything I'll ever be to Vince Hudson. He even looked out for my mother—as much as anyone could—while I was gone."

"Do you stay in touch with him?"

"Oh yeah. Our deal was that if I let him pay for my mission, he'd have to let me pay for his oldest son's when the time comes. So he's not going to get rid of me anytime soon."

Billie smiled, grateful that Nathan had been blessed with a good role model at a crucial time in his life. "It's good that your father was able to overcome his problems with drugs and alcohol. It kind of gives the story a happy ending."

Nathan's expression darkened. "My father died of liver disease if you call that a happy ending. And the improvements he made at the end of his life can't make up for my nightmarish childhood. You were raised in a happy family with parents who loved you and loved each other. I don't know if it's possible for you to imagine how it was for me."

"I'm trying," Billie pointed out.

"I was so alone," he whispered. "Night after night I'd wait in the dark, wondering if my mother would come home and if she'd have a strange man with her." He glanced over at Billie. "It was hard to know what to hope for."

"But it's over," she said. "You survived."

He didn't look convinced. "Things like that have a lasting, detrimental effect on people."

"Nathan, I know you'll never forget the past completely, but you can put it behind you. After all, we have been *commanded* to marry and have children."

"Special situations are taken into consideration," he said with a hint of belligerence.

She thought about this for a second, then shook her head. "The only 'special situation' I've ever heard mentioned from the pulpit is for people who remain single because of circumstances beyond their control."

"My parents were certainly beyond *my* control!"

"Your parents' weaknesses don't excuse you from your obligations."

"Are you setting yourself up as my judge and jury?" he demanded, angry now.

Billie wanted to retreat but felt that she couldn't. "I'm not claiming to be perfect, Nathan. But when I make a mistake, I don't tell myself it's my parents' fault. At some point we have to take responsibility for ourselves and our own lives."

"Do you know the statistics on abused children, Billie? A huge percentage grow up to abuse their own children. And the figures are no better for parents with chemical dependencies," he said vehemently. "My decision to live my life alone isn't a selfish one."

"I think the reason you've chosen to be alone is because you're scared," Billie replied.

"I am!" he agreed. "For my hypothetical wife and children!"

He was breathing heavily, and Billie regretted that she had upset him but still refused to back off. "The Lord doesn't ask us to do things we can't do, Nathan. You know that. If you try to obey any commandment, the Lord will help you—even with marriage and parenting, regardless of your tragic childhood."

"Billie, please . . ."

"And if you go through life running from your responsibilities," she continued, "responsibilities like a relationship with your brother, then you're no better than your father."

Nathan was quiet for a minute, then he sighed and said, "That wasn't a nice thing to say to a guy who just fixed you breakfast on Christmas morning."

Billie turned away. "I think I'm falling in love with you, Nathan. You don't have to accept my advice or my heart, but you have to know how I feel. And if you reject me, it has to be with your eyes wide open, fully aware of what you're giving up."

He didn't say anything for a long time. "Like you said, we probably won't live through the week, so all of this is moot."

"I'm not kidding, Nathan. I believe we could build a happy life together."

"I wouldn't ask you to settle for me, Billie."

Realizing that she had pushed him far enough, she sighed. "Maybe we could turn on the TV now."

They watched a couple of Christmas cartoons, then Billie fell asleep during a football game. Nathan woke her up with a gentle shake. "Time for Christmas dinner."

She opened her eyes and saw that he had a big Wendy's bag in his hand.

"What? No turkey and cranberry sauce?" she teased him with a sleepy smile.

"You are a hard woman to please," he replied, shaking his head. He distributed the food. "I did get frosties for dessert."

She opened one and took a big bite. "Better than pumpkin pie." After they finished eating, Billie leaned back, satisfied. "So what are we going to do with the rest of our afternoon?"

Nathan pulled out another sack, this one small with *Hometown Drugstore* written across it in red letters. "I'm glad you asked that.

After our little face-to-face encounter with our pursuers at the Winn Dixie yesterday, I think we need to alter our appearances—again."

"Cut my hair?" she guessed.

He pulled a box of Miss Clairol from the bag. "And go blondish."

Billie took the box from him and was examining it when he said, "If it makes you feel any better, I'm going to dye mine too."

She smiled. "What color?"

"I figured if we cut your hair, we could both split that same bottle. It should lighten yours and darken mine."

"Autumn chestnut," she read off the box. "Let's get started."

Nathan approached Billie's haircut as though he were installing a million-dollar security system. He measured and calculated for ten minutes before he finally picked up the scissors.

"If you don't hurry up and cut my hair, it's going to grow and mess up all your figures," Billie said impatiently.

He ran his fingers through the long tresses. "I'll bet you've never gotten it cut before."

"Just trims," she admitted.

"It's a big responsibility, being the person to cut it for the first time."

"I've been trying to find the courage to cut it for months," she told him. "You're doing me a favor, even if it turns out crooked."

"Really?" Nathan asked, picking up a heavy lock with his hand. "Why would you want to cut it?"

Billie remembered Camille's stinging remarks that last night at the chamber offices. "Because long hair is old-fashioned. I want to be more sophisticated or modern or something."

"I love your hair," Nathan said in complete sincerity. "And I hate that we're having to change you, even superficially."

"A little change never hurt anyone," she assured him. "Cut away."

Two hours later, they studied themselves in the mirror. Her now shoulder-length hair was several shades lighter than its natural color while Nathan's hair was several shades darker. The change really was amazing.

"I like it," she said, touching her shorter tresses.

He drew her into his arms and pressed her face against his chest. She wasn't sure if he was comforting her, apologizing for the necessity of cutting her hair, or trying to find solace, but she enjoyed the close contact. Finally he stepped away. "You haven't mentioned your nose itching in days."

"That's because it stopped," she told him.

"When?" he asked.

"Once I figured out that *you* were the good thing that was going to happen to me."

Nathan shook his head. "If your nose told you that these past few days were going to be good, heaven help you if you ever get a sign that bad things are in your future!"

Billie laughed, then stood and rubbed her hands together. "Okay, we've altered our appearances, and you've changed the license plate on the car. Now we just have to decide which way to go."

"It's your turn to pray," he said as he bowed his head.

Billie said a quick prayer, then waited a few seconds before saying, "South," with conviction.

He nodded. "That's what I think too." He pulled out his wallet and counted their money. "We have close to a hundred dollars left."

"That's pretty good." She tried to be positive.

"It's got to last us four more days. At the rate we've been spending, we'll be completely broke by this time tomorrow."

"We'll find a way to conserve," Billie told him with more confidence than she felt.

"I think we should sell the car."

"Then we'll be stranded!" she cried in alarm.

"We'll have to buy another one. But if we trade for a cheaper car, we can make some cash on the deal. Driving in a different vehicle will be a safety precaution, and if we buy from someone a little unscrupulous, we won't have to give them our real names."

"We'll have to buy from a place worse than Eddie Frank's?" Billie asked, then waited in dread for his answer.

He nodded. "We'll drive south through the night and should be able to reach," he glanced at the map, "Montgomery by morning. We'll find something there."

They took turns driving and pulled into Montgomery at daybreak. After a breakfast, they found a huge flea market. Nathan gave Billie some of their dwindling funds to buy a change of clothes.

Then they got two rooms at the Sleep Inn on North Road and slept for several hours.

When Billie woke up, she took a shower and changed into her fresh clothes. Then she knocked on Nathan's door. He was wearing the same clothes he'd had on the night before and looked tired.

"Did you sleep at all?" she asked.

"A few minutes," he said as he led her inside. "I've found a couple of used-car lots that I think might do business with us. I figured we'd have our prayer, then leave just as it's starting to get dark and drive by these places until we find one that looks right."

Billie rubbed her hands up and down her arms. "This part of town is creepy in the daylight. Why do we have to wait until night-time to do our shopping?"

Nathan gave her an apologetic smile. "So it will be harder for anyone to get a good look at us."

They got dinner in a drive-through line and ate in the car, then started their tour of north Montgomery used-car lots. One of the places on Nathan's list was closed and another was too busy for comfort. But when they pulled in front of the third one, Nathan nodded. "This one has possibilities."

He parked the Impala up near the office door as a small man with beady eyes and slicked-back hair emerged.

"You stay in the car and try not to let him get a good look at your face," Nathan told Billie as the car-lot owner approached. Nathan opened the door and climbed out as the man reached them.

"Howdy folks," he said with a smile that exposed crooked teeth. "Name's Wendell Hicks."

"Nice to meet you," Nathan replied, the omission of his own name obvious.

Wendell's little eyes narrowed. "What can I do for you?"

"We'd like to trade in our car for something else," Nathan told him.

"You looking to move up to something nicer?" Wendell inquired.

"No, actually we'd like to clear a little cash on the deal."

The man considered this for a few seconds, then nodded. "Let me show you what we got."

Billie watched through the window as Wendell led Nathan around the small lot. They stopped for several minutes beside a light-colored truck, and Billie assumed they had agreed upon a trade when they climbed in and drove it to the front. They got out, and she heard Nathan ask, "How much can you give us for the Impala over the value of the truck?"

The man scratched his stomach. "It's probably worth another five hundred dollars after processing fees," Wendell said. "But this is kind of a dangerous neighborhood, so I only keep a couple hundred in cash on the premises after dark. The banks are closed now, but if you want to come back in the morning . . ."

Billie wanted to mention the miracle of ATMs, but Nathan had asked her to stay quietly in the car, so she bit her lip.

"That's fine," Nathan said, as Wendell knew he would.

The car dealer pulled two crisp one-hundred-dollar bills from his pocket and they exchanged keys.

"Do I need to sign anything?" Nathan asked.

"Naw," Wendell said with a shake of his head. "I like to keep paperwork to a minimum."

Nathan nodded, then walked around and opened Billie's door. After she got out, he reached inside to retrieve his suitcase and the map. Once the car was cleaned out, he led the way to the truck.

"You've made a wise choice," Wendell assured them as he followed along behind. "This is a fine vehicle. Almost hate to let it go." He frowned as if he was beginning to regret the decision to sell the old truck. "Pleasure doing business with you!" He called out as they climbed into the truck. Nathan gave the man a vague wave, then started the truck and headed toward the entrance to the interstate.

"I know he had more cash than he gave us." Billie glared at the vanishing figure of Wendell in the rearview mirror. "And the car was worth *much* more than this thing."

"We weren't in a position to negotiate," Nathan reminded her. Once they were on the outskirts of Montgomery, he said, "I think we should call your friend Edgar again."

Billie frowned at this suggestion. "That didn't work out very well the last time."

Nathan looked over at her. "If Edgar's involved with the people who are trying to kill us, we can buy ourselves some breathing room by giving him false information."

"I hate to think that Edgar is trying to kill me," Billie whispered.

"He may not be directly involved, but it's possible that our pursuers are monitoring his phone calls. Either way it might help us."

Billie was impressed. "That's a good idea. I might use that in a book sometime, if you don't mind."

"Robert Ludlum already has." She pulled a face, and he smiled. "But I'll bet Regina St. Claire has some interesting plot twists of her own. When I get back to Utah, I'm going to order the whole collection."

Billie gave him a weak smile. The mental picture of him at home in Utah was not a particularly happy one, even if he was reading her books while there. A few minutes later, Nathan pulled into a busy gas station and parked beside a pay phone. Once again, he stood beside her as she dialed Edgar's number.

The call was answered promptly, but not by Edgar. "This is Conrad Lockhart," the voice on the other end identified himself.

"Oh, Mr. Lockhart," Billie said. "It's Billie. I'm sorry to bother you at a time like this, but I really need to speak to Edgar."

"Edgar is unavailable at the moment, but I'll be glad to help you," Mr. Lockhart offered.

"Oh, I couldn't ask you . . ."

"I insist."

Billie covered the receiver and whispered to Nathan, "It's Mr. Lockhart, Camille's uncle. He says that Edgar is unavailable."

"Stick with the plan," Nathan whispered back.

Billie chewed her lip for a second, then said, "I'm in a bind and Edgar was going to wire me some money."

"I can handle that if you'll give me your current location."

"I've got enough to last for a little while. I'm headed to Miami, and as soon as I get there I'll call back. Then we can arrange to have some money wired."

"I'll be waiting to hear from you," Mr. Lockhart said.

"Thank you," Billie replied. "And when you see Edgar, tell him I called."

"I will," Mr. Lockhart agreed. "I'd really like to talk to you about Camille, if you have time."

Nathan tapped his watch and Billie cleared her throat. "I'm so sorry, Mr. Lockhart, but I really can't right now. I'll call back later."

She hung up the phone quickly and turned to Nathan. "I wonder where Edgar is?"

"I'm sure Mr. Lockhart will get the information to him."

"I really hope Edgar isn't one of the criminals," Billie admitted.

"Remember Cowboy's advice—trust no one."

She raised an eyebrow. "What about you?"

He pulled a lock of her shorter, darker hair. "I'm getting shot at as much as you are. That proves my innocence." He reached over her and put some more coins into the pay phone.

"Who are you calling?"

"I thought as long as we've risked detection, I might check my voice mail and see if Kip has been found."

Billie waited while Nathan listened to his messages.

"Well?" she prompted, and he shook his head.

"Kip's still missing."

"Now can I check my voice mail?" she asked, and he handed her the phone. After she had listened to her messages, she hung up and looked at Nathan. "I had an urgent message from an Agent Loring Gray of the FBI office in Atlanta. He said that my friend Cowboy worked for the Treasury Department and they believe me about the GFL. He wants to talk to me—said it's a matter of life and death. Should we risk another phone call?"

Nathan frowned. "Not from here. Let's drive south for a few miles, like we're on our way to Miami. Then we'll stop at another pay phone. After our call to the FBI, we'll head . . . anywhere but toward Miami."

They drove for about an hour then stopped just outside of a city called Troy to make their phone call. Since it was close to nine o'clock, Billie didn't expect the FBI agent to answer, but he did.

"Miss Murphy," Agent Gray said in salutation. "I'm so glad to hear from you."

"I'd like to talk to Cowboy," she requested.

"I'm afraid the man you know as Cowboy is unaccounted for and feared dead," Agent Gray told her solemnly. "More lives, including your own, could be lost if we don't stop the criminals behind the GFL. That's why it's imperative that you return to Atlanta immediately."

"What good will that do?" Billie asked.

"If you'll give me a statement, we might be able to get a judge to issue a search warrant for the GFL offices."

"I don't have any actual proof," Billie explained. "Just what I can remember about an e-mail Cowboy sent me. And we're afraid to come back to Atlanta. Someone, I guess the GFL, is trying to kill us, and by returning to Atlanta we'd be putting ourselves within their reach."

"The FBI will guarantee your safety," Agent Gray assured her.

"How will you do that?" she asked.

Billie glanced at Nathan, who mouthed the words, *Trust no one.* She nodded, then concentrated on Agent Gray again.

"I'm sorry, but I can't do that. As much as I want to help you stop the GFL, my main concern right now is staying alive."

"I understand your concerns, and I want very much to keep you alive as well. However, if you don't cooperate with us, there is little I can do to protect you from the criminals or from any legal action the state of Georgia or the federal government may decide to take."

"Are you threatening me?" she asked.

"I'm *warning* you, Miss Murphy. You need to come to Atlanta immediately."

Billie chewed her lip as she looked to Nathan. He shrugged, then whispered, "It's up to you."

Finally Billie frowned at the phone. "I'll call back," she promised and hung up. Once they were back in the old truck, she said, "I can't defy the federal government. It goes against everything I believe in."

"We've prayed for guidance and safety," Nathan reminded her. "Maybe Agent Gray can provide both."

She nodded. "I guess there's only one way to find out. We'll go to Atlanta."

"Now?" Nathan asked.

"Yes, but I think we should take the long way."

Nathan smiled. "You're good at that."

She gave him a quick smirk as she picked up the map. "If the GFL people think we're going to Miami, we might be able to slip into Atlanta unnoticed." She studied the available routes and finally said, "Take 29. That will take us to the Georgia state line. Once we reach Eureka, we can figure out how to approach Atlanta."

He gave her an approving look. "You're a brave girl."

She shook her head. "I'm just trying to impress you."

He reached over and stroked her cheek. "I'm impressed. Now get some sleep."

* * *

The phone in the storage room rang, and Felix Hummer picked up the receiver.

"They've made contact with the Atlanta PD and the FBI," a voice reported.

Hummer cursed harshly, then spoke into the phone. "How much of a threat do they pose to us?"

"As long as they're on the run, very little. Now if they come in . . ."

"We've got to move quickly to prevent that. Arrange warrants for their arrest in connection with the deaths of Camille Lockhart and Jeff Burdick. By the end of the day, I want everyone in Georgia looking for them."

* * *

Billie guided Nathan to Eureka by using a series of back roads, and they arrived just after midnight. They found a motel on the outskirts of town and checked in.

"Not quite as nice as the place we stayed in last time we were here," Nathan said as he escorted Billie to her room.

She looked around and shivered.

"I'll turn up the heater," he said as he walked over and adjusted the unit under the window. "You want me to find a fast-food place and get us something to eat?"

Billie shook her head. "No thanks."

"Too tired to eat?" he asked with a sympathetic smile.

She nodded vaguely, unwilling to tell him that her feelings of anxiety were growing stronger the closer they got to Atlanta.

On Thursday morning, Nathan let Billie sleep in until almost noon. Then they ate lunch at Wendy's and headed east on Highway

82. "I thought we'd go as far as Dawson, then take 188 for a few miles and kind of meander toward Atlanta."

Billie nodded her consent. "Aren't we pretty close to Hugh and Thelma's dairy farm?" she asked.

"I think so," he confirmed. "They're probably packing their bags and getting ready to move out of that dump."

"I'm glad things are turning out well for someone," she said, staring out the window. "It sure is getting foggy," she added after a few minutes.

"Foggy?" Nathan repeated. He looked out her window, then swerved off the road. "That's not fog! It's smoke. Get out of the truck quick!"

Once Billie was standing several feet away from the smoking vehicle, Nathan used a T-shirt from his suitcase to protect his hand as he opened the hood. They could see flames mixed in with the smoke, and it all seemed to be coming from the engine. Billie used what was left of a bottle of water to douse the fire and they stood in unified dejection, watching the engine hiss and sizzle.

A cold wind whipped around them, and Billie pulled her coat tightly around her. "Would it be safe to wait inside while we try to figure out what to do?"

Nathan nodded, his face grim. "This is all my fault," he told her as they settled in the cab of the old truck.

She had to laugh. "*Your* fault? If it wasn't for me, you'd be back in Salt Lake installing expensive security systems right now."

"But once I decided to stay with you, I accepted responsibility for your safety. And I picked this miserable excuse for a vehicle."

Billie gave him a stern look. "I'm responsible for myself, and there wasn't a car on Wendell's lot that was any more dependable than this one. That's just one of the hazards of dealing with crooks."

They sat in silence until a new red truck pulled up beside them. The driver introduced himself as Ray Waltman and told them he owned the only service station within ten miles. "A passing motorist saw you pulled off on the side of the road and called me." He offered to look under the hood of their truck, and they accepted gratefully. After a few minutes he stepped back, shaking his head. "I'm not a mechanic," Mr. Waltman qualified his remarks, "but this thing is leaking oil like crazy. That's what caused your fire. The hoses are full of holes, patched up with electrical tape." He closed the hood. "You might be able to sell it as salvage, but I don't think you'll be able to drive this much farther."

"Where's the closest bus station?" Nathan asked with a sigh.

Mr. Waltman pointed to the east. "Dawson. About another twenty miles."

Nathan frowned. "You think it will make it that far?"

Mr. Waltman scratched his head and shrugged. "Maybe. Don't go more than about thirty miles per hour, and I'll follow you just in case."

"We couldn't ask you to do that," Nathan replied.

"I'm having kind of a slow morning anyway," the service station owner claimed as he swung up into his truck.

They made slow progress toward Dawson and had just parked in front of the bus station when the truck sputtered to a stop. "I only asked the Lord to get us this far," Billie told Nathan, and he smiled.

"No sense in asking for more than you need."

Nathan tried to give Mr. Waltman twenty-five dollars for his time, but the man wouldn't take it. "There's been plenty of times in my life when someone has held out a helping hand," he told them. "I'm glad I was able to do the same for you folks."

After they thanked him, Mr. Waltman drove off. Then Nathan and Billie walked into the bus station.

"What about the truck?" Billie asked.

"We'll just leave it there. After Saturday, I'll arrange to have it towed," Nathan replied as he approached the ticket counter and bought two one-way tickets to Miami.

"Why are we buying tickets to Miami with our limited funds?" Billie asked as they took seats in the waiting room. "Since we're going to Atlanta?"

Nathan glanced around before answering, "Just in case anyone tracks us this far, we want them to think we're headed to Miami. We'll wait here until they call our bus, then we'll walk out like we're getting on it."

"But what will we really do?"

"I've been thinking that we might call the Warrens since we're close to their farm. We could spend the night with them and maybe they'd loan us their car to get to Atlanta," Nathan said as they found seats in the waiting room.

As Billie considered this, she noticed a man across the room. She was certain that he had been staring at them, but when she made eye contact, he looked away. Leaning closer to Nathan, she whispered, "That man over there is watching us."

Nathan picked up a newspaper that had been abandoned in the empty seat beside him as he glanced over at the culprit. "Just ignore him," he advised. A few seconds later, he added, "I think I know why we're drawing attention." He held the newspaper over for Billie to see.

On the front page of the *Atlanta Constitution* were pictures of both Nathan and Billie. Nathan still had long, blond hair and she still had very long brown hair. "What does it say?" she gasped.

"We're wanted by the Atlanta Police Department for questioning in the deaths of Camille Lockhart and Jeff Burdick."

Billie felt all the air desert her lungs. As terrible as it had been to be pursued by criminals, the thought of being on the wrong side of the law was much worse. "What are we going to do?"

Nathan put a calming hand on her shoulder. "Let me think for a minute." Billie concentrated on breathing until he said, "I want you to get up and walk outside. Cross the street and meet me over there by that laundromat."

Billie narrowed her eyes at him. "Let me guess—you're going to stay here?"

"Just for a few minutes, then I'll follow."

"If I didn't know better, I'd think you were trying to get rid of me," she muttered.

"But you do know better," he said, inclining his head at the door.

Billie took a deep, shuddering breath as she stood, but before she could take a step, he reached out and caught her hand.

"If something keeps me from joining you, call Agent Gray." He took the pen from his pocket and carefully copied the number from the back of his hand onto one of the bus tickets before holding it out to her.

She folded the ticket and stuffed it in her jeans pocket. Their eyes met, and Billie bit her lower lip. "I don't want to leave you." In just a few short days, he had become incredibly dear to her.

"We'll be together again in a few minutes," he whispered. She gave him a look that she hoped expressed some of her feelings for him. He winked and nudged her gently toward the door.

Billie walked out the front entrance of the bus station and across the street, firmly resisting the urge to look behind her. Once inside the laundromat, she found a seat in a corner and waited for Nathan, her eyes focused on the door. After about five tension-filled minutes, he pushed open the door and motioned for her to join him. She stepped out into the cold December air and clasped his hand.

"I don't know when I've been so glad to see anyone," she told him. "Were you followed?"

"I don't think so, but let's get out of here just to be sure."

They walked down the street to a grocery store. Once they were inside and hidden by rows of canned goods, Nathan faced her. "Now that our pictures are on the front page of the newspaper, we've got to get off the street. Since we can't rent a car, I guess we'll have to call Hugh and Thelma Warren and ask them to come and get us. How far is their farm from here?"

Billie pulled the map from his bag and checked it. "They're about ten miles west on Highway 32."

"Good. It won't take them long to get here."

Nathan took her hand and led her to a public phone near the entrance. He called information, got the Warrens' number, and dialed. After he listened for a few seconds, the tension drained from his face and was replaced by irritation. "I got their answering machine," he whispered as he hung up. "We can't keep hanging around here. I guess we'll have to walk."

They bought sunglasses and baseball caps to further disguise themselves, then started down Highway 32.

"Ten miles?" Nathan confirmed.

"Maybe twelve." She gave him the best smile she could manage with numb lips. "At the end of which we'll both have frostbite."

"I live in Utah—I'm used to the cold. Now you, on the other hand, are a hothouse flower."

She raised an eyebrow. "Are you trying to make me mad?"

He shrugged. "I thought a little righteous indignation might help keep you warm."

"I don't think I *could* get mad at you," she told him, careful to keep her tone light and teasing.

He reached for her hand and tucked it with his inside his coat pocket.

After a few minutes, she asked, "What will we tell the Warrens?"

"Everything. It wouldn't be right to involve them otherwise."

"Then we'll borrow their car and head for Atlanta?"

"They might even loan us a little money."

"I'll write them a check, and they can cash it on Monday." Billie wondered if the Chamber would cover any of the expenses she was incurring on this little side trip.

"I hope we won't be putting the Warrens in danger," he said slowly.

Billie was philosophical. "We're out of options, Nathan."

It was almost ten o'clock before they reached the Warrens' farm, and all the lights were off in the ramshackle house. "It looks much more inviting now than it did a week ago," Billie whispered through chattering teeth.

Nathan pulled her against him and held her fiercely. "If we slept in the barn, we wouldn't have to wake them," he said against her ear.

She looked doubtfully at the dilapidated building. "Do you think it's any warmer in there that it is out here?"

He laughed. "Only one way to find out."

It was marginally warmer inside the barn since the wind was not a factor, but Billie could still see her breath.

"Look around for anything useful," Nathan advised.

She moved carefully, afraid she was going to find rodents and snakes who considered the old barn their home. She had just discovered a flashlight and two blankets when Nathan called quietly for her to join him at the back of the barn.

"This must have been the dispensary where they treated sick animals," he said, excitement on the edge of his voice.

Billie looked around at the huge metal sink and scarred wooden table. Then she saw the kerosene heater in the corner and smiled. "If it doesn't blow up when we light it, we're in business."

The heater didn't blow up, and soon the small room was nice and warm. Nathan brought in some hay and Billie spread out the blankets. Then they sat close together in front of the heater. Billie shined the flashlight's weak beam into Nathan's face.

"We could tell ghost stories," she suggested.

He rubbed his cheek against hers. "I don't scare easily."

"Or you could tell me about Diana."

He was quiet for a second, then said, "I already have."

Billie frowned in confusion before understanding dawned. "Diana was your mother."

"Yes."

"She broke your heart *and* taught you not to trust women."

"Yes."

Billie gave a contented sigh and settled closer to him. "Good."

He raised an eyebrow. "Good?"

"I'd rather compete with your mother than with another woman. It gives me hope."

He shook his head, but she could see a little smile at the corners of his mouth. Then he looked around the dreary little room. "Every time I think that things can't get worse, they do," he said, his tone discouraged.

"The smell's not so bad if you breathe through your mouth," Billie told him. "We need to get some sleep. You're exhausted."

"If I fall asleep, who's going to protect you from men with guns and from field mice and cockroaches?"

She shuddered as she closed her eyes. "You're right. Stay awake and prove you're a real man."

CHAPTER 10

Conrad Lockhart walked into the storage room without knocking. "Miss Murphy and Mr. Turner are headed to Miami," he reported, the relief obvious in his voice.

"You've confirmed that."

Conrad nodded. "The FBI tried to get them to come in, but Miss Murphy stalled. Apparently they're just going to hide until after Saturday night."

"So neither of them has a social conscience," Hummer said thoughtfully. "They're just going to let thousands of people lose their money—many lives devastated and fortunes ruined."

"That's the way it looks," Conrad agreed.

Hummer was silent for a few seconds, then nodded. "Let me know as soon as you have an exact location for our fugitives."

As the older man left the storage room, Hummer reached for the phone and dialed a familiar number. When the call was answered he asked, "Murphy and Turner are supposedly heading for Miami to hide out until after the festivities on Saturday."

"Supposedly?"

"I don't believe it. Watch all the roads that lead to Atlanta. I have a feeling they'll come back here and try to help the FBI close us down."

"They'd have to be crazy to risk driving into Atlanta."

Hummer glanced down at the copy of the *Atlanta Constitution* on the old desk. "Crazy or not, that's what I think they'll do. The press coverage has been good. Now I want roadblocks. These people need to be a nonissue by tomorrow."

"It's as good as done," the voice assured him.

Hummer hung up the phone and sighed. It was such a pleasure to be working with professionals again.

* * *

When Billie woke up on Friday morning, the little dispensary was cold. Apparently the heater had run out of kerosene during the night. Nathan was lying on the blanket beside her, and he looked young and unguarded in the early morning light. She reached out and touched his cheek as she watched him sleep, his mouth open slightly.

"Well, well, what do we have here?" a voice from behind her startled a little scream from Billie's throat. Nathan's eyes flew open, and they both jumped up. Hugh Warren was standing a few feet away, his hands on his hips. "I know I told you to come by and visit if you were in the area, but I meant for you to sleep in the *house*!" he emphasized.

"We got here late and didn't want to wake you," Billie explained, pulling hay from her hair.

Hugh wasn't smiling. "I read the papers," he told them. "But I wouldn't need to do that to know all about the trouble you're in. Now the television stations have picked up the story. You're on every channel."

"We didn't kill anyone," Billie said with conviction. "But the same people who killed Jeff Burdick and Camille Lockhart are trying to kill us."

"So we need to leave soon," Nathan added, looking toward the open door of the barn.

"Just the fact that we've been here could cause you problems," Billie agreed.

"Do you have a car we could borrow?" Nathan asked. "If anyone questions you about it, you could say we stole it."

"And could you loan us some money?" Billie added. "We'll pay you back."

"Whoa!" Mr. Warren held up a hand. "We'll get you whatever you need, but right now Thelma's got breakfast cooked, so come inside and tell us the whole story."

They followed the old man into the house. Thelma was in the kitchen and gave them both rib-crushing hugs, then settled them around the table. "Oh, if I'd known we were going to have company I'd have fixed something special!" she exclaimed as she heaped eggs and bacon and fluffy biscuits onto their plates. "Hugh, pour them some orange juice and coffee."

"No coffee, thanks," Nathan said. "But the orange juice sounds great."

"For me too," Billie added with a smile.

Once they had more food on their plates than they could eat in a week, they began telling their story. Thelma and Hugh would interrupt occasionally to clarify a point, but mostly they just listened with serious expressions.

"So now what?" Hugh asked when they were finished.

"The FBI has asked me to come in to their office in Atlanta," Billie said slowly. "I don't think we have much choice but to comply."

"If we can get to the FBI agent we've been talking to, I think he can stop all the accusations about us being involved with the criminals," Nathan added.

"At this point, the FBI may be the only protection we're likely to get."

Thelma shook her head. "Sounds like dangerous business to me."

Billie ran a hand through her matted hair. "For the last few days, just breathing has been dangerous for us."

"Seems to me like we've got to figure out a safe way to get you into Atlanta," Hugh said.

"The first thing we need to do is get them cleaned up and out of those dirty clothes," Thelma amended, wrinkling her nose.

Billie looked down at the straw still clinging to her flea-market clothing. "A hot shower sounds wonderful," she admitted.

Thelma stood and pulled Billie's chair back from the table. "You come with me."

Billie had the feeling that Nathan and Hugh were waiting for the women to leave before they discussed the more alarming aspects of their situation, but she was anxious for a shower, so she let Thelma lead her out of the kitchen.

The bathroom, like the kitchen, showed signs of care that weren't apparent in other areas of the house. Billie took a warm shower in comfort. After drying off, she put on the terry-cloth bathrobe provided by Thelma, then went down to the living room so that Nathan could take a shower.

"That's cute," Nathan said quietly as he studied the baggy robe that dragged on the ground. "Quite a fashion statement."

"Lately I've taken a lot of pride in my appearance," Billie responded with a roll of her eyes.

"Did you use up all the hot water?" he asked as he moved past her.

"I tried," she replied, and he gave her a quick smile over his shoulder.

Billie sat on the lumpy couch as Hugh came in from the kitchen and turned on the television. "Our reception out here's terrible, but you can at least listen." He switched several channels. "Not the news." Finally he settled on a game show.

Thelma rushed by with her arms full of their dirty clothes. She went into the kitchen, and minutes later Billie heard the washing machine start a cycle. Thelma came back with an afghan, which she tucked around Billie's legs, then offered to fix her a cup of hot chocolate.

"Thanks, but I'm so full after breakfast I may never be able to eat again. And I forgot to tell you that the sack lunch you fixed for us in Columbus probably kept us from starving."

"Just a couple of sandwiches!" Thelma cried. "If I'd have known what a mess you were in, I would have packed much more!"

Nathan walked in then, dressed in the sweatpants and T-shirt Billie had been using for pajamas. He sat beside Billie on the couch, and she spread one side of the afghan over him. Thelma watched this procedure and turned shrewd eyes back to Billie. "So, how long have you two known each other?"

"Almost two weeks," Billie replied, smiling at Nathan. "But it seems much longer."

Before Thelma could ask any more questions, Hugh came back in from outside and sat in a chair across from the couch. "I didn't see anyone," he reported. "So far I think you're safe here."

"We need to move on, just in case."

"You can't go until your clothes are dry," Thelma pointed out.

"And you need to have a plan," Hugh added. "With all this media coverage, if you try to just drive into Atlanta, you'll be arrested for sure."

"As long as it's the police who catch them, won't they be okay?" Thelma asked.

"There's no way to be sure. We were warned to trust no one," Nathan told her grimly. "So we assume that means that the criminals have people everywhere."

"And once we're in jail, we'd be easy targets," Billie added.

Hugh leaned forward and gave Nathan three hundred dollars in small bills. "This is all the cash we have, but we can go into town and get more."

Nathan shook his head. "This should be fine. We'll get the money back to you next week."

"I'm not worried about that," Hugh assured him. "You can take our car, and we'll pick it up on Sunday."

"That'll be a long trip for you," Nathan said with a frown.

"And how will you pick it up?" Billie asked. "Do you have another car?"

Thelma laughed. "No, but we have a hog."

Hugh seemed to think this was very funny. Billie and Nathan stared at both of them in confusion. "She means a motorcycle. This weekend there's a Harley Davidson convention in Atlanta, and me and Thelma are going. We can swing by and pick up the car on our way home."

"You and Thelma ride a motorcycle?"

"Not as often as we'd like, but we try to attend the big events— like the one on Saturday. We're meeting several of our friends in Americus and caravaning over."

A crazy idea started to form in Billie's mind. She glanced over at Nathan and saw the beginnings of a smile playing at the corners of his mouth. "What would you think about Billie and me riding the motor-cycle into Atlanta?" Nathan asked the Warrens. "I don't think anyone would even think to look for us in a group of motorcycle riders."

Hugh smiled. "You couldn't recognize your own grandmother if she was wearing a helmet and a leather jacket."

"You and Thelma could follow in the car. Once we get to Atlanta, we'll pull over and switch. You two can go on to the Harley party while we drive to the FBI office."

"Well, what do you think, Thelma?" Hugh asked his wife.

She grinned at their guests. "I think Billie and Nathan are in for the ride of their lives."

Since the motorcycle escort wouldn't be leaving for Atlanta until early Saturday morning, Billie and Nathan agreed to stay with the Warrens until then. Billie slept a good part of the day, but noticed that Nathan checked the windows constantly.

Hugh and Thelma ordered pizza for dinner, and Nathan insisted that he and Billie be completely out of sight when the delivery person came. After he left, though, they gorged on pizza and laughed at Hugh's outrageous stories.

When dinner was over, Thelma came into the kitchen carrying a big bottle of peroxide. "I think we need to lighten your hair a little more, Billie. And probably cut it short."

Nathan looked like he wanted to protest, but Thelma wouldn't hear of it.

"Billie can't wear the helmet after she gets off the motorcycle, and pictures of her with long, dark hair are all over the news."

Nathan sighed. "You're right."

Thelma went to work on Billie and entertained both her and Nathan during the process by telling them about a special she had seen on Lifetime TV. "It was all about people who were supposed to be in the Twin Towers on 9-11, but were delayed for some miraculous reason," Thelma told them.

She described several incredible incidences, and finally Nathan asked, "Were all these cases substantiated?"

"Heck no!" Hugh cried in disgust. "It was just a bunch of liars who wanted to get on television."

"Well, I don't know why you'd say that, Hugh Warren," Thelma defended the participants. "They also interviewed a man who missed the bombing of the federal building in Oklahoma by minutes, and two old ladies who had tickets for the Titanic but lost them . . ."

Hugh hooted with laughter. "The Titanic! Now I know that was a lie. They would probably be over a hundred years old."

"It is mathematically unlikely," Nathan told Thelma.

Thelma led Billie to the kitchen sink to rinse out the peroxide. "Well, no matter what you say, it was very heartwarming and shows that miracles can still happen."

"The fact that Nathan and I are still alive is proof of that," Billie said as the warm water ran into her ears and down her neck.

Thelma wrapped Billie's head in a thick towel. "You have a seat at the table," she told her. "I'll be right back."

"You want to know what will be a miracle?" Hugh asked once his wife had disappeared through the kitchen door. "It will be a miracle if Billie has any hair left after Thelma gets through with her."

Before either Billie or Nathan could respond, Thelma returned with a blow-dryer. She plugged it in and dried Billie's hair. When she was finished, she handed Billie a small mirror. "Wow," Billie said, staring at her reflection.

"You look just like that Meg Ryan!" Thelma cried, obviously pleased.

Billie turned to Nathan, anxious to get his reaction. "I don't know about that, but it's nice," he told her with a smile.

"You better watch out Nathan," Hugh warned. "If I wasn't a married man, I'd be tempted to give you a run for your money."

Billie laughed as Thelma hit her husband on the shoulder. "Hush up, you crazy old man. Don't you tease Nathan."

Hugh reached out and grabbed his wife around her waist. "You want to go upstairs and bleach my hair, Thelma?"

"You don't have enough hair left to bother with," she replied primly. "But we should leave these young folks in peace. Let's go on to bed."

Hugh followed his wife but smiled at them over his shoulder. "That's just an excuse to get me alone," he claimed.

They heard Thelma hit him again as he walked out the door.

Billie and Nathan exchanged an amused look, then walked into the den, and Nathan turned on the television. Their options were limited, so they finally settled on a rerun of *Walker, Texas Ranger*.

"On television the good guys always win," Billie commented as the criminals were rounded up and taken to jail.

"It's not like that in real life," Nathan replied. "I learned that lesson early."

After the program ended, Billie said, "I'd forgotten why I don't like TV. Now I remember." She glanced up to see Nathan watching her closely. "You keep staring at me. Does my new hair look that awful?"

"No, actually, it's really cute. Even better than Meg Ryan's."

Her fingers reached up and rubbed the short hair above his neck. "I miss your curls," she told him. "I can hardly wait for it to grow out so I can cut it again."

He made a face. "I'll never grow my hair out again, and the circumstances under which I'd let you cut it . . ." He shook his head. "Even after the last few days, I can't imagine being so desperate."

She laughed, then her fingers moved down and traced the small scar under his left eye. "How did you get this?"

He leaned back against the couch and drew her close to him. "When I was little I concentrated on survival. While my mother was entertaining I stayed hidden, no matter what. But right after my tenth birthday, I woke up to the sounds of fighting. When I heard glass break, I went to investigate. My mother's latest boyfriend had a broken Coke bottle and was threatening to rearrange her face. I told him to get out of our house, and he decided to teach me a lesson. I was lucky I only ended up with a few cuts and bruises. But the real interesting part of the story is that even though I had blood dripping off my chin, my mother left with her boyfriend, crying and apologizing to him as they went. It was a neighbor who took me to the local clinic and got my face stitched up."

"She had something wrong with her, Nathan," Billie told him softly. "Maybe it was the drinking or the drugs or a chemical imbalance or a mental illness. Whatever it was, it was *her* problem. There was nothing wrong with you."

"I understand that now, but when I was a kid it just seemed like I had to try harder to make her love me."

"You had a lot of responsibility for a little boy."

"Some guys have all the luck."

"But it made you strong," she pointed out. "Strong enough to survive the last few days and save my life in the process."

"Growing up like that might have left me damaged," he said carefully. "Like my parents. That's why I feel that living alone is my only choice."

"*Choice* is the operative word there, Nathan. You do have a choice."

They were quiet for a while, and finally Billie sighed. "We need to pray about our motorcycle plan."

"Is it your turn?" he asked.

"I've lost track," she told him with a smile. "Why don't you do the honors?"

After the prayer, they both felt that the plan was a good one. Relieved, Billie snuggled against him and said, "I'm anxious to see the new scanner my parents got me for Christmas." Then she paused as she realized the significance of her recent apartment robbery. "Although I won't be able to actually use it until I can afford a new computer."

"Maybe the police will be able to recover your old one," Nathan suggested.

"Or maybe Santa can bring me one next year."

"Aren't you a little old to believe in Santa?" Nathan asked with a smile.

"You never get too old for Christmas," she assured him. "Next year you can come visit us for the holidays, and we'll show you how it's done." She was careful to word the invitation casually, with no strings attached, and was pleased when he nodded.

"Sounds like fun."

She pulled her feet up onto the couch. "What did get your little brother for Christmas?"

"A savings bond," Nathan responded. "If I send him one for his birthday and Christmas every year, he should have a nice nest egg by the time he gets ready for college."

Billie twisted around so she could face him. "And nest eggs are *so* important to toddlers. Knowing they'll have some money when they start college makes them feel all loved and warm inside."

She sensed Nathan stiffening. "Someday he'll be glad I gave him the bonds instead of a bunch of toys that just end up broken."

"I'm not saying you shouldn't send the bonds," Billie clarified. "Planning for the future is important, especially since he doesn't have a father. But you should also send him a truck or a puzzle or a Tickle Me Elmo."

Nathan looked horrified. "I've never bought a toy in my life! I wouldn't even know where to begin."

"Toy shopping doesn't require much. All you'd have to do is go to a store and look at the boxes. They list the ages that each toy is appropriate for right on the front." She narrowed her eyes at him. "But I don't think that's why you settled for a savings bond." He wouldn't look at her, which convinced her that she was right. "A toy would have been too personal. As long as Cody remains a name on a bond—not a real flesh-and-blood boy—you can hold him at a distance."

"Of course he's real," Nathan said impatiently. "But he's got a mother to buy him toys for Christmas, and there's a great deal of distance between us, physically and emotionally."

"The distance isn't a big deal, and he's also got a brother. An irresponsible one."

Nathan sat up straight at this accusation. "I may be a lot of things, but irresponsible isn't one of them."

"Tell that to your little brother who's only seen you once and spent Christmas Day admiring the savings bond you sent him!"

"I don't want to talk about this anymore," Nathan told her firmly.

"I'll just bet you don't."

His eyes narrowed. "You can be very . . . aggravating."

"So my brothers tell me," she acknowledged.

He sighed. "This might be our last night alone together for a while, and I don't want to waste it fighting."

Billie took a deep breath. "What are we going to do if we can't fight? We can't talk about the future since we don't have one. We can't talk about the GFL since soon there won't be one. We don't want to watch television, and we've eaten all the pizza."

Nathan gathered her close. "Maybe we could just sit here quietly and enjoy each other's company."

She knew she shouldn't give in, but with a sigh, Billie relaxed against him. After a few minutes she said, "Nathan, would you say that during the past couple of days you have been under extreme stress?"

He nodded, his chin rubbing against her hair.

"You've been afraid and worried and frustrated," she continued.

He pulled away so he could look down into her face. "Not to mention enraged and guilt ridden," he agreed.

"And during this awful time, have you ever once felt the urge to take out your frustrations on me?"

A frown furrowed his brow as he considered this. "No. If anything, just the opposite was true. I felt even more determined to keep you safe."

Billie smiled. "Then I think you have proof that you're not like your mother, and you have a little inkling of how your father must have felt, knowing you were in a bad situation but helpless to save you."

She waited for him to reply, but instead he just pulled her back against his chest. Satisfied that she had scored an important point, she snuggled against him and closed her eyes.

* * *

On Saturday morning, Thelma woke Billie before dawn. "I hope you slept good, honey," Thelma said as she opened the old drapes to let in a little morning light. "Hugh and Nathan are downstairs eating breakfast and discussing their strategy for today." Thelma rolled her eyes. "Heaven help you if Hugh Warren is plotting your course. He was in the Korean War and thinks he knows all about military maneuvers." Thelma leaned close. "But just between you and me, his memory isn't what it used to be."

Billie sat up in the bed and smiled. "I'm sure Nathan will help him keep it simple."

Thelma nodded, then looked around with a worried expression. "I wish I'd had a chance to fix up a little before you came."

This time Billie laughed. "Oh, Thelma, if you could have seen some of the hotels we've stayed in, you'd realize that this room was a dream come true."

Thelma didn't look comforted. "Well, when we get moved into our new place, you'll have to come stay with us again so I can redeem myself."

Billie stood and approached the older woman. "I'll definitely come to see you, but not to take advantage of your hospitality again. I'll come to visit my dear friends."

Thelma smiled, then patted Billie on the back. "Well, for right now you need to get dressed and eat some breakfast. Your blue jeans are all washed and ironed," she said, waving toward a rocking chair in the corner. "I'll wait for you downstairs."

When Billie walked into the kitchen, Nathan and Hugh were staring at a small television set. Nathan reached over to turn it off, but Billie saw her own face and stopped him. "What are they saying about us?"

"They found the truck we left in Dawson," Nathan told her reluctantly. "They interviewed the local sheriff, and he said we bought tickets to Miami and they are checking now to see if we used them."

"How long will it be before they know we didn't?"

Nathan frowned. "They've probably already figured that out."

The general mood was solemn as they ate and prepared to leave. Thelma gave Billie a black leather jacket. "That's Hugh's," she said. "We figure it will fit you, and Nathan is going to wear mine."

Once Billie and Nathan had the jackets on, they walked out to the barn where the Harley was parked. "I liked to ride dirt bikes in college," Nathan said as Hugh approached the big motorcycle.

"That's like comparing a Volkswagen to a Cadillac," Hugh replied with a disparaging wave of his hand.

Nathan smiled. "But they both do drive pretty much the same."

Hugh gave Nathan a crash course in the operation of a Harley Davidson. Finally, when he started to repeat himself, Thelma stepped in.

"That's enough, Hugh. If there's anything you haven't told him, the boy can figure it out for himself."

"Can I take it for a test-drive?" Nathan asked, and Hugh nodded reluctantly. Nathan started the engine, and the sound reverberated on the walls of the barn. As he drove outside, the back of the motorcycle fishtailed in the straw.

Billie stood with the Warrens, listening to the sound of the engine in the distance. "I hope he's not having so much fun that he forgets we've got to leave," she muttered.

"Riding a Harley can be addicting," Thelma told her with a smile.

Hugh walked over to the barn door and watched Nathan. When the older man came back to stand beside the women, all traces of his earlier anxiety were gone. "The boy's a natural. He'll be fine."

Nathan returned a few minutes later, and Hugh helped Billie onto the seat behind him. "You follow us," Hugh told them. "Thelma will be watching out the back window in case one of you falls off."

Nathan waited as the Warrens went out of the barn and got into their Buick sedan. When the car moved toward the road, Nathan gunned the Harley's engine and took off. Billie clutched his midsection and held on for dear life.

A few miles out of Americus they passed two police cars headed back toward Dawson. Their lights were flashing, and Billie's heart skipped a beat.

"Looks like we got out just in time," Nathan hollered, and she nodded against the soft leather of his jacket.

Finally Thelma and Hugh pulled into a Cracker Barrel. Since hundreds of motorcycles dotted the parking lot, Billie assumed this was the meeting place for the Harley caravan. After Nathan parked the motorcycle behind the Buick, Hugh rushed back to check out his beloved machine. While her husband determined that the Harley was unharmed, Thelma introduced Billie and Nathan to the president of the Joy Riders Club.

Billie was expecting someone with long hair, numerous tattoos, and lots of gold jewelry, but the president was an oral surgeon from Columbus named Ed Potter. His hair was gray and sparse, he didn't have any visible tattoos, and the only jewelry he was wearing was a simple wedding band.

Thelma began an explanation of their plight, but Ed held up a hand. "The less I know about that, the better. I don't want to get our group into any trouble with the law, but you're welcome to ride along with us," he said. The unspoken *but if the police stop us you're on your own* was clear.

Mr. Potter introduced them to the other club members, and since Nathan was a relatively inexperienced rider they arranged for him to have a "protected" position in the pack. Once they were mixed in with over a hundred cyclists, Billie felt blessedly anonymous. She relaxed against Nathan and actually enjoyed the ride into Atlanta until they came to a roadblock.

Billie felt Nathan tense as they approached the line of police cars. The cyclists pulled to a stop in a tight group, and Billie wondered if they were trying to hide them. Thelma and Hugh had to pull over and the Buick was searched, but amazingly the officers waved the bikers through.

Weak with relief, Billie leaned back against Nathan. Thelma and Hugh caught back up a few minutes later, and they reached Atlanta just before noon. They stayed with the Joy Riders Club until the group reached the fairgrounds. Then, instead of following the other motorcycles, Nathan rode the Harley into a nearby parking deck. The Warrens' Buick pulled up beside them a few seconds later.

"So, how was the ride?" Hugh wanted to know as Billie and Nathan returned the helmets and leather jackets to their owners.

"I'm going to have to get me one of these," Nathan said in response, and Hugh smiled.

"Yeah, it doesn't take long to fall in love with a Harley."

Thelma stepped in between Billie and Nathan so she could give them both a hug simultaneously. "I feel so bad leaving you here like this." Her voice was thick with emotion.

Billie patted Thelma's back. "You and Hugh probably saved our lives."

"And we're just a few miles from the FBI offices," Nathan added.

"You're sure that you'll be safe once you get there?" Hugh asked.

"Not absolutely sure," Nathan admitted. "But we have to trust someone."

"I'll be praying for you," Thelma promised, and Billie felt tears sting the back of her eyelids.

Nathan cleared his throat. "The car will be at the FBI office. Here's the address." He handed Hugh a little piece of paper.

After another round of hugs and several admonitions of safety, the Warrens climbed onto their Harley and headed back toward the fairgrounds. Nathan and Billie left in the Buick a few minutes later. They hadn't gone more than a mile when they saw a blue and red light flashing behind them.

"What are we going to do?" Billie asked, the tears that had threatened earlier spilling onto her cheeks.

"We're going to stop," Nathan said with a frown. "We have no choice." He glanced over at her. "But don't cry. It will be okay."

He pulled the Buick off the road, and they watched a tall, African-American policeman approach. Billie wiped the moisture off her face, then whispered, "We almost made it." Nathan didn't answer, but she saw the muscles in his jaw tense as he rolled down the driver's side window.

Billie noticed that the officer had his gun drawn. "Step out of the car please." His expression and tone encouraged prompt obedience, so they both got out. "Can I see your driver's licenses please?"

While the officer examined their identification, Billie studied him. His badge was from Upton County, and his name tag identified him as Deputy Luther Briggins. The deputy looked up then and spoke to Nathan. "You're a long way from home."

"Yes, sir," Nathan replied simply.

"There's an APB out for a man and woman with your exact names," he told them conversationally. "Slightly different description though."

Billie stepped forward. "We haven't done anything wrong. We stumbled onto a plot to steal all the money generated by the GFL, and because of that, people are trying to kill us. We've been running for our lives since Monday."

The policeman regarded them steadily, and Billie waited for him to either get mad or laugh—but he did neither. "Who's trying to steal the money?"

"The people who started the league," Billie replied.

"You got proof?"

Nathan shook his head. "None, except that I've never had so much as a speeding ticket in my life and suddenly there's an APB out for me."

The policeman looked over at Billie. "What about you? Are you a career criminal?"

"No, sir. I *did* get a speeding ticket when I was in high school. I was going forty in a thirty-five mile-per-hour zone," she admitted. "But that's the extent of my lawbreaking."

The policeman considered this. "You say people are trying to kill you?"

Billie began to feel hopeful. "The fuel pump on my car was tampered with, causing it to explode on Saturday. Jeff Burdick and a coworker of mine, Camille Lockhart, were killed. Then Camille's car was blown up on Monday when the valet we hired at the airport tried to unlock it. And on Wednesday people shot at us at a Winn Dixie in Chattanooga."

The deputy frowned. "Where have you been since then?"

Billie looked at the ground. "We'd rather not say."

"Because you don't want to endanger whoever helped you," Deputy Briggins guessed as he rubbed his chin thoughtfully. "My mama taught me that there's no honor among thieves. According to the APB, you two are wanted for a series of terrorist car bombings and an attempted store robbery. You're supposed to be armed and extremely dangerous, but you don't seem to be either one. And if you're desperate criminals, what are you doing in downtown Atlanta where every living soul is looking for you?"

"We're innocent," Nathan assured him.

The deputy nodded. "I'm tempted to believe you."

At this point, Billie burst into hysterical tears. "I'm sorry," she sobbed. "I never cry. I don't know what's wrong with me."

Nathan accepted a crisply starched handkerchief from the deputy and gave it to Billie. "I feel like crying too," he told her gently. "But after I've spent several nights in awful hotels to prove what a man I am, I hate to ruin the image for you."

"Where are you folks headed?" Deputy Briggins asked.

"The FBI office," Nathan replied.

After another few seconds of contemplation, the deputy waved at his car. "Climb in. I'll take you there."

Billie looked at Nathan and he shrugged, then took her hand and led her to the Upton County Sheriff's Department vehicle.

Once they were settled inside, Billie thanked the deputy. "I know you're probably breaking some rules by taking us to the FBI, but we really appreciate it."

Deputy Briggins shrugged. "The Atlanta PD sent out a memo this morning demanding assistance. It said that they needed additional manpower and that cooperation was mandatory, so my sheriff sent me." Deputy Briggins looked at them in his rearview mirror. "I never have liked that word *mandatory.*"

Billie slumped against the seat, hoping that maybe things were going to be all right.

"Why don't you tell me your story while we drive," the deputy suggested.

Billie took a deep breath, then started by telling Deputy Briggins about her Internet friendship with Cowboy. She also explained

Camille's cruise-switching scheme and described the efforts the Georgia Chamber of Commerce went to on behalf of Blalock Industries. Deputy Briggins turned to Nathan. "This must be some kind of big plant you're planning to build."

Nathan shook his head. "Actually, it's not. It will employ about two hundred people once it's running at full capacity, but that will be three or four years from now."

"Two hundred new jobs three years from now," the policeman repeated, and Nathan nodded. "Did your company promise to donate millions of dollars to build a library or something?"

"No, nothing like that."

"Strange that the Georgia Chamber of Commerce was willing to invest so much money to entice you to build here when the payoff is so small," the deputy mused.

"It is a little strange," Billie sighed.

Deputy Briggins waved a hand in dismissal. "Anyway, go on with your story."

Billie described their trip to southwestern Georgia. She omitted the fact that somewhere along the way she had fallen in love with Nathan, but she saw the deputy look between them and realized he'd figured that out for himself. When she mentioned that Kip Blalock disappeared right before all their troubles began, the deputy stopped her.

"That name doesn't sound familiar, and I make a point of checking the missing persons lists every day. Let me call my dispatcher and have her check." The deputy used his cell phone to call the Upton County Sheriff's Department. After a brief conversation, he hung up and shook his head. "Kip Blalock isn't listed as a missing person in the state of Georgia *or* Utah."

"Kip's real name is Steven," Nathan provided. "Steven Kiplinger Blalock. Maybe it's listed that way."

"*No* Blalock is listed in either state," the deputy replied.

Nathan's shock was apparent. "But Mr. Blalock told me he was filing a missing persons report and asking for help from the FBI and the Atlanta police."

"He must have changed his mind," the deputy suggested. "And why does this Blalock guy need a bodyguard anyway?"

Nathan told the officer about threats made by the conservationists in Utah. "Kip and I are about the same size and have similar coloring, so Mr. Blalock hired me as his director of security. Then he asked me to dress like his son and go everywhere he goes."

"To protect him from the conservationists," the deputy clarified.

"As much to protect Kip from himself as any outside threat," Nathan admitted. "He's a compulsive gambler and always manages to find some kind of trouble. I'm sure his father is sick of bailing him out, but I can't understand why he wouldn't have the police helping with the search. Or why he would lie to me," Nathan added almost as an afterthought.

"Maybe Kip isn't really missing," Billie suggested, grasping at straws. "Maybe his dad just wants everybody to think so for his safety."

"But why keep that from me?"

"Maybe the dad has a big insurance policy on the kid and wants to end the problems he's caused once and for all," the deputy suggested.

Nathan paled. "No, that's not possible. The Blalocks are wonderful people."

"Okay, back to the GFL," Deputy Briggins returned to the original subject. "So you're saying that by the time the big game starts tonight, the organizers will have collected billions of dollars, and instead of continuing the football season, they plan to steal the money and disappear."

"That's basically what I think," Billie agreed.

Nathan leaned forward. "If it isn't true, why is someone trying so hard to kill us?"

The deputy rubbed his chin. "But if your Internet friend was really a government agent, why didn't he send this information to the FBI instead of you? And why did he say it was an idea for a book instead of an exposé of the GFL?"

"I don't know," Billie admitted. "At the time I thought it *was* just a book idea."

The deputy shook his head, then prompted, "What happened next?"

Billie put fingers to her temple, trying to think. "Camille was killed in my car, and my apartment was robbed. Edgar said the car exploding and robbery must have something to do with the GFL and Cowboy's e-mail."

"Who is Edgar?" Deputy Briggins looked confused.

"A chauffeur. He went with us on the business trip," Billie provided.

"So no one was chasing you at this point?" the deputy clarified.

"No, they thought they had already killed me, but it was Camille instead." Billie's voice shook a little, but she forced herself to go on. "Nathan and I drove toward Atlanta using side roads. We stayed in cheap hotels and paid cash for everything just as a precaution."

"But when you got to the airport on Monday, they were waiting for you?" Deputy Briggins asked.

Nathan nodded. "By then they had figured out that they'd killed the wrong girl. We've been running ever since."

"How did you get involved in the shoot-out in Chattanooga?" Deputy Briggins wanted to know.

"We called Edgar and asked him to wire us money," Nathan replied.

"So now we don't trust Edgar," Billie said sadly.

"When did you decide to come to the FBI office?" the deputy asked.

Billie shrugged. "We talked to an Agent Gray on the phone, and he pretty much insisted."

Deputy Briggins smiled. "The FBI can be quite convincing."

"We bought tickets to Miami and left word for Edgar that that's where we were headed, hoping to throw the criminals off our trail at least for a little while," Nathan explained.

Deputy Briggins glanced at their clasped hands in the rearview mirror, then asked, "So, are you two going to get married if you survive this?"

Nathan looked uncomfortable, but Billie gave the deputy a grim smile. "No, Nathan doesn't believe in marriage."

Deputy Briggins raised an eyebrow in Nathan's direction.

"That's not true," Nathan started to defend himself, but before he could say more Deputy Briggins got a call. As the deputy spoke into his radio, Nathan whispered to Billie, "Why did you tell him that?"

"To show you how stupid it sounds."

"Are you making fun of me?" he demanded.

She put a hand to her chest in mock horror. "Just because you refuse to marry and have children since your mother and father were rotten parents?"

"That's an oversimplification if I've ever heard one," he responded. Then he sighed. "I know you're upset, so I'll forgive you for that remark."

Billie sighed. "And I'm sorry that your association with me is probably going to get you arrested," she said as they pulled into an underground parking deck beside the FBI offices.

Deputy Briggins parked, then turned and spoke to them over the seat. "I want you to wait in the car while I check things out. I'll be back in a few minutes." He climbed out of the patrol car. "You said Agent Gray?"

"Yes," Nathan confirmed.

The deputy closed the door, and Billie and Nathan waited anxiously while he disappeared into the building.

"Do you think we should pray about this?" Nathan asked her. "It's not too late to run if we feel impressed to do so."

She took his hand in hers. "We've already prayed, and I feel good about it. I think we can trust Deputy Briggins."

Nathan squeezed her hand. "That's what I think too."

The deputy came back a few minutes later and opened the back door. "The coast is clear," he told them.

"You found Agent Gray?" Billie asked.

"Yes."

"And you checked his credentials?" Nathan verified.

The deputy laughed. "I did."

Nathan nodded. "Let's get inside."

They followed the deputy into the building and up to where a tall man with dark, solemn eyes was waiting. "Let me introduce Special Agent Loring Gray of the FBI," Deputy Briggins told them. He addressed the agent. "And this is Miss Billie Murphy and Mr. Nathan Turner."

"It's nice to meet you." The agent smiled, but his eyes remained somber.

"I'd like to see your badge for myself," Billie said, and Agent Gray raised his eyebrows. "I don't mean to offend you or Deputy Briggins, but people have been trying to kill me for a week, and I'm beyond social niceties."

The agent provided his badge, and once Billie was satisfied, he led the way to his office. Everyone settled around the cluttered desk, and the agent began. "It goes without saying that anything we discuss is privileged information."

"Don't worry," Billie told him. "Our life expectancy is minimal, so our opportunities to share secrets are limited."

"Please excuse her," Nathan told the agent with a frown in Billie's direction. "She's usually not this dramatic, but she's had a bad couple of days."

"I can speak for myself," Billie replied irritably.

"Lover's spat," Deputy Briggins told the agent. "Now, about your investigation."

The agent eyed Billie for a few seconds, then continued. "It's actually a Treasury Department investigation. They've been watching a known syndicate kingpin named Felix Hummer for years but never can get enough on him to prosecute. They had reason to suspect that he had ties with the new football league, so they put an undercover agent into the GFL organization."

"The undercover agent is my friend Cowboy?" Billie confirmed, and Agent Gray nodded.

"Since I'm with the FBI's Organized Crime Unit and the GFL is headquartered in Atlanta, the Treasury Department kept me informed as a courtesy." Agent Gray cleared his throat before moving on. "About a week ago, Cowboy reported that he'd overheard a discussion about a plot to steal money through the GFL. He didn't have many details, and the whole idea seemed so outlandish that I didn't put much credence into it. But the Treasury Department started a full-scale investigation, and then their agent missed his next check-in."

"Check-in?" Billie asked.

"Undercover agents have to check in on a regular basis to verify their safety and pass information. So their agent's failure to do so was very bad news."

"And he still hasn't checked in?"

Agent Gray shook his head. "No, and I'm afraid he isn't likely to. Felix Hummer isn't known for leaving loose ends."

Billie looked at her hands. "He's dead then?"

"Probably," Agent Gray acknowledged. "His disappearance strengthened the GFL heist theory but stalled the Treasury Department's investigation. Then we got your message. I checked both of you out thoroughly and called the Treasury Department to set up a little meeting. In the course of sifting through their information, I came across Kip Blalock's name and made the connection."

This comment got Nathan's attention. "Kip? What does he have to do with all this?"

Agent Gray looked reluctant to reply. "Kip Blalock is one of the crooks."

Nathan shook his head. "Kip gambles, but he isn't a criminal."

"A Treasury Department source inside Hummer's organization says Blalock owes Hummer a lot of money thanks to the gambling you mentioned. Apparently they offered him a chance to work off his debts by handling the computer transfer of billions of dollars at the exhibition game."

Billie wanted to laugh at the absurdity. "Kip Blalock could set up a complex computer program?"

But Nathan wasn't laughing, and he'd turned a little pale. "Actually, Kip is something of a computer genius."

Agent Gray leaned forward. "Why did Mr. Blalock come to Atlanta?"

Billie could tell that Nathan was uncomfortable with the question. "To look at possible sites to build a paper plant."

"But it's my understanding that neither you nor Mr. Blalock visited the proposed sites in other states."

Nathan nodded. "That's true." He took a deep breath, then faced the agent. "We weren't scheduled to come on this trip either. At the last minute, Kip decided he wanted to go."

"Which meant you had to go since you are his bodyguard."

Nathan acknowledged this with a brief nod.

"Hired to protect him from overly enthusiastic conservationist groups in Utah—or at least that's what Mr. Blalock Sr. told you."

Nathan frowned. "Why else would he hire Kip a bodyguard?"

"Maybe to protect him from the organized crime folks until he could make a deal with Hummer."

Nathan shook his head. "Mr. Blalock would have just paid Kip's gambling debts. That's what he always does."

"Not this time," the agent countered. "This time, Kip Blalock's debts were over a million dollars. Even someone as wealthy as Mr. Blalock couldn't cover amounts like that without selling off his company. So he hired you to protect his son."

"By taking a bullet for him!" Billie cut in, incredulous.

Nathan still looked confused. "Mr. Blalock wouldn't let me come to Atlanta under false pretenses. He's a very honest man."

"Who loves his son," Agent Gray said gently. "I'm sure he regretted the necessity of lying to you."

"So you're saying that Kip came to Atlanta with the *intention* of leaving us and going to work for the people who are planning to steal money from the GFL?" Nathan asked. "And Mr. Blalock knew this and gave his approval?"

"Maybe not his approval, but he accepted that this was the only way for Kip to wipe his slate clean with Hummer. The plant sites were just an excuse to get to Atlanta."

"Then Kip never was really missing. Mr. Blalock knew where he was all along." Nathan glanced over at Billie. "That's why he didn't call the police or the FBI. And I guess there's no private investigation firm looking for him either."

"Probably not," the agent agreed, then turned to Billie. "And your friend Camille Lockhart was involved in the GFL scandal up to her pretty eyebrows."

"She wasn't my friend, and I can't say that surprises me. She said she was trying to get a dream job within the GFL."

"More likely within Hummer's organization. We had enough evidence to arrest her for money laundering, but she died before we could act."

Billie shook her head. "So why did Cowboy send me the information in the form of a book idea? Why didn't he just give it to the Treasury Department?"

"He may have thought it *was* a good idea for a book. Or maybe he wanted to get the information out before he tried to leave, but he knew Hummer may have been watching him. So he sent it to you disguised as a book idea to protect both of you in case the e-mail was intercepted."

"So tonight, these criminals, with Kip's help, plan to steal all the money the GFL has generated thus far?" Nathan asked.

"That's my understanding," Agent Gray confirmed.

"Then the whole league will fold before any of the regular season games are played?"

Agent Gray shrugged. "We're not sure about that. We don't know if *all* the league organizers are involved. If some of them are honest, they might try to get some loans and keep the league afloat."

"Or they might just declare bankruptcy and cut their losses," Nathan said grimly.

Agent Gray nodded. "That's also a possibility."

"And the players and coaches who left their jobs in good faith will be unemployed," Nathan added.

"Yes," Agent Gray agreed. "And the cities who spent money on municipal improvements to qualify for a franchise will have wasted millions of taxpayer dollars."

"All the small-time investors who bought a piece of the action will be losers too," Nathan continued the dismal predictions.

"How do these people expect to get away with it?" Billie asked. "I mean, won't they all be the obvious suspects when the money disappears?"

"We figure that they've picked a fall guy." The agent glanced at Nathan. "Probably your friend Kip Blalock."

Nathan looked up sharply. "Kip?"

Agent Gray nodded. "Since he's the one who'll actually be doing the computer transfers, they could make sure he leaves a paper trail a mile wide."

"Then when the police come, they can turn him over and go home to count their money," Luther Briggins contributed.

"Exactly," Agent Gray agreed.

"So, what are we going to do to stop them?" Nathan wanted to know.

"There's nothing we can do," the agent replied. "Without proof we can't get a search warrant."

Billie frowned at this remark. "I thought you said my statement would help with that."

"I just said that to get you to come in so we could protect you," the agent admitted. "There's little chance that we'll find a judge who will issue a search warrant based on a deleted e-mail outlining a fiction novel."

"You lied to me?" Billie was aghast.

"Not exactly," Agent Gray defended himself. "I do want to get your statement, and I will request a search warrant—I just don't expect to get it. And after I saw the autopsy report on Camille Lockhart, I was convinced that you had to come in."

Billie felt a little wave of nausea. "Why?"

"Because whoever blew up your car wanted to make sure that you died. Jeff Burdick was burned terribly, but the driver's seat was saturated with an odorless but highly flammable substance so that Miss Lockhart's body was burned beyond recognition. The identification was made based on some jewelry that survived pending the arrival of her dental records."

Billie held up a hand to stop him. "So the criminals put something on my seat to make sure I'd be killed when the car exploded."

"That's the police department's theory," Agent Gray acknowledged.

"I'll never feel safe until these people are brought to justice," Billie whispered.

"But instead of trying to catch them, we're sitting here letting them steal billions of dollars," Nathan said bitterly.

The agent frowned. "I told you that this isn't my operation. But from what I understand, the Treasury Department is going to make one last-ditch effort to thwart the criminals."

"How?" Billie asked.

"Cowboy planted a virus in the system when he was setting it up. It's dormant and has to be activated, but once it has been, the whole interrelated computer network will implode."

"Self-destruct," Billie confirmed.

"Right. They've managed to get someone else inside the GFL to activate the virus."

Billie shuddered, thinking of Cowboy. "That sounds very dangerous."

Agent Gray acknowledged this. "It will be. To distract the criminals and give their man time to work, they've asked us to contact the GFL organizers. We're supposed to tell them that we've uncovered a plot to steal all the ticket proceeds and gambling bets. They'll be upset, of course."

"Yes," Billie agreed.

"They'll say it's not possible, but we'll tell them that we've not only found out the plans, but we know that the thief is Mr. Kip Blalock."

"You're going to accuse Kip?" Billie was confused.

The agent nodded. "It's the only way we can think of to get him out alive."

Nathan's hands gripped the edge of Agent Gray's desk. "They plan to kill him?"

"Mr. Blalock may not realize it, but I doubt very seriously that they would just let him walk away after the money is transferred," the agent confirmed. "And even though he's almost as guilty as the rest of them, we'd like to try to save him. Plus, the exchange will offer us the distraction the Treasury Department guy needs."

"What if they don't believe you?" Nathan asked.

"They'll comply anyway."

Nathan frowned. "So, you'll get Kip out safely and the virus may keep the money from being transferred, but the people who came up with the scheme won't be prosecuted?" Nathan verified.

Agent Gray grimaced. "We'll offer Mr. Blalock immunity to testify against the conspirators, but I'm not sure how strong a case we can build with just his word."

"So worst-case scenario is that the virus doesn't work, Kip gets killed, and the crooks avoid prosecution and live the rest of their lives in luxury thanks to the GFL's money," Nathan summed things up. "And they can keep hiring people to kill us from Morocco or the Cayman Islands or wherever they go."

The FBI agent shrugged. "I wish I could be more encouraging, but you're right. It's possible that they will get away with their scheme. In fact, we've been chasing Felix Hummer for ten years, and he always eludes us. But the good news is that either way, after tonight, Felix Hummer should lose interest in you and Miss Murphy."

"That's something anyway," Nathan acknowledged.

"We hope that the suspects will turn on each other to protect themselves after they're arrested during the exhibition game," Agent

Gray told them. "And even if we're never able to prosecute them, being arrested on national television will be a punishment of sorts."

"Why would the people who are planning to steal the money come to the game?" Billie asked in surprise.

"It's their alibi," Deputy Briggins guessed, and Agent Gray nodded.

"While the money is disappearing, they plan to be in full view of millions of people. I'd like to at least try to catch Hummer red-handed, but the Treasury Department has decided that keeping all that money from leaving the country is more important." The agent turned to Billie. "Unless you can provide us with any additional information."

"Me?" Billie asked in surprise.

"We're hoping that the book idea Cowboy sent you might have some specific information in it. Names, banks, even account numbers. If we had that kind of information, we'd know where to look for hard evidence."

Billie nodded. "Now that you mention it, Cowboy *did* name some of the characters." She glanced up. "I thought that he was just trying to put his mark on my book, but . . ."

"Those names could tell us who the local conspirators are," Agent Gray said with intensity. "Can you remember any of them?"

Billie concentrated, then shook her head. "I'm sorry, but I can't."

"Too bad," Deputy Briggins said.

The men were silent for a few minutes before Billie spoke to the agent. "What was his real name?" she asked quietly. "Cowboy's, I mean."

"Sparkman. Joseph Sparkman," the agent responded.

Deputy Briggins addressed the agent. "So you don't have any idea who the other conspirators in the GFL heist are? Besides the Las Vegas guy?"

The agent shook his head. "Nope."

"You might want to check out that chauffeur," Deputy Briggins suggested, then pointed to Billie. "What was his name?"

"Edgar Willingham," she provided.

The FBI agent made a note. "I will."

"So, what now?" Nathan asked.

"We'll contact the GFL about Kip Blalock, then work out details for tonight," Agent Gray replied.

"I want to be there when you arrest Kip," Nathan told him.

Agent Gray shook his head. "That would be very unwise, Mr. Turner."

"If Kip sees me with you, he'll know he can trust you," Nathan pressed. "Otherwise he might try to run or do something else desperate that will get him killed."

"If you go, I'm going too," Billie told Nathan firmly.

"That is out of the question!" Agent Gray was adamant.

Nathan tried a gentler approach. "There's no reason for you to take the risk, Billie."

"Except to be with you," she whispered.

Agent Gray cleared his throat. "Deputy Briggins, will you join me in the conference room across the hall? I have maps over there that we can use to plan the events of the evening. When you and Miss Murphy finish your discussion, we'll need you too, Mr. Turner."

"And I'm supposed to just sit here and do nothing?" Billie asked bitterly.

"You can pray for us," the agent told her. "And at this point, help from heaven may be the only hope we have."

CHAPTER 11

When Conrad Lockhart walked into the storage room, Hummer gave him an irritated look, then ended his phone conversation abruptly. "What?"

"The FBI just called. They say they have information that there will be a significant attempt to steal the ticket proceeds from the game tonight."

"Do they have any names?"

"Only one. Kip Blalock. They claim he's working for the GFL, and they want him turned over—immediately."

Felix Hummer tapped his finger against his fleshy lips. "That's perfect. Tell the FBI that we are grateful that their efficiency has averted a disaster. Tell them that we will be happy to set up a meeting with them to surrender the suspected thief."

"Won't we need him to make the money transfers?"

"Set the meeting up for a few minutes after the game starts so that Mr. Blalock will have time to complete his task beforehand."

"But Mr. Blalock could incriminate all of us," Conrad pointed out.

"After the computer transfers are completed, you take Mr. Blalock to meet the FBI. When you come into sight of the authorities, warn Mr. Blalock and encourage him to run."

"So the FBI will shoot him?"

"Precisely. I'll arrange for a backup in case the FBI misses."

Felix Hummer waited until the older man left, then picked up the phone. "I need a sharpshooter here as soon as possible," he said.

* * *

Billie paced anxiously around Agent Gray's office. Each time she passed the door, she would look into the conference room across the hall, hoping for a glimpse of Nathan. Finally Deputy Briggins left the meeting and walked into Agent Gray's office, effectively stopping her rounds.

"So, have you come up with a plan?" she asked him.

"The beginnings of one anyway," he replied. "I've been sent out to buy costumes."

"It could be worse," Billie pointed out. "You could be walking yourself dizzy in here with me."

Deputy Briggins laughed. "Why don't you sit down and write a book." He pointed at the computer. "I'm sure Agent Gray won't mind, and I'll bet your editor would be real happy."

Billie watched the deputy disappear down the hall. With a weary sigh, she collapsed into the swivel chair behind the agent's desk. Not that she would seriously consider working on one of her romance novels from an FBI computer, but . . .

The realization hit her so suddenly she was actually nauseated for a second. Then she jumped to her feet and rushed across the hall. When she burst into the conference room, the occupants looked up in alarm.

"Is something the matter?" Nathan asked.

"I just remembered," she gasped. "I sent a copy of Cowboy's idea to my editor at LoveSwift Books."

"An exact copy?" Agent Gray stood up.

She nodded.

"Well," the agent said with a small smile. "Let's call her and see if we can get her to e-mail it back to us."

* * *

Hummer answered his secure phone line. "Yes?"

"We've located them. They're at the FBI office in Atlanta."

"Out of reach?"

The man on the other end of the line laughed. "Are you kidding?" Hummer exhaled deeply. "Keep me posted."

* * *

"It's Saturday," Billie reminded the men. "My editor won't be at work."

"Give us her name and we'll come up with alternate numbers," Agent Gray told her.

"Margery Ross," Billie said. "She lives in Roanoke, Virginia."

The agent nodded, then hurried from the room.

"I can't believe I didn't think of this sooner," Billie whispered to Nathan as he came to stand beside her.

"I'm just glad you thought of it now. Maybe they'll be able to put these guys in jail."

A few minutes later, Agent Gray walked back in. He handed Billie a piece of paper with several numbers. "Start at the top of the list and see if you can reach her." Billie sat down in front of a telephone and started dialing. "Give her as little information as possible. Just ask her to forward the attachment to us at the e-mail address written on the bottom of that piece of paper." The agent turned to Nathan. "And I've got good news for you, Mr. Turner. The GFL has agreed to turn over Mr. Blalock at the game tonight."

"I guess that's good news," Nathan responded, but he looked uneasy.

"Of course it is. Mr. Blalock's arrest will give us a good excuse to cover all the exits, which will also prevent the conspirators from escaping." Agent Gray waved around the room. "And these Treasury guys don't have any objection to you tagging along."

Billie didn't even try to distinguish between the grim-faced men sitting at the table. "No answer at the first number," she told Agent Gray.

"Try the next one," he requested.

Billie nodded, already dialing. A few seconds later, Margery Ross answered the phone.

"Marge?" Billie confirmed.

"Billie?" the editor asked. "I was beginning to wonder if you had disappeared off the face of the earth."

Billie laughed, trying not to think how close that was to the truth. "Really you just thought I was ashamed to write back since my last book was late and my most recent proposal was so bad."

"It wasn't really bad," Marge hedged. "It needs some work, that's for sure. But it has possibilities."

Billie was astounded by this reaction. "Well, I'm glad you think so," she said. "Since that's the case, I wonder if you could do me a favor?"

"Sure," Marge agreed readily.

"Well, I've had some computer problems." She rolled her eyes at Nathan while making this horrendous understatement. "And I wondered if you could send that attachment back to me."

"First thing Monday morning," Marge promised and Billie winced.

"I actually need it sooner than that. It's kind of important."

There was a brief pause, and when Marge spoke again, some of the friendliness had left her voice. "It's the weekend, Billie. The office is a thirty-minute drive from here."

"I'm sorry for the inconvenience, Marge," Billie began carefully. Then she glanced at a note Agent Gray had written that said, *It could be dangerous for her if she knows the truth about that attachment.* Billie nodded, then continued. "In all the years we've been working together, have I ever asked for a personal favor?"

"Well, no," Marge stammered.

"I'm asking for one now. I need to see that attachment immediately. My muse is working overtime, and I'm afraid if I don't get my ideas down into the computer, I'll lose them forever."

After another pause, Billie heard Marge sigh. "I'll leave right away."

"Thanks, Marge. You're the best," Billie said in relief. Then she gave her editor the e-mail address Agent Gray had provided and hung up the phone.

"Good job," Agent Gray praised her as he led the group into his office where they all gathered in front of his computer. Forty-five minutes later, an e-mail popped up. "Here it is," the agent said. Soon, his printer started humming. Nathan gave Billie an encouraging smile and she tried not to cry. She kept thinking of Cowboy frantically typing the words into his computer just minutes before he died. Turning away from the men and the printer, she stared out the window.

Agent Gray glanced at the printout. "I think the names of the characters match the names of the local conspirators," he told Billie. "It's not hard evidence, but it gives us a place to start looking."

"I'm going to take a copy of this down to the boys in research and see what they can come up with," one of the men said as he took the e-mail and hurried out the door.

"Your friend wanted this information to get to them," Nathan comforted her, and Billie turned to face him. "They don't mean any disrespect."

"And he would want us to stop the GFL folks," Agent Gray added.

Billie nodded as Luther Briggins came back in carrying several shopping bags, which he piled on the agent's desk.

"What's all this?" Nathan asked.

"The stuff the FBI wants you to wear to the GFL game tonight," the deputy told him as he pulled nylon wind suits and Nike tennis shoes from the sacks. "He thinks it will help you fit in with the crowd at the Georgia Dome." He turned to Billie. "And since it hadn't been decided yet whether you were going, I got you some too. If you don't need a disguise, I guess yours will just be a token of the Bureau's appreciation."

"Hey, why do I have to be a fan of the San Francisco Tempests?" Nathan asked when Deputy Briggins gave him his clothing.

"It was all they had in your size," the deputy told him. "The sales-clerk said the suits are perfect for most weather conditions and are guaranteed to be comfortable. And together these two outfits cost more than my monthly house payment."

Agent Gray almost smiled again. "Why don't you go try them on?"

"Have you changed your mind and decided to let me go?" Billie asked hopefully.

The agent shook his head. "No, you'll be watching the game from the safety of this building. But we want you to show your GFL spirit."

Billie gave him a rebellious look but took her things and went into the ladies' room to change. From what she could see in the small mirror over the sink, they fit pretty well. She met Nathan as he was coming out of the men's room and couldn't control a laugh.

"What?" he demanded, looking down at his San Francisco Tempests jacket. "Do I have something on backwards?"

Billie shook her head. "I was just trying to imagine another circumstance that would convince you to wear that out in public."

He frowned. "There isn't one."

"Poor Nathan," Billie murmured as they reached Agent Gray's office.

"Well, don't you two look sporty," Deputy Briggins teased.

"If you even utter the words, 'Go Tempests,' I can't be held responsible for my actions," Nathan warned him.

While they waited to hear from the research people, the men rehashed their plans for the evening. Billie pushed her chair against the wall to get out of the way while the men pored over the diagrams of the athletic complex that included the Georgia World Congress Center, the Georgia Dome, and the Centennial Olympic Park.

"The GFL offices are actually in the GWCC," Agent Gray explained. "They'll bring Kip Blalock through the concourse and into this area, where we'll be waiting." He pointed at a spot on the map.

"Why can't we just meet them in the GFL offices?" Nathan wanted to know.

The agent shrugged. "This was the way they wanted it."

"Sounds fishy to me," Nathan muttered.

"We actually prefer to meet in the open," Agent Gray told him. "In their offices, we'd be trapped if something goes wrong."

Billie's attention drifted as they discussed the number of people to be stationed at each exit, coordinating FBI, Atlanta city police, and the Treasury Department, in addition to the security people at the dome itself. She thought about home—the smell of cinnamon rolls baking and the feeling of safety and security.

Finally Billie was so tired she couldn't keep her eyes open, so she walked out into the hallway and found a small lounge with a couch, television, and drink machine. She curled up on the couch and went to sleep. Nathan woke her a couple of hours later.

"We're leaving," he told her gently.

"Please be careful," she said, pushing up into sitting position.

"I'll be surrounded by law enforcement officials of every variety, so I should be safer than I've been in days. Try not to worry, and I'll get back here as soon as I can."

"What will you do then?" she asked, dreading his response.

"I'll have to get Kip back to Utah." Nathan reached into the pocket of his expensive wind suit. "There's something I want you to have just in case," he said. When his hand emerged from the black nylon, he was holding a hundred-dollar bill. "This is some of the money Hugh and Thelma gave us. I expect everything to go well tonight, but if something goes wrong, you might need it."

Billie tried to hide her disappointment as he pressed a quick kiss to her lips.

Agent Gray cleared his throat from behind, and Nathan stepped back. "This is Agent Shiver," the agent told Billie as he gestured to a woman standing with him. "She's been assigned to protect you while we're gone."

"Babysit," Billie amended.

"We're just being cautious," Agent Gray said.

She nodded in resignation as the men walked toward the end of the hall. Deputy Briggins gave her a little wave just before they stepped into the elevator and disappeared from view.

* * *

Felix Hummer picked up the phone after one ring. "I hope you've got good news," he said without preamble.

"I've got someone at the FBI office to handle Miss Murphy. I should have good news in a matter of minutes."

"I'll be waiting to hear." Felix Hummer put down the receiver and made another call. "Get Mr. Blalock started."

* * *

Agent Shiver was a middle-aged woman who encouraged Billie to call her Edith. After brief introductions she told Billie she was unhappy about working late. Billie apologized for the inconvenience, and Edith accepted with a resigned nod. "I always get the short end of the stick around here," she grumbled as she flipped a page in a *Soap Opera Digest* magazine. "I have two teenage sons who will eat everything in the refrigerator since I'm not home to stop them."

Billie considered apologizing again but decided to try a different approach. "I understand. I have four brothers."

Edith looked up from her magazine in horror. "Your poor mother."

Billie laughed, and Edith turned on the television. She chose a talk show and smiled as the host introduced the day's subject—siblings who wanted to marry. Edith nodded. "This ought to be good," she predicted as she collapsed on the couch beside Billie.

Billie stared at the screen in morbid fascination for a few seconds, then turned away in disgust as Edith's cell phone rang. The agent answered it gruffly. "My sister," she mouthed to Billie, then concentrated on the conversation.

Grateful for the excuse Edith's phone call provided, Billie turned off the television. Then she resigned herself to listening to Edith's real-life soap opera.

As Edith recounted the number of times her children had been arrested, convicted, and incarcerated, Billie realized that her brothers' exploits had been child's play. She vowed silently that if she ever saw her brothers again, she would hug them all soundly. Finally Edith hung up the phone and said she was going to the vending machines down the hall. "You want me to get you something?" she offered.

Billie was starving, so she asked Edith to itemize the choices. "They've got egg salad, ham and cheese, and the tuna salad is my favorite," Edith concluded.

Billie made a face. "I hate tuna salad when it's *fresh* and can't imagine eating it after it's been sitting in a vending machine for who knows how long."

Edith smiled at this. "After a while, you get to where you're not so choosy. They have cookies and candy bars—things like that too."

"I think I'll just wait until Nathan and Agent Gray get back," Billie decided. "Maybe they'll feel sorry for me and take me out to dinner." She glanced up at the agent and smiled. "And that way I'll be able to call 911 in case you get food poisoning from that tuna salad."

She could hear Edith's gruff laughter as the older woman walked down the hall. Billie settled back against the couch and wondered what Nathan was doing. Depending on the traffic, they might have had time to get to the Georgia Dome. A few minutes later, a trim woman wearing a small name tag that identified her as Treasury agent Rhonda Wallace walked into the lounge.

"I've been sent to take over for Edith," she informed Billie with a professional smile. "Apparently her kids are delinquents and her supervisor doesn't like to make Edith stay late."

Billie smiled. "I've heard all about them. I'm Billie Murphy."

"Nice to meet you." Agent Wallace extended a clear plastic container with a sandwich cut into even halves inside. "Edith asked me to give you this." The sticker on the front boldly proclaimed the contents to be a tuna salad sandwich.

Billie stared at the container and commanded herself to keep breathing. At one time she might have thought it was just a strange mistake, but after days of running for her life, she didn't dare ignore the sense of warning throbbing inside her. She had been very clear with Edith about her feelings for tuna salad—from a vending machine or otherwise. She was certain that Edith did not buy her a tuna sandwich, which meant Agent Wallace was lying or Edith had given the woman the wrong information on purpose. But either way, Agent Wallace was probably not trustworthy.

Refusing to allow herself to think about Edith and what had become of her, Billie took the sandwich. "Thanks." She put the container on the couch beside her and clutched her midsection. "I'm feeling kind of sick to my stomach. Could you point me in the direction of the nearest bathroom?"

The hesitation was slight, but Billie was watching for it. Agent Wallace had no idea where the bathroom was.

Billie rubbed her stomach and stood. "Never mind. I'll find it. Fast!" She covered her mouth, hoping to hide some of her anxiety. "And would you mind calling someone to see if they can bring me some Pepto-Bismol?" she added as she hurried down the hall.

The woman who claimed to be Agent Wallace stood and stared after her for a few seconds. Billie saw a dark hallway off to her right and turned back to the "agent." "Here it is!" she called, then turned into the hallway hoping the agent would think she had gone into the bathroom. The second she was out of sight, she started to run.

At the end of the hall, she found a flight of stairs and hurried down them, listening for the sounds of pursuit. She made it to the landing before she heard the door above her open. She didn't waste time looking up but knew that the fake Treasury agent was close behind.

* * *

Hummer dialed the number, then demanded, "Why haven't you called to tell me that the girl is dead?"

There was a slight pause. "The girl got away, but we know she's headed to the Georgia Dome. We'll handle her there."

"These are either the luckiest people on the face of the earth or my associates are the most incompetent!" Hummer yelled. "Take care of her immediately!"

"Once she's inside the stadium, there's no escape," the voice promised.

"Just handle it quickly."

* * *

Billie burst through a door at the bottom of the stairs and found herself on the parking deck. A dented Subaru pulled around the corner at that moment, and Billie ran straight into its path. "Are you an agent?" she asked breathlessly after pulling open the passenger door.

"Oh no, ma'am. I'm a janitor on the second floor," the kid replied.

Billie climbed into the seat beside him. "You're about to have the experience of a lifetime. Take me to the Georgia Dome, quick."

The boy paused for just a second, then pressed the gas obediently, and the Subaru shot forward. Billie ducked down in the seat as the door at the bottom of the stairwell burst open and "Agent Wallace" ran out.

"Are *you* an agent?" he asked as he slipped the car into the thick downtown traffic.

"Billie Murphy," she said, extending a hand in his direction and completely ignoring his question. "What's your name?"

"Rusty Herring."

"Well, Rusty, we'll have people trying to follow us soon, so you might want to take some alleys, back roads—that kind of thing."

Rusty's lips parted as he sighed, "Just like on television." He made a quick right turn, then added, "And I know my way around this town."

"Looks like it's my lucky day." Billie gave him what she hoped was an encouraging smile as he turned sharply onto a service road.

When Rusty got close enough to the complex to see the Georgia Dome in the distance, the traffic was so congested that Billie realized it could take hours for them to reach the stadium. "I may have to walk the rest of the way," she told him, keeping an eye on the mirrors.

"It's still two or three miles on foot," Rusty warned her, and her face fell. "But there's a Marta pickup point."

Billie smiled. The Marta shuttle would take her right to the front of the Georgia Dome. "Let me out here, Rusty, and then you get somewhere else quick. And when this is over, I'll let my friends at the FBI know what a big help you were to me."

The kid smiled. "Cool." He pulled over to a curb near the Marta stop, and Billie climbed out. She joined the crowd around the booth and watched as the next shuttle approached. It soon filled with the people in front of her, so Billie had to wait until the next shuttle arrived. With the passing of each minute, she was more certain that she needed to get inside the Georgia Dome and find Nathan. They were all in danger.

When the shuttle arrived, Billie climbed on and took a seat in the back, watching as they sped past the clogged traffic. The shuttle dropped them off at the front entrance, and Billie walked to the ticket booth. She asked for the cheapest ticket available as she pulled Nathan's money from her pocket.

"I'm sorry, ma'am," the ticket salesperson replied. "But the game is sold out."

Billie stared in horror at the woman. An attempt had been made on her life at the FBI offices. If the people who tried to kill her knew where she was, they also knew where Nathan was, and she had to warn him.

"I have to get into that game," she told the woman. "It's a matter of life and death."

The woman nodded as if she heard this regularly. "Try one of the scalpers."

Billie turned and saw several people standing by the ticket gate, waving tickets. She approached one of them. She could hear the visiting team members being announced and knew that the game would start soon. Nathan might already have Kip, and they might be about to leave the dome. But they wouldn't know that they were still in danger.

The scalper wanted a hundred and fifty dollars for his tickets, but after she gave him her Atlanta Competitors' jacket, he accepted the ninety dollars Billie had left after the shuttle ride. Since the game was about to start, she knew she could probably have negotiated a better deal but didn't want to waste the time.

* * *

"Is Blalock through with the transfers?" Hummer demanded into the phone.

"He finished a few minutes ago," Conrad Lockhart replied. "I'm about to personally escort him down to our little surprise meeting."

Hummer laughed, but it was an unpleasant sound. "Is Turner with the Feds?"

"Yes."

"Good. I'll have my marksman take him out along with Blalock. Then tell everyone to be on the lookout for the girl. I don't leave loose ends."

As Felix Hummer hung up the phone, the door opened. "I've never seen an operation so full of sloppy mistakes," he told his guest.

"It hasn't been pretty, but it's almost over, and you've made a tidy profit."

"So true," Hummer said as he stood.

"And not every member of your team is incompetent," his guest added with a smile.

Hummer nodded. "Let's get out of here."

They left the office, then turned down a dark hallway and walked out an emergency exit. The policeman guarding the door nodded to both and stared after them as they made their hasty departure.

* * *

As Billie pushed through the turnstile and entered the mass of people buying concessions, she looked around. She knew that there were FBI agents and policemen in the building. Agent Gray had said that they would be covering all the exits. But how would she know who to trust? Would she be able to look in their eyes and decide if they were honest? And if one of the crooks who was also around saw her, would he recognize her and shoot her on the spot?

Billie mixed in with the flow of people milling around and tried to remember their plans for the meeting with the GFL. It was to take place near a concourse. Looking around, she spotted a man with a broom and long-handled dustpan. The broom and dustpan moved continuously, but the man never looked down. Instead, his eyes constantly scanned the crowd. Billie said a quick prayer, then acted on her impression.

She made gradual progress toward the attentive sweeper, and when she was close enough, she asked him where the nearest pay phone was. He looked surprised, then pointed to a wall of phones about ten feet away.

"Thanks." Billie smiled, moving even closer. "I'm Billie Murphy, and I have important information that I need to get to Agent Loring Gray and the Treasury men. I know they're here arresting Kip Blalock. Can you show me where they are?" She resisted the urge to look over her shoulder. "And I'm probably being followed."

The sweeper didn't make a comment for several seconds. Since he hadn't killed her immediately, Billie knew he wasn't a bad guy, but she was beginning to wonder if he really was an innocent stadium sweeper when he nodded. "Come with me." The man abandoned the broom and dustpan, and they walked as quickly as possible through the crowded space.

A rock group had just completed their performance of the national anthem, and the noise was deafening. The crowd stood to watch the kickoff. The people on all sides stopped, focusing on monitors, effectively trapping Billie and the sweeper. He pointed forward, and, rising up on her tiptoes, she could see an area between a service stairway and an elevator that was roped off.

Agent Gray was there, along with some of the Treasury Department people. She couldn't see Deputy Briggins, and Kip was nowhere in sight, but she assumed that the heir to Blalock Industries was expected at any moment. Then her eyes found Nathan. He was facing Agent Gray with his back to her. Smiling a little, she felt herself relax. She was almost there.

Billie turned to her right and told the sweeper she could make it the rest of the way on her own. She watched him melt into the crowd, then as she turned, she saw a flicker of light above her. It was so brief that she almost ignored it, but her gaze settled on a security guard leaning against the second-story banister. Nothing seemed amiss, and she was about to return her attention to the men gathered by the steps when she saw the guard remove a gun from his holster.

Billie screamed, but the sound was swallowed up in the crowd noise. She pushed frantically against the people surrounding her. Some moved aside and others pushed back, but her progress was still slow. She looked up at the man with the gun. It was pointed at the back of Nathan's head. In horror, she realized that Nathan was about to die and she couldn't stop it. All she could do was stand by helplessly and watch.

Time seemed to stop. Her eyes focused on the black nylon collar of the San Francisco Tempests jacket pressed tightly against the tanned skin of Nathan's neck. The new haircut exposed pale skin that had previously been covered, making him seem more vulnerable.

Billie flinched as she heard the shot. But before the bullet could make contact with its target, a figure leapt from the stairway, knocking Nathan to the ground just as the bullet from the guard's gun arrived. The men by the stairs scattered as another gunshot rang out.

The security guard with the gun fell over the railing into the crowd. There were screams as people ran in panic, finally clearing a path to the stairs. When Billie arrived, she saw Nathan kneeling beside the crumpled body of Kip Blalock.

"Is he dead?" Billie whispered as she crouched beside them.

Nathan shook his head. "No." Then his eyes focused on Billie, and he pulled her roughly against himself. "What are you doing here? You were supposed to stay at the FBI offices where you were safe."

"A fake Treasury agent tried to get me to eat a tuna salad sandwich, so I had to run." Nathan's eyes clouded with confusion. "Never mind. I'll explain later." Her gaze moved to Kip.

"Did the bullet hit him?" Agent Gray asked from behind them.

Nathan nodded. "I think so, in the shoulder."

Agent Gray leaned over and examined the wound. "Just a scratch," he said. "Paramedics and an ambulance should be here momentarily. In the meantime, I've got arrests to make."

Kip's eyes fluttered open, and he gave them all a crooked smile. "Are you going to arrest me?"

"Maybe later," Agent Gray replied, then walked away.

"But right now you're going to the hospital," Nathan told his friend.

"Are my legs broken?" Kip wanted to know.

Billie looked down at Kip's legs, which were bent at odd angles and certainly fractured in several places.

Nathan looked too, but seemed unable to answer. Billie did it for him. "Probably."

"Seems like broken legs would hurt," Kip murmured. "But I don't feel a thing. You think that's bad, Nathan?"

Billie and Nathan exchanged a worried glance, then Nathan said, "We'll have to wait until we see what the doctors say."

When the paramedics and ambulance attendants arrived, Billie and Nathan stepped back. She took his hand, and he squeezed hers gently, then she watched as the men worked on Kip. They braced his neck, then bandaged the bullet wound and put splints on both legs without so much as a whimper from the injured man. As they loaded him onto the gurney, Nathan approached one of the paramedics.

"Is he going to be okay?"

The man shrugged. "Too soon to tell."

"Can we ride with him to the hospital?" Nathan reached for Billie and pulled her along as they moved toward the closest exit.

"One of you can," the ambulance attendant called over his shoulder as Agent Gray reappeared beside them.

"Have you seen Deputy Briggins?" Billie asked him while scanning the crowd.

The agent shook his head. "Not recently, but who could find anyone in this chaos?"

"They're taking Kip to the hospital, and Nathan wants to ride with him," Billie said.

Agent Gray nodded at Nathan. "You go ahead with Mr. Blalock. I'll take care of Billie."

"I thought you'd gone with the others to arrest people," Billie said as they walked toward an exit.

"The Treasury agents have that under control. I figure it's my responsibility to get you to a secure location."

"You'll be giving up exposure on national television to protect us," Billie pointed out. "It could mean a big promotion."

The agent nodded without looking at her. "Yeah, bitter enemies have cost me less." Then she saw that little half smile again.

Billie and the agent walked with Nathan to the ambulance.

"I feel kind of dizzy," Kip said as he was loaded inside.

"He needs to stay awake," the attendant told Nathan as he swung up into the emergency vehicle. "So try to keep him talking."

Nathan gave Billie a quick look before following the attendant into the ambulance.

"Did the computer virus work?" Billie asked Agent Gray once they were settled in the government car.

"Yes," the agent replied.

Billie was pleased. "So the criminals didn't get the money?"

"We saved most of it."

"Most of it?" Billie asked.

"The early investments and start-up capital were transferred a couple of days ago, but the bulk of the money is still in the accounts where it belongs."

"That's good then."

"Better than nothing," the agent agreed.

"But you didn't catch Felix Hummer?"

Agent Gray shook his head. "Oh no, he got away just like always."

When they got to the hospital, Agent Gray walked Billie into the emergency room where Nathan was waiting. The agent asked about Kip's condition, and Nathan shook his head. "They don't know anything yet."

"I'll wait with you for a while," the agent told them. "When I leave, there will be a policeman to guard Kip Blalock's room and another to take you two wherever you want to go."

"Thanks," Billie said. Then she asked, "Do you know what happened to Edith Shiver?"

Agent Gray looked embarrassed. "I'm so sorry about that. I didn't think you were in any real danger and left you with someone who wasn't trained for a violent situation. She was knocked unconscious, then bound with duct tape and stuck in a closet."

"Obviously she was well trained enough to make the fake Treasury agent think she was buying the tuna salad sandwich for me," Billie said, then proceeded to explain. Agent Gray seemed less humiliated when she finished. "I hope Edith's okay. I'd like to thank her personally."

"Don't worry about Edith," Agent Gray said. "She'll probably claim whiplash and take early retirement."

Billie smiled as she looked around the room. "I'm surprised Deputy Briggins isn't here. You still don't know where he is?"

Agent Gray shrugged. "If he's smart, he headed back to Upton County."

"I don't think he'd leave without saying good-bye," Billie said, then turned to Nathan. "Are Kip's parents coming?"

He nodded. "They were already in Atlanta, so they'll be here soon."

Just then, an orthopedic surgeon approached them. He introduced himself as Dr. Tidwell and shook their hands. "Mr. Blalock is a very lucky man," he told them. "The bullet passed through his upper arm without doing any serious damage. That's been stitched up and shouldn't be more than an inconvenience. His legs are a different story."

"They're both broken?" Nathan asked.

"Yes. The left is broken in two places, but the breaks are fairly clean and should set easily. But a section of the right fibula may require surgery."

"He said he couldn't feel his legs," Billie whispered. "Was there any damage to his spine?"

"As far as we can tell, there's no neurological damage, but we won't know for sure until he's able to get up and walk."

At this point the Blalocks rushed in. Mr. Blalock was a compact, well-dressed, and attractive man who appeared to be in his early sixties. Mrs. Blalock, however, hadn't aged as gracefully as her husband. She was pudgy with steel-gray hair and a face etched with wrinkles. She embraced Nathan, and so Billie liked her instantly.

The Blalocks gathered around while the doctor repeated his report on Kip's condition. "I'm glad that you're here," he told the Blalocks. "We'll need you to sign some forms, and we'd like to get a couple of pints of blood just in case surgery becomes our only option."

Mr. Blalock nodded. "We're both O positive, like Kip."

"I'll take you back to the lab, and after you give some blood I'll arrange for you to see your son for a few minutes. I have to warn you, though, he's groggy from the shock and the pain medication."

"I'm O positive too," Nathan told the doctor. "I'd like to give a pint," he volunteered.

The doctor smiled. "I won't turn you away."

The Blalocks and the doctor moved down the hall, and Nathan followed. He made it almost to the huge double doors before he remembered about Billie. "You'll stay right there with Agent Gray until I get back?" he asked, and she nodded. With a quick wave, he hurried to catch up with the others.

As Billie watched them walk, she felt Nathan slipping away from her, back into the Blalocks' world.

Agent Gray stepped up beside her. "He takes his responsibility to Kip Blalock very seriously."

Billie gave him a brave smile, realizing that he had picked up on Nathan's withdrawal as well. She looked around the dreary room. "I wish we could have gotten to a nicer hospital," she murmured.

"I asked about that, but the paramedics said that Mr. Blalock is in the best hands here."

"Really?" She was surprised.

"Yep. He said this place handles more gunshot wounds than any other hospital in the county."

Billie nodded, then looked toward the pay phones against the wall. "I guess it's safe to call my parents now?"

Agent Gray looked uncomfortable. "We're not really sure how safe you are. Felix Hummer may hold you partially responsible for foiling his plan. It will probably be weeks before any of us can truly relax."

"But I know my parents are worried."

Agent Gray frowned before handing her his cell phone. "Make it quick."

With a smile, she dialed her parents' number. Her father answered quickly, and she told him as little as possible but assured him over and over that she was fine. "I have to stay here for a little while, but then I'll be coming home."

Her father insisted that he was coming to get her. She warned him that she still had to talk to the police and didn't know how soon she'd be able to leave.

"I don't care," Rick Murphy replied. "I'm not leaving you and your safety in the hands of strangers anymore. I'll go to your apartment and wait until you're finished with whatever you need to do."

"The manager still thinks I'm dead," she warned him. "So if she asks any questions, you just say you've come to get some of my stuff."

"Won't she think it's strange that we want to pack in the middle of the night?" her father asked.

"People in grief do strange things, Daddy," she assured him. "I'll get there as soon as I can."

She returned the cell phone and Agent Gray immediately got a call. He answered it while Billie stared at the big doors that led into the emergency department, willing Nathan to walk back through them. A few minutes later the agent put away his cell phone.

"More news about the GFL?" she asked, and the agent nodded slowly. "Bad news?" Billie asked, concerned by the seriousness of his expression.

"Not bad news, but certainly startling. That was the Treasury agent in charge of the whole operation. He says that Kip Blalock was working for them. He was the one who activated the virus that stopped the money transfers."

"Are you sure?" Billie was astounded.

Agent Gray nodded, obviously also amazed as the big double doors opened and Kip's parents, followed closely by Nathan, emerged. Nathan led the Blalocks over, and they all took seats around Agent Gray.

Agent Gray cleared his throat, then said, "I've just been informed that Kip was the Treasury Department's inside man."

"Kip?" Nathan gasped, then he looked at Mr. Blalock. "Kip is a Treasury Department *agent*?"

"Of course not," Mr. Blalock replied. "He was just working for them on this one case."

Nathan spread his hands. "Why didn't I know?"

"I'm sorry I couldn't tell you sooner," Mr. Blalock apologized. "But it was a very dangerous situation, and we felt that the fewer people who knew, the better. In fact, only myself, Kip, and the Treasury Department agent in charge knew where Kip's true loyalties were."

Billie felt confused, but Nathan looked angry. "Can you tell me about it *now*?" He looked from Mr. Blalock to Agent Gray. "Any of you?"

"I'm as surprised as you are," the FBI agent assured him.

Mr. Blalock sighed. "I can explain. You knew about Kip's gambling debts?"

Nathan nodded. "Supposedly the gangsters offered him a chance to work off his debts by helping them steal millions of dollars through the GFL."

"That's all true," Mr. Blalock acknowledged. "After they contacted him, Kip came to me for advice."

Nathan's eyebrows shot up, and Mr. Blalock smiled.

"I know. It shocked me too. But it also made me realize how scared Kip really was. We talked about it, and I prayed about it and finally decided we had to notify someone in the government. I had my personal attorney check into the situation, and he recommended that we contact the Treasury Department."

At this point, Agent Gray took up the dialogue. "They suggested that Mr. Blalock follow Felix Hummer's instructions exactly."

"The Treasury Department asked him to risk his life?" Nathan looked angry again.

"When they made the arrangements with Mr. Blalock, the Treasury agent Miss Murphy knew as Cowboy was still in place. Kip was instructed to find him and offer assistance."

"So he was just there as insurance?" Nathan clarified.

"But by the time Kip got there, Cowboy was dead," Billie guessed.

Agent Gray nodded. "Fortunately, Mr. Blalock had been told how to activate the virus."

"So Kip is a hero," Billie whispered.

"He certainly saved the Treasury Department's operation," Agent Gray acknowledged.

"He took a terrible risk," Billie pointed out. "If someone in the GFL had found the virus . . ." Her voice trailed off as she shuddered.

Agent Gray nodded. "And because of Kip Blalock's bravery and service to his country, we don't plan to prosecute him for racketeering and the dozen other charges that we could have brought against him."

Nathan smirked. "That's nice of you."

"Gambling is a nasty business, Nathan," Agent Gray replied. "And believe me, Kip Blalock is getting a better deal from us than he would have from Felix Hummer. The presence of the gunman at the game tonight proves that they planned to kill him."

Mr. Blalock interrupted with a nervous glance at his wife. "I'm just thankful that things have turned out this well."

"I'll feel better once we hear from the doctors that they have Kip's leg set and that surgery won't be required," Mrs. Blalock said, wringing her hands.

"I feel pretty good about Kip's chances of a full recovery," Nathan said, then looked significantly at Billie. "How do you feel about it?"

She smiled, glad that he was still partly hers. "Kip's going to be fine."

The big doors swung open at that moment, and the doctor came out. "Both legs are set! Everything went well. We're very hopeful."

"Can we see him?" Mrs. Blalock asked.

The doctor nodded. "Follow me."

After the Blalocks left, Agent Gray cleared his throat. "I'm afraid I've got some more *bad* news for you, Billie." Billie turned to face him. "Conrad Lockhart was one of the GFL conspirators. In fact, he was probably the head guy."

Billie gasped for breath. "That's not possible. He loved Camille. He would never have harmed her." Billie shook her head. Such a thought was unimaginable.

"Of course not," Agent Gray agreed. "But remember, she was killed by mistake."

Billie met the agent's eyes. "While they were trying to kill me."

The agent nodded. "I'm sure he didn't want to kill you either, but it became a necessity. He was arrested along with the other suspected conspirators at the exhibition game. He was put in a cell, and apparently . . ." the agent paused, obviously reluctant to continue, "he committed suicide."

Billie started to tremble, and Nathan put an arm around her shoulders as the agent continued.

"Does Edgar know?" Billie asked as a tear fell down her cheek.

Agent Gray shrugged. "Edgar Willingham is unaccounted for."

"So Edgar and Conrad Lockhart were working together?" Nathan thought aloud.

The agent nodded. "It seems so. That must be how they were able to track you."

Billie swiped at the tears that wouldn't seem to stop. "All of this death for *money?*"

"A quick look at Mr. Lockhart's finances shows he was in terrible shape moneywise. He was about to lose his home and his entire way of life," the agent responded. "I guess he was desperate."

"What now? How safe are we?" Nathan asked.

"You'll need protection for the next couple of months until we're confident that Felix Hummer isn't bent on revenge."

Nathan frowned. "What kind of protection?"

"The police will provide protection to begin with. Later you'll want to hire someone privately."

Billie was already shaking her head. "I won't need a police escort. My father is waiting for me at my apartment. I'll just pick up a few things and then go home with him."

The agent considered this for a second, then nodded. "I recommend that you take a few weeks off work. Stay out of Atlanta for a while." He turned to Nathan. "And what about you, Mr. Turner?"

"I'll take Billie to meet her father, then I'll fly back to Salt Lake on the next available plane. I should be safe there."

Billie tried to hide her hurt. She had hoped that he'd stay around for a few days, possibly even come home with her for a late Christmas celebration.

"I'll have to notify the Salt Lake Police Department, and I strongly recommend that you accept any help they offer. And if I think of any more questions, I know where to find you," the agent said with a tired smile. "I've got a patrol car waiting outside for you." He turned to Billie. "I'll be in touch."

"I'd like to speak to the Blalocks before we leave," Nathan said as they stood.

Agent Gray nodded. "I'll check with the nurse."

"We never have heard from Deputy Briggins," Billie whispered to Nathan. "I'm getting worried about him."

"We'll ask Agent Gray to check on him," Nathan promised, but he didn't sound particularly concerned.

When the agent returned, he had a nurse with him. "This is Mrs. Dennis," he introduced briefly. "She's going to take you to Kip Blalock's room."

"You folks can only stay a few minutes," the nurse warned as they followed her.

Nathan nodded. "We understand."

CHAPTER 12

The nurse took them into a nice suite dominated by a hospital bed. Kip lay on the bed, swathed in white. The Blalocks were sitting on a couch across the room. "He's still doing okay?" Nathan asked as he stepped up beside the bed.

Mrs. Blalock nodded. "Yes, the doctors are very encouraging."

"That's good." Nathan walked over to stand near the Blalocks. "I'm heading back to Salt Lake tonight."

"Good," Mr. Blalock said. "It will give me peace of mind knowing you're there."

They heard a noise from the bed and turned to see Kip looking around. "Where am I?" he rasped.

The Blalocks rushed to his side. "You're in the hospital," his mother said with tears in her eyes. "You've got two broken legs, but the doctors think you're going to be fine."

"And you saved Nathan's life," his father added.

Kip looked over at Nathan. "He already got the girl. I didn't want him to get all the glory too."

Billie felt a blush rise in her cheeks as the Blalocks glanced toward her.

Kip's eyes fluttered closed. "Did I really save your life, Nathan?"

"You did," Nathan acknowledged.

"Where's Billie?" Kip whispered, his voice weak.

"I'm here." She stepped up to his bedside reluctantly.

Kip opened his eyes and gave her a sly smile. "I think you owe me something for taking Nathan's bullet."

She regarded him warily. "Like what?"

"Closer," he whispered.

She leaned down, afraid that he was going to require the kiss she had denied him earlier. But when her face was very near his, he said, "Tell me your real name."

She laughed softly. "Sybil."

"I won."

"Yes, you did."

"And I don't blame you for sticking with Billie." Kip's eyes closed again as the nurse walked in.

"That's it for a while, folks," she decreed. "Everyone out."

Once they were gathered in the hallway, Nathan and Billie said good-bye. With a little wave, he led Billie toward the elevator. A policemen met them at the emergency entrance and escorted them to a patrol car parked outside. The cool air felt good on Billie's face.

"Agent Gray told me to take you to the Chamber offices," the policeman said once they were settled. "He said you needed to leave your boss a note saying you wouldn't be in for a few weeks."

"That's fine," Billie told the policeman, then gave Nathan a rueful smile. "I guess Agent Gray is afraid if he doesn't make me do it now I might change my mind."

"Wise man," Nathan replied.

* * *

The new cell phone in Felix Hummer's suit coat pocket started to vibrate. He pulled it out and flipped it open, then pressed it tightly against his ear so he could hear the caller over the noise in the busy sports bar.

"Yes?"

"Mission accomplished," a voice said.

Hummer closed the phone without responding and addressed his companion. "For once, something in this miserable operation has gone right. I'll head to the airport while you tie up these loose ends. Meet me there as soon as possible."

Hummer paid their tab and left the bar. His companion waited a few minutes, then followed.

* * *

As they drove toward the Chamber offices, Billie stared out the window, trying to ignore the feelings of grief that threatened to overwhelm her.

Finally Nathan said, "Why are you so quiet?"

"Just tired I guess—and sad." She glanced over at him. "It's hard to believe that Camille's uncle was one of the criminals. And Edgar."

"And Camille herself," Nathan agreed.

"I find that less difficult to believe," Billie told him. "We don't even know where Deputy Briggins is."

"A lot of terrible things have happened," Nathan acknowledged. "But I'm too tired to think about that now, and since we don't have much time left together, you shouldn't be wasting it worrying."

She raised an eyebrow.

"I mean, don't you want to lecture me on the virtues of marriage or my fraternal responsibilities to lead, guide, and direct my little brother?" he teased.

Billie swallowed the lump in her throat, then forced herself to say, "Thanks for reminding me."

"Do you think your father has had time to get to your apartment?"

She checked the clock on the dashboard. "If he isn't there yet, he should be within the next thirty minutes."

"Maybe during this little vacation you'll hear good news from Randall House and won't even need your job at the Chamber of Commerce anymore."

Billie smiled. "I like a man who dreams big."

A few minutes later, the policeman parked the patrol car at the curb near the front entrance of the chamber offices. He accompanied Billie and Nathan inside, and as they entered the building, Billie stopped to speak to the security guard.

"Miss Murphy!" the man cried. "I haven't seen you in a while!" He glanced over at the small television set he had been watching. "Not in person anyway."

"I got in the way of the people who were trying to rob the GFL," she told him. "So they tried to make it look like I was a criminal."

"I knew you didn't do anything wrong," the guard assured her.

She smiled before moving toward the elevators. "Thanks. We're going up to my office for a few minutes."

The guard nodded, then turned back to his television.

When they stepped off the elevator, the policeman positioned himself by the door as Billie took Nathan's hand and drew him into the maze of offices. Billie faltered briefly when she saw Camille's desk but forced herself to walk past it into her own cubicle.

She paused at the door.

"Is something wrong?"

"I'm not sure, but I'm getting that uneasy feeling again." She flipped on the overhead light and looked at him. "The one I had when we were in danger."

"But the criminals have been arrested," Nathan reminded her.

She nodded. "I know. I guess it's just nerves." She sat at the swivel chair behind her desk and offered Nathan the chair across from her. "It will just take me a minute to type a memo to my boss. I know you're anxious to get to the airport."

She hoped he would deny this, but he didn't, so Billie turned on her computer. While she waited for the word processing system to come up, she put personal items from her desk into her purse. "Just in case I really don't come back," she told Nathan, and he nodded.

Billie typed a brief note explaining the circumstances and hit the print button, then continued her packing. When she opened the file drawer, her eyes were drawn to her junk folder. She opened it and pulled out the itinerary Camille had left on her desk. As she stared at it, she asked, "Did you think it was strange that some of Camille's jewelry survived the explosion?"

Nathan shook his head absently. "What?"

"Don't you think it's odd that Camille's jewelry didn't melt when my car exploded?"

Nathan shrugged. "I don't know what temperature it takes to melt precious metals."

"Camille showed me this itinerary the Saturday night before the trip was to begin. That was when she first mentioned trading trips, and she suggested that it was in my best interest since 'the owner's son' was available and rich."

Nathan frowned. "So?"

"I think Camille knew that Kip was coming on Saturday night."

"No one knew we were coming on Saturday night. Kip didn't even decide until Monday morning."

"Actually, that's not true. Kip knew he was coming long before then, as did Mr. Blalock and Felix Hummer."

Nathan's frown deepened. "So what are you saying?"

Billie looked down at the itinerary and tried to concentrate. "Do you like jigsaw puzzles?" she asked, and Nathan shook his head.

"I've never done one."

"We used to have one in progress all the time at our house," Billie continued. "One time we actually finished the puzzle, but every time I would look at it, I got the feeling that something about it wasn't right. It was several days before we realized that my youngest brother had forced a couple of pieces into the wrong spots."

"So even though all the pieces were there, the picture wasn't exactly correct," Nathan repeated hesitantly. She couldn't tell if he was following her train of thought or just humoring her.

"I think that's what's happened here," Billie told him. "We have all the pieces, but we've got a couple of them in the wrong spots." She tried to concentrate. "I don't think that Conrad Lockhart knew Kip was coming."

"Why do you say that?"

"Because when we were in Columbus, Edgar showed me a memo from Conrad Lockhart to Camille congratulating her for helping Blalock Industries choose a site in Georgia. He specifically asked Camille to give his regards to Cliff and Neal. Why wouldn't he mention you and Kip if he knew you were with us?"

Nathan frowned. "And why was he congratulating Camille?"

"Because she never told him that I was taking the tour for her like she promised she would. I think she planned to take my cruise *and* the credit for my success with the plant site." Billie glanced up. "But if Conrad Lockhart didn't know that Kip was coming, then how did Camille know on *Saturday*?"

"I'll admit that doesn't make sense," Nathan agreed.

"Unless she was working for Felix Hummer like Agent Gray suggested." Billie frowned in concentration. "And why was the

Chamber willing to invest so much time and money to convince your company to build in Georgia?"

"Unless the whole trip was just a way to get Kip here?" Nathan suggested.

"That's what I'm thinking. Even Camille's insistence that I change trips with her seems fishy now."

"How?"

"Cliff and Neal already had distractions. It was Christmastime and they were away from their families. That just left you."

Nathan nodded grimly. "So by sending a nice Mormon girl as our tour guide, they hoped to distract *me*." He glanced up. "And it worked."

Billie was too disturbed to see the compliment. "Camille was certainly not your type."

"So the crooks arranged the whole Blalock tour to get Kip here without causing suspicion," Nathan thought out loud. "But if Conrad Lockhart didn't know Kip was coming, who changed the itinerary?"

Soft laughter drifted toward them from the doorway of Billie's cubicle, attracting their startled attention. Then Billie gasped as she saw Camille Lockhart. "You never could just leave well enough alone, could you?"

Billie started to tremble as her eyes moved from the smirk on Camille's face to the ugly gun in her hand.

"Nathan, I'd like to introduce you to Camille Lockhart," Billie said slowly, staring at the woman, "who obviously didn't die in my car with Jeff Burdick."

Camille's eyes flickered over Nathan, and she gave Billie an unpleasant smile. "He *is* cute. Too bad your inability to mind your own business is going to cut both your relationship and your lives short."

Nathan didn't respond but sat quietly, watching the women.

"Who died in my car?" Billie hated to ask but had to know.

"I don't know." Camille tossed her hair carelessly. "Some homeless woman. Felix handled all that."

"Felix Hummer?" Billie repeated. "So it's true. You really are working for the Mafia?"

"I work for a genius," Camille corrected. "And the benefits are incredible."

"Why would the police assume the woman was you just because of some jewelry?" Billie asked.

"Felix had a detective on the payroll. He was assigned my case and closed it quickly without asking many questions."

Billie was shocked. "And no one else asked any questions either?"

Camille shrugged. "My death wasn't nearly as important as Jeff Burdick's. It was easily shuffled into the background."

Suddenly Billie felt very weary. "And I suppose you were a part of the GFL scheme from the start."

"Not from the start," Camille corrected. "The whole thing was Uncle Conrad's idea—which surprised me. I didn't realize he had that much imagination. He approached Felix and helped him set up a committee of local businessmen. I overheard Felix and Uncle Conrad talking one night and guessed what they were up to. I went to Felix and offered him my silence for a piece of the pie."

"But why did you fake your death?" Billie asked.

Camille frowned. "I didn't have any experience in crime and made some stupid mistakes, so the FBI was about to arrest me. Then Felix found an opportunity for me to disappear and join him in Las Vegas."

"You double-crossed your own uncle?" Billie was incredulous. "And helped to murder Jeff Burdick! I thought you loved him!"

"Jeff was sweet, but just a means to an end. It turned out that Felix could get me to that end faster." Camille's mouth formed a pretty pout. "And if Uncle Conrad hadn't gotten so stingy, none of it would have happened! He told me that he couldn't afford my *excesses* anymore. He said I was going to have to live on what I could make!" she informed them as if this were ridiculous. "So I really had no choice but to increase my income."

Billie clasped her trembling hands together. "We were told your uncle committed suicide."

Camille put a hand on her hip. "Let's just say he had a little help."

Billie's trembling increased. "You killed him?"

Camille gave her a scandalized look. "Of course not! Felix has all kinds of people to handle his dirty work." Camille glanced at a new diamond watch encircling her thin wrist. "And speaking of Felix, I'm supposed to meet him at the airport for our trip to Las Vegas in his private plane. And I guess the two of you will be accompanying me." She waved the gun toward the door. "You first."

"Why should we cooperate with you?" Nathan asked as he stood, then moved to put himself between Billie and the gun.

"Because if you don't, you'll be shot," Camille explained with exaggerated sweetness. "And although your protective gesture is very touching, I have *lots* of bullets in this gun. After I shoot you, I'll still have plenty left to kill Billie."

Nathan's shoulders slumped as he apparently realized the truth of Camille's words. Billie walked through the door and felt Nathan fall into step behind her. She couldn't help but wonder where the policeman was.

As if reading her mind, Camille said, "If you're looking for your police escort, he's right here." She pointed to the police officer waiting by the elevator. His gun was drawn, and it was pointed at Nathan.

Billie gasped. "You're helping *her*?"

"Meet the policeman Felix employs," Camille said.

Billie's eyes dropped to his name tag. "Davenport," she read out loud. "I believe we spoke on the phone a few days ago."

He nodded, but before he could speak, Camille broke in. "Let's go, *now*."

Officer Davenport waved his gun. "Please don't do anything foolish. If you cooperate, you won't be harmed."

Nathan took Billie's hand and followed Camille into the elevator.

When they reached the lobby, Billie looked for the security guard, but he was nowhere to be found. Officer Davenport led the way to his patrol car and opened the back door. Once Billie and Nathan were locked inside, Camille and the policeman got into the front.

As they drove toward the airport, Billie stared out the window at the dwindling traffic and tried to think. Their situation seemed hopeless, but there had to be a way out. They just had to find it.

Billie still hadn't come up with a reasonable idea by the time they reached the airport. Instead of going to the terminals, the officer drove around to the area dedicated to private planes. Once they were parked beside a hangar, Camille got out and told Nathan and Billie to do the same.

"Follow me," she commanded. "And remember that my policeman friend is right behind you."

As they walked across the tarmac, Billie glanced up at Nathan. He smiled, but his eyes were desolate, and she could tell he'd given up hope.

A tall man with dark curly hair and a deep tan stepped out of the hangar as they approached, and he addressed Camille. "The plane is all gassed up and waiting for us." Then he looked at Billie and Nathan.

Camille smiled as she handed him her gun. "Felix, let me introduce Billie Murphy and her faithful companion, Nathan Turner."

Felix Hummer regarded them with mild interest. "So, we meet at last."

Billie and Nathan stared back with silent resentment.

"You may not consider this much of a compliment," Felix Hummer continued after a few seconds, "but you've caused me more trouble and cost me more money in a shorter period of time than anyone I can remember."

"It's cold out here, Felix," Camille whined, rubbing her arms. "Hurry and get it over with so we can go."

Felix Hummer laughed and turned to the policeman.

"Should we take care of this now or in Las Vegas?"

Officer Davenport shrugged. "It's up to you."

Felix Hummer looked around. Except for the sound of his plane idling in the background, the area was eerily quiet. "No point in dragging our problems across the country. We'll tie up all the loose ends here."

Billie felt Nathan stiffen beside her. He squeezed her hand, then let go. She instinctively understood. Nathan wasn't just going to stand there and get shot. Taking a deep breath, she prepared to take action as well. Their chances were minimal, but they might as well die trying to escape.

"You or me?" the policeman asked.

"Why don't we split the difference?" Hummer said pleasantly. Then, in one quick motion, he aimed the gun Camille had given him and shot Officer Davenport right between the eyes.

The policeman stood motionless for a few seconds, a shocked look on his face.

"I don't know how you expected me to trust you," Felix Hummer told him. "The law-abiding citizens of Atlanta certainly couldn't."

"Yuck!" Camille cried as the policeman pitched forward and slumped to the ground facedown.

Nathan leaned his head close to Billie and whispered, "Run!" He then charged the man from Las Vegas.

Billie did run, but not away from danger, as she knew Nathan had intended. Instead, she ran toward Hummer from the opposite side. Felix Hummer swung the gun between Nathan and Billie as if trying to decide which one posed the biggest threat. A shot was fired, and Billie flinched, waiting for the pain. When it didn't come, she began to cry, assuming that Nathan was the one who had been hit. Then she realized that Nathan was still running toward Felix Hummer.

Hummer looked confused as another shot rang out, then he turned and ran toward his plane. Camille was already up the portable steps and ducking inside. Nathan grabbed Billie and pulled her down.

"They're getting away!" she cried.

"Yeah, but they're not shooting at us, so let's count our blessings."

"But who *is* shooting?" Billie asked, risking a look around.

Then they saw Luther Briggins step out from behind a luggage cart. He continued firing as he ran toward the airplane. Felix Hummer threw himself inside, and the door was closed quickly as the jet began taxiing. Finally Luther came to a stop beside them and dropped his gun.

"I missed him!" he said in despair.

"It's so dark," Billie comforted him. "And you probably saved our lives!"

Deputy Briggins didn't look consoled.

"Do you think he's dead?" Billie asked, careful not to actually look at the fallen policeman.

"Definitely," the deputy said, but he walked over and checked for a pulse.

"Where have you been?" Billie asked. "We've been worried about you."

"I was standing at my assigned security point at the Georgia Dome, wishing that I was inside where all the action was taking place," Deputy Briggins explained. "Then two people left through my exit. You remember I told you I check the missing persons lists religiously?" Billie and Nathan both nodded. "I also check the most-wanted list. Felix Hummer has been on that list several times, and I recognized him immediately. So I borrowed a vehicle and followed them."

"Who did you borrow a car from?" Billie asked.

"A UPS driver was picking up overnight mail from a drop box," Luther told them. "He left his keys in his van, so I took it."

"You stole a UPS vehicle?" Billie gasped.

Luther spread his hands. "I didn't have time to ask permission, and I couldn't follow them in a police car." He looked over at the brown van parked behind the hangar. "And that van was perfect for blending into traffic. Nobody gave me a second glance."

"Where did Mr. Hummer and Camille go?"

"To a sports bar. They sat there and watched the GFL arrests and confusion at the game for a while. Then Hummer got a phone call, and they left separately. I was in a better position to follow the woman, so I got behind her. She drove to the Chamber of Commerce, and I waited outside in my borrowed van. I was just about to give up my unsanctioned surveillance when she came out holding you two at gunpoint."

"It's a good thing you followed your instincts," Nathan told him. "Otherwise Billie and I might both be dead."

Billie gave the delivery van a nervous look. "And hopefully if Agent Gray explains everything to UPS, they won't press charges."

"I'm not worried about UPS," Luther told her as several airport security vehicles arrived. "I just wish I was a better shot."

The police and Agent Gray were called. Billie borrowed a cell phone and called her father to let him know she'd been delayed but would be at her apartment soon.

"Did you tell him what happened?" Nathan wanted to know when she returned to his side.

"No, I couldn't."

He put his arm around her shoulders and gave her a little squeeze. "Why didn't you run to safety when I told you to?"

She looked up at him. "If you haven't figured it out already, I don't like being bossed around."

When Agent Gray arrived, he consulted with the police for several minutes, then approached them. "I can't let the two of you out of my sight for a minute," he said with his characteristic half smile.

"Camille isn't dead," Billie blurted out, and the agent's eyebrows flew up. "Felix Hummer faked her death so she wouldn't be arrested."

"That policeman you sent to protect us was involved too," Nathan added.

Agent Gray cursed under his breath. "I am so sorry."

"It wasn't your fault," Billie told him.

"And I had Hummer in my sights, but I let him get away," Luther Briggins confessed miserably. "My shots went wild."

"Don't be too hard on yourself," Agent Gray told the deputy. "There's a lot of blood on the tarmac, which might belong to Deputy Davenport, but it's also possible that you hit Hummer. And there's something else even more important on the ground near where the plane was parked."

The deputy frowned. "What?"

"Jet fuel," Agent Gray informed him. "They've notified nearby airports to be on the lookout for an emergency landing. Felix Hummer will be in custody soon facing murder charges."

Deputy Briggins looked considerably relieved. "If they catch this Hummer guy, do you think they'll mention my name in the Atlanta paper?"

"I'll guarantee it," Agent Gray said. "The folks back in Upton County will be very proud."

Now Deputy Briggins was grinning. "Maybe it wasn't such an unlucky day when I ran into you two."

Billie felt her throat choking with emotion. "It was more than a lucky day for us."

Agent Gray addressed the deputy. "I've got an agent waiting to take you to the Georgia Dome to collect your squad car." He indicated toward a man standing beside a nondescript government sedan. "You need to get back to Upton County and start buying newspapers. I'll handle the return of the UPS van."

Deputy Briggins nodded, and after a handshake from Nathan and a big hug from Billie, he climbed in the car and rode away. Once the deputy disappeared from view, Agent Gray faced Billie and Nathan. "Okay, are you folks ready to go?"

"Do you have another policeman waiting to escort us?" Billie teased.

"Oh no," Agent Gray told her. "I'm sticking to the two of you like glue until you're out of my jurisdiction." He pointed to another car behind him. "I'm ready to go when you are."

"Have you found Edgar yet?" Billie asked as they walked toward the car.

Agent Gray shook his head. "If he was involved, he's probably hiding. If he wasn't, he's probably dead."

Billie winced. "Now I don't know what to hope for."

When they were settled in the backseat, Billie gave Agent Gray directions to her apartment. He made a phone call, giving her and Nathan a measure of privacy.

She leaned her head on Nathan's shoulder, and he put his chin against her cheek. "Are you tired?" he asked.

She nodded. "How about you?"

"I'm so tired I can barely think," he admitted. "The last few days have been grueling, both physically and emotionally."

She snuggled closer. "It's funny, but even though what we've been through is anyone's idea of a living nightmare, I honestly have to say it was also the best two weeks of my life."

"You're just thinking of all the material you collected for future books," he teased.

"I'll admit that's part of it," she returned. "But the company had a little something to do with it too." They were quiet for a few minutes, listening to Agent Gray describe the events at the airport. Finally Billie said bravely, "So, I guess you're anxious to get back to all that work that's been piling up on your desk while you've been driving around Georgia with me."

He nuzzled her temple with his cheek. "I'm not exactly anxious, but it's inevitable. Will you be glad when you finally get to your parents' house?"

"Yeah, I'm dying to open my presents." She smiled over at him. "The suspense is killing me."

He smiled back. "I'll probably be spending quite a bit of time in Georgia once construction begins on the new plant. We'll see a lot of each other."

Billie nodded, then looked out her window. She didn't know how she would bear being parted from him for a few days, let alone the rest of her life. Over the past week, he had become a part of her, but he couldn't commit, and it was time for her to accept that fact.

When they reached the apartment complex, Billie pointed out her parents' car parked in her spot. Agent Gray parked his car and followed them up the stairs, discretely staying a few yards behind. At the door, Billie just stared. "I hate to sound like a coward, but I'm not sure I can go in," she whispered.

"Having spent the past week with you, I know you're not a coward," Nathan said with certainty. "And I don't blame you for not wanting to go inside. We'll ask your father to come out."

Blinking back her tears, Billie nodded, then knocked on the door to her apartment. There was a scuffle on the other side before the door was finally jerked open by her youngest brother, Calvin. His short hair was mussed and his cheeks flushed with excitement.

"Your apartment is totally trashed!" he told Billie. "This is the coolest thing I've ever seen!"

Billie was overwhelmed with tenderness for the boy and embraced him fiercely. Calvin endured the excess affection politely for a few seconds before pulling back. "Come on, Billie. You know I can't stand that mushy stuff."

Austin, the brother two years older than Calvin, appeared in the doorway. "Billie's here!" he announced, and soon Billie was surrounded by her family.

"Your hair!" Nan Murphy cried as she gathered her daughter into a hug.

Billie put a hand to her head absently. "I had to cut it."

"Now Billie can tell us if blonds have more fun!" Calvin said happily.

Billie laughed, then turned to see that the older Murphy men were staring at Nathan.

"Nathan Turner," he introduced himself, extending his hand toward the curious group.

Billie extricated herself from Nan and moved over to help Nathan. "Nathan could have gone back to Salt Lake and let me deal with my own problems, but he chose to stay, and he saved my life many times over the past few days." Billie saw her father's features relax marginally. "And this is Agent Gray from the FBI," Billie added as she waved the agent forward.

After a brief pause, Billie's father accepted Nathan's hand. "Rick Murphy." He shook hands with Agent Gray and expressed his appreciation to both men, but he still looked wary.

"Miss Murphy did a good job of taking care of herself, but she attracts danger, and I'm relieved to have her back to you safely," the agent said, then turned to Nathan. "I'll wait for you in the car."

As the agent left, Nan joined them and ran her hands along her daughter's face, then smiled. "I've been dreaming of this moment all week. And as each day passed, I started to wonder if it would ever happen." She had to pause as a sob rose in her throat. "I'm just so glad to have you with us again."

Billie reached for Nathan's hand. "Mama, this is Nathan."

He extended a hand. "Mrs. Murphy."

"Call me Nan," she requested.

"And my brothers Austin, Philip, Jesse, and Calvin." Billie pointed at the various young men with a wry smile. "If you still had anything valuable, I'd warn you that they have a tendency to break things, but under the circumstances . . ." She shrugged. Then she looked into her ransacked apartment and shuddered.

"Let's get out of here," Rick Murphy suggested.

"Yeah, this place is creepy," Austin concurred.

"I've already packed you some things," Nan told Billie. They closed the door and moved down to the parking lot. "Will you come home with us, Nathan?" Nan invited. "We've saved our Christmas celebration."

"Mama won't let us put a single ornament on the tree until you're there," Calvin complained. "Every needle will probably fall off by the time we get it decorated."

"She's been worried sick about you," Rick Murphy said with a smile.

"I'd love to," Nathan told Nan. "But I've got to get back to Salt Lake. I'll be coming to Georgia often in a few months, and I'd be glad to visit then."

"You're leaving now?" Nan looked out at the dark sky. "In the middle of the night?"

Nathan nodded. "Agent Gray is going to take me to the airport. Then I'll try to get a red-eye flight."

Nan glanced from him to Billie. "Well, I hope you have a nice trip home." She turned to her husband and sons. "Why don't we wait in the car?"

Once the Murphys were in their Suburban, Billie faced Nathan, keeping her shaking hands in her pockets.

"We aren't really saying good-bye," he began.

"I'm going to miss you," Billie predicted through her tears.

"Don't cry," Nathan pleaded, his own eyes suspiciously damp. "I'll come back when construction starts on the new plant. We'll go out to eat at a nice restaurant, and there won't be anyone following us or trying to kill us."

"That would take all the fun out of it," Billie said lightly, then walked over to the railing and looked out at the star-studded sky. She had imagined this moment many times. The best plan she had been able to think of was simply to beg him to stay. Now she closed her eyes briefly and prayed for inspiration. When she opened her mouth to speak, a wonderful calm came over her.

"We're good together," he began. "We can be great friends, and who knows? Maybe someday . . ."

"No, Nathan," she said, then forced herself to turn around and look at him. "It won't work. You don't want a permanent relationship, and casual dating with you would break my heart over and over again instead of just this once. The time I've spent with you has been," she paused, looking for the right word, "incredible. But it's over." She saw the surprise register in his eyes as she continued. "You'll go back to Blalock Industries, and in a few weeks I'll be nothing more than a pleasant memory. Eventually I'll find someone else. He won't make my heart pound the way you do," she added with a shaky laugh, "but he will believe in marriage, and we'll raise a family together." She leaned up on her tiptoes and kissed him gently on the lips.

"So this is good-bye?" he asked, looking confused.

"Have a good life, Nathan," she said. After one last lingering gaze, she left him standing on the dark sidewalk and joined her family.

She put on her seat belt and refused to look back at Nathan as her father pulled out of the parking lot. The boys demanded that Billie retell her story, so she talked until she was hoarse and her brothers were asleep. When she fell quiet, her mother smiled at her. "You've had such an awful time."

Billie considered this. "In retrospect, it doesn't seem so bad. We did help stop a major robbery."

Nan reached over the seat to pat Billie's hand. "We're very proud of you, dear. And Nathan seemed like a nice young man."

"He is," Billie agreed. "I'm in love with him."

"Oh," Nan said with a quick glance at her husband.

Billie sighed. "But it's over."

Rick Murphy gave his daughter a sharp look in the rearview mirror. "He doesn't love you back?" he demanded.

Billie sighed. "Actually, I think he does. But his childhood was a nightmare, and he's afraid to trust anyone, even himself."

"Maybe he'll come around," Nan suggested hopefully.

Billie smiled. "Maybe. But it's a decision he has to make alone."

It was very late when they reached their home. Nan led her daughter into the house while her husband roused the boys. Billie took a long, hot shower and changed into her own pajamas for the first time in over a week. Then she crawled into the bed she had slept in as a child, burrowing deep into her pillows and savoring the feeling of safety. As she drifted off to sleep, she wondered if Nathan was still in the Atlanta airport waiting for a flight or if he was already on his way to Salt Lake.

* * *

When Billie awakened on Sunday morning, the sun was up and the house was quiet. She found her mother in the kitchen, but the rest of the family was gone. "We decided you needed the sleep, so Daddy said you could skip church. Just this once." Her mother smiled as she poured a mug of hot chocolate for each of them. "Want an orange roll?" She extended a foil pan half full of homemade pastries.

Billie shook her head as she took a sip of hot chocolate.

"How do you feel this morning?" her mother pressed.

"Tired, disoriented, empty," Billie admitted, then took a deep breath. She had promised herself that she wouldn't cry.

"You miss him very much."

Billie winced. "I know it sounds silly. I only met him a couple of weeks ago, but we've been through so much together and, well, it's like he's the other half of me. And now that he's gone, I feel like I'll never really be whole again."

"Oh, Billie," her mother whispered.

Billie clutched her hot chocolate mug. "I don't know how I'll face each day without him. I just know that somehow I have to."

"You'll find the strength. I know you will," her mother assured her, but there was concern in her eyes.

The discussion then moved to Billie's recent experiences, and Billie wondered aloud if Felix Hummer and Camille had been arrested.

"I don't know, dear. I haven't watched television this morning."

Billie called Agent Gray's number and wasn't surprised to find him at his desk on a Sunday morning. "So," she prompted after identifying herself, "did you catch Mr. Hummer and Camille?"

"They were arrested in Shreveport, Louisiana, around midnight," Agent Gray confirmed. "Hummer's lawyers are making all kinds of noise, and it's true that we don't have enough hard evidence to pin the GFL scandal on him."

"So he's going to get off after all?" Billie was shocked.

"Oh no," Agent Gray assured her. "His only mistake was shooting a police officer. Security cameras recorded the whole thing, and we have three eyewitnesses not counting Camille Lockhart, who is already trying to make a deal with the federal prosecutors."

"That's Camille," Billie said, shaking her head. "She always lands on her feet."

"She's going to have quite a few legal issues to deal with over the next few months and will be lucky if she doesn't spend time in jail," Agent Gray replied. "But I think we've finally got Felix Hummer, and you know, it's sort of funny."

"What?"

"Some of the best federal agents have been chasing Hummer for years. Now, he's finally brought down by a sheriff's deputy from Upton County and two civilians running for their lives."

"The Lord works in mysterious ways," Billie concluded.

"Amen," Agent Gray agreed.

After ending the conversation, Billie asked Nan to call the hospital in Atlanta and get a report on Kip Blalock's condition.

"Don't you want to talk to him yourself?" Nan wanted to know.

Billie shook her head. "I'm not up to a conversation with Kip right now."

Nan considered this, then nodded. Billie waited in the living room, where her mother found her a few minutes later. "Mr. Blalock said to tell you he's able to move his toes."

"That's good," Billie said with relief.

"And why does he call you Sybil?" Nan asked. "I thought you hated that name."

Billie laughed. "He's the only person on earth who currently has permission to use my real name."

"Well, why don't you get dressed, honey? Your father and brothers will be home soon. Since we didn't get to have a real Christmas dinner, I've cooked a turkey. Then we'll decorate the tree and open presents."

Billie looked at the nearly bare branches of the dying fir tree in the den. "I'm sorry I spoiled Christmas for everyone," she said softly.

"Christmas wasn't ruined," her mother replied. "It was only delayed, and there was certainly nothing you could do about it. Now hurry and get dressed so you'll be ready to celebrate when everyone gets home."

Billie put on some makeup and brushed her hair. Then she started to put on her red sweater, but since it reminded her of Christmas and Nathan, she settled for a pair of jeans and a faded Georgia Tech sweatshirt. When her father and brothers returned home from church, she joined them in the den and did her best to show enthusiasm as they decorated the tree.

Then her mother called them to dinner. The food smelled wonderful, but she found it hard to swallow, so she just pushed it around on her plate. She saw her father watching her carefully several times throughout the meal, and afterwards he had a whispered conversation with her mother by the sink. He was scowling as they began opening presents, and Billie knew he blamed Nathan for her unhappiness.

"Your father and I have been talking," Nan said after Billie unwrapped her scanner. "I've been thinking about getting a new computer and thought you might want my old one. It's nothing fancy, but . . ."

"I can manage, Mama," Billie said.

"You have to write," her mother pointed out. "And I really have been planning to get something more modern."

She knew she did have to write, so Billie accepted her mother's generosity. "Thanks."

Billie was quiet while the rest of the presents were opened, but her brothers' exuberance more than compensated. They had gotten dirt bikes and were anxious to try them out. Rick went over all the rules while Nan supervised the donning of protective headgear. Finally they burst outside, leaving a heavy silence behind them.

"Well," Nan spoke into the quiet.

"I hope they realize that I'm making an exception by letting them ride today," Rick said to no one in particular. "Dirt biking is not an acceptable Sabbath activity."

Before his wife could respond, Calvin dashed back into the house. "Billie!" he yelled breathlessly. "That guy you were with last night just pulled into the driveway!"

"Nathan?" she clarified, and Calvin nodded. Billie let his words sink and shook her head. "It must be someone else. Nathan is in Salt Lake."

Calvin was already on his way back out the door. "I'm telling you, it's him," he called over his shoulder.

Billie hurried to the front door and stepped onto the porch. Sure enough, there was Nathan, still wearing his San Francisco Tempests wind suit, standing beside a rental car. Without stopping to think, she ran down the stairs and into his arms. The tears she had successfully controlled all day fell down her cheeks.

"I was hoping to see you again," she told him. "But I never dreamed it would be this soon."

He clung to her desperately but didn't speak.

She pulled back and examined him. He hadn't shaved, and his eyes were bloodshot with fatigue. "Are you okay?" she asked, leading him to the swing on the front porch.

"I'm not sure," he said as he sat down beside her. "I got to the airport last night and found a flight leaving at midnight. While I waited for my plane, I made a list of things that needed to be done when I got home, planning to slip back into my regular routine." He looked up at Billie, and she nodded for him to go on. "When my flight was announced, I got on the plane and waited for takeoff."

Just then, the front door opened, and Rick Murphy walked out. He gave the couple on the swing a brief glance, then headed for his truck parked on the gravel driveway. Billie and Nathan watched as he propped open the hood and stared at the inner workings of the old Ford.

"Is your father making repairs on his truck?"

Billie couldn't control a little laugh. "Even if my father knew the first thing about truck repairs he wouldn't do them on Sunday," she told him. "Daddy's keeping an eye on us."

"He hates me," Nathan whispered.

"He doesn't *hate* you," Billie hedged. "You're a stranger, so he doesn't really trust you yet."

"He'd like to dissect me with a dull knife," Nathan muttered as Rick glanced in their direction.

Stifling another giggle, Billie gave the swing a gentle push with her foot. "He's more bark than bite."

"If I'm lucky."

"So you were on the plane," she prompted.

Nathan leaned forward and rested his elbows on his knees. "As soon as we were in the air, I started to panic. I'm terrified that I'll be a bad husband and a worse father, but on that plane I realized that there was something that scared me even more." He took a deep breath, then continued. "The thought that I might never see your face again." He risked a quick glance at her. Billie stared back. "Or even worse, that I might run into you one day and find out that you're someone else's wife and the mother of his children." He shuddered.

"And that's when I knew I couldn't leave you. I wanted to go up and ask the pilot to turn around, but people are so jumpy in airplanes these days. Getting thrown in jail would just lessen my chances, so I sat there. It was the longest flight I've ever been on. Each minute was taking me farther away from you when all I wanted was to get back. As soon as I got off the plane in Salt Lake, I bought a ticket for the first flight to Atlanta. The connections were terrible, and I had to change planes three times."

Billie contemplated all the information. "You spent the night flying back and forth between Atlanta and Salt Lake?"

He nodded. "With stopovers in St. Louis and Houston, I think. It's all kind of running together."

She didn't know what moved her more—the fact that he hadn't taken the time to change out of the clothes he'd been wearing for thirty-six hours or the tears that were pooled in his eyes. "Are you asking me to marry you?" she said gently.

He covered his face with his hands. "Oh, gosh, is that what I'm doing?"

She laughed. "I think so."

"Well," he peeked between his fingers, "will you?"

"Yes. But we're not going to rush into this. I want you to be perfectly sure."

His face grew serious. "Both my parents were addicted to alcohol and drugs. I don't know about my grandparents. Chemical abuse could go back for generations!" he exclaimed. "You'd be taking a terrible risk!"

"Your father beat his addictions," Billie pointed out.

"They killed him anyway," Nathan countered.

Billie considered this for a few seconds. "Nobody's family is perfect, Nathan. Everyone has something they need to overcome. That's why the gospel and the Atonement are so wonderful. Now, kiss me and then we'll tell my parents."

Nathan glanced at Rick Murphy, who was scowling at the truck's engine. "You're sure about this?"

Billie threw her arms around his neck and kissed him soundly. "Life with you might be hard, but without you it would be unbearable."

"I guess I'll take that as a compliment," he said as she pulled him to his feet.

"Right now we'll tell my family that we're engaged, then first thing tomorrow we'll go shopping."

"For a ring?" he asked.

"No, for toys for your little brother, Cody," she clarified with a smile, then turned and called to her father. "Come on inside, Daddy. Nathan and I have an announcement to make."

ABOUT THE AUTHOR

Betsy Brannon Green currently lives in Bessemer, Alabama, which is a suburb of Birmingham. She has been married to her husband, Butch, for twenty-four years. They have eight children, one son-in-law, and one granddaughter. Betsy is an assistant nursery leader in her ward.

Although born in Salt Lake City, Betsy has spent most of her life in the South. Her writing has been strongly influenced by the small town of Headland, Alabama, and the gracious, generous people who live there.

Her first book, *Hearts in Hiding,* was published in May 2001. *Never Look Back* was released in January 2002, *Until Proven Guilty* in August 2002, *Don't Close Your Eyes* in April 2003, and *Above Suspicion* in October 2003.

Betsy enjoys corresponding with her readers, who can write to her in care of Covenant Communications, P.O. Box 416, American Fork, UT 84003-0416, or e-mail her via Covenant at info@covenant-lds.com.